1

# USED

## By
## Allison Agius

Cover photograph taken and styled by Jonathan Raper

Typesetting and formatting by Sarah Patrick

Printed by Peppermint Books

**WARNING: this book contains content of an adult nature and sexual violence**

Other books by the same author:

Fiction:

Treading Water
The Cross Over
The Lost Voice

Non-fiction:

Hidden Secrets Buried Treasure
Five Simple Steps to Success
The Seven Day Guide to Meditation

The author would love to hear from you. Go to her website to find her other books and contact her.

www.allisonagius.com

Or find her on Facebook: Allison Agius Writer

*With Thanks*

*I have so many people to thank for this book.*

*Graham Leggett-Chidgey for his patience and kindness. He gave up hours of his valuable time to show me round the Butterwick Hospice and talk me through life there. It's an amazing charity that makes a huge difference to so many people.*

*His equally patient wife, Nurse Julie Leggett-Chidgey, for letting me pick her brains about what could be possible with the plot in terms of care in the community. It is an infinitely better book for her saying 'No, you couldn't do that,' or 'No, that wouldn't happen,'.*

*Sarah Patrick for doing a beautiful job of typesetting the cover.*

*Dot Long for the the great proofreading.*

*Peppermint Press who always do a fantastic job of the printing.*

*And finally, to my amazing husband Jonathan. He is my first reader, the photographer for the cover of all my books and my daily inspiration. Thank you for telling me I can do it on those days when I thought I should quit and go get a job in Edinburgh Woollen Mill.*

*For all our daughters...*

*When your heart stops beating*
*Will you be happy, with the things you've done.*
*When it's all over*
*Will you lie back and say the time has come.*

*Song Lyrics, Suzy Agius Beaverstock*

# Thursday

## Lottie

'Want more coffee?' Lottie Logan asks, as she picks up the pot, trying to ignore the fact that this is possibly the biggest day in their five years of married life.

Dan fails to respond. She could understand it if he had his head buried in the newspaper or a book, but he just stares out of the window, chewing on his toast. She notices crumbs in the corner of his mouth.

'Dan?'

He turns. 'What?'

His face holds the expression she dislikes the most, pinched and hard. Then it softens as he realises where he is. He drifts away more often with each passing week, but perhaps the results today will bring him back for good.

'Coffee?' she shakes the pot at him.

'No. Thanks.'

She doesn't ask what's wrong any more, there's little point.

'Where were you?' she asks instead, hoping he's thinking about the same thing. That would be something at least, his answer deflates her.

'The front lawn needs cutting.'

She gets up from the table and takes her coffee to the sink to pour it into her travel mug.

'You off? he asks.

*At least he noticed I moved.*

'Yeah, I'll drink this in the car on the way.'

'Have a good day,' he says, and returns to his contemplation of the lawn.

She doesn't want to do this, but once again he has left her no option.

'Shall I meet you at the clinic then? 4pm?', ' she adds, in case he's forgotten and needs to ask. She couldn't bear that.

He nods without looking at her, it hurts but she pushes on. 'Meet you there then,' her voice is upbeat, breezy.

He nods again. Lottie leans forward, kisses the top of his head and leaves disappointed.

*It'll be better when we know*, she thinks, as she drives away.

Despite her earlier start there's heavy traffic and it's after nine when she finally gets into the office.

Her PA and their receptionist, Sandra, beams a welcome at her. 'Good morning part timer,' she quips.

'All the perks of being the boss,' Lottie says, they both know she is usually the first in and last out. 'Any messages?'

'No, not yet.'

'Good, I have a ton of emails to get through.'

'Serves you right for rolling in at this time.'

Lottie laughs as she makes her way down the corridor to her office.

She enters, stows her handbag in the bottom drawer of her desk, switches on the coffee machine set up the night before, hangs her coat on the back of the door and finally sinks into her executive chair in front of her desktop, the familiar morning routine a balm to the strain of life at home.

*This is going to be a good day,* she thinks, and pushes all doubts to the back of her mind.

As if Lottie has sent this out on the ether as a challenge to the universe, Miriam Winston's sour face appears at the office door.

*Oh god, that's all I bloody need.*

'Morning Miriam, how are you?' she asks brightly.

Miriam has the sculptured physique of a keen runner and the eyes of a magpie. No piece of glinting gossip escapes her. If that wasn't enough to irk Lottie, the woman had a 'can't do' attitude  reserved especially for her.

The woman strides in. 'Fine, fine. The staff meeting?'

'Team meeting,' Lottie corrects her.

'The *team* meeting this week.'

'What about it?'

'I'm sorry, I can't make it.'

Lottie wonders if this is another one of her games and disdain for this woman prickles her body. She has picked a subject for a fight, and Miriam knows it. As relaxed as Lottie is as a boss, there are the two things she insists on: they follow process and everyone attends team meetings.

Miriam has been passed over twice for Lottie's position, and within a week of Lottie starting Miriam informed her she felt someone on the recruiting panel of the board had it 'in for her'. If they did exist outside of Miriam's imagination, Lottie would happily shake the person's hand.

'I'm assuming, Miriam,' she says, her voice tight. 'That there is a very good reason.' She contains her anger, just, but it hisses out with her words like a pressure cooker with the lid on wrong.

Miriam smiles. 'Of course,' her tone is treacle. 'Doctor's appointment.' Her chin juts out and Lottie is tempted to give it a jab.

'I see. And is it an an urgent appointment, or routine?'

'It's personal,' she says, and waits to see what Lottie will do next.

Miriam has had her faults, but she hasn't been like this before. Lottie wonders at this new tack. She takes a breath, unclenches her hands and places them on the desk top so she's not tempted to damage the woman.

'Is it absolutely unavoidable Miriam? You know how important I think it is for the team to meet together regularly. We have lonely roles, we need each others support.'

'I appreciate that only too well, however in this instance there is nothing I can do about it,' her tone is haughty.

Lottie nods, recognising defeat when she sees it. 'Well, thanks for letting me know, although it is disappointing.'

'As I said, it is unavoidable.'

It crosses Lottie's mind that Miriam might genuinely be ill, but one look at her triumphant face suggests she isn't. Still, Lottie can't be sure.

'And that other thing?' Miriam asks.

'Other thing?' Lottie says, playing for time.

'Yes, we were going to discuss following process, or rather, the lack of it.'

She is referring to a small breach of process one of the family workers has made and Miriam has just revealed her hand. Lottie relaxes, the woman is not ill, at least not seriously.

'I hadn't forgotten,' she says. 'But after some reflection I thought it would be better to address all the staff together, rather than individually. It's the major agenda item at the next team meeting. The one you are unable to attend. Sandra will provide you with a copy of the minutes, and if you have any questions she'll find you some time in my diary. Now, if you don't mind?'

Miriam's face puckers as she leaves and Lottie remembers something Winston Churchill said about nothing being so exhilarating as being shot at without result. Smiling she returns to ploughing through her emails.

'Thanks for doing this,' Lottie says later that morning, standing up from the table in her office and stretching. 'Especially on your day off. Coffee?' she asks, as she moves across the room to the coffee machine.

'Please,' says Poppy. She runs a hand through her spiky red hair, scribbles something on a piece of paper, then throws down the pen and leans back. 'It's no biggie,' she says, and gives the piercing in her lower lip a quick twist. 'I didn't have anything else to do. Stevie's spending the day with a friend. Suppose I'll have to get used to spending half terms on my own in future. I can't believe she's twelve next month.'

Lottie switches on the machine and returns to the table, running her hand over her head to ensure her hair is still neatly in its pony tail, pulling

13

on her fringe to fan it across her forehead, is long hair still appropriate at thirty-four?

'It's my mother's birthday today,' she says, surprising herself.

'Don't suppose you sent her a card?'

Poppy knows the whole story. Well, nearly. They shared their histories one night over a couple of bottles of wine. Lottie shakes her head and the two women sit in a silence disturbed only by the gurgling of the coffee machine. The smell of the grounds fill the room

'It's a good bid,' Poppy says, indicating the paperwork strewn between them on the table.

Lottie nods and the conversation peters out again.

She glances across at her friend. They met at a networking event a year ago and became friends instantly, though no one would think it to look at them. Poppy looks intimidating if you didn't know her, but Lottie learnt to look past the obvious a long time ago. It's why she's good at her job.

The coffee machine bleeps, and she brings the pot over to the table.

'Does it bother you?' Poppy asks, as Lottie fills the cups set on the table.

'What?'

'Not having your mother in your life?'

'No,' she replaces the pot and sits down.

'Yeah, I can see the benefits. There are times when I wish mine wasn't, especially when she bangs on about my love life.'

Grasping the life line Poppy has thrown her Lottie laughs and says, 'What's a love life?'

The two women smile and sip their coffee. Poppy knows about the strain between her and Dan too.

'But like I tell her, I'm married to my job,' says Poppy.

Silence descends. The mention of her mother's birthday hangs like an unwelcome spectre, flattening the atmosphere. It seemed she would never be rid of the woman.

'What does she look like?' Poppy asks, as if she too can sense the woman's presence.

'Nothing like me,' Lottie says. *I look dull and staid in comparison, like a hen next to a macaw.* 'She was...stunning.'

'Stunning?

'Yes. And when she smiled it was as if...as if the sun was shinning just for you.' Lottie stares into the distance, clasping her cup, remembering the feeling. Then she sits up straight and looks at Poppy. 'Until you got to know her.'

'Books and covers, eh?'

'Something like that. She was...how do I describe it...?'

'Like dog shit wrapped in Christmas paper?'

14

Lottie laughs. 'Poppy!'

'What?'

'Okay. Crude, but accurate,' she says. 'Shall we get back to it?'

Two hours later, after much coffee, laughter, a sandwich and some more work, Lottie sees Poppy out with the promise of a night out sometime and heads off to her next meeting.

Memories threaten. Bad ones mostly. Even after all these years, but as she presses down on the accelerator she pushes them away, she has bigger things to focus on today.

# Thursday

## Andrea

Andrea Parker hates this smell of death that lingers around her. A putrid smell that no washing can eradicate. It's different from immediate death, from a blood loss death. The iron in the air, the raw meat of it. In her experience there's something pure about that. Not like this...this...rotting. She is ashamed to be associated with it.

'Just gently,' nurse Jean says, as she rolls her onto her side to put the towel underneath her. 'Need to get you clean, make you more comfortable, eh?' She rolls her onto the other side.

If Andrea had a granddaughter she imagines Jean is her, though she's a little too plump for her liking. Hippy and big arsed, she decided yesterday, as Jean left the room. She'd have to say something, if she was her granddaughter.

'How's that?' Jean asks, when she rolls Andrea onto her back.

'Fantastic,' she says, sarcastically. Jean looks at her and smiles, then leaves the room to get the water.

No sense of humour Andrea decides, and confirms with a glance that she does indeed have a bigger than average arse for her body size. Shame, she'd look good with a few pounds off. Still, Andrea likes her better than any of the others.

'You heard anything about that daughter of yours yet?' Jean asks, as she carries the bowl in. She places it carefully on the trolley at the end of the bed.

'Yes. I've got a number.'

Jean wrings out the flannel, but doesn't say anything more.

'I'm going to ring her tomorrow, when I feel better.'

Jean nods and falls silent. Andrea wants to say something, anything to take the attention from the fact that she's washing between her legs. This is no way to spend your last birthday on earth. No one tells you about this part of illness, about these embarrassments and inconveniences. Like no one tells you when you're pregnant that after the birth if you want to take a crap you'll have to take the baby in with you.

'You married Jean?'

'No, I told you.'

'Just checking.'

She drops the flannel in the bowl and dries the area that she has just been washing.

'Checking what?' she asks.

'Checking you're not lying to me.'

'And why would I be doing that then?'

'People do.'

'About being married?' she sounds incredulous.

'Perhaps not,' Andrea doesn't want to shatter the poor girl's illusions, but Andrea's met many a man who's lied about that, and more. Cal for one. Was she really to blame for all that carry on? She knows she invited him in, introduced him, agreed with his plan for Lottie, sort of, but Lottie didn't have to go through with it, if she hadn't wanted to. She was old enough to make up her own mind, wasn't she? It just...got out of hand...that's all.

'Andrea?'

'What!' She hears the snap in my voice. Jean takes a step back. It's the first time Andrea has let the mask slip and Jean's face tells her she's still as terrifying as she ever was, if she wants to be, indeed even if she doesn't it would seem.

'Sorry,' she says. 'I'm very uncomfortable today.' It's true, though not for the reason Jean thinks.

Jean smiles. 'Don't give it another thought. I don't think I'd be the nicest person to be around if I were in your shoes,' she blushes when she realises what she's said. 'Sorry, I didn't mean...I mean, I'd be much worse than you...oh dear,' she puts hand in front of her mouth.

Andrea wants to laugh at the silly girl's softness. Boy oh boy, life is *really* going to chew her up.

She waves at the girl. 'Don't worry about it, I know what you mean.'

'I was trying to remove your nightie so I can wash under your arms,' she explains.

'Must you?' Andrea asks, feeling tired by it all.

'Well, I'm supposed to, but I guess I could leave it just this once,' she says, doubtful.

'Would you?' she pleads with her best pleading eyes. 'It's all just such a chew on, and I'm not convinced it makes any difference.'

'You'll get sore if we don't wash you, ' Jean explains. 'You need to be clean, it's important.'

'I know, but does it have to be done *every* day? I mean, I'm hardly training for the Olympics am I?'

Jean looks vague.

'Exerting myself, you know, working up a sweat?'

'No, I guess it can't hurt just for once. But you mustn't tell a soul. I could get into a lot of trouble.'

'It's a deal.'

She pulls Andrea's nightie down, rolls her over to one side and then the next, removing the towel from beneath her, and then helps her get comfortable. 'Better now?' she asks.

Andrea nods.

17

'It should be fine, with these new mattresses and all,' Jean smiles with satisfaction and takes the towel and wash bowl out of the room. Andrea lays her head back and wonders when all this humiliation is going to come to an end. And if they're right about this afterlife, when she can join Andrew.

Assuming she will be in the same place as him. She has done so many bad things in her life. Taking the money was only the half of it. She shouldn't have taken the money, she knew she shouldn't. She shouldn't have blamed Lot's boyfriend, she knows that too. But she was already in so deep by then. Cal owned them, taking the money didn't make any difference. She has to believe that. She has to.

Oh for the joy of just being snuffed out. This elongated death, this time for reflection, it's ridiculously overrated. Things she'd forgotten pop up to torment her.

Funny how one small incident in your life, one apparently minor decision, can snowball into another and another and another. How one apparently minor decision can impact on the rest of your life. So Andrea has to reel all the way back, start at the beginning, or one beginning. You have to start somewhere.

So for her the beginning started when Andrew met Rosie, before Lottie was even conceived...

### Andrea 1964

It was a Saturday night in the Red Lion. Smoke hung like a low cloud in the middle of the room and Diana Ross creamed out 'Baby Love' from the juke box as I made my way through the crowded pub. In the snug at the back I found Andrew sitting there with his mate, Mark Harvey.

'Hey hey, hey, she's here,' Andrew declared, when he saw me.

I felt tantalising and sexy as I joined them at the table, aware that Mark checked out my legs as I sat down.

'Drink?' Mark asked.

I looked at him and gave him my best smile. I knew I looked hot tonight. I was wearing a new midi dress I'd bought off the market that day. Navy with white panels down each side that emphasised my already thin waist, and my knee high white boots showed off my legs perfectly.

'Love one,' I said, a little breathless, on purpose, not because I was out of breath.

Andrew laughed and rolled his eyes and I shot him a glance of annoyance.

'What'll it be?' Mark asked.

'Port and lemon or larger and lime, depending on how generous you're feeling.' I smiled, knowing he'd bring back a port and lemon, they always did.

Mark left to go to the bar.

'Haven't seen you at home much lately,' Andrew said, offering me a fag. 'What you been up to?'

'Not much,' I leaned in to light it. 'Dad's been on my back a bit so I thought I'd keep my head down.'

'It's not difficult you know?'

'What isn't?' I asked, taking a long drag and holding in the smoke.

'Keeping on the right side of him.'

I blew out a long stream of smoke before I spoke. 'Speak for yourself, he thinks the sun shines out of your proverbial.'

'That's because I've got that apprenticeship lined up. Get a job, start paying some board and he'll leave you alone.'

'Said I'd meet Hayley here, you seen her?' I asked, changing the subject. I'd looked around but didn't fancy much. Hayley was working at Paton and Baldwins but I didn't fancy factory work. I wanted to be a secretary, but my typing was dreadful and I got bored practicing.

He shook his head, his eyes squinting at the smoke from the fag hanging from his lips. I leaned forward and pulled it from his mouth.

'Hey!' he said, his forehead creasing 'What yer think yer doing?'

'It looks uncouth,' I told him, handing it back.

'Who d'you think you are? The Queen of bloody Sheba?' he snarled.

'No, and you're no James Dean either. Yer daft sod.'

Mark came back with my port and lemon.

'Thanks,' I said to Mark, and I smiled at Andrew. He shook his head again and laughed. He was never angry with me for long.

'I've applied for the police,' Mark said, when he sat down.

'I thought you already were?'

He shook his head. 'Nah, just a cadet at the moment. I'm applying to be a police constable.'

I raised my eyebrows. 'OOOHHH, did you hear that Andrew?'

'Yeah, they'll take anyone these days.'

Mark playfully punched Andrew and the two men laughed.

'So when do you hear?' I asked.

'I've got an interview next week.'

'So...do you get a uniform?' I smiled slowly, I quite fancied dating a man in uniform.

He grinned, 'I already have one.'

In truth I'd had a bit of a thing for Mark for a while, uniform or not, but I'd been playing it cool. I'd seen some of the girls throwing themselves at fellas and it always ended in tears. I wanted to be a little more...careful. At least, at first. I knew he liked me, but oh my god was he shy! We had been playing this daft damned dance for weeks now, or had I been playing it too cool?

'Andrea,' he paused, and I held my breath. Surely tonight he would ask me, for god's sake give him the courage to ask me. 'Andrea, I was wondering-'

'Hey there's Johnny Caldwick,' Andrew said.

*Oh for the love of god!*

I had my back to the entrance of the snug so with clenched teeth I turned round to look. 'Johnny' was a wardrobe of a man, with a mop of black hair and shovels for hands.

'Who's that with him?' Andrew asked.

He was referring to the woman standing beside Johnny. A petite framed dark haired doll, with pixie features, all neat and in place. She looked tiny in comparison to him. She wore a black midi dress with pearls. Very classy, I thought, a bit too classy. I'd heard about her, all airs and graces that were neither necessary nor welcome round here.

I saw Mark looking at her. 'It's Rosie Pickles,' I said.

'D'you know her?' Andrew asked, not taking his eyes from her.

'Sort of, I've heard she's a stuck up cow,' I said, and turned back to my drink.

'So...' I said to Mark. 'You were going to say something?'

He was still looking at Rosie.

'Mark?' I barked.

I smiled as he turned to give me his full attention and raised my glass.

'Yes?' he said.

'Nothing, just trying your name out on my lips.'

Normally Andrew would have made some quip at this point, but he said nothing. I glanced at him and my insides froze. He didn't seriously want to be messing with Rosie Pickles.

'Leave it Andrew,' I said.

'Huh?' he said, turning to me at last.

'I said, leave it.'

'Leave what?' he laughed.

'Rosie bloody Pickles, that's what.'

He laughed again and picked up his near empty pint.

'She's Cal's girl,' I warned.

'Not for long,' he said, draining what was left. 'My round I think.'

Andrew left with his empty glass and I turned back to Mark. He was looking over my shoulder, watching Andrew make his way to the bar, a frown crinkled his forehead.

'You look worried,' I said.

Mark shrugged. 'I'm sure he'll be alright,' he said, picking up his drink.

I raised my glass. 'Yeah,' I said, a knot forming in the pit of my stomach. Everyone knew Johnny Caldwick's reputation, and no one with any sense messed with him.

That night was the night Mark *finally* asked me out and we started dating. In the weeks that followed I barely saw Andrew. I was convinced he was avoiding me, and the rumours that Cal and Rosie had split up made me nervous.

For our three month anniversary Mark was taking me to the Eastern Promise on Grange Road, a Chinese that hadn't been opened long and was considered very exotic. Not many people I knew had been and when I told my friend Hayley she nearly bust a gut.

'No! God you're sooo lucky. I've been dying to go there.'

'I know, aren't I?'

'God, Andrea, everything always works out for you.'

I smiled. She was right.

'It's just being gorgeous,' I told her, with a laugh. I was only half joking, I knew it helped.

I preened and prettied myself all afternoon, excited about going out to a restaurant. This was the life I wanted. Restaurants and glamour, not my mother's life of ironing and a trip to the seaside once a year, and definitely not kids, all we seemed to do was stress her out.

When we entered the restaurant the lights were low and strange music was playing in the background. We were led to our table. Mark had reserved a booth.

'What d'you want to drink?' he asked.

I shrugged. 'Wine?' I said, not really sure.

When the waiter came over Mark looked me straight in the eye and ordered a bottle of Blue Nun. I rewarded him with my best smile. Once I'd chosen from the menu with, 'anything you want', ringing in my ears, and the wine was poured and sipped, conversation inevitably turned to Andrew.

'Did he tell you he was seeing Rosie?'

I shook my head. 'I've barely seen him to be honest. You probably see more of him than me. What about it?'

Mark shook his head. 'Nothing.'

'What do you know?'

I saw the struggle on his face and then he shook his head. 'Doesn't matter,' he said eventually.

'I'm not some fragile flower that needs protecting, you know,' I said, my anxiety rising.

Mark looked at me for a long time without saying anything. I don't generally get uncomfortable with people looking at me, usually I like it, but his expression made me shift in my seat and clear my throat.

Mark looked away, shook his head and finished his wine quickly. He refilled the glasses, the air thick around us. I waited, unsure what to say.

'I'm sorry,' Mark said, after taking a drink. 'It's just that...Andrew's talking about getting engaged.'

Surprise replaced concern. 'What? That's nonsense. They hardly know each other.' Andrew would have told me, besides, my brother had always been the more sensible one. I was the impulsive twin, the one everyone shook their heads and rolled their eyes at.

We sat in silence as we waited for the meal to arrive. There were times, I thought, when being a twin was a pain. There's no you, it's always two and it seemed I couldn't even go on a special date without Andrew lurking somewhere in the background.

Mark leaned over and took hold of my hand and I felt relief. I wanted to get this night back on track, not talk about my bloody brother and I found myself wishing, just for once, that he would disappear for awhile.


The following day I was making a cheese sandwich when Andrew came into the kitchen, Mark's comment *had* bothered me, so I asked him if it were true.

'Yep,' he said, as simple as that.

He picked up the kettle and filled it. I waited for the thunder of the water to finish before I continued.

'You two are *actually* getting engaged?' I asked, eventually.

'Yep,' he put the kettle on the stove and struck a match, lighting the gas ring under it.

'Bit soon isn't it? You barely know her.'

'I know enough.'

I tried a different tack. 'You're treading on dangerous ground,' I said.

He knew what I meant. 'Aw, Andi, what's he gonna do? Thump me?'

I watched him walk across the kitchen, shake the match dead and throw it in the bin. He was thin, lanky and pigeon chested, whilst Cal was a big, robust, shed of a man. It would be like pitching a whippet against a bull dog, and I didn't fancy Andrew's chances if it came down to a scrap. When I factored in Cal's reputation for fighting dirty, I was nervous for my brother.

'I just don't think Cal's going to let this go.'

He pinched a piece of cheese and threw it into his mouth.

'I agree,' he mumbled, his mouth full.

'So? Doesn't that worry you?'

He shrugged. 'A bit, but what can I do? If Cal's decided I need a good kicking, we all know that's what I'll get.'

I put the knife down, turned and leaned against the counter so I could get a proper look at him.

'You know what they say about him don't you?'

'That he's an evil piece of shite? Yeah, even more reason for Rosie not to be seeing him. She's too good for him.'

'And you know he could hurt you? They say he's got policemen in his pocket, that he *knows* people, that he's *done* things. Things we only read about in papers.'

He just shrugged.

I sighed. 'Tell me one thing Andrew, is she worth it? Do you really think Rosie Pickles is worth taking a kicking off Johnny Caldwick for?'

'Abso-bloody-lutely,' he grinned. He picked up a mug and waved it at me. 'Fancy a brew?'

I shook my head in exasperation and turned back to making my cheese sandwich. The daft sod could go to hell.


The night it happened started out as any other Saturday night. Mark met me under a town clock festooned with Christmas lights. When we arrived at the Red Lion Andrew and Rosie had seats saved for us in the snug. I joined them whilst Mark went to the bar.

'Hi, Andrea,' said Rosie.

I nodded at her as I sat down. I had nothing against Rosie personally, but I would have preferred it if she *wasn't* dating my brother. I could only see bad things coming out of it. I turned to Andrew.

'How are you?' I asked, I had barely seen him since our last conversation.

Our Mam hadn't said much about the engagement, but I could tell by her tightened lip when Rosie's name was mentioned that she wasn't happy about it either.

'Grand, you?'

'Alright. I never see you these days.' It came out as more of a rebuke than I intended.

Andrew just laughed.

'Hayley's in,' said Mark, coming up with the drinks.

My heart sank. 'Oh god, where? Did she see you?'

'Of course. She's at the bar,' he put the drinks on the table. 'I told her to come on over.'

'Why did you do that?' I hissed at him.

Mark stepped back. 'What's the matter with you? I thought she was your friend?'

I rolled my eyes. 'She's been such a pain recently, moaning *all* the time.'

'She does have a lot on her plate,' it was Rosie, in that simpering voice of hers. God! What did my brother see in her?

'I know that,' I told her. 'She is *my* friend.'

'So what's going on with her?' Mark asked, as he sat down.

I didn't say anything, I had no idea, so I just shrugged.

'Come on,' Mark said, laughing. 'Spill.'

'I'm off to the ladies,' I said, to buy some time.

I passed Hayley at the bar and stopped to ask her how she was.

'Oh, you know? Same.' She handed over the money for her drink.

'What's going on?'

Her eyes darted to the people around us. The bar was smokey, crowded and noisy.

'I'd rather not talk about it here,' she said, casting her eyes to the floor.

I stepped closer and smiled. 'Hayley, no one's listening to us, look around.'

It was true, everyone was engrossed in their own conversations. Hayley took her change from the barmaid and put it in her purse.

'Is it serious?' I was curious now, and wondered how Rosie knew something I didn't. How had she wormed her way into our social circle like this?

'I'm...' she shook her head, looking around again. 'I told you.'

I struggled to remember, but nothing came to mind.

I shook my head. 'You pregnant?' I asked.

Her eyes opened wide in shock. 'No! Of course not.'

I didn't think so, unless it was the immaculate conception, but it was all I could think of. 'Then what is it?'

'You don't remember?'

'Hayley, you talk about lots of things, how can I possibly remember *everything* you tell me?'

'I suppose,' she sounded dejected. 'But all the same, I'd rather not talk here,' she stood squirming on the spot.

'Oh, so you'll tell Rosie Pickles but you won't tell me, your best friend,' I knew I was being unfair, but I had to know what was going on. 'At least, I *thought* you were my best friend. Still, suit yourself.'

'Andrea, it isn't like that.'

'No? That's what it looks like to me.'

'No, it's just...here, now, I'd rather not.'

I shrugged. 'Okay, as I said, suit yourself.'

I turned to walk away and she grabbed my arm. 'Wait,' she said.

I stopped and faced her. 'So?'

She leaned towards me and lowered her voice. 'I'm having surgery.'

'Nooooo. What for?'

'I...I may lose my foot.'

'Your what?' I said, loudly. People looked round at us.

Hayley shushed me.

'My foot,' she hissed under her breath. Of course, I had heard her, I was just shocked. Shocked she might lose her foot and shocked that it had passed me by. How had that happened?

'But...but...why?'

'I have a neuroma.'

'A what?'

'It's like a thickening of the nerves, or something. An inflamed nerve I guess, between my toes.'

I must have still looked confused because she added, 'a tumour?'

It was then I remembered Hayley had started limping, and vaguely remembered her mentioning it, but I hadn't taken much notice. I thought she was just doing it for attention.

'But your foot?'

She nodded, and tears started to form in her eyes.

'God, don't cry Hayley,' I was sorry I had asked now, I didn't want a scene in the pub, and I didn't want to see her upset either. I never knew what to do when someone started to cry.

'Sorry,' she said, and put her head back, as if gravity would stop the tears from falling.

'When did you find out?'

'I've know for months, the doctor's been trying some different things to see if the swelling would go down, but last week he told me they would have to operate.'

'And will you *definitely* lose your foot?' I wanted to make sure she wasn't being melodramatic.

'There's a strong possibility, because of the position of the neuroma.'

'God! Really?'

She nodded.

I didn't know what to do next. So we stood at the bar, Hayley sipped her lager and lime, I stood looking around. I knew I should invite her to sit with us, but I really didn't want to. I was uncomfortable around this sort of thing. Maybe that's why I hadn't remembered her saying it, I must have blanked it from my mind. It wasn't my fault I wasn't nurse material.

'I'm off to the ladies,' I said eventually, and left her standing at the bar. I'd get her something nice, I decided, to make up for it. Not shoes, obviously. I knew it was mean, but the thought did make me smile.

When I got back she was sat with Mark, Andrew and Rosie. I joined them. They were talking about her impending surgery, which I knew they would. This was going to turn my stomach and put a proper damper on the evening. Brilliant!


We left the Red Lion about ten thirty and headed across town to Shades Nightclub. Hayley, to my relief, went home. Unfortunately Rosie didn't.

Mark and I walked behind Andrew and Rosie, they were holding hands and I realised Mark wasn't reaching for mine the way he usually did. Now I thought about it, he had seemed a little off with me in the pub too.

'You alright?' I asked him.

He nodded, but he didn't look at me.

I stopped walking and after a few steps he did too. He turned to face me.

'What you stop for?'

'What you sulking for?'

'I'm not sulking.'

'You look like you are, what's wrong?'

Mark shrugged.

'Look, I'm not asking again, either tell me what you're sulking about, or I'm going home.'

'Suit yourself,' he said.

I was so angry I turned and stormed off in the direction of home, not having enough for a taxi I realised I was going to have to walk, which made me even more angry. After a few moments I heard his footsteps behind me and smiled with relief. I wouldn't have to walk home after all. He grabbed my arm and swung me round.

'Wait!'

I stopped. 'What the hell for?'

'God, Andrea, you are hard work sometimes.'

'Oh, right, is that your idea of an apology?'

'No, it's just...'

'What?'

'It was you.'

'Oh, again, apology accepted...!'

'Hang on,' he said, as I turned to leave.

I waited.

'Look, I'm...I'm sorry, alright?' he said.

'What's the matter with you?'

'It was the way you were with Hayley, and Rosie for that matter. I just...didn't like it.'

I shrugged. 'I don't know what you mean.'

'You left Hayley standing at the bar on her own for a start.'

'I was going to the loo! You'd already invited her to join us. I just thought she would. It's hardly my fault if she just stood there like a spare part besides, she did join us.'

Mark paused, thinking about what I had said. It wasn't entirely the truth, but it sounded better than what had *actually* happened. I *had* left her there, I *had* hoped she wouldn't join us. I knew it wasn't the kindest thing to do, but I didn't want to be talking operations and amputated feet all night. I *was* sorry for her, but it turned my stomach. What with that and now a moody Mark, this was not turning into the night I had looked forward to.

'And Rosie?' he asked.

'What about her?'

'You ignored her for most of the night.'

I paused, giving myself some time to think. Bloody Rosie!

I decided to be honest. 'I don't like her going out with Andrew,' I said. I put my sweetest voice on, I couldn't have him thinking I was a complete cow. 'I'm worried for him Mark, after what you said.'

I could see he was softening.

'You can't treat her like that, Andi,' he said.

'I know, I know it's silly, but I thought that if I could push her away then Andrew would dump her and be...safe? I wasn't trying to be mean.' It wasn't all the truth. I didn't like how Mark laughed hard at her jokes and I hated that I didn't see Andrew any more, but it was enough of the truth.

'I know, baby,' he said, pulling me towards him. 'But you have to let him go out with who he wants.'

I sighed into his neck, and pushed against him. I knew exactly what I was doing and I could feel that I was having the desired effect against my stomach.

He pulled back and coughed. 'Erm...we'd better catch them up,' he said.

I nodded.

'Andrea?' he said, as we walked hand in hand.

'Yes?' I still had my simpering voice on.

'I...I think I love you,' he said.

I smiled. Of course he did, but it was nice to hear. 'We'd better run,' I said. 'To catch them up?'

He nodded, looking disappointed, and we ran hand in hand until we caught them. Andrew looked back at us as we approached.

'I thought you guys had headed off home.'

'Since when have you known me miss the chance of a dance?' I asked, breathless.

He laughed. 'We did think it odd.'

My teeth clenched. I didn't like the 'we', nor the idea that they had been discussing me. Bloody Rosie!

'You okay?' Mark asked.

I forced a smile and nodded. 'Sure.'

He leaned over and kissed me and my heart fluttered.


Mark and I had danced hard, I was sweaty and hot, and the alcohol was making my head spin.

I leaned over and shouted, 'I need some fresh air.'

He looked at his watch. 'It's nearly kick out time, you want to go now?'

I nodded, then pushed between Rosie and Andrew.

'Andrew, we're going.'

He nodded, went to Rosie and said something in her ear, then shouted to me. 'Wait for us, we're just gonna finish these,' he picked up his glass. 'Won't be long.'

Mark and I left, collecting my coat on the way out. Outside I welcomed the cold December air against my skin.

'Ahh, that's better,' I said, my ears still thrumming.

'Put your coat on,' Mark suggested, as the noise of the music turned to a muted throb through the closed door.

'I'm fine.'

'Snow's forecast tonight.'

'Doesn't feel like it,' I said, but I pulled on my coat anyway.

Mark grabbed my hand and pulled me to him. 'Give us a kiss,' he said.

I giggled and kissed him. It was sweet, and lingering, and I found myself out of breath when we'd finished.

'Wow,' he said.

I leaned back in his arms to look at him. 'What?'

He shrugged. 'Just...wow,' he smiled, and leaned in to kiss me again.

I didn't resist. This time when we were finished I found I'd got hot again, my heart was thumping hard and I knew what I wanted. My head spun at the excitement of it. I untangled myself from his arms and grabbed his hand.

'Hey!'

'Come on,' I said, and pulled him off the main street.

'What about Andrew?'

'He'll wait,' I called, as we headed round to the back of the club.

Once there I pushed him against the wall and we kissed deeply. He moaned and I knew he was as excited as me.

We stopped kissing, and he said against my lips, softly, 'I don't want our first time to be like this, Andi.'

I pulled away. 'Isn't that supposed to be my line?'

He laughed and shook his head. 'What am I going to do with you?'

'I'll show you...if you like,' and I started to undo his trousers.

Within minutes it was over and we were tidying ourselves up. Mark had been right, behind the club in an alley that smelt of stale beer and piss wasn't an ideal setting for our first time, but the recklessness of it was exciting, and I knew Mark was smitten, it would be okay.

When we had rearranged our clothes and were decent again Mark took my hand and pulled me towards him. 'Andrea?'

'Yes?'

'What I said earlier...'

'What bit?' I asked, knowing exactly what he was referring to.

'That bit about I love you?'

'Oh that,' I smiled. 'What about it?'

'I meant it you know?'

I laughed. 'There's no need,' I said.

'Don't do that.'

'What?'

'Push me away.'

'I'm not pushing you away, I'm just saying.' But he was right. I *was* being cautious.

'You're a queer fish.'

I leaned forward and kissed him on the nose. 'Good,' I said.

29

The sound of shouting and arguing floated over to us.

'Typical bloody Saturday night,' Mark said, with a groan.

I laughed. 'When you're a bobby are you going to sort it out?'

'Too bloody right I am. Come on, let's go and find the others, they'll probably be waiting for us by now. '

'Make sure your flies are done up, can't let Andrew know what you've been doing with his baby sister,' I said.

He laughed, grabbed my hand and we walked round to the front of the club. I think that walk was the last time I was genuinely happy.


I couldn't believe the effect Mark was having on me, he was making me soft and there's a danger in that. I'd seen it in other girls, from goddess to doormat in the blink of an eye, so even as the euphoria of feeling I might be falling in love hit me, a voice in my head reminded me to tread carefully.

When we rounded the corner a crowd had gathered and I was curious. Mark tried to hold me back, he wasn't much of a spectator, but I liked to get a front row seat. I pushed my way through the crowd, releasing Mark's hand as I progressed forward and as I reached the front I saw a body in the gutter. A frisson of excitement ran through me, immediately followed by a fervent wish that what I saw wasn't true.

My heart slowed, the blood stopped and my brain didn't quite compute what it saw at first, didn't want to recognise the body in the gutter. The red stream was mesmerising. I tried to dismiss it, what would Andrew be doing lying there like that anyways?. Then the mist of alcohol and after sex glow cleared, and it dawned on me that yes, that was the body of my brother lying there, bleeding.

My legs gave way and I found myself kneeling beside him, lifting his head up and cradling him to me, calling his name. His eyes fluttered so I knew he was still alive, even though there seemed an ocean of blood flowing from him. That's when I lost it.

'Phone an ambulance! Phone a fucking ambulance for fuck's sake!' I screamed.

Then Mark was by my side. 'Oh shit,' I heard him say, then he too knelt down beside me.

I could feel a lump, a hard lump of something painful in my chest and screamed out again. 'Will some fucker phone the ambulance!'

A voice from the crowd told me they had, and it took my fight away. Everything that could be done had been done, so now all I could do was hold the head of my bleeding twin and pray that he wouldn't die right there in my arms.

I pulled him up and wrapped my arms around him, aware now of the cold hard pavement against my knees laddering my tights, the sex juice dribbling into my knickers. Mark sat beside me, his hand on my shoulder, rubbing from side to side, but instead of it comforting me it irritated. I wanted to lash out and punch him to make it stop, instead I shrugged his hand away.

Someone walked from the crowd and stopped at Andrew's feet. I took in the shiny pointy shoes and knew who it was without looking up, so I didn't. I didn't want to see his shitty cunt of a face.

'Well, well, well, what do we have here?' he asked, his voice bass drum deep.

I didn't know where Mark was, and regretted shrugging him off. I was suddenly afraid. I knew who had done this to Andrew and I found myself incapacitated with fear, fear that he was about to do the same to me. Slowly I looked up the length of his body, until I took in the ugly features of Johnny Caldwick. I noticed Rosie was stood behind him, looking pale as a ghost.

'So, someone did poor Andrew in did they?' he said, as if he didn't know anything about it, whilst his demeanor said different. 'Just shows you, doesn't it, Andrea?'

I just stared at him, unable to say anything. Fear and grief and anger clogging my throat.

'Yep,' he said, with a sigh. 'Just shows you,' he turned. 'Come on Rosie love, let's get you home.'

I watched him as he put a proprietary arm round Rosie's body. To my surprise she pulled away from him.

'Don't touch me!' she said, her face now reddening as she turned and looked directly at me.

She mouthed something but I couldn't make it out. She repeated it but I shook my head. Cal grabbed her arm and growled a warning I couldn't make out.

She pulled away again and pushed her way through the crowd with Cal following close behind. My heart jumped in fear. Once she might get away with, but twice, and in public...she was either very brave or very stupid.

Breathless she crouched beside me. 'He'll pay for this,' she whispered quickly, but before I could say anything Cal grabbed her and hauled her off her feet and back through the crowd.

I wondered if I would ever see her alive again, but as I returned to cradling my brother, I realised I didn't care.

A few minutes later the ambulance arrived and Andrew and I were hurtling through the town towards the hospital. As I held his hand and watched him slip away to the sounds of the sirens overhead, I wept and made two vows: Nothing would hurt me like this again, and no matter what the cost, Johnny Caldwick would pay one day.

**Lottie**

The room is warm, a woman from the Job Centre is droning and Lottie's eyes feel heavy. Her mind wanders to the possible results of the appointment, going over the ramifications of each for Dan and herself.

In an effort to stay focused she straightens up in the chair and looks round the table. There are twenty professionals here, and she starts to tot up the cost, not convinced of the effectiveness of this multiagency board. She pushes the cynical direction of her thoughts aside as they move to the next item on the agenda: A new initiative called the '80/20 Programme' launched by the council.

'So, the idea is that 80% of your work, your sales, or our problems in this case,' the project lead begins. 'Comes from 20% of your inputs. For this initiative we've set up a task force and made a list of the 20% of families who, potentially, cause about 80% of our workload and cost. Obviously we can't be that exact, but you understand the principle we're working to. The three problems we've specifically targeted for this trial are,' she pauses, looks down at her papers for reference, and then continues. 'Truancy, substance misuse issues, and petty crime.'

'That list has been circulated as a confidential paper to all members of the board,' the Chair informs them.

Lottie is relieved to see she isn't the only one who fumbles through the papers to scan the report. She knows she should read these papers before the meeting, but she never seems to find the time.

'To use an example, the Craig family has been identified as one who would fit into the 80/20 project,' Helen Jackson from probation, says, looking up from her papers.

Lottie's ears prick. Her organisation has been working with the Craig family for the past six months and she has a personal interest, one which she hasn't disclosed to anyone.

'Just to remind members,' the Chair says. 'We have agreed to use names in the meeting, but we will not be minuting them.'

The Chair gives the floor to Debra Wood, the Craigs' social worker.

'The father is in prison at the moment. The mother is a heavy drinker and drug user. The three boys, ranging from eight years of age to thirteen, have a history of truancy and petty crime.'

She is interrupted by a policeman, whose name has escaped Lottie.

'Looks like they're following into the family business,' he quips. He grins and a dimple appears. His attitude makes Lottie's skin bristle. *What is his name?*

'Quite,' Debra continues, her tone like lemon juice in a paper cut. Lottie bites back a smile.

'But it's the eldest child, Jenny, who we're most concerned about,' she says. 'Jenny Craig is fourteen and sexually active. That's not unusual on the estate, but we think there may be sexual abuse in the family, an uncle, the brother of the father. We suspect the mother knows about it and could be taking money for it, but we have no proof.'

Lottie's hands ball up into two tight fists.

'Possibly to fund her drug habit,' adds the woman from the Drug Action Team.

'Yes, very likely,' says Debra.

'Can't we *do* something about this?' asks a thin haughty woman, the councillor for that ward, directing the question at the policeman.

'We're unable to prove anything, and until we do our hands are tied,' he shrugs, and Lottie can't help thinking that actually, he really doesn't care, and she wants to use her balled up fists on his face. 'We can't very well go round arresting people without evidence,' he says, somewhat defensively.

Dave Sunders! That's it. Lottie examines the policeman further. He has dark handsome looks, spoilt by the look of entitlement he wears. She's seen that look before, and decides she doesn't trust him.

Debra continues, ignoring the glares between Dave and the councillor. 'Jenny rarely attends school and was recently pulled in front of the truancy board with her mother.'

'And unfortunately I have to agree with Dave,' Debra adds. 'There is very little we can do at this stage. We're working closely with Lottie's team at Children First.' She glances over at Lottie who nods in response. 'All we can do is continue to work with the family and hope something comes to light before it's too late.'

'Exactly,' this is the council's project lead again. 'The point today is not to ascertain what can be done, we'll set up a sub committee for that.'

Lottie groans inside, another bloody committee and she's bound to be expected to attend.

'What we're doing today is simply explaining the basic premise of the 80/20 project, and highlighting the initiative to the board, so the sub committee can report back.'

Lottie zones out as the Chair summarises the discussion for the minutes. She thinks of Jenny, in front of that truancy board with her mother, and aches to do more. More that is, than sit on another bloody committee.

## Lottie - 1980

'I don't know what to do with her,' my mother said.

It was the eve of my fifteenth birthday and we were sitting in front of three stern figures that made up the truancy board. They glared at me, demanding to know why I had not attended school, as I sat and listened to my mother's lies.

'I've even taken Lottie right up to the school gates.'

My mother was rarely out of bed before noon, sleeping off the effects of the previous night. Even later if she'd brought a man home with her. It was a small house and no amount of anything stuffed in my ears would drown out the sound of her moans. I doubted if I would *ever* get that enthusiastic about *anything*. The day after she always emitted a musty pungent smell. I loved that smell, associating it as I did with her being in a good mood.

Mum was still talking. 'She's in one door and out the other. I blame this new boy she's taken up with.'

There was no boy. I fancied Baz, Barry Johnson, off the estate, but every girl did, and I had as much chance of going out with him as flying to the moon. He'd spoken to me a couple of times in the street, well, shouted after me. He made my heart hammer and my face go red. But I ignored him, just put my head down and walked faster. I knew he was just setting me up for a laugh, the latest victim in some elaborate joke. Girls like me didn't date boys like Baz. So my mother was lying, there was no boy, we both knew the real reason I wasn't at school. Her.

'Do you have anything to say for yourself, young lady?' It was the balding man. An overweight barrel with a wobbly chin. The tiny glasses perched on the end of his nose gave him a pinched look. An unremarkable man, I decided unkindly. I knew he was doing his best to look stern, but he didn't have a hope in hell of scaring me. None of them did. They had a long way to go before they even came close to Mum. They were predictable, but my Mum...Mum might do just about anything.

I shook my head. There was little point. I'd tried to get help before and it always ended badly. Keith, my last social worker, had been my final attempt. I'd asked him for help but asked him *not* to tell mum, he ignored me. It took me a week to recover from that beating. My left ankle still buckled when I ran.

My Mum was cleverer than she looked. It was a dangerous combination and no match for anyone we had yet to meet. People underestimate the intelligence of a beautiful woman. They underestimate the evil of one too. And Mum was as ruthless as she was beautiful.

The words 'nothing at all?' brought me back to the room. It was said by the bird like woman with a beak for a nose. Her eyes glinted and I could

35

see her loathing, feel it stick and cloy. I didn't blame her. From the outside I looked unkept and insolent, shabby and rude, and people rarely looked beyond the outside.

Then, briefly, I did care, I wanted to explain myself, tell the truth, until I felt my eyes prickle and slammed the door on it. I didn't have the kind of life where I could care, and if I cried I'd be in for it.

I pushed my chin out in an effort to keep the tears at bay. 'No,' I said.

'Even though you have caused your mother such distress?' said bird woman.

My mother was weeping next to me. A new emotion started to erupt, a boiling lava that caused my teeth to fuse. This was so unfair, and there was nothing I could do about it.

'Perhaps one word, one *very* important word?' the woman's voice cut through the lava.

I turned my attention to her. She clearly wanted something from me and I scrambled about in my fog of emotion.

'There isn't *one word* you'd like to say for *all* the distress you've caused to your mother and your teachers? For wasting the precious gift of an education?'

Then the fog lifted and I nodded, swallowed and spoke. 'Sorry?' I whispered.

She banged her papers together, clearly still not happy despite the fact that she'd just got what she wanted. I had a teacher like that, Mr Rowell, pain in the arse he was. Come to think of it, I had a mother like that. The thought made me smile.

The bald barrel spoke now. 'This is not a laughing matter, young lady,' he began. He went on about the importance of education, its value, passport to a better life, blah, blah, blah. I watched his jowls wobble as he spoke and nodded where I thought I should, but it was all white noise to me.

These people, my teachers, my social workers, none of them got it. None of them understood that my life, at least for now, was squarely in the hands of the broken woman sitting next to me, and until she decided she was done, or I grew old enough and lucky enough to find a way out, there was nothing I could do.

The thin younger man at the end spoke for the first time, giving us a final warning. If my truancy levels persisted to this degree, they would have no option but to 'intervene'. I liked the word and made a mental note to look it up.

'We would have no choice,' he repeated. His voice was monotone, lacked authority and I wondered how he got his kids to do anything he told them. 'We would have to remove Charlotte and take her into the care of the authorities.'

I had been in care before, at the age of seven when my mother was admitted to the psychiatric ward for slashing her wrists on the stairs. They came and took her away and put me in a home. One of the staff fingered me. He smelt of onions. I did not want to go back there.

Still, it wasn't up to me.

### Lottie

Lottie and Dan sat on red plastic chairs, the ones you find in every NHS waiting room. The ones that seem to cut into the back of your legs. They have waited so long she has tingles in her right foot

In the last six months they had been to this clinic several times to be probed, prodded and tested. It was the culmination of desperation. The previous four, of their five years of marriage, had slowly filled with home ovulation tests, morning thermometer readings and temperature charts. They used to cuddle after sex but now, on the more and more infrequent times they managed it, Lottie held her legs in the air to help the sperm on its journey to her, hopefully, waiting fertile egg. So far, all to no avail.

When they first came here they held hands, hopeful, expectant, but now, weary of the journey, they read magazines in their separate bubbles. Whether it was them or the process wasn't clear, and Lottie tried not to think about it

No one tells you how hard it is to have a baby. Teenagers are told 'don't have sex!'. But the secret truth is, as Dan and she had learnt to their cost, there's only two or three precious days in every cycle. A small window of opportunity. You have to be really lucky, or really unlucky, to hit that. And no one warns you that when you're thirty-four and aching for a child, trying to hit it will consume your every waking moment.

Dan's fertility was okay, he'd been tested and given the thumbs up. Today it was her turn. She was waiting to hear if she'd passed a test that she'd had no opportunity to prep for. She had never failed anything in her life, nothing she had set her mind to anyway. No exam, driving test, job interview, nothing. Up to now. And now, when it really mattered, when there were no re-sits or second chances, and no opportunity to do some last minute swotting, she realised she had absolutely no control over the result and it was terrifying.

She looked at Dan engrossed in a classic car magazine. Would he stay if she was barren? Barren. What an ugly word. It was right up there with spinster. Did they do that on purpose?

Her thoughts were interrupted when they were called into the doctor's office, and as she stood a wave of nausea threatened to upend her.

'A pelvic what?' asks Dan.

'Pelvic Inflammatory Disease or PID. It's an infection of the upper female genital tract. This includes the womb, fallopian tubes and ovaries,' the consultant explained.

'How did she get this? I mean my wife…' Dan's eyes dart to her and she can feel heat rising in her cheeks.

'It's a sexually transmitted disease.' The doctor says this in a perfunctory way.

'A what?' Dan looks incredulous. 'That's impossible,' he turns to Lottie. 'Tell him.'

Lottie opens her mouth but the words stick in her throat.

'Tell him!'

The doctor tries to smooth things over, misunderstanding Dan's upset. 'Mr. Logan, this disease was contracted a *very* long time ago.'

Lottie knows exactly when and the heat deepens as she watches Dan grapple with the news.

'How? When?'

The consultant takes a breath before speaking. 'Mrs. Logan has chlamydia.'

'Wouldn't she know?'

'Not necessarily. Some people have no side effects. If left untreated it can cause infertility. So whilst we can't give an exact time, we do know, because of the damage, that it was contracted some time ago.'

Dan falls silent and Lottie steels a glance. He is gazing out into the car park, wearing the same far away look he wore that morning, and Lottie fears for their future.

'There are other things we can do, treatments we can try,' the consultant ventures.

'Is it…is it hopeless?' Lottie finally asks.

'Well, we never say never, but frankly, given the amount of scarring on your fallopian tubes I'd say it was virtually impossible for an egg to travel down into the womb.'

'But not totally impossible.'

He smiles kindly, and leans forward. 'In my professional opinion, it is virtually impossible and it would be cruel of me to suggest otherwise.'

Lottie hears a door slam and voices travel along the corridor, rising as they neared and falling away again into the distance.

'And there's nothing we can do?' It was Dan, returning from wherever he had been.

'As I said there are fertility treatments-'

'I mean about *her*?'

His last word cuts into Lottie's flesh.

'I...I...no, I'm afraid not,' the consultant says, clearly taken aback.

Dan stands. 'Thank you for your time,' he says, and leaves without looking at her.

Lottie smiles an apology at the consultant and quickly follows, her heart beating, her mind whirling. This is not going to be easy to explain.


They drive for a few minutes in silence, Lottie holds her breath, waiting for the inevitable, hoping it won't come.

'So...' Dan says, at the first set of red traffic lights, yanking the handbrake on. 'What the doctor said...?'

He leaves it hanging, waiting for her to fill in the space.

'What about it?'

'What's going on?'

'Nothing's going on.'

'Something happened.'

'It's not important.'

'Then tell me.'

She looks at him for the first time since they left the doctors. His eyes glare at her with such intensity she has to look away.

'Lights,' she says, with relief.

He releases the handbrake and pulls away.

'I always thought...' his voice is just above a whisper.

'I know.'

'So?'

'It was a very long time ago. Before I met you.'

'Why didn't you tell me?'

'I didn't know until today.'

'I don't mean that, for christ sake!'

She knows he doesn't but she can't think of anything to say, can't think of an explanation except the truth, and she can't bring herself to tell him that, for surely that would be the end of everything.

'I'm your husband,' he says, softer now.

'You weren't then.'

'But I am now, and this affects our life.'

He flicks on the indicator and the sound fills the car until the car turns and it clicks off. The engine picks up as Dan pushes down on the accelerator. She can't think about what happened, what it now means, so instead Lottie focuses on these sounds.

'Lottie.'

'I don't want to discuss it.'

'Damn it Lot, don't shut me out like this.'

It's the final straw for her and she turns. 'You mean like you have recently?'

'I don't know what you mean,' he says.

There's a falter in his voice that makes Lottie wonder if it's been something else that has pushed him away, that it isn't the strain of the fertility tests at all.

'You do know what I mean.' Her voice is soft.

'I've had a lot on at work.'

'I'm not talking about your physical absence, although god knows there's little enough of that, but even when you're home you're mind's elsewhere.'

'Can you blame me? All we ever talk about is babies and fertility and cycles. It's like coming home to Doctor Spock.'

'Doctor Spock wasn't a fertility expert, he advised parents in the sixties. Anyway, it's all over now so you don't have to worry,' the last word catches in her throat. It is all over. Done. Gone.

'What's that supposed to mean?'

Lottie takes a deep breath to steady herself. She has to be a grown up about this. 'As I can't have children the subject's off the table.'

'Jesus! This isn't just happening to you, you know?'

'But you...' she stops herself. It won't help to say it.

'What?'

'Nothing.'

'What? Come on, say it.'

'Nothing.'

'For christ sake Lot! Stop playing silly buggers.'

Okay, he asked for it. 'You never really wanted them anyway. I expect you're relieved.'

'What? What an outrageous thing to say. I have never said that. When did I say that?'

'You didn't have to!'

The silence hums, the air molecules agitated not by the shouting, but by what isn't said. They remain like this for the rest of the journey. When they pull up outside the house Dan doesn't switch off the engine.

'You not coming in?'

Dan shakes his head. 'I need some time. There's a lot to...to take in.'

Lottie doesn't protest. It's better this way, this way he might leave the past where it belongs. She gets out of the car and bends down.

'There's nothing to tell,' she says, by way of a reconciliation. 'It was a long time ago.'

'Yeah, you said,' Dan says, facing straight ahead, refusing to look at her.

She sighs, stands upright and closes the door. The car speeds off and Lottie turns towards their home. This wasn't the end to the day she had hoped for.

Several hours later, when Lottie puts the phone down she can't quite take it in. It's as if something isn't in the place it ought to be. She goes over the experience in her mind.

Did the man on the phone really say that? Her brain scrambles round trying to make sense of it, put it somewhere, file it away, but it doesn't fit anywhere. She hasn't had this sort of experience since she was a child, since...Cal.

Then the upset comes up, grows into panic and frustration, like when you're a child and you get your head stuck in a jumper. You pull and pull, and the more you panic the more you feel stuck. She is like that now, trying to escape from the feelings that threaten to overwhelm.

Her heart thumps and her hands start to shake, tears threaten so she stands up.

'Don't be silly, it's only words,' she says out loud.

But they stick, those words. They make her feel tainted, used.

She feels assaulted, just as sure as if the man were right here in her home, and today of all days. With the news, and the memories, and Dan not being here.

*But then, he never is these days*, and tears form again. She goes and checks the doors are locked and comes back to the sofa.

*I was rude,* she thinks. *I told him I didn't want to speak to him - that's rude.*

'I'm not interested in speaking with you, please remove my details,' she had said.

'What are you not interested in?' he kept asking. So she kept repeating it.

She said it three times.

Until he said, 'and are you not interested in sucking my dick!'

41

She hung up.  Now she wishes she'd said something cool like, 'I doubt I'd be able to find it' or...or...something like that.

She just hung up.

She just hung up.

And now the phone is ringing again, and she's afraid and her mind takes her back to another place, the day she met Johnny Caldwick.


**Lottie 1980**

It was the day after the truancy board, my fifteenth birthday, when Mum told me she had got me a job on a used book stall.  I was to start the following Saturday.  I thought all my Christmases had come at once.  It was easily the best present I had ever got and she *even* gave me a card.

I hugged myself tight, then tried to hug Mum.  'You're the best,' I said, clinging awkwardly to her shoulder.  I was going to work on a book stall! A book stall!

She stepped out of my grasp and looked at me.  'Don't let me down now.  I called in a favour at The Lion.'

'I won't, I won't,' I hopped round our kitchen, barely able to contain myself.  Oh the joy, the absolute sheer joy of it.  I couldn't believe it!

'Yeah alright, well, calm down and make us up a cuppa.'  She sauntered off into the living room, lighting a cigarette as she went.

I took time over her tea.  She liked it a particular way, the colour just right, a deep brown with plenty of milk, so the tea had to be really strong.  I'd been scorched a few times by a badly made cup of tea and I wanted to get it spot on today.  Not just so's I could avoid getting burned, though that would be a bonus, but because today I just wanted to do something nice for her, the way she had for me.  Besides, when she was in this good a mood she sometimes gave me a ciggie.  Anyways, even if she didn't, nothing could stop this feeling.  Nothing, I decided.  Not even a scalding cup of tea.

Later that day, Mum made me my favourite: spaghetti Bolognese, and we sat with it on our knees in the living room while she explained.

'It's a second-hand book stall on the market,' she said, round a mouthful of food.  'For a fella I know called Johnny Caldwick.'

The name slowed my blood.  I'd heard of Johnny Caldwick on the estate, there were rumours he'd murdered someone.

'Not *the* Johnny Caldwick?'

'Sure,' she waved her hand to dismiss my concerns and lit up.  'It'll be fine.  I've known him for years.  People exaggerate.  Anyways, he needs someone to look after the stall when he's not around,' she took a deep drag off her ciggie.

Suddenly I forgot any concerns I had. 'So...so, I'll be running the stall?'

She pouted her lips and blew out a long stream of smoke. I wished I had such a pretty mouth. 'I doubt it,' she said. 'Not at first anyway, but given time, yeah, maybe.'

I was going to run a book stall, not just work on one. 'Great! Can't wait,' I said, how could this not be amazing?

'He'll be here to pick you up Saturday morning.'

I tried to ignore the knot of anxiety in the pit of my stomach.

Mum knew him, I reminded myself. It would be fine.


Johnny Caldwick, Cal for short, was a large man who came up the path like a moving wardrobe. His brow protruded in the way I'd seen pictures of cave men in the books at school, and he had the same thick lips. His hair was thin, greasy and slicked across his balding head.

There was something menacing about him, nothing specific, but I felt ever so slightly nervous in his presence. I decided it was because of his eyebrows, they met in the middle and gave him an angry look. That and probably the fact that there was talk he'd killed someone. He looked like someone who would kill someone.

Mum was up, which was odd. It was all odd. Mum awake, dressed and made up. This large man entering our home. A taxi ride to work. A job on a book stall.

I wasn't used to men much. Occasionally Mum would bring a fella back. Sometimes she told me to 'fuck off up to bed', and at other times she hissed at me in the hallway 'Don't you dare fucking leave me'.

These men were strange creatures of the night, with a noticeable need for sex and an apologetic shameful air about them, and they were gone as quick as you like the next day. But not this man.

This man stood in our hallway and took up all the space, sucked up the oxygen, making no apologies for his presence. He had a large stomach, huge hands and wore a suit, shiny from wear. When he moved the skin under his chin wobbled.

'Here she is,' Mum said, standing behind me, hands on my shoulders, presenting me. It reminded me of the television programme 'Upstairs Downstairs', when the daughters were presented at the coming out ball.

43

I was suddenly nervous, fearful now not of him, but that he wouldn't like the look of me and would not give me the job after all. Perhaps, despite wearing my tidiest jumper and jeans, he would think I was too shabby to serve his customers. Maybe he, like the truancy board, would only see some insolent little oik and leave, taking his job and his taxi with him.

I smiled my best best smile, desperate that he wouldn't leave and take all this new and exciting stuff with him.

'What d'you think Cal?' I heard the nervousness in my mother's voice and realised that for once, she knew how important this was for me, how much I wanted it. My heart squeezed with gratitude and in that moment, for all her faults, I truly loved her.

Cal swiped long greasy strands of hair across his balding head and peered at me. He towered over me as I waited, his eyes moving up and down my body till they landed on my face. There was something in his gaze that made me uncomfortable and I instinctively went to step back, but my mother's fingers dug hard into my shoulders as she thrust me forward.

'Well?' she said, a little breathless now. I couldn't see her face, but I could hear the smile in her voice.

'Might work,' he said. 'We'll have to see. Take it slowly.'

He might think that, but he didn't know how quickly I picked things up, I'd show him. I'd show them both.

My mother's fingers relaxed. 'Agreed.'

'Right then, you,' he said to me, pointing. 'Ready to sell some books?'

I nodded and grinned, all discomfort forgotten. I was going to work on a book stall. A book stall!


Cal's second-hand book shop was a stall in the inside market in the next town.

'The rates are cheaper,' he explained, on the taxi ride there. I hadn't ridden in many taxis before. They were too expensive. So I was impressed by this apparent wealth. Wealth he was spending on me. I could have easily got the bus but decided not to tell him that. It was raining and in here it was warm, dry and there was the radio.

Otis Reading's 'Dock of the Bay' played in the background. It was one of my favourites, but I tried to ignore it and focus on what Cal was saying instead. Still, despite my best efforts part of my attention stayed with the music.

'I've ran it for about four years now. Canny little number.'

Cal explained that customers bought books at one price and then, on return, they received a small amount back in credit against their next purchase.

'What's your maths like?' he asked.

I stopped listening to the radio and my mouth ran dry, because of course, since missing so much school, my maths had suffered. I'd been in the top set when I started the secondary school, but at the beginning of each year I was moved down, and now I was languishing at the bottom in the CSE class. I wasn't going to stick around to do exams anyway, and I hated maths, but now... Now maths suddenly became vital.

I shrugged, deciding that all I could do was brazen it out. I'd seen my Mum do it often enough. 'Okay I guess, how hard can it be, right?'

He nodded. 'S'pose. As long as you can add, and do percentages, that's pretty much the top and bottom of it.'

My stomach clenched. Percentages! All that dividing by this and multiplying by that confused me. I was convinced I'd only been in the top set in the first place because they'd made a mistake. I blamed Mr. North from my junior school. He was always telling me I was brighter than I thought. He was probably responsible for the top set mix up, thinking he was doing me a favour.

Bugger! I thought a love of books would be enough to work in a book shop. I hadn't figured on the maths bit. I'd just have to wing it, until I could pick it up. God, I hope I could. I just had to hope Cal didn't rumble me before I did.

'I'll stick around for awhile, till I know you've got the hang of it. Then, if all goes well you'll be on you're own. Okay?'

I nodded, I wanted the earth to open up and swallow me. How was I going to pick it up with him hanging around? The thought sat heavy on my stomach for the rest of the journey.


I needn't have worried. Within a few weeks I was at home on the book stall and Cal wasn't nearly as scary as I'd first thought. Neither was the maths. It was simple. Twenty-five percent back on the purchase price if they were buying another book, ten percent back if not.

My tasks were simple: stamp new books inside with the purchase price and the two return prices; serve the customers; update their card with their returns and purchases; take their money; file returned books; keep the stall tidy and, if Cal was there, do any errands he sent me on.

I soon got into a routine and it wasn't long before he left me to get one with it. I arrived, unlocked, stored the heavy boards underneath the stall, (my least favourite job), and then I'd sort through the books that had come in during the week.

Tony, who owned the fruit and veg diagonally opposite to ours, would help me with the heavy boards when he could, and he often brought me coffee. We'd stand and chat about how business was going. I felt grown up, as if I really did own the stall. Sometimes, at the end of the day, he'd give me a juicy peach or a soft banana.

All my earnings were handed over to Mum of course, but I didn't mind. All day I got to read books, talk about books, handle books, smell that musty smell of the browning paper, feel the soft suede of the worn pages, learn new words. I would have paid Cal to be there, though I never told him that of course.

Cal started visiting Mum and me at home. Bringing beer or wine for mum, Cresta for me, Our electricity was reconnected so we didn't have to plug into next door to watch the TV. Mum bought herself a new dress. Smiled more, gave me more ciggies. Food started to appear regularly in the house. I didn't ask how we could afford it at the time, and if I'd thought about it I'd have realised that my Saturday wages couldn't pay for it all, but it never occurred to me.

In short, I was happy.

Everything just seemed...easier in my life since Cal appeared. He was like this great big fat angel, so I couldn't believe the things I'd heard about him. The whispers, the rumours, I dismissed them all.

After the first two weeks Mum stopped getting up when the taxi came for me and went back to sleeping late. I preferred it that way. It unnerved me to see her up and about before noon, it was like seeing some creature outside of its natural habitat, like a lion walking up the high street. It just wasn't right.

After the first couple of weeks I was never sure if Cal would be in my taxi but this week, my fifth, he was there when I climbed in.

'Now then Cal, alright?'

'Can't complain. You?'

'Alright.'

'Been up to much?'

'Finished that Jane Eyre book. It was brill. You read it?'

'Nah, not my cuppa tea. Bit of a girl's book that. I like Ian Fleming.'

We chatted about nothing for the twenty minute ride and when we arrived Cal sent me off to get a tea and coffee whilst he unlocked the wooden panels. I was pleased. It was the one bit of the job I struggled with. They were heavy and I was just over five foot two with stick arms and legs, so I always staggered under the weight of them.

I came back with two teas and a coffee, and nipped over to Tony with one of the teas. He was busy with a customer so I left it by his till and started back to the book stall.

'Hang on a minute love,' he called to me, then turned to his customer and asked them to wait.

'Alright Tony?' I said, returning to his side, surprised he would interrupt a sale.

'Yeah, fine, thanks pet. What's his nibs doing here?'

'Cal?' I shrugged. 'Usual I guess, just checking up on his best store girl,' I smiled at my own joke.

'You just go careful pet.'

'What d'you mean?' There was something in his tone, his demeanour that took my smile away.

'Just,' he patted my arm. 'Just promise me you'll look out for yourself. Okay?'

I looked over to see Cal looking across, something in his expression told me he didn't like what he saw. I hurried back to the stall, a tightness in my stomach.

'What was all that about?' Cal asked.

'What?' I said, buying some time, not sure what was going on, but getting the same creeping dread I got sometimes with Mum's moods. It was a feeling I'd learnt to trust.

'Tony over there. What's he say?'

I started going through the books that had come in and needed stamping and pricing. This was my favourite part, deciding how they should be 'categorised'. It was a new word, categorised, and I liked it.

'Just thanking me for the tea,' I said, without looking up.

'Does he need to put his hands on you to do that?' There was a snarl in his voice and I looked at him in surprise, my stomach tightening further.

'Eh?' I said, not sure what else I could say.

'His hands. On you.'

'He only patted my arm,' I said, but I could feel my face flush.

'Yeah well, you just watch him,' he growled, as he turned back to his tea.

It struck me as odd, how each man had warned me about the other, and yet how different each had made me feel. Against my better judgement I chose to ignore the nagging fear in the pit of my stomach. Cal was okay, I kept telling myself. Until I saw his gun.

When Cal didn't come to the stall he would drop by our house on the Sunday to pick up the takings. I'd been working for him for six weeks and this was the best Saturday so far. He was pleased when I handed it over. Mum never messed with the takings and I got the impression that she was more wary of Cal than as I was.

He handed me an extra fiver as a bonus for doing so well, which would have been great had he not done it in front of mum. I saw the greedy glint in her eye and knew she'd have it off me as soon as he left.

'Go and put the kettle on,' Mum said, and I left them alone. I could hear the murmur of their voices but not what they were saying. I'm not sure what made me do it, but while the kettle was boiling I crept into the hall and listened at the living room door.

'...might be too early,' Mum said. 'A little more time perhaps?'

There was a long silence then Cal spoke again. 'We have an agreement,' his voice was hard and fear crept through me, tingling my fingertips. I'd never heard Cal speak in that tone.

'I'm going down the smoke on Thursday and I need fresh meat, Andrea.'

'Okay, yes,' Mum said impatiently. 'But not straight away. This has to be done...slowly.'

The piercing whistle of the kettle shattered my insides making me lift off my feet. With a thumping heart I ran back to the kitchen to make the tea. As I did so I reflected on what I had heard.

What agreement did Cal and Mum have? And what did she mean by too early, what was too early? And what was that about smoked meat? Did Cal have a butchers business? Was he going to let us have some bacon maybe? That would be lovely. I loved crispy bacon. I took the tea into the living room and handed the mugs out to Cal and Mum, then sat down.

'You not having one?' Cal asked.

I shook my head. 'I don't like tea and we don't have coffee. Too expensive.'

Cal looked at Mum. 'Get the girl some coffee,' he instructed her. Mum nodded. Her easy agreement unnerved me.

He leaned forward to put his tea on the coffee table and the left hand side of his jacket flopped open. That's when I saw it.

Shock must have registered on my face because Cal looked at me and followed my eyes, but instead of hiding it quickly as I'd expected, he put his hand in and withdrew the gun from the underarm holster.

He held it out to me. 'Here,' he said. 'Take hold of it.'

I didn't do anything at first. Just looked at the large dull metal gun, hardly believing my eyes.

He weighed it in his hand. 'Go on,' he urged.

I looked at Mum and saw fear in her eyes, but she raised her eyebrows in an encouraging manner. She was clearly as afraid of this thing as me, but wanted me to indulge Cal.

I stretched out my hand and took it from him. The first thing that struck me was how heavy it was. Very different from the plastic guns I'd handled in toy shops. And it was icy cold, deathly cold.

'Why do you have a gun?' I asked.

'Protection,' he said. 'And to make sure no-one messes with me,' he glanced at Mum and she flinched.

'It's...heavy,' was all I could think to say, and handed it back. I didn't want to hold it any longer.

Cal laughed. 'Can really make a mess of someone, take their face right off.'

I nodded.

'Need it for the smoke,' he said, placing it back in its holder. 'In case anything kicks off.'

'The smoke?'

'London, love.'

So it wasn't smoked meat then. I was disappointed, probably meant we wouldn't be getting any bacon.

Later, when he'd left, Mum lit a ciggie and offered me one. We lit up and I asked her if she knew Cal carried a gun?

'No,' she said. 'No, I didn't.' She stared straight ahead, her hand was shaking as she lifted the cigarette to her mouth.

'Did you know he owns a butcher's?'

She shook her head, it was obvious she wasn't really listening. We smoked in silence.

Cal was becoming a different person. He visited London, took cabs, carried a gun, ran lots of businesses, all this information rattled through my mind and I wondered what else I didn't know about this man my mother had invited into our lives.


The sound of the phone brings Lottie back to the present. She tries to ignore it; afraid of what it might bring, but after six rings she has steeled herself. This time she'll give the little pervert a shock. She wasn't ready before but this time, she tells herself, as she pulls herself off the sofa and crosses the living room, she'll scare the little bastard witless.

**Andrea**

On the rare occasions in her life when she has reflected, she always remembers Andrew's contorted face, the blood, the terminally long ride in the ambulance and the sharp slice of pain when he finally slipped away. Watching your twin die, not just someone you love, but someone you have shared a womb with, a whole life with, someone you consider to be the other half of you, and in her case, the better half, watching them die...well, it never leaves you. Never.

Something in Andrea died with Andrew. He made her want to be a better person, and with him gone, he took what little good she had in her with him. But she was getting ahead of herself.

She wants to tell Lottie everything so they can put it behind them, Lottie can move on and she can die in peace. Is this for her or for the girl? She shrugs, maybe it's both. It doesn't have to be one-sided. No one has to be the winner. Not anymore. Andrea stopped playing that game a long time ago. Though perhaps she shouldn't have left it so long before she called...

Still, she always was one to avoid something if she could.

**Andrea 1964**

The weeks following Andrew's death were a haze. No one knew anything, no one had seen anything, no one was talking, but everyone knew who'd done it.

I tried to tell the police but there was no evidence, just the ramblings of a young grief stricken sister. I realised how it looked and so did Cal. Which was why he wasn't worried. He swanned round town as if nothing had changed, carting a pale Rosie on his arm as if she were something he'd won at the fair. My hatred for him deepened.

The day of the funeral arrived. Mum was glass eyed, Dad gruff. I had never been close to either of them. In my opinion they both worked too hard, had too little ambition and very little to say of interest, but my heart softened that day, recognising how old they had become in the weeks since Andrew's death.

When we got out of the car I stepped between them, holding out my arm. They didn't move, just looked at me.

'Mam?' I said, indicating my arm. The message got through eventually, as if it had been transmitted through thick fog. She took my arm and I turned to my Dad on the other side. 'Dad?'

'Thanks love,' he said.

As we walked towards the crematorium entrance together I saw Mark standing off to the right. He nodded at me and I nodded back. It was the only communication we had exchanged since the night at the club. I didn't want to see him, didn't want to speak with him, and I hoped he wouldn't try to approach me later.

I caught sight of Rosie and felt a jolt of surprise that she had braved the wrath of Cal to be here today. I didn't look at her directly, until a movement caught my eye and looked to see *him* walk up and stand beside her, his hands in his pockets, a sly smile on his face and a glint of malice in his eyes. The fucking bastard, I thought, but fought to bring my attention back to my parents.

I knew they must be hurting. They adored Andrew, 'not a jot of trouble' I'd heard my mother say many times, casting a glance at me. I heard the message, knew that I had given them nothing but, and now they were left with me, and I with them, and the only thing that bound us together, was the pain we shared at the loss of Andrew.

Through the service my mother wept quietly to my right, my father took his handkerchief from his pocket and wiped his face discreetly a couple of times. I didn't take much of it in. I couldn't. I was afraid that if I let even a little of the words in they would undo me and I would crumble. Watching the coffin slip behind the curtain created a catch in my throat and I looked out the window, praying for it all to be over.

After the service we went to the function room at the club. It was a huge room with a bar at one end and a large stage at the other. Long formica tables bridged the gap between the two, stopping just before the dance floor at the foot of the stage.

The room had a dour air. It smelt of smoke and stale beer and the light was dingy. Along the far wall a table had been set up with a buffet of sandwiches, sausage rolls and cheese and pineapple on sticks.

Dad went to the bar to get us some drinks whilst Mum and I made our way to the front of the room to sit at the table near the dance floor. The dance floor was sticky as we crossed it and I couldn't help feeling Andrew deserved better than this for his wake.

People started arriving and making their way to the bar. Of course, we couldn't turn anyone away, but I hoped Cal would have the decency to avoid the wake.

'Alright Mam?' I asked.

'Aye love, holding up, you know.'

I nodded. We sat in silence, watching Dad with the drinks clasped in his hand, chatting with people as he made his way from the bar. Eventually he made it to the table.

He sat down and took a long drink from his pint.

'Go careful, John,' Mam said.

51

'Canny turn out lass,' he said, ignoring her comment.

'He was a popular lad, everyone loved our Andrew,' Mam's eyes started to fill.

'He was that. Here, get that down yer,' he said, indicating the port and lemon he'd put in front of her.

Neither of them addressed me directly and I was relieved. I wouldn't have known what to say.

The three of us sat in abject misery, our loss insufficient to bridge the distance between us. People came and said words, dull words, predictable words, and my parents lapped them up. Desperate to escape, when I saw Mark I forgot my earlier reluctance and made my excuses.

'Hi,' I said.

'Hi. How you holding up?'

I shrugged. We stood side by side, taking in the room.

'Rosie was here,' he said.

'I saw.'

'And Cal.'

'I know.'

'They've gone now.'

'Good.'

There was a pause until Mark spoke again.

'Where's Hayley?'

'Recovering. She had her op a couple of days ago.'

'Oh, yes, I forgot.'

'She kept her foot.'

'Good...that's good.'

I sipped my port. Watched my parents talk to one of the neighbours, my mother nodding her head furiously, agreeing with something, my father sucking on his pint which he'd nearly finished, Mam would give him hell about that when she noticed. Though, maybe not today, maybe today he would be allowed to have another without the grief. There was enough of that today, surely.

'Andrea, about what happened that night-'

'It's done.'

'But it isn't.' He turned, but I refused to face him. I couldn't do this today, so I stayed looking out into the room while he talked.

'What happened between you and me, it was...'

'Fun.'

'Well, yes, but that wasn't what I was going to say.'

'Over?'

'I hope not.'

Finally I glanced at him. He looked in pain and for a moment I felt a flicker of sorrow for him. 'What d'you want Mark?'

His answer nearly broke me.

'Us.'

I bit my lip, swallowed hard and took a breath to steady myself before I spoke. 'Mark, I don't think we're on the same wave length, we want...different things.'

I couldn't tell him that every time I looked at him I was reminded of Andrew lying in the gutter, bleeding to death. I couldn't tell him of the guilt I carried around. I didn't have the words to explain. The feelings were too big, and I didn't have any room inside to think. But as always, he knew.

'It wasn't our fault,' he said, breaking into my thoughts.

'I know, but he was waiting for us. If he hadn't been outside then, or if we'd been there to meet him, or if...I just wish-'

'If wishes were horses, beggars would ride.'

At that I turned to him. 'Eh?'

'Wishing doesn't change anything, action does.'

'And?'

'I'm getting out of here, Andrea. I leave for the police in a couple of weeks.'

'So?'

He sighed. 'You really are hard work you know that?'

I nodded. 'It's been said.'

'I want you to come with me, I want you to...to be my wife.'

My insides shrank back at his words. How could we? How could he?

'I mean, I know the timing's not that great, but sometimes, well, sometimes you've got to grab the bull by the horns, you know? Make something good come out of something bad.'

'Marrying you will not make up for losing Andrew.'

'No, I don't mean that. And I vow I will do everything to make Cal pay, one day. What I mean is...well, we deserve some happiness, Andrea.'

'I buried my brother today.'

'I know, I know it's not great timing, asking you now. But I've tried to see you and you've been too busy.'

'Busy burying my brother.'

'Andrea, please.'

'No, Mark, no. What we did that night meant I lost Andrew.'

'No, it didn't'

'Yes! It did,' my voice had risen and people were starting to look round.

We stood side by side again in silence. I finished my drink.

'Want another?' he asked.

'No, thanks. I should get back to mam and dad.'

As I went to walk away Mark caught hold of me. 'Think about what I said, please?'

I pulled my arm from his hand, nodded without looking at him, and walked back to the table.

'Everything all right?' my father asked, as I sat down.

'Yes, everything's fine.'

'I'm just off to the bar, want one?'

I nodded. 'Why not?'

I caught my mother scowling at me but chose to ignore it. Today of all day's I needed a drink.

I didn't even realise until it was too late. Mark had left for his police training. He wrote for awhile but communication goes both ways and as I didn't answer any of his letters, I guess his new life started to fill the void left by his old one. His letters stopped and we lost touch. It was inevitable.

I was glad. It had been wrong to be doing what we were doing when Andrew was in trouble. It was all just a question of timing.

So by the time I realised I was pregnant it was too late, and it didn't change anything anyway. Mark being off the scene just made it easier.

Can't say I wasn't horrified when I realised, and for about three hours I considered a back street abortion, then I remembered Jenny Dobson. There were too many horror stories going round for me to consider it seriously. I was too afraid, not of infection itself, but the pain and risk of dying. So I tried all the things that are said to 'dislodge' it: hot baths, gin, curry, running, castor oil, bouncing on the bed, I even went horse riding, and I hadn't done that in years. Ironically, I think Mam thought I was getting back on the straight and narrow. Nothing worked. The thing was jammed in there good and tight, and after two weeks of stress I realised there was only one way it was going to come out, and I'd just have to deal with it.

As if our lives hadn't been shitty enough these past few months. As if they needed any further proof that they had lost the best child, I not only had to tell them I was pregnant, but I didn't know who the father was.

I walked downstairs and stood in the hall stairwell, between Dad in the living room reading his paper at the front of the house, and Mam in the kitchen at the back. I can remember the smell of chips frying for tea, the forget-me-nots on the wallpaper, the sounds of Dad's paper as he turned the pages.

My parents and I barely spoke. It had always been that way, Andrew was the oil that lubricated our relationship, and without him cracks had started appear over the last few months. Strained conversations that trailed off. I wasn't sure how to tell them, so I stood there, waiting, for inspiration I guess. I stood there a long time and nothing came. I was just thinking of going back upstairs when Mam came out of the kitchen abruptly and full of bustle.

'Andrea! Goodness, what you doing lurking here?' before I could answer, she went on. 'Call your Dad, yer tea's ready.'

Dad and I were sitting at the table, the fourth place empty. Mam had stopped setting a place for Andrew, although it had taken weeks for her to break the habit.

She put the plates of sausage, egg and chips on the table and then joined us, picking up the teapot and pouring strong brown tea into our mugs.

'Dig in,' she instructed.

We ate, the only sound the scraping of knives and forks on the china.

I kept opening my mouth to tell them but nothing would come out. Not a single sound. What was I so afraid of? I knew I would disappoint them, but I'd done that before, many times. Still, nothing like this. Again I kicked myself for being so bloody stupid. It was all my doing, Mark even tried to resist, not very hard but still...If only we hadn't left early, if only I hadn't pulled Mark round to the back of the club like that, if only I'd listened to his soft protests, ...Andrew might still be here, this dilemma definitely wouldn't be. *If wishes were horses...*

'I'm pregnant.' I didn't even realise I'd spoken until the words were out there.

All movement stopped. The words hung, suspended in the silence, observed, like some curious exhibit in a museum.

Finally my mother spoke, her voice calm. 'Are you sure?'

'Yes, I'm sure.'

'And who...'

'That doesn't matter.'

'It bloody well does lass,' my father said, his knife and fork clattering down onto his plate. He was more incredulous than angry.

I felt relief that they knew. I could relax now, we could sort it out and I could get on with my life.

'This is very disappointing.'

'I know Mam, I'm sorry.'

'Sorry!' It was my father.

I turned to him. 'Yes. *Sorry.* I know it's only a word, but I am, and it's all I can think of to say.'

My father's face was bright red and going redder by the minute.

'John, calm down, it won't do your blood pressure any good, you remember what the doctor said?'

55

'Bloody easy for the doctor to say.'

'John!'

'Sorry love, blame intense provocation.' He scowled at me. I told him to fuck off in my head.

'Still, let's keep our manners,' my mother said.

He nodded and picked up his knife and fork.

'Of course, I'll get the baby adopted when it comes. I can go to a home for the last few weeks, they sort out everything. You needn't worry.'

'You'll do no such thing,' said my mother. 'It isn't ideal, but we'll deal with it.'

'But it's usual in...these sorts of cases,' I insisted.

'You seem to know a awful lot about it,' my father said.

I looked down at my plate, the chips congealing in the fat. 'It's just what I've heard. From friends.'

'Interesting company you keep,' he picked up his mug and drank his tea, glaring at me over the edge.

I ignored him. 'But Mam, why would we want to keep it? Think of the scandal.'

It was her turn to glare at me, 'Perhaps you should have thought of that before?'

I lowered my head again, normally I was up for a fight, but I was on shaky ground for an argument.

'It's flesh and blood,' she said. 'And god knows there's not enough of that in this house.'

'But-'

'Enough, you heard what your mother said. We're going to make the best of this.'

So that was it. I would have gladly given it away, but my mother insisted we keep it, perhaps as some sort of second chance, perhaps as a punishment for me. Who knows? My mother condemned me to motherhood, and what she might have thought of as a second chance, I saw as the death penalty.


So I was stuck with it and my life became narrower and narrower. As soon as I started to show I had to lock myself inside to avoid the shame and condemnation. I had to give up my stupid job at Paton and Baldwins of course, which I didn't mind except it added fuel to an already growing gossip fire. A prisoner in that house, with only my parents for company, I felt caged, trapped and desperate.

The thing grew inside me, making my belly swell and my body hurt in paces I didn't even know existed. Growing inside, eating the food I ate, drinking what I drank, sucking everything from me, narrowing my life and reminding me daily of what Mark and I had done.

So naturally for the remaining five months, I cursed that child every day it was in my womb and prayed daily it would not survive.

The day of the birth was looming and the closer it got the more afraid I became.

'Oh, don't be so daft,' my mother said, when I finally voiced my fear. 'Millions of woman do it all the time. In Africa they just go and drop them in the fields.'

I didn't think they did, but I didn't argue with her. I didn't have the energy and besides, she was missing my point. I've never had a very high pain threshold, and the thought of another human being tearing me in half to get into the world did not appeal in the least. I didn't even want the damned thing to be in my world anyway!

When the day finally came the pain was shocking, it took over every fibre of my being and shook me until I felt traumatised by it. At one point I was terrified I was going to die, an hour later, I begged to.

We both survived and I gave birth to a healthy girl weighing in at seven pounds, two ounces. They turned it upside down, slapped its arse and its bald cry filled a room that smelt of sweat and blood. To my relief they took it off to the nursery and my mother trotted along behind, leaving me some time to get cleaned up and try to gather myself together. I had done battle with some demon in the under world and needed to straighten my hair.

When my mother reappeared at my bedside thirty minutes later beaming, I wanted to slap her. She had no idea what she had put me through, what she had done to me, my body, my life and I didn't think I could ever forgive her.

'What you going to call her?' she asked.

'I haven't thought about it.'

'Andrea!'

'What?'

'I'd have expected you'd have given it *some* thought.'

I didn't say anything.

'She needs a name,' she insisted.

'I know, I'll think about it,' anything to deflect the questions.

Later the nurse arrived carrying a squawking bundle and informed me that 'baby needed feeding'. When I held her I felt numb.

'Isn't she beautiful?' my mother gushed.

She was a mewling burden with grasping hands and a desperate mouth. A red raw trap, an alien that would always want something from me and I shuddered.  I didn't see beautiful, I saw something that had ruined my life.

I handed her back to the nurse.  'Give her a bottle,' I said, turning away.

'I'll do it,' my mother said, jumping up.  I laid my head back in relief.

It was the first of my many steps away from the child.


A few weeks later I still didn't have a name for the baby and Mum suggested we call the baby Charlotte.

'It means tiny and feminine,' she said.

I agreed, it was as good a name as any.  We registered her together, I'm not sure she trusted me to do it and time was running out.

Mum pretty much took care of the child, I hovered round the edges, not keen on getting involved if I could possibly help it.

There were some humdinger arguments, mostly my father telling me what a waste of space I was and asking when was I going to face up to my responsibilities.

'I didn't want any responsibilities, remember?' I shouted.

'Andrea, you are *such* a disappointment.'

'Oh, tell me something I don't know,' I said.

'You know you're problem?'

'No, but I feel sure you're going to tell me.'

'You're too damn smart for your own good.'

'John! Language,' my mother cut in.

'Is that my problem?  I'm *smart*?'

'You think you're better than everyone else, when really you're just a whore.'

'John! No!'  It was my mother again.

Her sanctimonious hypocrisy was too much, and I turned on her.

'Oh, for fuck's sake mother, stop it!  You agree with every word he says, at least he's got the guts to say it.'

I was pleased to see tears spring to my mother's eyes.

'Don't you talk to your mother like that,' my father said.

'Why not?  It's her fault we're all in this fucking mess!'

'Mess, this isn't a mess,' she said.  'Charlotte is a beautiful baby.'

'She's a rock round my neck,' I said.

'Andrea!'

'Leave it love, you'll not get any sense out of her.  She's a bad un through and through.  Don't listen to her.'

I could see in their eyes that same message, why Andrew, why him, why did she survive, and every time I saw it I felt the need to push them even further away. Prove them right.

'I hate her!' I said, pointing to the baby in the walker, dribbling on a plastic rattle. 'And there's nothing you can say that will change my mind.'

It was true, and after every argument I hated the child even more, I couldn't help it. I tried to love her. I picked her up and fed her on occasions, cleaned her arse, bathed her, nothing happened. There was nothing inside of me. I didn't feel connected to her, and besides, Mam did it much better than me, all of it. What could I give her that my mother couldn't, and a hundred times better? I looked at the kid and to me it was just another something in the world that told me how I had failed.

When the child was about a year old she started to talk. Her first words sounded like 'dadda' and for the briefest of moments it pulled at my heart, made me think there might have been a different outcome if only...I wondered where Mark was, what he was doing and who he was seeing. I wondered what might have happened if I'd told him. I remembered the day of the funeral, and wished I could go back, talk to him, have the chance again. I wished I had told him, perhaps we could have worked it out between us.

Then I pushed it out of my mind. What was the point of dwelling on ifs and buts? *If wishes were horses...*

I was here, stuck with parents who thought I was a disappointment, a ruined reputation and a child I didn't want. This was my life, not the champagne and silk sheets of my dreams. Nor even a respectable life carved out with someone I liked by my side. This was it, right here. My mother, in her wisdom, had condemned me to exactly what I didn't want, a life less than hers, and I hated her for it. And I hated the child just as much for enabling her to do it, and what capped it all? I could wave goodbye to any hope of seeking revenge on Cal. Bile thrashed thorough my body. I hated everyone.


Hayley visited about this time.

'I'm sorry I haven't been before,' she said, in that simpering way she had. I'd have much preferred it if she could just be honest. She didn't want anything to do with me now I was 'shamed'. As if she were so bloody marvellous.

We were sitting on the sofa in the front room. Mam and Dad had taken the baby out and I had been enjoying having the house to myself for a change until Hayley arrived.  I didn't offer her a drink, she wouldn't stay so long that way.

'I've been so busy.  Gone back to college you know.'

'No, I didn't.'

'I'm studying to be a legal secretary.'

'Right.'

'It's a long course, but I think it will open me up to new opportunities.'

She sounded like an advert.

'After the scare with the foot I thought, god, I'd best *do* something, you know?  With my life?'

Was she having a laugh?  I wondered.   I looked at her properly. There was something different about her, she'd done something with her hair, or maybe it was the clothes she was wearing.  Something was different anyways.

She smiled.  'How's motherhood?' she asked.

'Shit,' I said.  One of us had to be honest.

Her eyes widened in surprise.  'I...what?'

'Shit.'

She giggled as if I'd made a joke.   'I guess you must be tired though.'

'Yeah, knackered.'

The conversation halted and I watched Hayley look around the living room.  Finally her eyes rested on me and she smiled.  I didn't return it.

She stood up.  'Well, Andrea, I should be off.'

'I'd like to say this was nice...' I said, at the door, but didn't have the heart, or maybe it was the energy, to finish the statement.  Besides, one look at Hayley's face told me she knew what I thought.

I closed the front door behind her with a sigh of relief, and returned to the living room, unsure why I hadn't enjoyed seeing her more, not realising that I would never see her again.


A year later my father and I buried my mother.  Cancer.  It came quickly, raged through her body like a fire in a barn of dry straw.  And all we could do was stand by and watch it devour her.  Turning her from a robust woman to a skeletal cadaver.

The day after the funeral it was just the three of us in the house: me, Dad and Lottie.  She was cranky and awkward that day, as if she knew Mam had gone.  I couldn't do anything with her, nothing appeased her two year old temper, and in the end I lost mine and slapped her across the legs.

60

My father flew into a fury, calling me names and shouting words at me I didn't even know he knew, and without my mother to temper the flow, he unleashed years of pent up anger that not even I could rail against. Lottie screamed in the corner. I stood in the centre of the maelstrom, shrunken with grief and humiliation and desperation.

An hour later, when it was all over, my father came and sheepishly apologised.

'That's okay,' I said, but we both knew it wasn't. It never would be, nor could it be. His words had lodged inside me like shrapnel, they chafed when I moved, and I could not look at him without it causing pain.

Two days later I was on the housing list, and within months Lottie and I had moved out. I never gave him our address and we never saw him again. Another door to the past closed.


### Andrea

Andrea presses the bell. It takes them a long time to come, longer than she thinks it should. When they do it's the dark haired skinny one with pursed lips. They don't get on.

'Can I have the phone?' Andrea asks, in her softest voice. This one doesn't like her. If it was Jean she wouldn't have to beg.

'It's very late.'

'I know, but it's important,' she can see her waver and pushes her slim advantage. 'Please?'

'Alright but keep it brief, I don't want you disturbing the other patients.'

Andrea nods and looks around at the others while she waits. *Not likely. Most of them look half dead*, she thinks. Then she realises they probably think the same about her.

Finally the nurse brings the phone to her bed, plugs it in and leaves her with it. Andrea stares at it, wondering if she can do this, and knowing that really, she has no choice.


### Lottie

The sound of the phone brings Lottie back to the present. She tries to ignore it; afraid of what it might bring, but after six rings she has steeled

61

herself. This time she'll give the little pervert a shock. She wasn't ready before but this time, she tells herself as she pulls herself off the sofa and crosses the living room, she'll scare the little bastard witless.

'Lottie?'

The female voice at the other end of the line is vaguely familiar but Lottie can't quite place it, not the little pervert anyways. She lets out the breath she didn't realise she was holding.

'Lot? Lot is that you?'

That's when it comes to her, bringing it all screaming back, and it takes all Lottie's effort to breathe, let alone speak. The voice is rougher than she remembers, older, but it's her alright.

'Yes,' she manages, finally.

'Lot, it's Mum.'

'Yes.'

'I'm dying.'

Lottie doesn't say anything.

'Lot? Are you there?'

'Yes.'

'Did you hear what I said?'

'Yes.'

'Lot, I'm dying.'

For the third time today her brain tries to handle new information. She fears something might burn out in there.

'Mum?'

'Yes. Will you come?'

'I...I...-'

'Do you have a pen?'

Lottie automatically pulls a biro from the jar of pens that sit by the landline and bends to poise it over the messages pad.

'Yes.'

Her mother reels off an address and phone number and Lottie lays it down, stroke by stroke, until it sits in front of her. She adds, as if she might forget, 'Mum' on the top of the page, and underlines it neatly.

'You got that?'

'Yes.'

'Good. When will I see you?'

'I...I...don't know,' she mumbles something about work, but she's not sure what she says.

'Don't leave it too long,' her mother says, before ringing off.

When Lottie switches off the phone she has to sit down for a moment. Her legs won't support her.

She hasn't seen her for...she passes her hand over her face as she does the reckoning. Nearly twenty years? Not since the week after Lottie shaved her head.

The next morning Lottie had woken up and her mother was gone. That wasn't unusual. But after a week she still hadn't returned. She had left her there. Left her for Cal.

*And now the bitch is dying, and she's sent for me.* Lottie immediately shrinks in shame at the thought. It is her mother after all. And she *is* dying.

# Friday

## Lottie

On impulse Lottie picks up the phone to ring Debra, the Craig family's social worker. Even though she knows shouldn't, that this is a breach of protocol, she has to do something, the call from her mother last night has brought the memories flooding back, and she needs to help someone, needs to fix something, needs to make sure someone doesn't fall, or if they do, she wants to catch them.

She dials quickly, before she can change her mind, and Debra answers after three rings.

'I'm calling off the record,' Lottie explains.

'Oh?' She can tell from Debra's tone that she is intrigued.

'About the Craig family?'

'Oh yes?' now she sounds wary.

'What the latest on them?' Lottie asks. There is a long pause.

She knows it is wrong, she knows she is being unprofessional, but she can't help it. After years of pristine professionalism it is as if she's gone on a bender, like a dieter who has gone mad for doughnuts after years of denial, it is a compulsion, she has to do something.

'I usually talk to Hilary.'

'I know.' She knows what Debra is going to ask next, and her mind darts round, frantic to find an answer, she should have thought this through before she rang, had a more convincing explanation, but then she wouldn't have rung at all if she'd thought it through.

'I'm sorry,' Debra laughs, obviously embarrassed. 'I don't mean to be rude but...really, why are *you* ringing? Is there a problem?'

Lottie laughs to buy some time, and then the answer drops in, like magic. 'Oh no, sorry Debra, I should have explained, my fault. I was in the CTB meeting yesterday. The family were mentioned so Hilary and I have been looking at this particular case more closely, part of the 80/20 project?'

Debra relaxes. 'Oh right.'

'As primary partners I want to see it get off to a good start, so, I thought I'd have a little more…"hands on" approach so to speak, you know, try to see if there's anything in our process we can improve upon, fresh pair of experienced eyes, that sort of thing,' she holds her breath and waits.

'That's fantastic!' Debra says and Lottie relaxes. 'Unfortunately, as you'll be aware, that particular family has many challenges. The children have a chaotic lifestyle and the boys school attendance is dismal.'

'And the girl, Jenny?'

'Well, her school attendance is always worse than the boys. She's the primary carer and assumes a lot of the responsibility for the home. Not unusual in cases like these.'

'No, I understand that. How do they manage financially?'

Her answer makes Lottie's heart stop beating for a moment.

'Surprisingly well. Which leads us to suspect another source of income.'

The implication of what Debra is saying hums between them. Lottie's worst fears are realised.

'And there's nothing we can do?' she asks, even though she knows the answer.

'Nothing.'

Lottie thanks her and rings off. Her heart sinks, her worst fears have been realised and the need to help gnaws at her further. An old familiar helpless feeling rises...too much has happened in the last twenty four hours. The news of her fertility, the argument with Dan, the obscene phone call, her mother's contact, and now her inability to help Jenny are all too much for her body to contain.

She gets up from her desk, walks over to her office door and crouches behind it to weep. Not a lot, but just long enough to let out some of the pressure.

'It's better than shaving my head,' she whispers moments later, as she stands, straightens her skirt and returns to her desk.


## Andrea

Andrea wonders if she did the right thing, ringing Lottie like that. But if she didn't do it quickly, she might never have done it at all, like pulling off a plaster it was best done without thinking about it too much. Now all she can do is wait, and remember...


## Andrea 1968

The first three months were hard. It wasn't just the adjustment to living alone with the sole responsibility of a kid. In the last three years my life had reduced to a house and a baby. No brother, no boyfriend, no friends, no mum or dad. I didn't even have the freedom of a job. As if it

65

wasn't shit enough, I had the reputation of having a bastard. That didn't worry me much, but I couldn't even have a bit of fun.

On the rare occasions I got out for the night that bastard acted like some ancient talisman that warded off good times. Any man I met scarpered as soon as they heard I had a kid. It wasn't as if I was asking them to marry me. All I wanted was a little fun, a few drinks and bit of a laugh, some adult conversation, maybe even someone to hold me for a while. Something that lasted more than a night or two.

But once they knew of Lottie's existence their attitude changed, I guess they assumed I was an easy lay, and I suppose I was in the end. For the first couple of years, when I met someone new I thought, 'this time it will be different'. But it wasn't. So I stopped thinking it might be, and began to grow numb inside.

I took what I could get from them: drinks, dinner, dancing, gifts, money and I gave them what they wanted in return. It seemed a fair exchange until I woke the next morning beside some stinking stranger and wondered where my life was going.

The black hole inside me got bigger and I grew more numb to fend it off, felt a little less than I had the day before. I had to. So when Lottie called for me in the morning, I'd rise from the temporary shared bed and have a little less to give her. Not that I'd ever had that much in the first place. But each time I was a little more ashamed of myself, saw a little more disappointment in my dead mother's eyes, and with what was left inside, keened at the loss of my brother.

I saw Cal once, walking across the market square with Rosie. They were married now and my blood turned sour watching them. I hadn't forgotten my vow. One day. I hadn't forgotten what Rosie said either, but some people said things they didn't mean. She was clearly one of those people, but my vow stood. One day he would get what he deserved, and in the meantime I drank and fucked to forget.

As the inside became hollow and dark and vulnerable, the outside grew harder. Slowly, like a dung beetle, I grew a shell, until eventually, I couldn't feel anything. No one could get in, no one could hurt me and finally, I was safe.

When Lottie was three and that shell was good and thick and tight, that's when I saw Mark.

'Andi!'

The voice from my past was like an arrow piercing my armour. It was the high street on a quiet Wednesday afternoon, so there was nowhere for me to hide.

So I turned and there he was, his face bringing so many sweet and bitter memories that for a moment I faltered.

'It's me...Mark?' he said, misunderstanding my hesitation.

I forced myself to smile. 'Hi, yes, Mark. How are you?'

He was walking towards me, closing the gap between us. 'I'm good. Wow!' He stopped in front of me. So close I could feel his body heat. 'It's great to see you, you look fantastic!'

I smiled, for real this time. It was a long time since I'd trusted a compliment and it felt refreshing.

'Thanks.'

'What you up to these days?'

I shrugged, retracting. I couldn't have this conversation, I had to keep schtum or something vital would slip out.

'This and that,' I said, deliberately vague.

Mark looked stung, misunderstanding my reticence, and we stood in awkward silence. I couldn't trust myself to say anything and it was clear Mark thought I was snubbing him. Probably for the best, though I couldn't help wishing again that I'd handled a million things differently.

'Do you...I mean if you're not busy, do you...fancy a drink?'

He was tenacious, I'd give him that, and he'd obviously overcome some of his shyness, but Lottie needed collecting from nursery and I was already running late. I could see Mrs Robinson's scowl, Lottie waiting in the cloakroom with her coat on, the usual scene. If I turned up late *and* smelling of alcohol Mrs Robinson would have a fit.

'I can't,' I said. 'Sorry.'

Mark kicked the pavement and blew out air, his lips making a raspberry sound that made me think of kissing. I jerked my handbag strap higher on my shoulder.

'Got to go, running late,' I said.

He nodded, his eyes scanning my face. 'Andi?'

'Really, I have to go.' There was a warning bite to my voice.

'Another time perhaps?' he said and I nodded.

'Sure. Got to go.' I walked away quickly, before I did or said something irreparable.

'Andi?' I turned. 'It was good to see you.'

I waved and turned away.

'You too,' I whispered, and just for a moment I thought I would break.

## Lottie

'You were late back last night,' Lottie says, as she places the bowls of spaghetti and meatballs on the table in the kitchen.

'Yeah.'

'Where did you go?'

Dan shrugs. 'Just drove round.'

Lottie sits and picks up her cutlery, casting a glance at her husband. He has a furtive look about him, as if he's guilty of something. *Probably the way he behaved yesterday*, Lottie thinks and decides to leave it at that. She never was one for picking at scabs, things healed more quickly if left.

She wants to tell him about the phone call from her mother last night but she isn't sure where to start.

'I'm off on Jack's stag night tomorrow, remember?'

She had forgotten. 'Yes,' she says, realising that this would be her last chance before he left. 'My mother phoned last night.'

To his credit he puts down his knife and fork and looks at her. 'Your mother?'

She nods.

'After all this time?'

'She's dying.'

He takes a sharp breath in.

'And she wants to see me.'

'And?'

'And I don't know what to do.'

She waits.

'What do you want to do?'

'I don't know, I *really* don't know.'

'If you go and see her what have you got to lose?'

It's a fair question, but she bites. 'You mean, I've lost so much already?'

He pauses. 'No, that isn't what I meant.'

She wants to apologise, but it sticks to her. She wants to apologise all the time these days, but especially after yesterday.

'I just meant...' he tries again. 'I just meant, well, would it be so bad to visit a dying woman?'

It sounds different when he puts it like that, but it isn't that simple. This isn't just *any* dying woman.

'I'm not sure I can,' she says. 'You don't know what she's like?'

'No. You've not really said much.'

'What's to say?'

Dan picks up his cutlery and resumes eating.

'Do you think I should go and see her?'

Dam chews, swallows and says, 'Only if you want to. If you don't, then...don't. But...' he stops.

'What?'

'Well, I think if you don't you might regret it. You'll always wonder.'

She pauses and then says, 'I wonder if she ever loved anyone.'

'Love means different things to different people.'

It strikes her as an odd thing for him to say.

She starts to eat, the food tasteless but necessary. She can't afford to get sick right now, not with everything that's happened recently.

She's not sure talking to Dan has helped, but what would? This is a decision only she can make, and as Dan intimated, one she will live with for the rest of her life.

And what makes it all the more difficult is, Lottie isn't sure how long she has left to make that decision.

At least he hadn't brought up the fertility question again. Then she wonders if that is such a good thing.

# Saturday

## Andrea

Andrea wakes to another day of the same. Lot didn't come yesterday, perhaps she'll come today, perhaps tomorrow, perhaps never. It strikes her as funny how people come when you don't want them to and don't when you do. Or is that just her?

## Andrea 1975

It had been over seven years but my heart still skipped when I saw him in the doorway.

'What you doing here?' I said, when I meant to say so many other things. Better things.

'Looking up an old friend,' he said, grinning. 'Gonna make me a cuppa?'

I hovered, wondering what to do. It was dangerous seeing him standing on the doorstep like that. It weakened me, and I didn't have a life that allowed me that luxury any more.

'Andrea, I've come a long way,' he said. He held up one hand and showing me the palm, 'I come in peace?'

I pulled the door open and let him in, beckoning him to my kitchen.

Luckily Lottie was at school today. It was one of those rare mornings when I'd managed to get up in time. She was ten now and bright enough that she could miss a bit of school from time to time, but I was glad this wasn't one of those days. I didn't need him putting two and two together and asking awkward questions.

'Sit down,' I ordered as I filled the kettle, lit the gas stove and threw the dead match into the sink with the others.

I didn't look at him, I couldn't. Instead I busied myself making tea, surreptitiously taking in my surroundings with fresh eyes. There was a film of greasy dust across every surface and the room smelt of stale frying. It angered me that he had found me like this; dull, badly domesticated and unsure of myself.

'So, how've you been?' he asked.

'Alright. You?' I scooped out the soggy matches from the sink and dumped them in the bin. *It was a start,* I thought as I rinsed my hands.

'I'm fine.'

I wiped my hands on the tea towel then faced him. 'What d'you want Mark?'

'To see you, for old time's sake.'

We looked at each other for a long time and I could feel the shell starting to crack. If he held me would it make everything all right? Could we reset the clock and start afresh? Would it be possible for me to live an ordinary life?

'Andrea, I-'

The kettle started to whistle, a low sound building up. I watched him, willing him to speak now, quickly, before it reached its crescendo and drowned him out, but he didn't. I turned away and took the kettle off the stove.

The silence created a void, a chasm between us, as I knew it would. My shell reset and I finished the tea, handed him a mug and joined him at the table.

'It's been a long time,' I said.

'Over ten years.'

I nodded. Sipped my tea. Listened to the sound of the TV that I'd left on in the living room.

'Doing much?' he asked.

'This and that, you know,' I said. Best to keep it vague, keep the distance. 'You?'

'Got promoted.'

'I heard.'

'Oh?'

I shrugged to hide my error. I didn't want him to think I was interested. 'People talk round here, and you're a copper.'

He smiled, nodded, looked down at his tea.

'So,' he said, eventually. 'You doing okay?'

'I am, yes. Never better.'

'Good, good.'

He sipped his tea.

'What do you want Mark? Why are you here?'

'I told you, I'm looking up an old friend, making sure you're okay,' he paused before adding. 'Andrew would have wanted me to.'

'And nothing else?'

He played with the condensation on the side of his mug and I held my breath, not daring to hope.

Finally he looked at me. 'No,' he said. 'What else is there?'

So he was here for Andrew. Nothing else. The thought snagged on my heart and I thought again how different things might have been.

I stood up. 'I have to be at work soon,' I lied, before I could make a fool of myself.

He jumped up. 'Right.'

'Sorry, but, you know…?'

'Yes, no, I mean…' he laughed, then looked straight at me and I thought I felt his dark eyes trace the contours of my face, just as clearly as if he'd done it with his fingertip. 'It was good to see you, Andrea,' he said.

I smiled for the first time since he'd appeared on my doorstep. 'You too,' I said, then I turned away and lead him to the front door.

He stood on the step. 'Take care of yourself.'

'Will do,' I took a deep breath to steady me. 'Sorry Mark, I've gotta run.'

He nodded. 'Sure.'

I closed the door as he turned away and caught a glimpse of an expression I didn't understand. I forced myself to keep closing the door on him, then turned and leaned my back against it, catching my breath. *If wishes were horses Mark…*


## Lottie

'I won't have any reception on my phone so don't expect to hear from me,' he says as a parting comment and then he's gone. He doesn't kiss her.

The stag weekend in the Lakes was likely to consist of hiking, biking and too much booze. From habit as she watches him drive away, she thinks about the effect of the latter on his sperm count, then remembers with a pang that it doesn't matter anymore.

As she returns to the empty house, she decides it will do them both good to have some time apart. The news is fresh, and when she reflects on what else the doctor said, it doesn't feel so final. It *wasn't* impossible, he had said, there were *other* things they could do.

Determined to keep busy and catch up on all the things she means to do but never gets round to, she makes straight for the utility room to tackle the laundry.

They don't have to give up hope, she thinks as she pulls the darks from the washing basket, not yet. She hasn't said as much to Dan. There hasn't been the right moment and besides, his smarting point about coming home to Dr Spock, however ill conceived the idea, still stings. She will not to bring up the subject of babies until he does.

She pulls Dan's jeans from the basket and checks the pockets, remembering that she has plans to go out with Poppy tonight. She can forget about everything then.    Work, the lack of family, her mother...everything.

She retrieves a piece of paper folded into four from Dan's jeans and distracted, instead of dropping it in the bowl for him to sort later, she unfolds it.

When she thinks back she'll wrongly remember she opened it slowly, carefully, as if it were some ancient parchment with a message from the oracle.    It will be a moment of slow motion that will draw a line between her life before and her life after.

She reads it not once, not twice, but six times, and she still can't take it in.    It can't be.    But the female hand, the name '*Ruth*' and the kiss that seals it, all say differently.

She reads the note one last time, slowly, word by painful word, each one pushes deep into her body, bleeding her from the inside, until finally they shatter her heart.


For two hours she sits on the utility floor in front of the washing machine and cries, shouts, spits, kicks, rails and cries again.    And when she is throughly exhausted and the cold of the floor has seeped into her bones she stands up, groups the fragments of herself together and goes upstairs to run a bath.

An hour later she is sitting at her dressing table, washed, warmed and wrapped in a towel. Her face in the mirror haggard by tears and pain.

There is no doubt that Dan is having an affair, and small nuggets of realisation keep dropping in. The day he went missing for the afternoon and Lot couldn't reach him on his mobile.

'It was dead,' he said, when he got back and she told him.

The necklace she saw in his briefcase.

'Leaving present for someone at work, I was volunteered to pick it up.'

The late nights and missed dinners.

'It's frantic at work, all hands to the pump.'

She has swallowed it all, hook, line, sinker, the lot. Is he really away with the lads this weekend, or is that another line too? Her mind fills with images of him with her. Naked bodies entwined, drinking champagne and laughing. It doesn't matter that she doesn't know who she is, nor that Dan hates champagne. The image is as real to her as if she were watching it right there in front of her, and the shards cut deeper.

Her numb mind begins to fill with questions. Who? When? How? And the most obvious and yet easiest for her to answer...why?

73

She knows why, and as tears blur her vision she begins to punch her stomach repeatedly.

'Bastard body,' she wails, the sound distorting her mouth into obscene shapes.

She makes sounds that frighten her, sounds she didn't know a human could make, as she slides off the stool and crawls across the floor towards the bed. But before she can make it she collapses, sobbing. Lost in the darkness of her new world.

When Lottie arrives Poppy has her head buried in her phone, no doubt checking her work emails even though it's Saturday night. A pint of beer and a glass of red wine sit on the table in front of her.

Lottie sits down and Poppy looks up in surprise. 'Hey! I didn't see you come in,' she says.

'I'm not surprised,' Lottie scolds.

She puts her head down in a fake apology. 'I can't help it, I'm addicted.'

'I know,' Lottie says, taking a sip of her wine. It is a deep bodied Merlot and the tang works her taste buds on either side of her tongue as she swallows. 'God, that's good.'

Poppy puts her phone away. 'I'm expecting news of a bid I put in last month but nothing's come in.'

Lottie looks at her watch. 'Not likely to over the weekend.'

'I know, wishful thinking. So, how are you?'

'Okay.'

'Okay? Why am I not convinced?'

Lottie wants to tell Poppy about her discovery but it is just too awful, too raw. She almost cancelled but she needed to get out of the house, and make-up can cover a thousand pains.

'Oh, you know...work and that.'

She nods. 'Ah work...and *that*.'

Lottie looks at her and Poppy smiles back. She won't ask, she knows when Lottie is ready she'll tell her and until then she won't pry.

'So, where are we going to eat?' Lottie asks.

'I booked a table at the Latin American place in Skinnergate, Habanero's? Food's good and cheap, and their cocktails are fab and Jim behind the bar knows his beers. We could get lashed, around the world in eighty beers.'

'I'm not sure I'll need eighty!' she says, horrified. Poppy can drink, and Lottie has long since learned not to try to keep up with her. It always turns out very messy if she does.

'Okay, around the world in eight beers then,' she suggests.

'You know, getting lashed is probably exactly what I need right now.'

They sit in silence for a few minutes sipping their drinks.

'I'm sorry.' Lottie says.

'About?'

'I don't know I just...I'm just...I'm not very good company,' she says, eventually.

'But you're *never* very good company. That's why I hang out with you, you make me look good.'

'Oh ha-bloody-ha,' she says.

They laugh and the tension has gone.

'Tell me more about this bid,' Lottie says, and Poppy launches into her second biggest passion after her daughter.


It is late in the evening, and Lottie is on the dance floor a little worse for wear when she spots him. Naturally she assumes he is looking at Poppy, unless of course he's having a laugh at her expense. Lottie hates dancing, she looks like someone whose limbs have just been rehabilitated, but Poppy loves it so she endures it for her.

With a second glance she realises that this man standing at the bar watching them dance isn't looking at Poppy, he is looking at her, and quite pointedly. In fact, so obviously that it is beginning to get uncomfortable.

Lottie leans into Poppy. 'Shall we go?'

'What?'

'I said, shall we go?'

'Go?' she looks puzzled.

Lottie nods.

'Why?'

'It's getting late,' she points at her watch.

She shakes her head and points to her ears, then walks off the dance floor and waves Lottie to follow her. Her body quivers as Poppy heads to the bar right towards the man who's been staring at her. Now he is bound to think she's said something and they are heading over to talk to him.

*This is not what I need right now*, she thinks, as she reluctantly follows.

75

Poppy stands at the bar next to him and Lottie can feel her face grow crimson, glad it is too dim for anyone to see, and she deliberately positions herself so Poppy is between her and the man. She notices her heart beat is just a little higher than it might be through dancing alone.

'What'll you have?' Poppy asks.

With the alcohol, the music and the heat, not to mention the attention of this dark stranger, her head is already swimming.

'I think I'll shoot off,' she says.

'Already? It's only,' Poppy inspects her watch, 'Well, it's not even one yet. Come on, I hardly ever have a night without Stevie. Pleeease?'

Lottie hesitates. She really doesn't want to hang round here, but she knows Poppy doesn't get much grown up time.

'Okay, but why not go somewhere else?'

'Lot, do you really fancy walking across town for one last drink?'

There is no easy way out of this so she relents. 'No, I guess not.'

Her friend beams. 'Great! Same again?'

Lottie nods. *In for a penny...*

Poppy leans over the bar and orders two Bees Knees, and in doing so, clears the way for the man and her to look at each other. He is about her age, with deep lines running down either side of his mouth, thick sensuous lips and large dark eyes. Handsome, she decides. Dressed in a black shirt, with his dark hair cropped into a stylish spike, he clearly takes care of himself. He looks dark skinned, but whether that is the result of a recent holiday, his natural colouring or, god forbid, sun beds, she can't tell.

He gives her a lopsided smile and raises one hand, waggling his fingers in a wave. It is a cheeky childlike move and she can't help but smile back at him. He then waves the barman over and she turns to face the dance floor, leaning her back against the bar to catch her breath and still her pulse, she is not prepared for this kind of reaction to a man.

She didn't even feel like this when she first met Dan. She waits for Poppy to finish ordering, trying to get herself straight. She wants him to leave her alone, but she knows she'll be bitterly disappointed if he does. She begins to chew her lip, suddenly unsure how this evening is going to end, or even how she *wants* it to end.

*I'm married*, she reminds herself. *Only just*, she answers.

Poppy turns and hands her the cocktail. Lottie takes a deep breath before taking a sip, knowing this drink will be the undoing of her. To her surprise Poppy takes a step back from the bar so the man and she are facing each other, and the three stand in a triangle. Lottie, Poppy and the man. Then Poppy turns to him.

'Thanks,' she says.

'You're welcome,' he says, with a smile, the lines around his mouth deepening. Lottie wonders how often he smiles. He has a deep timbre to his voice with the twang of a Middlesbrough accent. *Local then.*

'So,' Poppy says, often blunt. 'What do you want?'

The man rests his dark eyes on Lottie and says, 'Your friend.'

A frisson of excitement shoots through Lottie's spine and turns her stomach to liquid.

'Ohhhh,' says Poppy, looking between them, grinning. 'Good answer.'

Lottie is unable to speak and he doesn't say anything either. They just look at each other and for the briefest moment the world falls away and it is just him and her.

'Shall I give you a moment,' Poppy says, laughing, and her words bring the room back into focus.

Lottie breaks the gaze and looks down at her drink, still unable to find anything to say. Surprised at what just happened. She didn't know it really could.

'I'm Poppy, this is Charlotte, Lottie or Lot, depending on how well you know her. I'd hazard a guess you're at Lottie already.'

*Thanks Poppy!*

'Murtagh,' he says, stretching out his hand. 'Murtagh O'Sullivan.'

'Interesting name,' Poppy says, taking his outstretched hand and shaking it. Lottie thinks it is rather a formal and old fashioned gesture, especially for the environment, especially for Poppy.

'It's Irish, my father was Irish,' he says, turning with his outstretched hand towards me.

'What's it mean?' asks Poppy. 'Irish names usually mean something, right?'

Lottie stares at his hand, wanting to take it, terrified of doing so.

'"Muir" means "sea", and "ceardach" means skilled. Murtagh implies skilled in the ways of the sea.'

He doesn't take his eyes off Lottie as he says all this, with his hand still outstretched, waiting for her to take it. Anyone else would have become embarrassed by now and removed it, but he just holds it there, waiting.

'You're not a sailor by any chance?'

Lottie has never heard Poppy talk so much to a stranger, but then she reminds herself, it isn't usually Lottie they are interested in. She is grateful.

'No, I'm a teacher, at Middlesbrough College.'

He raises one of his dark eyebrows, a request to take the hand and Lottie finds herself slipping her hand into his. His warm fingers close round hers and the room tilts slightly. It's the alcohol, she tells herself.

'Pleased to meet you...Lottie?'

She nods and smiles, but still no words. He releases her hand and when it comes to rest by her side, it feels as if it no longer belongs to her.

'Odd place to come on your own,' Poppy says. 'Out trawling?'

Murtagh throws back his head and laughs. 'Are you always so blunt?'

'Yes, are you always so evasive?'

He laughs again. 'I'm out with a friend, he's dancing with someone he just met.'

'And you fancy my friend?'

'Poppy!' Lottie glares at her.

She waves her away. 'She's very shy,' she says.

'I can see that.'

Lottie glances at him, he is still looking at her.

'You want her number?' she asks.

'Poppy, please!'

She ignores Lottie's outburst.

'Very much,' Murtagh says.

Poppy turns. 'Lottie?'

'What?'

'Are you going to give the man your number?'

'We need to go.' Lottie puts her empty glass on the bar. All the alcohol is catching up with her and she is beginning to feel queasy.

'So soon?' he says, his voice reverberating through her body in spite of the background music.

'Yes,' it comes out as a whisper, without conviction. She looks at Poppy. The room is starting to spin.

Poppy nods. 'Okay,' she drains her glass. 'We should go.'

'Your number?' he asks, leaning towards her. Lottie catches the smell of a musky aftershave and it makes her head spin a little more. She really needs to leave, and quickly.

She is married. Two wrongs don't make a right. It really isn't sensible...she has so much on her plate already... she doesn't need this complication...her life is already so...so...he holds out his phone and before she knows what she has done she enters her name and number, and returns it to him.

Then she throws up on his shoes.

# Sunday

### Andrea

Andrea wakes at four in the morning with a start. The pain fogs her brain and it hurts to breath. Did she nearly go? Was that what woke her? She's not ready to give up, not yet. She is holding out for Lottie. There's a country song in there somewhere: Holding Out for Lottie.

Yesterday she was angry with her, but today she aches to see her, she wants to make it right, she wants her to know the truth, whatever that means. And yet, she knows, deep down, that it is impossible to make it right, any of it. All she can do is her best. It's all she's ever done, surely it's all anyone ever does? Even if that best is, at times, shit.

And her best has been terrible, many many times. Is that why Lottie doesn't come? Is that why she is going to die alone? And really, when she looks at herself honestly, and all she has done, does she deserve anything else?

Perhaps she should just close her eyes now and give up? It would be so easy. All she has to do is close her eyes. How many times in her life has she wanted to do that? Just close her eyes and die? When she lost Andrew, then Mark, and when Cal was in their lives she wanted to do it every time she looked into Lottie's eyes. She stopped looking in the end. Self preservation.

She closes her eyes, sinks and surrenders to whatever comes when she opens them: death, or a new day to struggle through, it's all the same to her now.

### Andrea 1980

It was another five years before I saw him again. He didn't see me. I was sitting in the back of the Red Lion in town with Jimmy and a few of the other regulars I'd struck up a friendship with. It was a loose term really, drinking buddies would have been more apt.

We could see the door from where we sat but people couldn't see us, not straight away anyways, so we liked to sit there and gossip and giggle about folk who came in.

I saw Mark enter straight away and my treacherous heart did that flip it always did when I saw him. He wasn't alone. A woman was with him. Petite, with mousey hair and pale complexion. Thin mouth but good cheek bones. She was quite pretty, in a plain sort of way.

79

At first I hoped they worked together, but the proprietary air in which he guided her to the bar, his hand in the small of her back, told me otherwise. There was an intimacy there and I flashed with anger, imagined her bleeding at my feet.

I looked away, trying to focus on something Jimmy had just said that had the others roaring with laughter, but I didn't have the heart. I wanted to leave but I was trapped. If I ventured out towards the exit Mark would spot me and, while I didn't look too bad today, I didn't want to meet *her,* and I knew he would insist on introducing us.

I stole another glance and watched them chatting easily at the bar. He leaned forward and whispered something into her ear, she lifted her head back with laughter. It made my heart pull. He was funny, Mark, he always managed to make me smile, always managed to pull me from my dark place and I burned with envy and regret.

I picked up my lager and lime and took a mouthful, swallowing all the emotions and memories down before they could engulf me. It was all a long time ago. He was different, I was different and we hadn't seen each other for very long. I'd be a fool to think there was anything left of us. A memory of Mark visiting a few years back, standing on my door step with his lop sided grin spitefully resurfaced. I took another drink. He was there out of duty for Andrew, he'd almost said as much.

'Hey, Andi, slow down love we can't keep up,' Jimmy shouted across the table.

I forced a laugh and raised my glass at him, aware in my peripheral vision that Mark's head had turned in our table's direction. My heart was a mixture of excitement and dread. I didn't know if I wanted him to see me or not, and the confusion made me swallow another mouthful of lager. The bubbles got stuck and burned my throat, and for a moment I thought I was going to choke.

There was movement in the corner of my eye and my heart raced. He was coming over. I didn't know how to be. Should I pretend I hadn't seen him and wait for him to tap me on the shoulder and then effervescently be surprised, or should I spot him coming towards me and throw him a seductive 'well, hello' smile as he walked across the floor towards me?

A tap on my shoulder brought me out of my reverie with a start and I had run out of time to decide. I put my empty glass on the table and stood up.

'Can I buy you a drink?'

Flustered, all my plans aborted, my voice came out higher than I'd have liked. 'Mark? Hi!'

He smiled. 'Hello, Andi. How are you?'

'I'm good, good. Yes, how are you?' I took a breath, trying to slow down my breathing, my heart, everything.

'I'm alright.'

I looked over his shoulder. 'Who's your little friend?' I didn't mean it to come out as spiteful as it sounded, but then, I never do.

He turned and raised a hand to let her know he'd be there in a moment, then turned back. 'That's Christine.'

'She seems…' I didn't finish, it wasn't going to be pleasant and for once I was doing as my mother had taught me, the 'if you can't say something nice…' advice.

He laughed. 'She is, in fact we're engaged.'

If he had hit me with a baseball bat it would have been easier to stay standing.

'Well, congratulations,' I managed.

'Thanks. That's why I'm home. She's meeting mum and dad.'

'How are they?'

'Still going strong, they'll outlast me.'

I nodded.

'How's your dad?'

'My dad?'

'Yeah, I heard he'd been in hospital recently.'

I hadn't seen my father since Lottie was two and I didn't think much about him anymore. Mark brought him back, and for a moment I wondered whether I should go and see him, whether it was too late...

'Andi?'

'Oh, okay, you know,' I lied. I didn't want to tell him I didn't know my father had been ill, I couldn't explain without it leading to all sorts of questions.

'I heard you had a kid?'

'Oh, where'd you hear that?' I asked, wary now.

'I bumped into Hayley, she told me.'

Someone else I hadn't seen for years. Not since that rather uncomfortable exchange at my mam's.

'I heard she'd moved to London?'

Mark nodded. 'Yep, married a barrister. Has two kids now.'

'How'd you bump into her?'

'She was up visiting her folks.'

'I hear your girl's in her teens now. Pretty girl, I hear.'

'You've heard a lot,' I said, a sharpness in my voice.

'Keep your hair on, just making conversation, catching up.'

I nodded, feeling relief that he hadn't guessed.

'A word of warning,' he said. I leaned closer, could smell his after shave, the hairs on my arms prickled at his proximity. 'Cal, remember Cal?'

I leaned back, repelled by the name. 'How could I forget?'

'Of course,' he shook his head. 'Dumb thing for me to say, sorry.'

I nodded and leaned back in.

'We've got word that he's been...now you have to keep this confidential, okay?'

I nodded, wishing him to get to the point.

'We've been given a tip off that he's been messing around with underage girls. We can't prove anything at the moment, but it's only a matter of time. Keep an eye on her, eh? Stay well clear, the pair of you.'

I nodded. 'I haven't seen him in years.'

'Best keep it that way.'

'It's the same story all over again with Cal, isn't it?'

'Huh?'

'Cal gets away because the cops can't prove anything.'

We exchange a long look, reliving the night when I lost my brother, Mark lost his best friend and we lost each other.

'Another drink, Andi?' Jimmy shouted, breaking our connection. 'It's my round.'

I turned. 'Go on then Jimmy, I'll just have one more, then I've got to get back.' I turned back to Mark, 'and you'd better get back to your fiancé,' I said.

He nodded. 'Good to see you, and take care of that girl of yours.' *Ours.*

'Thanks, will do.'

Mark nodded and made his way back to the bar and his future. I sat back on the stool, exhausted from the exchange, as if I'd done a round in a boxing ring. By the time Jimmy arrived with the drinks Mark and his fiancé were leaving the pub.

'Thanks Jimmy,' I said, taking my drink. I moved onto the bench, the stool no longer feeling stable enough to support me, and laid my head back, gathering myself.

The whole meeting had flustered me, but there was something amongst all the emotion and words, said and unsaid, that had pricked an idea. I ran through the encounter moment by moment, picking through it like a panner for gold. What had Mark said that had momentarily made me jump? It had been something to do with Cal, but whatever the idea was that had stirred, I couldn't grasp it now.

'You gone to sleep?' It was Jimmy.

I lifted my head and smiled at him, 'Nah, Jimmy, just resting my eyes,' I quipped. Jimmy laughed.

I pushed it to one side for now, whatever it was could wait. No good wasting the rest of the night.

## Lottie

By lunchtime Lottie is up and about and whilst she doesn't feel the best she's ever felt, she can at least cope with moving her head, as long as it's slowly.

She rings Poppy.

'God I feel awful,' Lottie tells her.

'Mmmm, don't feel so great myself but you, you were a demon. What were you thinking?'

'I was trying not to.'

'Of course,' Poppy says, then Lottie remembers her drunken sobbing break down in the cab on the way home, after giving her number to Murtaugh and vomiting on his shoes. Then throwing up again on the grass verge at the bottom of the street while Poppy held her hair.

'God, I'm sorry,' Lottie says, shrinking in embarrassment.

'I don't think we can go back there for a while, but there's no need to apologise to me. It's nothing I haven't done with you…well, apart from the vomming bit,' she laughs.

Lottie remembers Poppy's last break down and smiles in relief.

'So, what are you going to do?' she asks.

She's not sure whether Poppy is referring to Murtaugh or Dan or her mother.

'I dunno. I really don't know.' It works for all.

'Well, I'll tell you one thing for nothing. Drinking isn't the answer. You're a bit crap at it.'

Lottie laughs. 'I know.'

'So, throwing up on a bloke, I've never thought of that as a put off,' she says.

'Oh, please don't.'

'No, seriously, good job.'

'Ha ha, very funny. I think it's safe to say he won't be calling me.'

'He might send you a few hate texts.'

'Or a bill for his shoes.'

When Lottie hangs up she slinks back under the womb like duvet and the oblivion of sleep.


That afternoon the rain lashes against the house and Lottie is curled up under a blanket on the sofa, in front of a roaring fire, half watching 'The Guns of Navarone'. Her hangover has subsided and she is starting to feel human again. She had thought she was going to die that morning and she is once again reminded of her mother, lying somewhere with lung cancer, waiting.

But today she needs to take care of herself, it would be a bad idea to go and see a dying woman when she feels *this* ill. Besides, her husband will be home in a few hours. Her cheating husband. There's only so much one woman can shoulder at a time. Her dying mother will have to wait. Ignoring the justifications, she forces herself to refocus on the movie.

The hidden explosives are about to be triggered and once done, all hell will break loose. *I know how that feels. Tomorrow, I'll go tomorrow,* she tells herself. *When I'm feeling stronger.*

But it nags at her, interfering with the film. *Damn that woman!* Seriously, after everything the woman has done why does Lottie feels she has to go to her? Because she'll be haunted for the rest of her life if she doesn't. But tomorrow is soon enough, surely?

Moments later she flings back the blanket in a temper and stomps up the stairs to get dressed, glad her head has cleared at least.

*I can't believe I'm doing this*, she thinks later, when she's in the car. Somehow that woman always got her own way, with everyone, with everything. She made it your fault if you didn't do what she wanted. Clever woman. Wasted talent really. With all that charisma and manipulative power, she could have done so much. Politics comes to mind, but on second thoughts, her mother didn't have the self control, probably still doesn't. Is probably why she's got cancer. This last thought shocks her and she feels herself shrink in shame.

Lottie flicks Radio 4 on but it's Gardeners Question Time, so she switches over to the local station. A song from her youth comes on, Buddy Holly 'True Love Ways'. It was her and Barry Johnson's song. The memories stab at her and she pushes the accelerator down as if speeding can get her away from them. Of course, nothing can now. They all come tumbling out of the cupboard since HER call. God, she hates that she can do this to her!

More importantly, why does she let her? What is it in her that can't say no to that woman? She owes her nothing. Nothing!

She takes the next exit off the motorway, swings round the roundabout and takes the turn that leads her to the hospice.


A volunteer wearing a pink overall has signed her in and is escorting her to her mother. The rotund woman stands at least three inches shorter than Lottie which she finds unnerving, at five foot three Lottie rarely towers over anyone.

'I always say to new visitors it's like a rabbit warren in here,' she says. 'But you soon get used to it.'

'Is that so?' says Lottie, trying to be kind, show an interest, when really she hasn't a spare speck of attention for this lovely volunteer who is taking her to her mother.

'Lifts just here,' she says. 'So you'll be able to find it next time.'

*Next time?* Lottie isn't even sure she'll get through this time.

'Not many hospices are on two levels. We're an old building. Most of them these days are purpose built.'

The doors open and they enter a creaking lift. Lottie is unsure and it must show.

'Perfectly safe,' the lady smiles and Lottie notes her name badge, Jenny, knowing she'll forget the moment the woman leaves. Feeling guilty she makes some effort on this short journey to remember.

*Jenny, Jenny, Jenny, Jenny.* Then it occurs to her that it's the same name as the Craig girl at work and she relaxes. She won't forget.

'You're Mum's on the last ward we have now,' Jenny is saying. 'Course, we're modernising. Down to just that one now, all the rest have been converted.'

'Into what?'

The woman, Jenny, laughs. 'Private rooms, silly. We'll convert the last next year, just as soon as we've raised the funds. I'm chair of the fundraising committee.'

'Really? That's...very good of you. Jenny.' It sounds false.

'Oh I don't know, keeps me busy. Here we are,' she says, needlessly as the doors open onto the first floor landing.

'There's a coffee machine over there,' she points to the machine in the corner.

They pass through double doors and she points to a kitchen on the right.

'The machine's not bad but can get a bit pricey, so you're more than welcome to make a cuppa in the kitchen. All we ask is you bring in a few bits and bobs from time to time.'

'Bits and bobs?'

'You know, tea, coffee, sugar. Whatever you fancy. It's not compulsory, but it keeps costs down. Us being a charity an' all.'

'Yes, of course.'

'You're Mum's in the ward I was mentioning.'

'Is it far?' She feels as if she has been walking forever.

Jenny stops. 'No, she's in there. Far corner. If you need anything just give us a shout.'

'Thank you. Jenny,' Lottie forces herself to smile but thinks it might be more of a grimace.

'No problem at all,' the woman says.

Lottie watches her walk down the corridor and back through the double doors.　She wants to ask her to come back and hold her hand. Instead she turns to the open door, takes a deep breath and steps inside.

## Lottie

'Mum,' Lottie nods curtly. Her heart feels too big for her chest as she tries to take in the woman that was once her mother, still is really.

There's that smile, though it has to work harder to improve the face, struggle through the crags and the wrinkles. *God she's aged.*

'Lot! I didn't think you'd come.'

'You do surprise me.' There's a tang in Lottie's tone, a poison, lashed out on her snake tongue. By way of apology she remembers her gift.

'Brought you some grapes,' she says, and rummages in her bag. 'It's what you do...isn't it? When someone's ill, I mean?' Lottie pulls them out and looks at her mother.

'I'm not ill, I'm bloody dying.'

'Yes, well, I think it's still grapes. I'll leave them here,' she says, placing them on the bedside cabinet. It seemed appropriate when she stood in the shop deciding, now it seems lame and childish. Flowers would have been better. More appropriate.

'Sit down then. I'd get up but, well, you know.' Andrea laughs and then starts to cough. It hacks away at her insides until Lottie thinks she might turn inside out. She stands watching, not unmoved though you'd never guess by looking at her. She's learnt to hide a lot.

The nurse flits into the room and to Andrea's side, tweeting and twitching in vain attempts to comfort her. She's a pretty plump young thing and Lottie aches to be young again, to have another go, to do things differently. Still, it would have turned out the same regardless, she has a defective womb, thanks to this woman.

When the coughing spasm is over Andrea is out of breath and lies back to recover, giving Lottie a chance to get a better look at her. The skin slides back, stretches over those high cheek bones that gave her such beauty in her youth. You can see what her skull will look like when the rest is gone. The thought disturbs Lottie and she looks out the window, but not for long. Andrea is mesmerising, like a road accident, and Lottie doesn't want to slow down and look, but she can't help it.

Then it strikes her hard in the chest. *She is dying and I will lose her.* Suddenly she regrets all the time wasted hating her. But what else can she do? If she lets her in she will destroy her, like she did before. The thought makes her turn and leave.

### Andrea

Lottie just stands there, staring, while Andrea coughs so hard she thinks a lung might just pop up there on the bed between them. What had started as the tap tap tap of an incessant and unproductive cough has now developed the ability to wrack her whole body on occasions. Trust it to chose *this* occasion.

*She's got hard. It doesn't suit her. Her face is pinched and old. To old for her years.* Her daughter's looks have always been a disappointment. She was pretty enough and Andrea admits she envied her youth, but Lottie never really did shine. And now she's lost the bloom of youth she hasn't got much going for her.

Jean takes care of her body as it wracks with the coughing. Sweet thing that she is, she doesn't know what to do with herself when Andrea gets like this. Still, it's nice to get a reaction from someone. Lot just stands, watching.

When the coughing is over the pain is unbearable and Andrea has to lie back to catch her breath. She needs to be stronger to face Lottie, they have a lot to talk about. Andrea hears her moving and when she opens her eyes, to her dismay, Lot is gone.

### Lottie

Dan empties the contents of his case into the washing basket. She has to give him credit, his washing certainly looks like he's been romping across fields rather than in his lover's bed.

'Good weekend?' Lottie asks.

'Yeah, really good.'

'What did you do?'

'The usual. Walks, bit of canoeing, pubs, that kind of thing.'

'Bit cold for canoeing isn't it?'

'Not really.'

She knows he's lying. It's all lies. He doesn't look at her while he speaks. How could he?

'Thought anymore about visiting your mum?' he asks.

'No.' Two can play this game. 'Who went?'

He glances at her. 'The usual. Why?'

'Just wondering.' She sits down heavily on the bed and his case bounces gently.

'You okay?' he asks, straightening up. Perhaps he senses the change.

Lottie nods. 'Yes, why?'

He shrugs. 'You just seem...different,' he says.

She stands and turns to face him squarely, the bed between them. 'Different how?' Lottie asks. It is a challenge and he knows it.

Dan takes a step back. 'Hey, what's with the attitude?'

'I didn't know I had an attitude.'

He pauses, uncertain. She watches, waits for his next move, not sure what hers will be.

'What we having for tea?' he asks.

'Fuck all.'

His eyes widen and his brows shoot up. Lottie smiles, waiting, arms folded.

They stand, facing one another. Lottie feels eleven again and rock hard. He looks eleven and lost. For a moment she remembers her Dan, her soft, trustworthy, kind Dan, and she nearly flounders, until he speaks.

'What the hell's got into you?'

She doesn't trust herself to answer without telling him what she knows, so she turns and leaves him to his unpacking.

# Monday

### Lottie

Lottie feels hung over at the Monday morning staff meeting. She couldn't sleep next to Dan last night, knowing what she knew, and ended up finishing a Jo Nesbo and falling asleep on the sofa.

Now, in a fug, with an almighty crick in her neck, she stands before the twelve staff she inherited a little over a year ago, and just for a moment, quails. In that brief moment her confidence deserts her, she can't do this, one of them is going to stand up and call her out.

She shakes her head, blaming it on lack of sleep, her mother's call and the subsequent aborted visit, the memories that have started to haunt her again, Dan's betrayal.

In an attempt to pull herself together, Lottie takes a deep breath as she looks around the room at her team. She spots Miriam's sour face. *Oh god, that's all I bloody need.*

'Lottie, can we get on?' It is Miriam. Of course it is.

*Her voice can cut glass,* Lottie thinks, but it's the push she needs. There is nothing Miriam would like better than to watch Lottie fall apart before her.

'Yes. Right. Right folks, good morning,' she says, her voice is overly bright. 'Let's get this show on the road,' she claps her hands and smiles and then kicks herself for using such a cliche. *I sound like that manager from The Office,* she thinks and cringes. What was the matter with her today?

But she knows what this is, this is operating on only four hours sleep. This is having her mother back in her life, even if it's only on the periphery. This is being betrayed by her husband and her body. This is Cal haunting her again. This is feeling cornered, feeling so alone you can barely breathe from the pain of it but she forces herself to push it all to one side and focus on her team.

An hour later, with the meeting over, she can breathe again. It went well, considering, even Miriam behaved herself for once, but there's one more thing she needs to take care of that's been at the back of her mind throughout the morning.

'Hilary, can I see you for a minute?' Lottie asks, as the team start to leave.

Hilary Collins is one of four development workers. They are assigned to work directly with specific families. Hilary works with the Craig family, and after the mention of them at the meeting last week, Lottie can't seem to let it go.

Hilary takes the empty seat beside her, looping her hair behind her ear, leaning forward and smiling. She is good at her job, she gets results and Lottie can see why. When Hilary's with you, it's as if she doesn't have anywhere else more important to be. Lottie takes in the earnest blue eyes set in a long slim face. *You feel as if she would catch you if you fell,* Lottie thinks, and hesitates before she speaks, afraid she might unravel right there in front of her.

From the corner of her eye she spies Miriam watching as she leaves, so she waits, making sure the meeting room door is firmly closed before she starts.

'Okay,' she says, when she has steadied herself and she's sure they're alone. 'The Craig family were mentioned at the Children's Trust Board last week. No names minuted of course,' Lottie quickly reassures her. 'They've been selected as one of the families for the council's new 80/20 project. Where are we with them?' She keeps her personal interest to herself.

'Father is still in prison, due to be released in a couple of months. Mother is in a substance misuse programme, but I think she's just going through the motions.'

Lottie nods.

'There's a benefit threat if she doesn't cooperate. We've improved the school attendance levels of the three boys, but it's still nowhere near where we'd like it to be.'

'And Jenny?' Lottie asks, trying to hide her impatience.

Hilary looks pained for a moment. 'Nothing I'm afraid.'

'Nothing at all?'

She shakes her head sadly. 'I can't seem to make progress. She's as tight as a clam. I'm wondering if Bob is dealing Tracey drugs.'

Bob is the uncle they suspect of abusing Jenny, Tracey is her mother. Just hearing her name makes Lottie shudder.

'Jenny is precocious, she knows far more about life than you'd want a fourteen year old to know, but it's still conjecture. All I can do is keep talking to her, and try to get her to school.'

'How's that going?'

Hilary screws up her nose. 'Not great.'

Lottie stares down at the table for a moment or two, trying to gather her thoughts, trying to decide what to do for the best. She doesn't usually get this involved with cases, there's just something about Jenny...she reminds Lottie of herself when she was young, and the truth is, she's more than a little curious about Tracey. She'd like to see that bitch again.

Of course, from the moment she recognised her six months ago she was curious, but recent circumstances has exacerbated it, and before she realises what she is doing she says: 'Can I accompany you next time you visit the family?'

She can see surprise register on Hilary's face. 'Well, I...' Lottie can tell she wants to say no. 'Well, it's unusual,' she says, instead.

She should say no, it's not appropriate to take someone along for the ride, even your boss, not without a good reason, and Lottie's been in this business long enough to know that. She wouldn't have allowed her manager to come on one of her visits, not under these circumstances, *but Hilary isn't me*. Lottie wants to give her a good argument to help her, but she doesn't have one, so instead she just waits it out, knowing Hilary will capitulate.

'Okay,' she says, finally.

'Good, check my diary with Sandra and make it soon please.'

Hilary leaves and Lottie decides to sit in the meeting room to gather her thoughts before returning to her office and the onslaught of the day.

*What do I hope to achieve?*

Is it just macabre interest, or does she want Tracey to know that she, Lottie Logan, or Parker as it was then, made something of herself. Perhaps it's even to gloat at Tracey, show her what she's become? No, not that. That wouldn't be right...

And what of Jenny? Does she want to save Jenny in a way that she couldn't save herself? Or is she using her to remember what her mother did, so she doesn't weaken and visit her again? Or is it all simply a distraction for what she really ought to be facing....her own past.

'Pull yourself together, woman,' she mutters, as she stands up and returns to her office.

The memory of Tracey follows her.

### Lottie 1980

I dropped into my seat and waited for our form tutor to arrive, rooting in my bag for my rough book. I didn't use mine much, but I had a vague memory that I had got some notes in that might help with my first lesson. The school had recently stopped giving them out, something to do with the new government and Margaret Thatcher. The first female prime minister and she stopped free exercise books. Great!

It felt strange being back here after missing school for over three weeks, but I'd been in this place before. It would settle down in a day or two. I didn't think Mum realised that when she kept me off school I perpetually feel like the new girl.

And it was hard making friends, at least if I really were a new girl they'd be some intrigue. Intrigue, I mulled the word round, wondering where it had come from, who had decided it was even a word.

A jolt in my back interrupted my thoughts.

'Oh, oops, sorry,' it's Tracey Craig and it's not a sincere apology. 'I didn't see you there, this desk's usually empty.'

I looked up but didn't respond. Jane Waugh and Susan Bickerton stood either side of her, set slightly back and both wearing the uniformed sneer of Tracey's gang. I wondered again if Tracey was such a cow because she was fat, you know, the 'be a bully or get bullied' philosophy.

'Oh, cat got your tongue?' she asked.

'Fuck off, Tracey,' I said, before I had engaged my brain.

She stepped closer, I could smell the cheap perfume a lot of the girls got off the market.

'What the fuck did you just say to me?' she hissed.

Oh, here we go again, I thought. I wasn't afraid, not really. Tracey had no idea what I had to contend with at home, none of them did, and they had no idea what I was capable of. Still, I didn't like confrontation and I *didn't* like fights. Not any more. Not since Paul Hammond.

I made the decision to leave the fighter in junior school the day I calmly beat Paul's face off his desk until his nose popped. It was the blood that stopped me in the end. I was horrified, it made me feel as if I might be becoming like my mum, and I didn't want to be that way.

I was sent to the headmaster's office of course. When I explained that Paul had been calling me names he recited in a sing song voice, 'Sticks and stones may break my bones, but names will never hurt me, Charlotte.'

'Names do hurt sir,' I insisted.

'Nonsense, Charlotte.'

I thought for a moment about how I could prove my point. 'If I called you a fat old bastard, I bet that would hurt your feelings,' I said, eventually. He was fat. He was old. He gave me a detention. That made him a bastard in my book, though I wasn't sure I had proved my point.

It was then I decided I would reinvent myself in secondary school. Not because of the headmaster, but because of what I was becoming. Still, it was harder than I thought it would be, and every now and again there was a piece of me that forgot. Now was one of those moments.

I lowered my head in supplication. It worked.

Tracey stepped closer, pushing her bulk of a body into me. I could feel her warmth, her soft belly pushed into my shoulder. She bent down, her breath on my face as she whispered in my ear.

'Listen, you fatherless bastard, if you dare speak to me like that again, I'm going to mash your ugly little face in, you understand?'

I nodded, but didn't look up. I was afraid I'd punch her, especially after what she'd just said. It cut deep, that missing person in your life, especially when the one who stayed clearly would rather you didn't exist.

When I was younger I'd ask Mum about him but she just cut me dead, even when I told her what the other kids said.

She was another one. 'Sticks and stones, Lot,' she would say, and then consider the subject closed. I knew better than to try to continue once she'd said that, but it was a stupid platitude and I never understood it. Names hurt, more than any beating.

Tracey's voice brought me back to the present. 'Understand?' she said again, for emphasis.

I nodded and whispered, 'Yes.'

Mrs Collinson came in at this point and, satisfied, Tracey backed off. The other two girls made spitting noises and then turned away. I didn't think they'd actually spat on me, I hoped not.

'Alright now, quiet,' the form tutor's voice rose.

Tracey's barb about my father cut but I tried not to think about him. Sometimes, in the dead of night, when I couldn't sleep I'd allow myself the indulgence. Who he was, why he left, where he was now. I fantasised that he was rich and successful and would arrive one day in his open top car with soft leather seats and whisk me away from all this. I dreamed of golden gates, and sweeping lawns, cool marble bathrooms with lashings (I loved that word), of hot water and bowls of tutti frutti sweets, the purple ones. It was a pleasant way to pass the time until sleep came for me.

Mrs Collinson cut into my daydream. 'Quiet, I said!'

I settled myself down for another stint at school, unsure how long I'd be here, wishing Mum would just let me do this one thing like other kids.

### Lottie

On the drive home Lottie thinks about options for dinner, about collecting her dry cleaning at the weekend, even Murtaugh, anything in fact, except her mother and her husband. Yet they keep resurfacing like something that won't flush down the toilet. A constant uncomfortable reminder that caused discomfort and embarrassment.

Why should she tell Dan about what happened, even if it did impact on their lives now? It was still none of his business. Besides, he wasn't telling her about shagging someone else and that was happening *now*, and impacted just as much if not more, on their lives.

Why should she visit a dying woman just because she gave birth to her? That's where her mother's responsibility for her began and ended, the gestation period. She barely remembers any sweetness, any kindness...except at the end, and what good did that do? She abandoned her. It was as if her mother was allergic to love.

As she pulls up outside the house and walks up the garden path Dan's words come back to here. *'Love means different things to different people.'*

Why did he say that? Was he going to leave her? How did she feel about that? Did she love him the way she had?

As she puts the key in the door she realises that she does still love him, she wants to make it work. Why else would she pretend she didn't know what she did?

She would make him something nice for dinner. One of his favourites. Corned beef pie, she hadn't made that during the week for a long time. If she made a little effort then maybe…

She thought of what it all entailed. Making pastry, cooking the filling, pulling it all together and then preparing veg. She'd have to make gravy too. She glanced at her watch. It was already six. They wouldn't eat till eight and she was ravenous. She'd have to prepare some sort of snack to keep them going. It was a lot of work and the idea weighed heavy on her. It would be easier to take something out of the freezer.

No, she thought as she reached the kitchen and dropped her bag on the table. Tired as she felt, she would do this for him. Start building the bridges to a new life. This affair would burn out, it was bound to. They could find a way out of this mess. Other couples did.

She didn't bother to get out of her work gear, instead she pulled out the scales from the cupboard before she could change her mind again. She had to reach into the back of the cupboard for the plain flour, it *was* a long time since she'd done this.

As she straightened up, flour in hand her phone bleeped. It was a text from Dan.

'Something come up. Have to work late. Don't wait up. x'

'Must be *some* emergency if you couldn't even find the time to call,' she whispered to the empty kitchen as she bent down to return the flour to the back of the cupboard.

# Tuesday

### Lottie

Lottie's heart leaps into her mouth and her throat closes over her words mid-sentence. Poppy turns to look at the entrance doors to the hall.

'Oh,' is all she says, then turns back and smiles, one eyebrow raised.

They are sitting at one of twenty round tables set out in cabaret style in a room dominated by a domed ceiling and halogen lights.

'What was I saying?' Lottie asks, shaking her head and turning back to face Poppy.

'I'm not sure it's that important,' Poppy says.

'Behave!' Lottie hisses. 'He's coming over!'

Poppy laughs and Lottie scowls at her.

'Ladies, what an unexpected pleasure,' says Murtaugh O'Sullivan.

Poppy nods. 'Nice to see you again. Will you excuse me for a moment,' and before Lottie can stop her Poppy heads off in the direction of the ladies.

'Was it something I said?' His voice is creamy and smooth and runs across Lottie's body, disconcerting her.

'What are you doing here?' she asks, ignoring his question. The memory of throwing up on his shoes makes her colour up.

'It seems we have more in common than we might have first thought.'

'Perhaps.'

He laughs. 'Are you always so…?'

'What?'

He pauses, she waits.

'Closed?'

'Yes.' *That should sort it.*

He raises one eyebrow. 'Good.'

'What?' The man is infuriating.

'I like a challenge.'

Before she can respond Poppy returns and the MC for the day asks them to take their seats.

Lottie is both relieved and disappointed when, instead of joining them, Murtagh returns to his colleague and takes a table two rows behind them. She takes a moment to observe his companion and her heart sinks. Slim, mid-twenties, smartly dressed in a blue pin stripped skirt suit, coiffured hair, a little make up but not too much, matching black briefcase and low heeled shoes; sensible yet still a little sexy.

Lottie turns to face the lectern as the first speaker is introduced and, determined to focus, she picks up her pen, poised to take notes.

96

Ninety minutes later and Lottie didn't find it as hard to focus as she thought she might. Pages and pages of her spidery writing sit before her to prove it. She feels a moment of compassion for Sandra, who will have to make sense of it all to type it up.

'Coffee?' Poppy asks.

Lottie smiles and follows her from the quiet room into the corridor outside and the assault of the chatter of the delegates. A long table has been set up with stacks of white cups and saucers in neat rows at one end, six plunge metal flasks stand sentry-like at the other. They collect a cup, and queue to get their coffee. Lottie eyes the plates of milk and dark chocolate digestive biscuits.

'Interesting stuff,' Poppy said.

Lottie nods. 'I've got some great points I think we can use in that new bid.'

'I thought so too.'

They reach the front of the queue and help themselves to coffee. Lottie resisting the biscuits, helped by her skirt biting into her waist. Not wishing to return to the conference room where they have spent most of the morning, they make their way through groups of people chatting, to stand by the railings.

The wall ahead is made of glass and curves seductively in waves below. The Sage in Gateshead is a feat of architectural engineering that astounds Lottie, seeming to defy gravity to her layman's eyes.

Through the glass the river Tyne ribbons past, the Tyne bridge to their left. It is a crisp bright day and Lottie finds her heart lift momentarily. Water and the sun will do that, and she promises herself a trip to the beach this weekend. It is the least she deserves after everything that has happened recently.

'So, what do you think to his nibs showing up?' Poppy asks, breaking into her thoughts.

'Who?'

Poppy laughs. 'You don't fool me that easily.'

Lottie smiles. 'I don't think anything of it. Coincidence, that's all. Besides, wouldn't matter if I did think something of it, I'm married, remember?'

'Yes, and be fair to the man, you did throw up on his shoes,' she giggles.

Lottie joins her. 'God, don't remind me.'

They turn back to the view. Lottie can feel her shoulders slowly unwind as she sips her coffee, squinting across the river, taking in the sun drenched view.

'Hello,' says a familiar voice, and she turns to face Murtaugh's dark eyes sparkling with mischief.

She steadies her heart, determined that he won't see the effect he has on her.

'Hello again.' From the corner of her eye she sees Poppy sidle away and vows to kill her next time they are alone together.

He turns to face the glass wall.

'Wonderful view. Inspiring.'

It gives her a brief opportunity to look more closely at this man who has inadvertently got under her skin.

He is shorter than she had thought in the bar, and the daylight reveals deeper lines. The thought pulls her up short, in this light he will surely see the mistake he made in the bar in asking for her number. Either that or he'll finally spot her wedding ring. It suddenly feels tight, heavy, uncomfortable on her finger.

Stifling a sigh she turns to face the view, she is married anyway, so none of it really matters. 'Yes,' is all she can find to say.

'I was surprised to see you here.'

'Me too. You, I mean.'

He laughs. She feels him look at her and she holds her breath, waiting. Surely now he will walk away.

'What now?' he says.

She looks at him in surprise. 'What?'

'What now?'

'Erm...I think there's a talk on pedagogy by a professor somebody or other, I don't have the programme with me.'

'I'm not talking about the conference agenda.'

'I...I'm sorry, I don't follow.'

'Well, I am ridiculously attracted to you, despite you throwing up on my shoes.'

'Mmm, yes, sorry about that.'

'And I think, without being too conceited, that you are somewhat attracted to me too. So I was wondering...what now?'

Lottie feels as if someone has stolen all the oxygen. She takes a breath, trying to arrange her muddled brain into some sort of order so she can sound reasonably intelligent when she responds.

*This is the point when you tell him you're married, Lottie*, she thinks.

'But you never called,' she says instead, not wanting this game to end.

'No, the number you put in was unobtainable. I thought it was your way of getting rid of me, that and throwing up on my shoes. I should imagine that puts most men off.'

She turns. 'About that, could you refrain from mentioning every opportunity you have?'

He laughs. 'Sorry, but you do have to admit it's funny?'

Lottie nods. 'It is, but still…'

'Anyway, I did *try* to call.'

Lottie pauses, not quite sure that what she is about to do, is the right thing to do.

'I'm glad.'

'So I'm not wrong then?'

She shakes her head. 'No, you're not wrong…' she pauses again.

Is she really going to turn this man down? She has never felt like this before, not even with Dan. Doesn't she want to explore it, even a little bit? Is she really going to close the door and walk away?

'I feel a 'but' coming on,' he says.

'It's complicated.'

He nods, plucks his cup from its saucer and turns back to the view. 'I understand.'

She isn't sure what that means but decides not to pursue it. After all, it really isn't fair to give him some idea that something might happen between them when clearly nothing can.

'Excuse me,' she says. 'I just have to…' she points in the direction of the ladies then walks away.

She knows he is watching her, and as she places her empty cup on the table and makes her way to the ladies, she prays that for once she won't make a fool of herself and trip over her own feet. She makes it safely to the toilets and leans against one of the sinks, taking deep breaths and steadying herself for the remainder of the day.

During lunch Murtaugh doesn't approach them at all, although he does nod across the room when they catch each other's glance.

'What did you say to him?' Poppy asks.

Lottie shrugs. 'Nothing.'

'What, nothing at all?'

'No, nothing.'

Poppy shakes her head in despair.

'What?'

'You're a big fat idiot.'

'That's very grown up of you, Poppy.'

'Just saying it like I see it.'

'I'm *married*, Poppy.'

'Oh yes, I forgot. And does your husband know?'

'That's not fair!'

'That's exactly my point.'

Lottie has to admit she is disappointed he doesn't try again, but what can she expect? Looking at his colleague is she really that surprised? Besides, not only has she thrown up on his shoes, she *has* told him she isn't interested.

As they file back into the conference hall for the afternoon session she sees Murtaugh sitting beside his colleague chatting. She is beautiful, she concedes. Lottie really needed to update her wardrobe, maybe get a hair cut, put on a little make up.

*God, what am I saying? I don't have time for all this silliness. I have an organisation to run, a failing marriage to patch up, and a dying mother to attend to...or not. Which is exactly why you said no. Give your head a shake, woman.*

But despite her protestations, it has reminded her of another person who made her feel like this before. Before Cal did what he did. Before she stopped believing in love.


### Lottie 1980

I had been working for Cal for a couple of months when Barry Johnson walked up to me as I was leaving the shop on our estate.

'Alright?' he asked, nodding his head.

I stopped and looked behind me, checking it was me he was talking to before I answered. I didn't want to look like an idiot.

I nodded. 'Yeah, you?'

'I'm good. What yer got in the bag?'

'Milk and eggs,' I said, feeling dumb.

'Right. For yer Mam?'

I nodded.

'You don't call her that 'dyer?'

'What?'

'Mam.'

I shook my head, the power of conversation seemed to have deserted me.

'You call her "Mum",' he said, in a mimicry of a posh voice.

So that's what this was, a piss taking session. I felt more comfortable now I knew and I set off in the direction of home at a fast pace.

'Hey! Where you going?' he asked, catching me up and trotting alongside me. 'Slow down.'

I didn't respond. I'd found it to be the best tactic if I didn't want to get into a fight.

'Hey, hey, hey, I'm sorry. Did I upset you?' he asked. 'I'm sorry. Slow down, I just want to talk to you.'

I glanced at him, he did *look* sorry. I kept walking but slowed my pace, curious to know what he wanted.

'Word out is you're working for Johnny Caldwick.'

'What of it?'

He shrugged. 'It's cool is all.'

I thought of Cal's gun and wondered how cool Baz would think *that* was. Very, I decided. Was this what this was about? I stopped and turned to him.

'What do you want Barry?' I was angry, and in no mood for anymore jokes. What he said next took my breath away.

'I wanted to ask you out.'

I just stood and gawped at him.

He grinned, his dimple appearing. 'Well? What d'you say? Wanna go out with me?'

Barry was top dog on the estate, he'd only gone out with hot girls in the past. So I was sceptical.

'Why me?'

He laughed. 'What?' he said, as if he hadn't understood the question.

'Why me?'

''Cause I fancy you, you daft arse!'

'Really?'

'Yeah, course. Why else would I ask you out?'

'For a joke maybe? To make fun of me.'

'God, no, fancied you for ages.'

'Oh.' I thought about those times he'd shouted after me in the street.

'So, how about it? D'you wanna go out with me?'

'Why now?'

He shrugged. 'Why not? Seems as good a time as any. What cha say?'

'Sure, yes, okay, that would be fine.' I felt myself go pink.

'Great. Can I walk you home?'

'That'd be a good start,' I said, with a smile.

He smiled back and there was that dimple again, and I felt a hundred butterflies tumble through my stomach. We walked side by side in silence for a while.

'So, why do you call your Mam, Mum?'

I shrugged, 'Dunno, I always have.'

'You know, some people say she's got airs and graces, like she thinks she's a bit better than everyone else.'

My insides shrank at his words and I felt hot with anger. How dare they! What did they know about anything? Barry must have sensed something was wrong.

'What?'

I shook my head, 'nothing.'

'No, really, what is it?'

I stopped, we had reached the end of my street and I didn't want Mum to see Barry, not yet. I had this feeling that she'd spoil it for me, and whilst I knew she'd find out eventually, I didn't want her meddling fingers in this just yet.

I looked at him, my jaw set tight with anger. 'I think they're jealous, because she's got class and they don't,' I said. 'Got to go, see you around?'

'Hey! Come here.'

He started to follow me, so unless I wanted to lead him straight to our door, I had no choice but to stop.

'Do I need to apologise? Again? So soon after the last one?'

I looked at him, his big eyes so sorrowful. It made me laugh.

'There you go,' he said, smiling now. 'So, I'll call for you later, okay?'

'No!'

'What?'

'No, I'll meet you somewhere,' I didn't give him time to argue. 'Where?'

'Erm, alright, club car park? About six?'

'Make it seven,' Mum would have gone out by then and there wouldn't be any questions.

'See you,' he said, and walked off, raising a hand in goodbye.

I turned down my street with my heart soaring. I was Barry Johnson's girlfriend, I had a job on a book stall and I was going to school. Life wasn't half bad right now.


I spent the rest of the afternoon in a daze, watching the clock slowly work its way round, barely listening to my mother. Eventually she left and the time arrived.

I was in the club car park as arranged and when I saw him strut towards me I forgot everything else. My heart swooped in my chest and I was so happy I thought I was going to throw up.

'We're going to the reccie?' he said and I nodded, not daring to speak.

We walked for a while in silence. I couldn't find anything to say in my scrambled egg brain. This was our first date and I didn't want him to be disappointed, but I couldn't find a single thing to talk about.

'You go to Bellway school?' he asked.

'Yeah, I do,' I paused, frantic for something, anything I couldn't ask him the same question because he didn't go to school. Everyone knew that. I'd look like an idiot if I asked him that. But just as the panic was being to reach crisis mode Barry started speaking.

'I've been expelled from three of the four schools in town now. Bellway's is the only one left.'

'You going?' I asked, and my body started to relax.

'Nah, I'll not bother now, it's not worth it.'

'So, what'll you do?'

'I have plans, you know?' I didn't, but I didn't doubt it. Baz had a fierce reputation on the estate and the way he held himself, you just knew he'd be okay.

'How was Borstal?' I asked. There was silence for a moment and I froze inside. Was it an inappropriate question? It stretched between us and then, reaching for my hand as we walked, he broke the silence.

'That's what I like about you, Charlotte.'

'Oh?' I wasn't clear what he was getting at.

'You're dead honest. I've noticed it in the gang.'

Gang? I was part of a gang now? Was he referring to the group of girls who kicked my sorry arse every time I got to school?

'Really?'

'Yeah, the other girls, they giggle and joke about, twiddle their hair and wear the latest fashion no matter how daft it is.'

I'd have done the same if I could have kept any of the money I earned.

'But you, you're serious. You listen. Talk about stuff.'

I wasn't sure what 'stuff' he was referring to, but I let him burble on. I didn't often hear someone singing my praises and I liked it.

'You ask direct questions. You have...an inquiring mind.'

I didn't tell him it was enquiring, I didn't want to stop his flow.

'That's why I wanted to get to know you. I bet you read books.'

I nodded. 'I work on a book stall on Saturdays. In Stockton market. A place called The Shambles?'

'What types of books do you read?'

'All sorts. The classics of course, just to see what everyone's banging on about, but I like reading modern stuff too. What about you?'

'Nah, my reading's not too good. Missed too much school and now it's a bit late for all that.'

I thought about maths again, my exams, my future, then pushed it to one side to concentrate on Barry.

'What are you going to do if you can't read?'

'I didn't say I couldn't read,' he snapped, and I realised I'd touched a nerve. 'I'm not fucking stupid nor nothing.' Baz had a reputation for having a bad temper. I'd heard a rumour he'd put a lad in hospital, but I didn't know if there was any truth in it.

'I didn't mean anything by it,' I said, just to be on the safe side.

He squeezed my hand lightly so I guessed it was over. We walked quietly.

'Charlotte?'

'Yeah?'

'Are you a virgin?'

I stopped and pulled my hand away. 'What?'

He looked confused. 'I just thought, seen as you'd asked me a direct question, I could ask one of you.'

I glared at him, not knowing whether to walk off and leave him there and then, or hit him first. Chances were, he'd hit me back. Would his punch hurt more than mum's? Possibly.

'I'm sorry - I didn't mean any harm by it.'

Again he looked genuinely sorry, so I dropped my shoulders. He was right, if I was going to ask personal questions then he should be allowed to too. It was just his seemed so much more...personal than mine. Still, I guessed it depended on your definition of personal.

'Friends?' he asked, his head popped to one side, a cheeky grin exposing his adorable dimple.

I nodded reluctantly and he took my hand again, pulled me along to walk with him.

'Come on yer daft lass, the gang'll wonder where we're at.'

His words made my heart sink. 'The gang', we were off to meet 'the gang'. Whoopy fucking doo.


We were meeting The Gang on the reccie. The reccie was a wide open space made up of compacted black kind of mud stuff where nothing grew. None of us kids knew what had caused the reccie to be the reccie, and none of us thought to ask, but the deep peaks, troughs and dips were great for bike stunts.

'The gang', whom we ended up spending every night with, included none other than my arch nemesis Tracey Craig, along with her two lackeys: Susan Bickerton and Jane Waugh.

My heart sank as we approached, sure that this was where it all ended. This was where Baz turned round and laughed in my face for believing he'd ever go out with me, swiftly followed by a good kicking. So I was shocked when Tracey lifted her chin in acknowledgement.

'So, you two an item then?' She shifted the bulk of her body from one foot to the other and looked me up and down.

'That's right,' Baz said. 'What of it?'

'Keep yer 'air on I'm only asking.'

'Where's the others?'

Tracey indicated with her head, her hands firmly stuck in the pockets of her black Harrington. 'Out on the reccie.'

'Brought their bikes?' Baz asked.

'Yeah.'

'So where's Dunny.'

'Running after them, the daft sod.'

Baz turned to me, 'Dunny can't ride a bike, never learnt. We tried to teach him but he was hopeless.'

Tracey chuckled. 'Thick as pig shit,' she said, there was that familiar snarl I knew so well. It was unpleasant, even when I wasn't at the receiving end.

I took the opportunity while they talked of checking out all the girls. I hadn't had a chance before, for fear of having my head caved in.

Susan, a tall thin girl looked translucent with her pale skin, pale hair and pale face. I swear I thought I could see the blue rivers of her veins under the skin of her forearms. She reminded me of the willow trees by the river in the park.

Jane in comparison, looked like Susan's negative opposite. Her deep dark eyes, set beneath thick black eye brows, black hair and dark skin, gave her a Spanish or Italian look. She was curvy, with amazon strong arms and legs.

Tracey was big, with at least three rolls of fat around her waist. She had no chin, buried as it was within the folds of her neck, and her eyes had been squeezed. She looked like a small person who had been consumed by a much larger one, and I wondered how she moved about. It looked uncomfortable carrying all that weight, but she was surprisingly agile for her size.

'What you looking at, Bitch?'

*Don't know, they don't label shit.* I shrugged and turned away.

'Craig, enough,' said Baz. 'She's with me.'

I glanced back and watched Tracey take it all in. She never struck me as a bright girl, but surely even she could see it would be dangerous to continue to taunt me. I waited.

'Alright?' she said eventually.

'Yeah fine thanks,' I said.

'Rowell was a pain in the arse today, eh?'

'Rowell is always a pain in the arse,' I said.

To my surprise the girls laughed. The tension in the pit of my stomach began to ease and I joined in the laugher. I hadn't been joking, he was, but it felt good to make them laugh. Baz reached out and squeezed my hand.

'Yer alright, you,' he said. 'Isn't she lasses?'

'Aye, she's not bad.' It wasn't a ringing endorsement from Tracey, but at least she wasn't going to kick my head in at the first opportunity Which was progress.

'She's canny.' It was the first words Susan had spoken since I arrived, and I realised that I had never heard her speak before. Her voice had an angelic sing song ethereal quality. I ached to hear her say something else.

'Jane?' said Baz.

'Yeah.' It came out gruff and snappy, as if she had been stopped in the corridor by a teacher and asked for homework.

My acceptance was tentative and based on Baz's demand. I didn't feel reassured but it didn't really bother me. Everything was transient, why should this be any different?

At that moment Gary Donald and Peter Harvey arrived on pushbikes, braking side ways and showering us in a plume of black dust. All except Baz that is, who had let go of my hand and, clearly anticipating what the boys were about to do, took several steps back out of range.

'What the fuck!' said Tracey. The other two joined in, lamenting loudly, spitting and coughing for effect. I decided it was best to just brush down my jeans and try not to breathe too deeply until the dust settled.

John Dunn, Dunny, who had been running up behind them, arrived and bent over, his hands resting on his knees to catch his breath. He let out a silent laugh, his shoulders bouncing up and down, reminiscent of Muttly. Even his dark curly hair was like the cartoon dog.

'Shut yer face, Dunny,' Tracey ordered.

Dunny wasn't the sharpest tool in the box, he was what my Mum would call 'a pork pie short of a picnic', but I had always liked him, and I didn't like Tracey speaking to him like that. It soon became clear I wasn't the only one.

'Tracey leave the poor little fuck alone,' said Gazz, swinging his bike back and forth between his legs. He had a shock of red hair that seemed to spring out of his head in all directions and so many freckles they had begun to join so he looked as if her had a blotchy tan.

'Oh, right and what you gonna do about it then?'

'Seriously Tracey, shut the fuck up,' this was Harvey, the tallest and broadest of the boys. He had sharp blue eyes, blond crew cut and massive lugs. He wore turned up jeans and burgundy doc martins.

'Oh yeah, come on if you think yer hard enough,' Tracey shot back.

Gazz and Harvey exchanged glances and my stomach clenched again. These boys were ex-Borstal, both had criminal records and were as scary as shit to watch in a fight. There were no boundaries for these guys. They didn't see any stop signs. In short, they had fuck all to lose so you didn't mess with them. Any of them. So there was no doubt in my mind they were hard enough.

Harvey got off the bike and handed it to Baz. 'Fancy a go?' he said, ignoring Tracey's outburst.

I couldn't believe Tracey was giving them so much lip, and I couldn't believe that they were taking it. I held my breath waiting for it to kick off, waiting for a fight to break out or someone to start screaming, but it just died away as quickly as it had ignited.

We spent the rest of the night sharing two bikes between the seven of us, I say seven but it was really only five because Tracey and Susan refused to take part. Baz taught me to do some of the stunts and we played chicken, pedalling as hard as we could at each other and seeing who would chicken out the soonest. I won every time, and at the end of the night even Tracey came and patted me on the back.

As I walked home to a dark empty house about ten that night, I was tired, dirty, aching and starving, but I felt on top of the world. I was now knocking about with the elite crowd on the estate, and I was in the thick of it all.

There wasn't much in the way of food in the house, so I made a sugar sandwich and ate it while I did my homework, slipping to bed just before Mum was due home. She was unpredictable at the best of times, but when she'd had a drink she could be especially volatile, or maudlin, and either would spoil my night.

As I lay in bed, listening to the kick out of the club across the road, I started to ask myself what I might do with my life. School was coming to an end in the summer, but before I could answer, and being only vaguely aware of Mum's key in the door, I slipped into sleep.

The following day, with Tracey and the girls off my back, school wasn't bad at all. I even started to enjoy it. The things the teacher said were becoming clearer, and I loved turning over the puzzles in my head, feeling that click of understanding. It was like putting a jigsaw together.

Each time I understood one piece, something else clicked. I was making progress, and I didn't need anyone to tell me so. I knew it. If I could get some qualifications, then maybe I would have some choices. The teachers banged on about it enough, perhaps it was true after all, even for kids like me.

# Tuesday

### Andrea

Jean plumps up Andrea's pillows. She's a little sweetheart, Andrea's favourite. Nothing is too much trouble. She's going to get walked over in life. Old fashioned name, Jean. Probably named after some ageing rellie, poor thing. At least she didn't do that to Lottie. Then she remembers she didn't give Lottie her name, so no credit there then.

'Has your daughter been back to see you yet?' Jean asks, breaking into her thoughts.

'Not yet,' Andrea says, and Jean goes silent.

She knows what she's thinking, she knows how this looks. Andrea looks like a saint while Lottie looks like an evil wicked daughter. It's the roles they have often played, usually instigated by Andrea, but this time it isn't her fault. Well, it sort of is, she realises.

'It isn't her fault,' she says, in an attempt to right this small wrong.

'I didn't say anything,' Jean says, straightening her covers and tucking in the corners at the bottom of the bed.

'You didn't have to,' she tells her.

She straightens up. 'It isn't my place to judge,' she insists.

'Doesn't mean you're not though, eh?'

Jean smiles. She really has a lovely smile.

'You don't know the full story,' Andrea pauses. 'I wasn't the...best mother in the world.' Which she knows to be a gross understatement, but it's all she's capable of today. For some reason she wants this young woman to like her. She doesn't usually have this need, perhaps it's because she's dying.

'Well, no doubt you made mistakes, we all do. My mother has had her moments I can tell you, but she's still me mam and you only have one.'

Andrea can't argue with her logic and besides, she's tired. It's Tuesday night and Lottie still hasn't returned. Perhaps she never will, maybe she won't give her that opportunity to make it right. Then it occurs to her, maybe she can't.

### Andrea 1980

It was a couple of days after bumping into Mark that the idea came to me, fully formed and, like most good ideas, obvious once you'd got it. I needed to get inside Cal's business and bring it down from the inside, find something on him, some evidence the police could use. And I knew how.

All I needed now, was to find Cal.

My skin crawled even at the mention of his name, let alone what I was planning to do. Even in such a small town, I had successfully managed to avoid him over the years, but now I would have to actively seek him out, make friends with him, more importantly, make it look like we'd bumped into each other by accident.

It was dangerous and Mark's warning surfaced once in awhile. If Cal suspected, even for a moment...I knew what he could do. I *was* afraid, I'd have been foolish not to be, but I finally had a chance to get him and I couldn't pass this up. It felt like this was why everything had turned out the way it had. Having Lottie, losing Mark, it had all led to this and I owed it to Andrew to try.


I 'ran' into Cal a couple of weeks before Lottie's fifteenth birthday, and I'd had a few drinks. For courage. I wanted to see him suffer, I wanted to bring him to his knees.

'Well, well, well,' Cal said, when he saw me. 'Look what the cat dragged in.'

'Hello, Cal.'

'What brings you to this part of town?'

I shrugged. As he came closer the small hairs on the back of my neck lifted and my muscles ached to lash out. 'Fancied a change.'

'Sick of slumming it, eh?'

'Something like that,' as he came and stood beside me, I felt as if a malevolent cloud surrounded him. An unspoken warning that he could hurt you, and hurt you bad, and he would.

I shrugged it off as imagination. He couldn't hurt me anymore than he already had. Besides, I could handle myself. Johnny Caldwick was a man wasn't he, and men frequently fell at my feet, why would he be any different? He had a cock didn't he?

'Drink?'

Pushing my feelings aside I turned to him and gave him my best smile. 'Thanks, I'd like that.'

He raised an eyebrow in surprise and smiled. 'What'll it be?'

I raised an eyebrow in return. 'Port and lemon?'

He laughed, 'By, that takes me back. You serious?'

I shook my head and laughed. 'No. I'll have half a lager and lime, thanks.'

Cal ordered and I started to relax. Not totally. There was still a tightness, a fear lurking inside.

He turned to me. 'I hear you've got a kid.'

*Here goes.* I nodded.

'A daughter. Pretty little thing by all accounts.'

'That's what they say,' I said.

'She got a name?'

The conversation was going exactly as I had predicted. 'Lottie.'

'And how old is little Lottie then?'

'Fourteen, fifteen next month, why?'

'I might have a job for her.'

'What kind of a job?'

The barman put my drink on the bar and Cal dipped into his pocket, rummaging through the change in his hand.

'I own a book stall,' he said, without looking up.

I hadn't expected that. 'Really? That's not what I heard,' I'd had a few drinks and caution was thrown to the wind. I was on dangerous ground with Johnny Calwick.

Fortunately he laughed. 'You shouldn't believe everything you hear, love. I own a lot of things.'

'And people...?'

He passed the correct money to the barman.

'Come on, let's get a table,' he said, ignoring my comment.

We sat down and I took a sip of my drink before placing it on the table in front of me.

'Fingers in many pies, eh?' I said, changing tack.

'You better believe it,' he winked at me, and I remembered it all. Saw Andrew's blood, his contorted face, the ambulance ride. I shook the image away.

'So why Lottie?'

'I heard she was bright, pretty and I need an assistant. Thought she sounded about right.'

'And you want her to work on your...book stall?'

He looked at me for a long moment then said, 'Initially, yes.'

I sipped my drink. Buying time, trying to decide whether I could go through with this. Then I realised I couldn't.

'Look, Cal,' I said, putting my drink down. 'Never mind my daughter, *I* need a job.'

'You? On a book stall? I don't see it, love.'

'Yeah, me, and I'm not talking about a book stall either.'

He looked at me for a long time before he spoke. 'What's wrong, state don't pay enough all of a sudden?'

I shrugged, deciding to ignore the jibe. 'Teenagers are expensive.' As soon as I said it I regretted it.

'There's the book stall job,' he said. 'Make her pay her way.'

'I owe money,' I lied. He would never have believed anything else.

'To who?'

'That doesn't matter.'

He pulled on his pint and watched me over his glass.

'I'm very...adaptable,' I said, and gave him one of my best flirtatious looks, cocking one shoulder up.

He licked his lips, they glistened and my stomach turned over at the thought of what he might make me do. Why did I never learn? Why did I never think before I acted?

'Your past you're sell by date,' he said at last.

His words sliced me and I gasped. 'What? I'm not even thirty!'

'Pull the other one,' he picked up his pint and watched me as he drank.

'Okay, but I don't *look* my age.'

He put his pint down and looked at me. 'I'll give you that,' he conceded. 'But I still don't have a market for you.'

I had reached a dead end. If I couldn't get inside Cal's business I couldn't get anything on him. If I couldn't get anything on him, my plan, such as it was, was finished.

'There's always the book stall job for your little Lottie,' he said, with a grin.

My intuition was sounding off like a submarine making a dive. Whilst Lottie had been part of my plan originally, now I was faced with Cal in the flesh I couldn't do it. Yet, there was another part of me that didn't want to go away empty handed.

Right there in front of me, for the first time since I lost Andrew, was an opportunity to get what I had always wanted. Cal. Revenge for Andrew's death. Surely I could manage Cal? I knew what I was doing. There was risk involved, but it was manageable. And the payoff, the idea of giving the police what they needed to finally nail this bastard...all I had to do, was say yes...

So I agreed, and Cal saw that I agreed. But I underestimated Johnny Caldwick,.

# Wednesday

### Lottie

They're not offered tea, despite the evident affection for Hilary they are not real visitors. Lottie sits on the edge of the sofa beside her, her coat clenched round her, even though it's far from cold. Her heart is starting to return to its normal level and her breathing has levelled out. The excitement replaced with shock.

Tracey sits in the armchair, drawing great drags off her cigarette. She is unrecognisable, and if Lottie didn't know who she was, she would pass her on the street without a second glance. Tracey is a scrawny woman now, with deep wrinkles that make her look more like a woman in her sixties than her thirties. Is it poverty, six children, the death of two of them, or her predilection for her addictions? Probably a combination Lottie decides.

The difference in their appearance gives her a momentary shiver of pleasure, marred only by the realisation that Tracey is now a broken woman. Any feelings of revenge Lottie might have harboured have evaporated.

'Do I know you, love?'

Lottie's heart beat quickens and she shakes her head. It isn't a lie. She doesn't know her, never has. If she asked her if they'd met before, that would be different.

She wanted to show Tracey that she'd escaped this life, but for what? At least Tracey is surrounded by life. It is teeming. Her children play fight at her feet, knocking into her. She lashes out with a slippered foot and catches one of them.

'Fuck off out to play,' she shouts, and the boys rise and shove each other into the passage and out the front door, shouting their goodbyes to Hilary and slamming it as they go. A silence settles like ash from a bonfire.

'Little bastards,' Tracey mutters, but there's affection in her voice. She turns her attention back to her visitors and peers at Lottie.

'You sure I don't know you?'

Lottie smiles. 'I'm sure,' she says.

Tracey seems satisfied by her answer and turns her attention to Hilary.

'So, how've you been Tracey?' Hilary asks.

'Not bad love, you know.'

'You know why I'm here?'

'Yeah love, me benefits.'

Hilary smiles. 'Among other things, Tracey.'

'I know pet, the boy's school, but you can see how they are.'

'Yes,' she laughs now. 'A bit of a handful, eh?'

'Fuck me, you can say that again. Sorry, pet,' she says to Lottie.

Lottie smiles an acceptance of her apology. Hilary and Lottie agreed on the way here that Hilary would introduce her, but she would say nothing.

'There's also a matter of *your* welfare Tracey, and Jenny's, of course. Your health is very important to the family.'

'I'm grand.'

'You missed one of your meetings, for your programme?' she reminds her.

'Aye, I know, I wasn't well.'

'You need to keep up with them Tracey, otherwise I can't help you.'

'Understand love, don't want to get you into any trouble, but I was ill, like I said, straight up.'

Hilary makes a note then looks up and says, 'And what about Jenny?'

'What about her?' Tracey's eyes narrow and the affable exterior evaporates.

Hilary pauses before answering. 'She hasn't been in school,' she checks her notes, even though she doesn't need to. Hilary can recall all the stats about this family at the drop of a hat. Of all her families come to that. 'Six weeks. The truancy board will be calling her up soon if she doesn't go.'

'She's not keen.'

'That's understandable,' she laughs. 'Not many kids are. I hated it. Still, fact remains that legally she has to attend and, I'm afraid Tracey, as her parent, you have to ensure she goes.'

'She won't listen to me.'

'Do you want me to have a word with her?'

'You can have a go, but you'll be wasting your breath for all the good it'll do.'

Tracey leans her head back and bellows. 'Jenny!' She repeats this three times until they hear a faint shout back.

Lottie's heart quickens. At last she is going to meet Jenny, see her, be in the same room. She'll be able to assess her, see what is going on beneath the surface, figure out how they can help her escape.

She hears whispers in the back of my mind, *escape to what?* but pushes it aside. It will be different for Jenny. She *will* go on to have a family, a full life, not live the half life Lottie will now experience. She curses recent events.

But for Jenny it will be different. Lottie hears her feet on the stairs and then, there she is, standing before them all.

She is taller than Lottie expected, and heavier. Her upper arms are on the verge of flabby and her vest is pulled tight over a bulging gut. Her shoulder length hair hangs limp, thin and greasy. Her pudgy face has a vacant look that warns against expecting much more than trite and garbage to spew from her mouth.

What stands before her, is the image of Tracey at the same age. The image of everything Lot has despised. Her tormenter, her torturer, her enemy.

Something inside her closes down and without a thought, she stands up and leaves.


Hilary comes out to the car about ten minutes later. Lottie knows she has cut short her visit on account of her and she is glad. Standing by the car waiting, being watched by the kids in the street, and possibly by people in the houses surrounding her, makes her feel exposed.

Anyone watching wouldn't have believed that this was where she came from, that once upon a time, these were her people. But then, she never belonged here then either.

Hilary doesn't say anything for the first few minutes of the drive back to the office, but once they are off the estate and on the main road she says, 'You okay?'

'Fine,' Lottie says. 'Sorry.'

'It's not a problem,' she says, although her voice is tight. She's angry and Lottie can't say she blames her. 'Want to talk about it?' Hilary asks, after a few moments.

Lottie has long exercised the principle of not developing personal relationships with her staff. She's learnt from experience that it can get messy should there be any disciplinary issues. So she is surprised by her response.

'My mother is dying, I came from an estate like that, I wanted to rescue Jenny, help her escape like I did, but one look told me that won't be possible. Besides, I'm beginning to wonder if there is such a thing. As escape I mean.'

It is a lot of information to take in and to Hilary's credit she pauses before responding. *She's a real professional, not like me*, Lottie thinks.

'We can't make an assumption about someone because of how they look, or where they come from,' she says.

'I know, but you can see the girl lacks intelligence.'

'That isn't the only measure of someone's worth.'

Hilary is shaming her and quite rightly, but for some reason Lottie persists, as if she has to prove a point, be right about something.

'I know the type.' She colours but it is too late. It's been said.

She hears Hilary take a breath and waits. Hilary drives in silence until she pulls up at a set of traffic lights.

She turns to face Lottie. 'She has the patience of a saint and the compassion of a nurse. You should see how she looks after that family. Her common sense, patience and understanding keeps that family together. Her mother relies on her for *everything*. I've watched that girl clean up mess after mess.'

Lottie doesn't say anything. She knows what she wanted to see, she knows why she's behaving this badly, but she can't put it into words. It comes out distorted and ugly, or perhaps it comes out how it is.

'I'm appalled,' Lottie says, by way of an apology.

Hilary misunderstands. 'I've seen worse.'

'Not with *them*, with *me*,' she explains.

'There's none of us perfect,' she says. 'It's one of the joys of being human.'

The lights change and Hilary puts the car in gear and removes the handbrake.

Lottie hopes that means this will stay between them, and she relaxes. Well, as much as her shame will allow. Another shame to add to the many recently, funny, she always thought she was the good guy. Her life is topsy turvy these days. Much like the last time her mother was part of it.


### Lottie 1980

Despite my misgivings about Cal, life was taking a turn for the better. In truth I wasn't sure if it was Cal's appearance, or the truancy board's threat, but I'd managed to get to school almost every day for six weeks and the work was becoming easier with each passing lesson. Not maths. Maths was still a mystery to me, although I now had a desire to learn fractions and decimals that I'd never had in the past. But anything to do with shapes or simultaneous equations still baffled me. It might have been my inability, no matter how hard I tried, to see any point in them whatsoever.

'I'm never gonna need this in life,' I told Mr Wright.

He sighed heavily and scratched his head. He had black springs for hair that stuck out in all directions.

'What about working out the area of a room so you can buy carpet, Charlotte?'

'I'll just get the man in the shop to do it for me.'

'But don't you want to be able to do it yourself? Don't you want to be able to make sure you're not having the wool pulled over your eyes?'

'He wouldn't dare!' I said, with indignation. The class laughed behind me.

Mr Wright smiled. 'No, I dare say you're right. Still, you'll need it for the exams. You're bright enough you know?'

'Doubt that, sir.' It was Tracey Craig. I'd recognise her voice anywhere and my stomach turned over. It would seem that I wasn't entirely off the hook, despite Baz's endorsement.

'That's enough.' Mr Wright said, over my head.

Exams. They were months away but they kept banging on about them, although I was coming round to the idea more. Since working on the book stall I realised that having a few qualifications might not be such a bad thing, and as school didn't seem as confusing now, I thought I might even have a chance at getting one or two.

I wasn't sure how long it would last before Mum would start keeping me off again, but I decided that for now at least, I'd see if Mr Wright was...well, right.

Maybe I was brighter than I thought? Not top set bright obviously, but a little bit brighter than where I was languishing now...maybe. Besides, I wanted to show that Tracey Craig. Stupid fat cow. And then there was Barry of course.


It was already dark when I met Baz by the big oak next to the Skerne bridge that night. He was alone.

'Alright,' he said, as I approached.

I shrugged. 'Yeah. Where's the others?'

'Gone to the reccie.'

I started in that direction.

'Not tonight,' Baz said.

I turned and must have looked confused because he held out his hand for me and said, 'Just us eh?' and smiled.

I smiled back and felt a flutter of pleasure as I took his hand.

We walked by the river in silence. It burbled alongside us and you could hear the odd car pass in the distance. I pulled my coat round tighter against the nip of the wind. It was October and the trees had lost their leaves. The gang were planning to go 'penny for the guy' the following week, and as I'd never been before I was looking forward to it.

'Fancy going to the park?' Baz asked, breaking into my thoughts.

'At this time of night?'

'Why not?' he smiled, and his dimple made him look cheeky and cute.

'Okay.'

We changed direction and picked up the pace, heading towards the park. I hoped they hadn't locked the park gates because I hated climbing over the fence. It was high, I was small and I wasn't very good at climbing. I had a scar along the top of my arm to prove it.

My heart sank as we rounded the corner. The gates were locked, of course they would be, it was dark and any hope I had was false hope.

'Bugger!' I said, then wished I hadn't, I didn't want to look like a spoils sport.

Baz pulled me closer to him, put his arm around me and squeezed me into his side. I could smell tobacco on his clothes and a dampness, as if his clothes had been left too long to dry.

'It's okay Munchkin, fret not. I know where there's a break in the fence.'

'Really?'

'Yep, come one.' He broke away and pulled me behind him as he quickened his pace. About three hundred yards past the vaulted victorian gates he let go of my hand and disappeared into a large overgrown bush that grew through the railings and spilled onto the outside pavement.

It had green spotty leaves and I'd walked passed it a million times before. Now it seemed like some secret night portal to the park, and Baz was sharing it with *me!*

He reappeared. 'Come on,' he whispered, even though it was clear there was no-one around. I dived into the bush after him and after fighting my way through a few branches I found myself on the other side of the fence.

'How?' I looked back to see that some of the railings had rusted and the force of the bush growth must have pushed them apart. 'How come the parkie hasn't seen this?'

'Dunno, but I'm glad he hasn't.' He grinned at me.

I smiled. 'Me too!'

'Swings or lake?'

'Swings?' I ventured. People rarely asked me so I was anxious to get it right.

'Good choice,' he said, and we headed to the swings hand in hand.

I was so happy my heart felt too big for my chest. So this was what love felt like.

**Lottie**

'I'm taking Friday off work to play golf,' Dan tells her that night.
Lottie stops, with the dirty plates suspended mid-air in her hands.
'You're what?'

Dan looks up. 'It's alright isn't it? You'll be at work. I'll be back
by the time you get home.'

Frustration bubbles up. Is he playing golf, or seeing *her?* She
swallows and forces her body back into motion. Dan returns to the
newspaper. She carefully loads the dishwasher, whilst in her mind she's
crashing them against the wall, screaming at him that he's a lying cheating
bastard.

They had made plans to watch a movie together tonight. He'd
picked it up on his way home. 'One you've been wanting to see,' he'd said,
beaming, eager to please.

Her heart had soared. It was over, he'd come home to her, they were
back on track. But now she sees the gesture for what it is and it burns her
heart.

She closes the dishwasher door and washes her hands, drying them
carefully. Then she leaves the kitchen, plucks her coat off the hook in the
hallway and picks out her car keys from the bowl on the table.

'Lottie?' Dan calls. 'What you doing? You ready to watch this film
then?'

She opens the front door and leaves, with no idea where she will go,
but with a need to get out of the house before she does him some damage.
Not sticks and stones damage, real damage.


'I've developed the uncomfortable habit of running out on people
recently.'

'Oh,' Poppy says, sipping her red wine and reaching forward for
another piece of her chicken peri peri. 'Who are the lucky people?' She
grins at her own joke.

Lottie found herself heading for Poppy's. It was the only place she
could think of going and the thought makes her feel sad. Is her life really
that narrow? She thinks about Tracey and the teems of people surrounding
her and suddenly the woman doesn't look as broken.

'I'd laugh but it's not funny.'

'So who?'

'Mum, Dan, a home visit at work, I could go on…'

'Well, the first two deserve it. I can't comment on the home visit,' Poppy says now. 'Except to say there's been a few I've wanted to walk out on.'

'But that's just it, you didn't.'

'So?'

'So, I feel...I feel as if I'm losing it.'

Poppy doesn't say anything for some time, just chews on her chicken. Lottie waits, knowing what she has to say, when she finally gets round to saying it, will be worthwhile.

Finally Poppy swallows, looks at her and says, 'Fuck 'em.'

Lottie laughs. 'What?' she asks.

'Fuck 'em, bake a big bloody fuck off pie.'

'A...a...what?'

'Fuck off pie. Never heard of it?'

Lottie shakes her head, wondering what on earth Poppy is going to say next.

'It's easy. You take one cup of see if I care, a dash of kiss my arse, add some fuck yous, then stir in a wedge of shove it up your arse and finish it with a sprinkling of fuck-offee.'

Lottie laughs again. 'Poppy! That's hardly constructive.'

She points a peri peri chicken wing in Lottie's direction, the thick red sauce makes it look as if it's just been slaughtered. 'That, dear Lottie, is your fundamental flaw.'

'What is?'

'Your almost OCD need to be constructive, to fix it, to make things right for everyone. It's why you keep returning to people who've hurt you, it's as if you've got some pathological need to be kicked.'

She doesn't know what to say to this. She digests her words, before she finally speaks. 'I don't *need* to be kicked.'

Poppy looks at her. 'Lottie, I love you, you know that, but it drives me mad to see you take the blame for *everything*. It is *not* your fault your mother's dying; it is *not* your fault your husband is a cheating twat, and it is *not* your fault that Miriam is a cow. You. Didn't. Do. Anything.'

Poppy returns to gnawing her chicken wing and Lottie sips her wine. She's right of course, Lottie does take it all on her shoulders, everything. At least, it's her initial reaction, until she's managed to reason it all out. But at first it's all her fault, it's always been all her fault.

'Dan isn't a cheating...twat' Lottie says quietly. She can't help but defend him. 'We've had a lot of...pressure recently.'

'Yes, "we", but you didn't go and shag someone else did you?'

'No,' she says, carefully, slowly.

Poppy's right. Lottie doesn't know why she has this compulsion to control and fix everything. Then she remembers that horrible night, and she knows why.  If she keeps everyone happy, if she fixes all the broken wings, then maybe, just maybe, no one will hurt her like that again.

But she can't tell Poppy, she can't tell anybody.  There's only one other person who knows about that night and she is on her death bed.  Will her secret die with her mother, or has she already told someone else?

Poppy's next question breaks into Lottie's thoughts.  'You going to leave him?'

'I don't know, I have a lot on my plate right now.  I really don't know if I could deal with that as well.  I keep thinking he might just stop it, that it's just a fling.  Then I think I'm fooling myself and being a mug. Ohhhh, Poppy,' she wails.  'What do you think?'

'You know what I think.'

'I *think* I know what you think.'

Poppy laughs.  'It's beginning to sound like a comedy sketch.  I think you think that I think you know what I think,' she laughs.

Lottie finds herself smiling even though she doesn't want to.  'You have peri peri in your teeth,' she tells her friend.

'Fuck it!' Poppy says, and her grin widens.

Lottie shakes her head but can't help laughing.  She is sorry she hasn't told her friend the whole story.  If Poppy knew Dan was the only lover she had ever had, she might understand Lottie's reluctance to leave, but that would only lead to more questions, and Lottie can't bring herself to reveal why.  And to think, it had all started so...innocently.


### Lottie 1980

Cal began to come to work more often.  Some weeks I could feel Tony watching us, whilst Cal watched Tony.

I wondered why Cal was there at all, he didn't do anything except sit and read the paper, stand up and hoist his trousers over his belly, then sit back down and drink tea and eat bacon butties.  Occasionally he'd have a bit of banter with his regular customers.

'Nice to see such a pretty face on the stall, Cal.'

'Yeah, and the lass isn't bad either eh?' Cal fired back.

It was all harmless fun, but I could feel Tony's eyes taking it all in and he was even beginning to make *me* feel uncomfortable.  When Cal caught him looking he'd shout over 'wanna picture Tony pal?' and Tony would hastily turn away.

It went on like this for a few weeks, the tension building, until I thought something had to happen to clear it, like the building of a storm.

Then one afternoon Cal revealed an aspect of his business I'd rather not have known about.

It was late in the afternoon and Cal had sent me off to get the drinks. Tony was ill so he wasn't in this week, his wife was manning the stall and it was clear there was no love lost between her and Cal. She was always pleasant to me, but looked like thunder near Cal so, though it felt mean, I only got drinks for the two of us.

I loved the warmth of the polystyrene cup in my hands, the knowledge that it was fragile, that I could squeeze it, but if I squeezed it too hard, it would break beneath my fingers. I was engrossed in this when Cal reached under the counter and pulled out a brown paper bag. He then leaned one cheek of his arse on the counter in his familiar way.

'Hey, want to see something weird?' he asked.

I was sure I didn't, but I said okay.

'Come here,' he looked about him conspiratorially. It was quiet today. You could hear the rain pounding on the plastic roof, hammering through the damp hall. It was a cold, bleak October day and soon we'd have to think about Christmas. I wanted to do something a bit different on the stall, perhaps dedicate a section to gift ideas, but I hadn't run the idea by Cal yet, so I was pleased to get an opportunity to butter him up. If he were in a good enough mood on the way home then I would ask him. Mind you, I'd never known him in a good mood when business was this slack, and the rain *always* kept people at home.

He dipped his hand into the bag and pulled out a magazine. I knew instantly what kind of magazine it was.

'Don't look like that,' he said, 'these women are professionals. They're paid a lot of money for this sort of thing. It's an art form.'

I didn't want to look prudish or childish so I said, 'Sure, I know, was just...surprised that's all.'

'Ever fancied being a model yourself?'

'Me?' I wasn't sure I'd heard him right.

'Yes you. You're a pretty lass,' he tapped the magazine with his forefinger. 'There's uglier lasses than you in here you know?'

I wasn't sure it was a compliment, but I thought maybe it was. Models were pretty, right? And Cal had just asked me if I'd ever thought about being a model, *and* he'd said I was prettier than some models he'd seen so...so...so he must think I'm pretty enough to be a model.

'Not that sort though,' I said.

'Why not?' he sounded incredulous, like I'd said I didn't want to keep my head.

'Well, it's a bit...' I couldn't find the right words, I didn't want to look foolish and it didn't help that Cal's eyes were glued to me, waiting. In reality, I wasn't sure why.

'It's modelling,' he said. 'Modelling's modelling.'

'Yeah, but that's not modelling clothes is it or...' I tried to think of other types of modelling. 'Fridges,' I said, thinking of Sale of the Century.

'Fridges!' he laughed. 'Who'd want to model fridges?' He stopped laughing and leaned close to me. 'This is the highest type of modelling,' he said. 'This is the modelling of self. No gimmicks, no clothes to hide behind, nothing. This is modelling the woman. It is modelling in its purest form, and that, lass, is why this,' he stabbed at the magazine again, 'is art.'

I wasn't sure how to respond to that. I'd never seen pornography as art. I just thought it was something men looked at to jerk off to. Never imagined it had some higher calling, but the way Cal put it, he made it sound...decent.

'Really?' I asked.

'Really. And another thing, it pays. Pays really big.'

'How big?'

He opened the magazine to a woman knelt facing us, her white shirt unbuttoned and half way down her arms so her breasts were exposed. They were small, with pink pimply nipples. Mine are bigger, I thought with pride. She had her thumbs tucked into the top of her white panties, as if she were about to remove them. She was half smiling, but biting her bottom lip as if she wasn't sure what to do next. I felt the same way.

'That lass there would have earned about a hundred nicker for doing that. A hundred nicker for a couple of hours work.'

I couldn't imagine that. I earned a fiver every Saturday and thought it a fortune. At least I would of, if I'd got to keep it. Last tatty picking season I got seven quid a day for picking a full length pitch. It was back breaking work. She didn't look like her back would break doing what she was doing.

'And lots of actresses who are famous now did this sort of thing first you know?' I didn't. 'That's how they broke into show business.' He closed the magazine. 'Think about it,' he said, and smiled at me as he returned the magazine to its paper bag.

I did think about it. Couldn't stop thinking about it. I wasn't naive enough to think that taking your top off earned you that kind of money, I'd seen those magazines and the other kind of poses those woman did. Henry Johnson brought one into school once, flogging individual pages for ten pence to the lads. But I couldn't quite shake off the idea of all that money. I wouldn't have to do it for long, I could save money, buy a nice house, I could get away from the estate we lived on. And it wouldn't matter if my maths wasn't that great - I wouldn't even have to *do* exams...

Cal broke into my thoughts. 'And one more thing,' he added. The magazine was stashed away and he was back perched on the stall with his tea in his hands. 'If you *are* interested, I could help you break into the business. I know a few people. I own a shop that sells that kind of stuff.'

'A sex shop!' I said, a little louder than I had intended. I looked around and saw Tony's wife scowling over. I didn't think she heard me, she always scowled in this direction.

'Alright, don't broadcast it lass. Yes, a sex shop. So I have a few contacts down in the smoke.'

The Smoke, there he went again talking about London, he went there regularly and I ached to have that life. I had the Houses of Parliament in a snowstorm globe on my bedroom window sill and I longed to visit London, the Smoke. I'd called into the bus ticket office in town once to find out how much the bus fare was. It was sixteen pounds. Sixteen pounds! And it took six hours to get there. You'd have to stay in a hotel for at least one night and I wouldn't ever be able to even find the fare, let alone the money for a hotel. It had always been beyond my reach but now, maybe not?

And maybe I could buy my own book stall or even better, a book shop, one with armchairs so the customers could rest and enjoy the books after they bought them.

Maybe I could go on holiday, on a plane, like I'd seen in the adverts on Boxing Day. Walk on the sandy beaches, have a cocktail with a brolly in it, maybe ride a horse through the mountains. I'd never ridden a horse, but I could get lessons.

My mind tripped over possibility after possibility, galloping in directions it had never been allowed to travel before. Suddenly, I had choices.


I was tired the following Saturday morning as I climbed into the back of the cab. Cal was there. I knew he would be, I knew he would be there every Saturday, until I gave him an answer. The trouble was, I wasn't sure he'd accept any answer other than yes, and the feeling of having choices in my life was rapidly vanishing.

We didn't say much on the way that day. Clearly Cal didn't want to talk about anything else and I didn't want the cab driver (or anyone else for that matter), to know.

We set up the stall. I went for the drinks and passed Tony on the way back. He nodded, I smiled, but we didn't talk. There wasn't anything to say.

All morning we worked alongside each other in silence. We were busy so it wasn't too awkward. At one point a woman in heels walked past and I noticed Cal couldn't take his eyes off her. She seemed to have some power over him, his desire pronounced, and I envied her.

I wanted men to look at me that way, I wanted that power. I wanted to walk by and have men's eyes follow me. I wanted, I realised, what my mother had. Perhaps Cal could give me that. Not in the real world, but in that make believe world of those magazines he had shown me.

It wasn't until Cal was sitting sipping his tea late afternoon that he said what we had both been waiting for him to say.

'Well?'

'Well what?' I said, though I knew fine well what.

'Don't play games with me, missy,' he growled, and I felt that familiar tightening inside. I hesitated for a moment and then I decided to be honest.

'I'm worried,' I said.

'About?'

'About whether I could do it. I don't want to say yes and you get studio time and a break for me and then I can't do it and let everybody down.' It came out in a tumble, words over words.

'What don't you think you can do?'

'That,' I said, pointing under the stall, where he'd put the magazine last week.

'But what couldn't you do?'

He really didn't get it 'Take my clothes off,' I muttered. 'Move like...that.'

'Don't worry about that. I can teach you. You think those girls just did it? Nooooo. All of them felt like you at first. In fact, I coached a few of them myself.'

'What, in that magazine?'

He nodded. I didn't know whether to believe him or not.

'It's natural to feel the way you feel, but by the time I've finished with you, you'll be ready to go up against any pro.'

'Really?' He nodded. 'So...what do I do next then?'

'I'll pick you up Tuesday night and we'll do a little session at mine as a warm up.'

'What about mum? She'll want to know where I'm going.'

'Don't worry about that, I've squared everything off with her.'

I didn't know how he could when I'd only just agreed, but I had a more pressing problem, I needed to think of an excuse for Baz and the gang. The tiredness I felt that morning returned with a vengeance. Everything was getting hard, I decided.

Monday night was Halloween. We spent the early part of the evening hollowing out turnips with some knives Dunny had brought from home to make them into lanterns. I suspected his mum didn't know about it. The rest of the night we went knocking on doors. Mostly they told us to fuck off, and we stoned their windows and ran off laughing. Some gave us money or sweets. One fella gave us an orange, which outraged Gazz.

'A fucking orange. What we supposed to do with that?'

'Shove it up yer arse,' Tracey said, and everyone laughed, including Gazz.

He peeled it and handed it round to everyone. The feeling of camaraderie and belonging heightened the sweetness of the orange. It would never taste this good again, I thought.

At the end of the night I told Baz I had to go to my auntie's the following night. He was okay about it. He was okay about a lot of things actually. He walked me home, kissed me and then left. We'd been going out for a couple of months now and he never tried to force anything. It was...gallant, romantic, unexpected, and I thought perhaps there was more to him, that like me, he could have been a better person if he'd had a different life.

Tuesday night Cal arrived in a cab just after seven. My Mum had been fussing round me like I was going to a prom or something. I don't know what Cal had told her.

'Trust me,' she said, thrusting a carrier bag at me as I was about to leave.

I clearly didn't because I looked in it. 'Mum what...? Really?'

She nodded frantically. 'Just take it. Trust me.'

I knew I didn't have a choice if I wanted to leave the house without a scene, so I took it.

'Good girl,' she said, patting my hand.

She stood in the doorway, the light behind her so I couldn't see her face clearly, but she seemed anxious. I wasn't used to seeing her anxious, so I smiled to reassure her. She smiled back, and looked so small and lonely I didn't want to leave her.

'Go on,' she said, shooing me away and I hurried down the path, obeying without thinking.

I got in the cab with Cal and when I looked back, just before we turned the corner, she was still standing there, waving, making me more nervous.

We drove in silence. It didn't take long to get across town. I had expected Cal to live in a big house, but he lived in a house much the same as ours. A little bigger, and in a nicer part of town, but really not much different.

The house was in darkness as Cal guided me up the path. He held my arm as if I were old or infirm. He fumbled a bit with the door keys and my insides suddenly felt loose and uncomfortable, as if they might run out of me. Cal hadn't said a word since picking me up, and I couldn't think of anything to say to shatter the silence between us.

The house had the same layout as ours. Small square hall, stairs directly ahead of the front door, living room to the left, kitchen to the right. Cal took off his coat and indicated with his hand that I should go to the left, into the living room.

He clicked on the light and as he set about closing the curtains I took in the room. It ran from front to back, a big modern room. The sofa was dark brown with matching armchairs. The chimney breast and alcoves were covered in a large flowered orange wallpaper. They had a radiogram in one alcove and a teak TV in the other, each framing the stone fireplace. Above the fireplace was a picture of white stallions running through the sea. It was a picture my Mum had wanted for some time. The smell of furniture polish was strong, and the wood gleamed. I wondered where his wife was.

Cal clapped his hands, making me jump, and then rubbed them together as if he was chilly.

'Right then, shall we get started?'

I couldn't move, the implications of what I was about to do hit me properly for the first time. I didn't want him to see me without my clothes on. I didn't want *anyone* to see me without my clothes on.

'Come on lass, I know you're shy, we talked about this. It's natural, remember?'

I nodded.

'There's nothing to be nervous about. It's just you and me. No one else tonight, alright?'

I nodded again, but I still couldn't move.

'Let me take your coat and I'll get the camera.'

I put down the carrier bag my mother had given me before I left and eased off my coat, my heart pounding in my ears as I handed it to him.

He disappeared for a few minutes and I just stayed standing in the middle of the room, wondering. Wondering what I was doing here, how I had agreed to this, what was going to happen next, if I could go through with it, what would happen if I couldn't, how I would get home...I was wondering so much I felt sick with it.

Then Cal was back in the room with a polaroid instamatic in his hand. I'd seen them on the telly, they were expensive. How much money did he have? Did he have one of those new Sony Walkmans too? Perhaps I could buy one...if I could find the courage to do this.

I turned my attention back to the camera. I was curious to see if it really did work like the advert said, one click and the photo was supposed to slide out and appear in minutes before your eyes. The curiosity helped with the sick feeling.

'Alright now, I haven't got much film so what I want you to do is take off your top and get used to being around me in your bra before we take photos, yeah?'

I nodded, that didn't sound too bad, I thought, and pulled off my jumper. I stood in my t-shirt and jeans.

'T-shirt too, love,' he said impatiently.

I didn't want to piss him off so I folded my jumper, put it on the arm of one of the chairs, then took off my t-shirt, but instead of folding it I held it up in front of me.

'It's alright, no one's going to hurt you,' Cal said.

I hadn't thought they were, so now I had something else to wonder about. What would I do if 'someone' was going to hurt me? It made my heart beat a little faster and my mouth cloy with glued up emptiness.

'Let me have the T-shirt,' Cal said, holding out his hand.

I handed it over then instinctively put my arms across my chest area, hiding my bra.

'If you're going to stand like that you might as well take your bra off too. I can't see anything love.'

It all felt terribly fast. I needed some time to catch my breath. I felt as if my head was being held under water and panic was starting to build.

'I...I...'

'Bloody 'ell lass,' he boomed. 'You'd be hopeless on set. They'd have packed up ages ago. You'd have to be a damn sight more professional than this.' He ran his hand through his thinning hair. 'D'you know it costs about £200 an hour for a studio to be up and running? You just cost 'em nearly a hundred nikker fannying on like this.' He hitched his trousers over his stomach and glared at me.

A hundred nikker! A hundred pounds! I wasn't ever going to be any good to anyone if I cost them that sort of money. I swallowed hard, determined to be brave, and slowly lowered my arms.

'That's a lass,' he said, the softness back in his voice. 'Sit on the sofa,' he commanded.

I sat on the sofa in my jeans and bra.

'How d'you feel?' he asked, after a few moments of looking at me.

I shrugged. 'Okay. A bit...strange.'

He nodded. 'Understandable, but you're doing good.'

He came and sat beside me and took my hand. 'If you can do this you could earn a fortune. More money than you can dream of.'

If it had just been about the money I would probably have backed out there and then, but it was about more than that. It was about choices, a new life, getting off the estate. This was my big chance to escape.

'I know it feels a bit awkward now, love. But soon it won't, soon it will feel second nature to you. You'll surprise yourself with the things you can do.'

Perhaps he was right, perhaps this would become easier the more I did it. A bit like my school work. I remembered then that I had a piece of history homework I needed to get done before tomorrow, giving me another reason to hope we wouldn't be too much longer.

'You ready for the next step?' he asked.

His voice was soft, my homework was waiting and I thought that it was probably better to just get on with it if I was going to do it at all. Get it over with. Besides, no one died from being naked, did they? Unless they were in snow of course, then they'd get hypothermia, I'd read about that. Another good word, hypothermia.

'Okay lass, off with those jeans.'

I slipped off my jeans, folded them with my jumper and sat back on the sofa feeling the air round my bare legs.

'Stand up,' he said. I did. 'Spin round slowly.'

I did as he asked, my hands clasped tightly together to cover my front, trying to fight the compulsion to grab my clothes and run.

'Well done, it's not so bad eh?'

'No,' I lied.

'Well, bloody smile then,' he said laughing.

I pushed the corners of my mouth up.

'Right, let's get a couple of pictures and see if we can relax you a bit. Sit on the sofa,' he got up and fiddled with the camera. He looked up at me. 'Okay, legs to one side, arms behind your head.'

I did as he instructed.

He looked and frowned and my stomach clenched. I wasn't doing it right. I couldn't do it. Part of me was relieved, maybe he'd give up on me and let me go home, another part didn't want to lose my chance of a new future.

'No,' he said, coming towards me. 'That doesn't look right.'

He pulled me into one pose after another, not taking any photos and not liking anything. I was getting more and more worried. This would be costing the studio a fortune and my history homework was calling out to me. Mr Bleasdon would go ballistic if I didn't hand it in, and the prefect badge I was working towards would be a step further away.

'I need your bra off lass,' he said, breaking into my concerns. 'Alright?'

He looked at me hard, my body tensed, but I knew he was right. If I was going to do this thing I had to do it. Now or never, we both knew that. The air in the room stilled, everything oscillated for a moment, we held our breath.  Cats squalled outside, someone shouted down the street, a door slammed.  Then I reached behind me and undid the clasp on my bra.

'Good girl!' he cried, as I slid the bra straps down my arm.  Emotion chocked the back of my throat but I fought against it, I couldn't cry, that would ruin everything.

He whistled and sang as he put me in similar poses as before, only this time he took a couple of photos.  It got easier, the desire to cry subsided, and after a few more minutes I almost forgot I wasn't wearing any clothes.  I felt happier, like I was doing it right now, I wasn't wasting anybody's time or money.  The studio would be pleased.

I felt the discomfort return when Cal asked me to cup my breast and try to lick it.  It felt difficult, awkward and odd, but he seemed pleased with the results and let out a whoop that reassured me.

He only took about five photos in all, even though I posed for a long time.

'What's in the bag?' he asked.

I'd forgotten about the carrier bag my Mum had given me.  Thinking she'd made a mistake I brushed it aside.  'Just my school uniform,' I said.

Cal's eyes lit up.  'Really?'

'Yeah, my mum said I should bring it.'

'Oh, your mum's a diamond isn't she?'

I shrugged.  I was used to the world thinking so, but I was yet to see it.

He glanced at his watch.  'Buggar, wish I'd known before.  Still, next time.' He looked at me.  'Get yer kit on lass,' he said, as if I was crazy to be sitting in his living room in only my pants.

I got dressed quickly, pleased to have my clothes wrapped round my body again.

'Cab'll be here in a minute  We'll have to do some more of this. You're nowhere near ready.'

I nodded.  I knew that.

'Bring this next time,' he said, handing me the carrier as a cab tooted outside.  'And I'll sort out another time with your mum.'

'Okay, thanks,' I mumbled, realising she must know what was going on.  Did that make it okay?

I got into the cab and the car pulled away.  I didn't feel any different for being naked in Cal's living room.  Nothing had changed inside me.  It hadn't been as bad as I'd feared in the end.  A few photos.  Then I realised I hadn't got to see the photos.  I shrugged it off.  It wasn't important.  What was important was my history homework.  I hoped Mum was out so I could get on and do it.  I spent the rest of the journey thinking about the Luddites.

# Thursday

## Lottie

Lottie is in the office even earlier than usual the following morning. She stayed at Poppy's and barely slept for the second night in a row. Her mind spins between Dan's affair, her mother and memories of an ugly past.

She pushes herself to focus. She has to prepare for an audit meeting with their major funders later this morning, and she needs it to go well. Not just for the organisation's future, but because she needs some confirmation that she is still in control of something. As she picks up her pen her office line rings.

'For Christ Sake!' she mutters as she picks up the receiver.

'How you holding out?' a familiar male voice asks.

For some weird reason she thinks at first it's Murtaugh and her heart speeds up, until she realises it's Dan.

'I tried your mobile,' he says.

'It must still be switched off.'

'You never came home last night.'

'I sent you a text.'

'Are you okay?'

'Fine. You?'

Dan doesn't say anything for a moment and she waits.

'Why don't we go out for food tonight?'

She lets all the air out of her body and asks herself, not for the first time, is this so he can go and see *her* tomorrow without guilt or because he's trying to find his way back?

'Are you still planning to play golf tomorrow?' she asks.

He ignores her question. 'Or we could watch that film we didn't manage to watch last night?' he says.

'Either's good with me,' she says, eventually.

Miriam appears at her office door.

'Look, I have to go. I'll see you tonight.'

Lottie's insides tighten as she puts down the phone. It must be trouble, and the syrupy tone of Miriam's voice confirms it.

'Charlotte. Unlike the rest of the staff she never did accept calling her Lottie.

'Miriam, to what do I owe this pleasure?' It comes out sarcastic and she regrets it immediately.

'Hilary tells me you went out on a house call recently, on one of her cases?'

Shit! Her heart flutters but she brazens it out and plasters a smile on her face, determined to show no weakness.

'That's right.' Less is more she decides.

'That's most...irregular,' she says.

'We live in interesting times,' Lottie tells her. *What the...what am I saying? I sound like a politician, a bad one.*

'Quite. What may I ask, is the reasoning for this change in process?'

'As I explained to Debra, th-'

'Debra? You phoned Debra?'

Shit, shit and double shit! 'I...'

They both know Lottie is on the back foot and Miriam's eyes narrow as she waits.

Lottie takes a breath and spreads her fingers across the desk in an effort to anchor herself. It's an old habit. Sometimes it works, this morning it doesn't. She can feel Miriam's eyes boring into her. She has caught Lottie off guard and she feels like a child again, small and vulnerable, her mind won't work fast enough to escape the adults. It's been a long time since she's been this defenceless.

'Are you feeling alright?' Miriam asks.

'Quite alright, thank you.'

'If you're making changes to process, fundamental changes, without informing the staff, then I must protest. We work with vulnerable people, they, and our staff, need protection, and a good process affords that protection.'

'I am well aware of what our clients and staff need Miriam,' Lottie says, her voice hard as glass. 'I put the process in place. Remember?'

Miriam pulls herself up and whilst Lottie despises her, she has to admit she is right and they both know it. By not following the processes that Lottie insisted on implementing when she first arrived, she is exposing everyone to risk, including herself.

Lottie sighs. 'I'm sorry,' she says. It won't do her any good to get on the wrong side of Miriam. She doesn't need trouble from her on top of everything else. 'I'm tied up right now preparing for a meeting. Can we discuss this another time?'

Miriam hesitates, but it's not a request.

'Thank you, we'll talk again later,' Lottie asserts.

Miriam nods curtly and leaves.

*Damn!* Just because she leads the organisation doesn't mean she shouldn't follow the rules and usually she does. It's just...a feeling of overload washes over her as the phone on her desk rings again.

Cursing she deals with the call then returns to her prep, or rather the few lines she has managed to scribble down this morning among all the interruptions.

If only she could cancel the damned meeting, but then Lottie never was one for quitting.

Later, after the meeting, a little of her old self returns. It went well, the funders left happy and it feels good to be back in control. She begins ploughing through her emails, but despite her small success her heart isn't in it. She defers as much as she can to tomorrow, flagging tasks and messages to come up as reminders in the morning.

The remainder all require some action from her today. She is half way through a response to the first one when Sandra appears.

'I need to talk to you.'

There's something wary in her tone and Lottie forgets her email. 'Oh? What is it?'

When Sandra steps into the office and closes the door Lottie's heart beats in alarm.

'What is it?' she repeats.

'I wanted to warn you...'

'Warn me?'

Sandra nods.

'About?'

She looks over her shoulder even though the door is closed.

'Miriam.'

'Oh god, now what?'

'I thought you should know, she's started...gossiping with the staff, about your...'

'What?'

'Your...behaviour.'

'What behaviour?'

'Can I sit down?'

'Yes of course, sorry.'

Sandra takes a seat at the meeting table and Lottie leaves her desk to join her.

'What's this all about?' she asks.

'It looks like she's concerned but, well, I know there's little love lost between you two.'

Lottie shrugs and nods, there's no use denying it.

'She's going round saying how worried she is about you.'

'Worried!'

Sandra nods, 'she says you're behaving erratically.'

'Really?'

'She's been saying she thinks the strain is getting to you and that you might...'

'Go on.'

'This isn't me saying this,' she adds quickly.

'I understand.  What is she saying?'

'She's saying that you might not be up to the task, you might not be able to take the pressure.'

Lottie sits back in her chair, unsure of her next move.  If someone accuses you of not being able to cope, of cracking under the pressure, then whatever you do can only confirm their suspicions.

'I see,' she says eventually.  'And what's the staff's reaction?'

'I think at first they just ignored her but now, well, some of them are wondering.'

'About?'

'The breach in protocol is...unusual for you.  And a few of us have noticed you looking more tired and distracted recently.'

'The Craig case,' she whispers, cursing her carelessness.

'And Miriam has pointed out that you have been going early on occasions.'

'I've racked up a lot of lieu time.'

Sandra put her hands up to ward her off.  'I know that, I know, and I told them, and I'm not saying you shouldn't, it's just, you haven't before.'

Lottie lets out a long breath.

'Mostly, I think the staff are just concerned for you.  Miriam is trying to stir things up but if it's any consolation, I think it might be backfiring on her, still...'

'Yes, except this Craig family thing.  On reflection I might have cocked up a bit there,' she says, deliberately not mentioning Jenny.

'Sometimes life isn't always as tidy as we'd like it to be.'

It is on the tip of her tongue to tell Sandra that her mother is dying but she stops.  It might get back to the staff and add fuel to the already wild speculations that she is cracking under the pressure.  Maybe she is?  She regrets her conversation with Hilary after the Craigs visit but it's done now, she can only hope she doesn't share it with anyone else.

'Thanks for the warning, I appreciate it,' Lottie says.

Sandra takes this as her cue to leave, as she is supposed to, and stands up.  'No problem, but if you do have anything bothering you...' she leaves it hanging in the air.

'Thanks, much appreciated,' Lottie says, as she stands up and pushes the chair under the table.  Her shutters back up.

Sandra stops at the door.  'Oh, and Lottie?'

'Yes?'  She is back behind her desk.

'Don't forget you have that bid to finish by tomorrow, the details are in the file.'

Lottie smiles.  'I hadn't forgotten,' she lies.

When Sandra's gone she rings Dan and tells him she has to work late, wondering as she does, if this is adding nails to the coffin of their marriage.

*At least I'm not lying.*


### Lottie 1980

When I saw Baz the following day I had to lie to him again. I hated to do it but I didn't have any choice.

'So what's wrong with her,' he asked, when I told him I needed to visit my sick aunt twice a week from now on.

'I dunno, they haven't told me. Something to do with her heart, I think.'

'Can't someone else visit her as well? I mean, two nights a week?'

'Dunno, me Mum's said I have to go so I have to go.' That bit was nearly true.

'It's a bit shit, I don't see you on Saturdays either.'

'I know, but we've got Sundays.'

'S'pose.'

I snuggled up to him. We were on our sofa, Mum was out so we had the place to ourselves. I had smuggled Baz in through the back door. Mum had met him, briefly one night when he called for me. She only spoke to him for a minute or so, but decided she didn't like him, said he was a bad influence and I wasn't to see him anymore.

'*And* you're doing homework now!' he said, as if I was doing it right there and then.

'Baz, I want to get on in life, you know, get somewhere and I, well, I might not be as daft as I thought.'

He laughed, not unkindly. 'You? Yer as daft as a brush.'

I punched him lightly in the arm and he wrestled me to the floor overpowering me. He sat on me, pinning my arms by my head, then he leaned forward and we kissed, my heart leaping in my chest. When he pulled back and I'd caught my breath I said quietly, 'Don't you want to get away from here, Baz?'

He got off me, helped me up and we sat back on the sofa, holding hands.

'Course I do. This place's a dump. I know it, you know it, we all know it, and I've got an idea for making a lot of money, then we can get away.'

I liked the 'we'. 'You have?'

He nodded.

My stomach clenched and I knew that whatever he was involved in, wasn't going to be legal, and I was probably better off not knowing.

Instead I asked, 'Is it dangerous?'

'Not if you know what you're doing.'

'And do you?'

'I think so.'

I didn't say anything to that. He seemed to know his way round and he could take care of himself, I wanted to know more but decided that, like me, he was entitled to a few secrets. It was probably better neither of us knew the whole truth, especially if it involved a plan for getting off this estate. Inevitably it would be something neither of us would be proud of, and if we managed to escape, would want to forget.

## Lottie

It doesn't take Lottie as long as she thought it would to finish the bid, another one. *It is all I seem to do these days, chase money.* There was a time when her work in the charitable sector meant something to her, now it was all reports, bid writing and crisis management.

She sits at her desk for an hour, the building empty, sipping coffee and soaking in the silence, reluctant to return home and face Dan. Until eventually she leaves the office and finds herself here. At this place. With her.

Andrea is sleeping when Lottie arrives. She looks smaller, shrunken somehow. It should please her, seeing the woman so broken, but strangely it doesn't, it doesn't at all.

She sits watching her chest rise and fall, it looks like hard work, like her body isn't made to do it anymore. It's then Lottie realises how quickly it's over. Life and death is merely the matter of a breath.

Her body takes a deep gulp of air at the thought. All working. But the feeling of her mortality hits her as she watches her mother struggle to hold onto life, and she realises she may not wake up to answer her questions.

Lottie may never know who her father is, or why her mother left, or why she did what she did. If she'd been a little braver, stayed last time or returned sooner, then she might now know, and she burns with regret.

It's the story of her life. If she'd been a little braver, asked a few more questions, demanded and expected more from life, then where would she be now? Would Dan be doing what he's doing? Would her mother have abandoned her the way she did? Would Cal have...

One thing she does know, she doesn't want to be her anymore, she just doesn't know how to be anything else yet. If only she had made better choices, trusted her instincts...

And the memory of what this woman and Cal did to her urges her to leave and never come back. This is not a place of answers, but recriminations. Lot will not find the peace she seeks here, her mother was never a source of comfort. Decision made, she picks up her bag and leaves.

## Lottie 1980

When I turned up at Cal's on the Thursday in the cab he sent for me, I didn't feel as nervous. I took my school uniform as he'd asked, though I didn't see the attraction myself. I knew about St. Trinian's and all that, I wasn't that lame, but I would have rather worn something more...grown up and womanly. Besides, I didn't think I looked a bit like any of the St. Trinian girls. When I said all this to Cal he just said 'Leave the thinking to me lass.' So I did. What did I know anyway?

Taking my clothes off wasn't as difficult this time.

Cal must have noticed because he smiled and said, 'More relaxed eh?'

I nodded. It really wasn't so bad.

He asked me to adopt the various poses he'd shown me before and he took a couple of photos. I asked to see them, but was disappointed. They were grainy and cheap, not at all like the glossy bright ones I'd seen in the magazine. Mine looked used, cheap.

'Cheer up,' Cal said. 'This is just practice runs yeah?'

'Yeah, I suppose.'

'You wait until you get them studio lights on you, make you look like the million dollar film star that you are.'

I felt my cheeks heat up with his compliment and I couldn't help smiling.

'That's better,' he said, chucking me under the chin. 'Now, what d'you say to another Tuesday and Thursday session?'

I didn't want to. I had hoped we could just keep it to one night a week. It was more comfortable this time, but it wasn't exactly my favourite pastime.

'Lottie,' Cal said, his voice serious. 'If you want to get a head in this business you need to work hard. Okay? I'm just trying to help you.'

I still hesitated, I wasn't sure about any of it.

'Course,' he said. 'I've much better things to do. And I have much more appreciative girls to help, if you know what I mean?'

I did so I nodded.

'Good girl, so Tuesday and Thursdays then? I'll send a cab.' He looked at his watch. 'Christ doesn't time fly when you're having fun? Come on love, get dressed, cab'll be here in a minute.'

I sighed with relief, another session done and I was still in one piece. I hadn't been struck down and when I looked at my reflection in the back window of the cab my face hadn't changed.

Perhaps I could do this after all, perhaps I would be a model, make lots of money, get out of this place, maybe even become a movie star. More important, buy my book store, a home, get married to Baz and have a family. A normal one. I started to feel excited and shiny about the future.

Tuesday played out much the same as previously so I arrived for my fourth session feeling much more confident about the whole thing. That was my first mistake. My second was to turn my back on Cal.

I was naked when he asked me to turn round and bend over the sofa. I did as he requested and heard him moving. I thought he was getting into position to take a photo, so I was surprised when I realised he was right behind me.

He reached out and stroked my naked buttock. I sucked in my breath and my whole body went rigid. What was he doing?

'Relax,' Cal said, from behind me. 'This is all part of the next step.'

'Next step?' It came out as a whisper, was he going to have sex with me? Was that what he expected?

He stroked my buttock again, as if I were a pet dog. 'Just relax.'

'But why do you need to touch me?' I asked.

'Photographers will move you into position from time to time. You won't have any clothes on. At some point in your career they're bound to touch you. You don't want to react like a little girl now do you?'

He was right, I didn't, and it made sense when he put it like that, but I didn't like it. Not one bit. I wondered how often it might happen. Still, at least he didn't want to have sex with me. That was a relief.

'Okay?' Cal asked.

I nodded mutely. I didn't want to agree, but I couldn't argue with him. He knew the industry inside out, he knew what I needed to be good at in order to make it, and he was right about one thing, I didn't want to act like a child when the time came.

'Good girl,' he patted my bottom. It was still stuck up in the air. I hadn't moved an inch. 'Okay stand up and turn around.'

I turned, he cupped my breasts in his hands and I flinched.

'Take a deep breath and relax,' he said.

I did as he said and he rubbed his thumb over my nipples. 'There, now that isn't so bad is it?'

I could feel his hot breath on my face, rancid with stale tobacco. My stomach turned over and for one awful moment I thought I was going to be sick or worse, burst out crying.

I think he saw because he stopped and pulled away from me. 'Get dressed,' he snapped, clearly angry.

I started to dress, pulling on my pants. He didn't speak to me again until I was almost fully dressed.

'I'm not wasting my time here am I, Lottie?' His voice was deep and serious.

'No,' I said. It came out as a wail and made me even more miserable.

'Because I've better things to do, you know?'

I did know. He was an important and busy man, and I knew I was lucky that he was spending time training me. It was just that, well, I didn't want to be ungrateful, but...I hadn't asked him to...had I?

139

'When you agreed to being a model, this is what you agreed to.' he said, as if reading my mind.

'I know.'

'It was *your* choice.'

I nodded. He was right of course, even if all of a sudden it didn't feel like that.

'Lottie?'

'Yes?'

'Am I wasting my time, love?' His voice was softer now.

I took a deep breath, pulled on my coat and turned to face him. This was my chance to get out of this before it went any further, but I had made a choice. I had made an agreement and I wasn't going to back out of it now like some...some...little kid. Just because it was a bit uncomfortable.

'No, I won't let you down,' I said.

His whole persona changed as he beamed at me. 'That's great. I'll see you Tuesday. Oh, and in case I forget, I can't make Saturday this week. Off to the smoke to finalise some deals, get some things lined up for when you're ready. You can hold the fort on your own can't you?'

'Sure.'

'Good lass,' he smiled again, his thick rubber lips pulled back over his teeth. I remembered the smell of his breath and my stomach turned over at the memory. A car beeped outside.

'Okay,' he said, coming close and patting my bottom. 'Cab's here, off you go. See you Tuesday, and bring Saturday's takings with you. I won't be able to collect them Sunday.'

'Okay,' I said.

'Oh, and here,' Cal said.

I turned round to see him holding out a fiver.

'What's that?' I asked.

'Candy floss, what's it look like?' he smiled at his joke.

'I mean, what's it for?' I assumed he wanted me to give it to Mum.

'You.'

'Me!' I stood up straight, not believing my eyes or ears. It had to be a dream.

'Go on then lass, take it.'

I inched forward slowly.

'Come on,' he said, waving it at me. 'I haven't got all night. Cab's waiting.'

I gingerly reached out and took hold of it, expecting something somewhere to happen. This couldn't be mine. All mine. A whole fiver!

'Wow, thanks,' I said, as he let go of it. I held it stretched out between my two hands, gawping at it.

'What's it for?'

'I dunno, call it an early Christmas bonus,' he said. 'You've done well, and there's plenty more where that came from if you keep it up.'

Warmth suffused my insides as I closed the front door behind me, but despite the money I was relieved I wouldn't see him on Saturday. In the cab ride home it occurred to me that the takings would be in the house for several days, within Mum's grasp. Then I reminded myself that she wouldn't dare touch them. Not Cal's money. It would be more than her life was worth.

Mine on the other hand was an entirely different matter, so I shoved the fiver deep into my knickers.

# Friday

### Andrea

Andrea feels her life has been reduced to waiting. Waiting for Lot to visit, waiting for the nurse to make her comfortable, waiting to die.

There's no love lost between them, so if there's any grieving on Lot's side, if she's giving her even a second thought as she lies here dying, it'll be because her daughter didn't get answers.

She could still take it all to the grave, and maybe that would be best, but she won't. She needs this one last act of selfish purging before she goes. If it's good enough for the Catholics.

She feels hazy today. A little more rubbed out. She thinks she might be dying a little bit more, so perhaps not much longer to wait.

Her breathing has deteriorated and comes in short breaths. They warned her that this would happen, but it isn't as she imagined. She thought she would be out of breath in the way you are when you've been running, but this isn't like that at all.

This shortness of breath is like a slow suffocation, like someone has their hand over her mouth, and she fights her imaginary assailant but of course, it doesn't do any good. If truth be told it makes it even harder to breathe.

'Just relax,' the nurses tell her.

Stupid bitches! She'd like to see them relax when they can't breathe properly.

And where the fuck is that dumpy daughter of hers? She needs her here, she needs to tell her the truth, she has to. Fucking Cal!

*I tried Lottie, I tried, I want to tell her,* but then I remember the truth...and I know that I didn't really.

### Andrea 1980

Cal had been in our lives for nearly two months but I still had nothing on him. I knew he was taking photos, but it was just my word, and possibly Lottie's, against his and it wasn't enough. Besides, I wasn't sure how much of a criminal offence taking photos of a fifteen year old girl was.

I was afraid I might have underestimated Cal's ability to resist my charms, and my world had tilted on its axis, like some natural law had been broken. He hadn't fallen for me, despite my best efforts, and I was stumped. What did ugly women do? I'd seen them in shops, towing their man behind them.  How did they do it?  What secret technique did they have?  I'd never had to do much more than smile or lean forward and lower my voice, but Cal...I floundered in a way I hadn't since I lost Andrew.

'You behaving yourself?' I asked him, the next time he was round.

'Yep.'  He was sat on my sofa with his head resting on the back.  I wondered if it would leave a greasy patch.

'Just photos?'

He raised his head to look at me and my heart stopped.  Had I gone too far?

'Just photos,' he said.

More confident I decided to dig deeper.

'No visits to "special friends",' I asked, using a smile and quotations marks with my fingers to avoid angering him.

To my relief he smiled.

'No, none.  All is as we agreed.'

'Could I...see one of these photos?'

He sat up and leaned forward, peering at me.  'Now, why would you want to do that, love?'

I shrugged.  'Curiosity, or maybe I just want to make sure.'

'Make sure what?'

'That they're...appropriate.'

Cal sat back and laughed.  I waited, my heart thumping.

'Of course they're not appropriate.'

I felt foolish and angry, but Lottie came in with the tea and I couldn't say anything else, wasn't sure what I would have said even if I had the opportunity.  He was right of course, why would he want to take appropriate photos of my daughter?  That's when it hit me, just exactly what I had done.  So I really don't know why I did what I did next.  I guess I just wasn't thinking.

## Lottie

Hilary is loitering at her office door when Lottie returns from seeing her eleven o'clock out.

'Okay?' Lottie asks.

Hilary looks worried so she closes the door.

'What is it?'

'It's the Craig family.'

'What now?'

'The mother's been arrested.'

'What? Tracey?'

Hilary nods.

'When? Why?'

'Shop lifting, this morning.'

'Why?' She is momentarily stupid.

Hilary raises an eyebrow and Lottie shakes her head, a gesture designed to ask Hilary to ignore her last remark.

'What about the kids?'

'The uncle has taken care of them.'

'The uncle…'

They are both silent for a while.

'What about Jenny?'

Hilary doesn't say anything.

'I know, I know I'm sorry, I don't know what's the matter with me today,' Lottie rubs her forehead. She's asking questions as if she's taken a stupid pill.

'Lottie are you okay?'

'Sure.'

'You just seem...'

'I've just got a lot on my plate,' she snaps, she doesn't want to hear what Hilary thinks of her right now, especially after the scene at the Craigs', after Sandra's warning yesterday. The carefully crafted walls erected between her and her staff are crumbling.

Hilary says nothing, waits for Lottie to continue. She doesn't, she just stands there rubbing her forehead.

'So, the Craig family. What's next?' Lottie asks, eventually.

'Nothing. I've liaised with the Craigs' social worker, and told her what I know. She hasn't got any further info for the time being so,' she shrugs. 'We'll keep a close eye on things but...'

'And Jenny?'

'There's nothing else we can do.' She shrugs again. 'Sorry.'

*There's nothing we can do.*

Lottie feels helpless, frustrated and bloody angry: about Dan, who is allegedly playing golf but is probably bouncing his balls off the arse of some young bitch! About her mother, who hasn't got the decency to not bother anyone and just die! But mostly about that girl's family and what they're doing to her. The fear brings demons storming back so hard Lottie thinks she might burst if she doesn't break something. Where is she? What *are* they doing to her? How can she stop them?

As Hilary makes to leave the office Lottie goes behind her desk and slams her hand down hard on it making everything jump.

'Fuck!' she says.

*When am I going to take charge of my life? When am I going to take matters into my own hands? When am I going to decide what happens to me?*

Hilary looks back in alarm, but Lottie doesn't care.

'Alright?' Hilary asks.

'Just go back to your office Hilary,' she tells her in a tight voice, her hands on her hips, her breath shorting through her nostrils.

*There's no such things as monsters in the night. They're not hiding in dark corners, wardrobes or under the bed. No. They're walking around looking like you and me. Just ordinary people living seemingly ordinary lives.*

Of course, she didn't know that at the time. Then she thought it was her fault, she thought she'd done something wrong, worse, she thought she had a choice and had made the wrong one.

Tears threaten but she refuses to crouch behind her office door to weep, instead she holds onto the desk and remembers Baz.


### Lottie 1980

I made us egg and chips for Friday tea, except there was only one egg left so I gave it to mum.    We sat in front of the telly watching Name That Tune.    I was rubbish at it, even if I guessed what the tune was, I couldn't remember what it was called. Mum got some right though.

'Here,' she said, handing me her empty plate when the programme had finished.

I took them into the kitchen and washed them up.    When I got back Mum was putting on her lipstick in the mirror above the fire.    I watched, mesmerised, knowing that no matter how much lippy I wore I could never look as beautiful as her.    She was like some screen goddess, classy, bold, fun, sassy. I dreamt of being Cinderella, but in our house I was an ugly sister, only kinder.

She pressed her lips tightly together to spread the colour then, satisfied, snapped the top onto the cylinder with a click.

'Off out?' I asked, needlessly. Mum didn't put lippy on for my benefit.

She was rummaging in her bag. 'Yeah,' she said, without looking up.

Great! I'd made arrangements to meet Baz. I might even be able to sneak him in later. There was bound to be something good on TV. Well, BBC1 or Tyne Tees, there was never anything good on BBC2, only Open University and boring history programmes.

I waited a good ten minutes after Mum had gone, just to make sure she hadn't forgotten anything, before leaving by the back door, the fiver burning a hole in my pocket. I had a suspicion that our neighbour Pat, was keeping an eye on me and I didn't want Mum to know I'd left.

Baz was waiting for me by the park gate as arranged.

'Alright?' he said, grinning, and kissed me.

He tasted of peppermint and tobacco.

'You hungry? Fancy fish and chips?' I said, grinning at his surprise.

'Whoa, big spender. Where's the money for fish and chips?'

'Don't ask,' I said, not wanting to lie anymore to him. 'Got enough for scraps too.'

'Scraps are free.'

I laughed. 'So, hungry?'

'I can always eat fish and chips.'

We walked along the park railings heading towards the chippie. It was only a short detour on the way to the reccie and I thought about the others.

'Shall we get the gang some?' I said, then laughed.

'What's funny?'

'I feel a little fraudulent saying 'the gang' like that.' Fraudulent was my new word and I was still playing around with it.

'What's that mean?'

I thought for a moment about how to explain it. 'It's a bit like a lie,' I said. 'Like pretending or...play acting.'

'What, like it's not really true?'

'Yeah, sort of, only...I don't think it's as bad as a lie.'

'Like a white lie?'

'I suppose.'

We walked along in silence for a while until we stopped to cross the road. Baz turned to me.

'What d'you think is the difference between a white lie and any other kind of lie?'

'I don't know, I've never really thought about it.'

We waited for a car to pass then crossed.

'I mean, do you think there's a kinda grades of lying?'

I thought for a moment. 'I suppose so. There's grades of crime after all. I mean, you get different punishments depending on what you've done, don't you? You know, the worse the crime the worse the punishment.'

'So the bigger the lie, the more the punishment you'll get?'

'Something like that.'

'So who decides? I mean, what make one lie worse then another?'

'Maybe it's about why you lie, you know, if it's to avoid hurting someone's feelings that might not be as bad as if you lie to them to get something out of them.'

I was uncomfortable with the conversation, especially after all the lies I'd been telling recently. Did he suspect something? It felt as if there was no one I hadn't lied to recently.

'Or to get someone to do something they don't want to do?' he said.

'I don't know, Baz,' I said, my tone frosty now.

'Okay, keep your hair on, I was only asking.'

We turned into the street where the chippie was, and with relief I could see the lighted sign like a beacon, the smiling blue fish stood up in his top hat, leaning on his cane.

'So shall I get some then?'

'Fish and chips?'

'Yeah.'

'Can you afford it? I thought you were joking earlier.'

I took the fiver from my pocket and rubbed it between my finger and thumb.

'Jesus!' he whispered. 'Where'd you get that from?'

There wasn't anything for it. 'Mum gave it to me,' I lied.

'Seriously?'

I nodded, hoping that would be the end of it.

'Why?'

I shrugged. 'I've been helping a lot round the house and stuff.'

'That's a lot of help.'

We'd reached the door and the smell of vinegar assaulted my nostrils, causing my mouth to water and my stomach to contract. I was hungry, despite the chips earlier.

'Well?' I asked, wanting to eat now.

'Is your Mam home?'

'No.'

'In that case no, let's get them wrapped and eat them at your place.'

My heart sank. It would take at least fifteen minutes to get home and I was starving.

'Don't worry,' he said, reading my expression. 'We can get two fish and chips wrapped and get a bag of chips open to eat on the way home.'

My heart swelled as I looked at his earnest face. How had I ever been intimidated by him?

Five minutes later we were heading home with a carrier heavy with our supper and sharing a scalding bag of chips in vinegar soaked newspaper. Baz told me stories that made me laugh so hard I could barely swallow. As I licked the salt and fat off my fingers I knew it was one of those perfect moments. One of those perfect moments that I would remember forever.

Later that night, as I watched Baz climb over the back fence, the moon lighting the overgrown garden, a chill in the air sent goose pimples up my arm and something Baz had said earlier sent a similar chill down my spine.

*The bigger the lie...the more punishment you'll get.*

# Saturday

### Lottie

Lottie wakes the next morning in an empty bed, exhausted but with a new resolve. If she is going to survive she needs the old Lottie, the young Lottie. Not the secondary school beaten and down trodden Lot, but the one before. The scraper, the fiend, the one always in trouble. If she is going to survive, she needs her. Whatever she decides to do about Dan, and she doesn't know what that is yet. She needs her.

So by the time Dan returns home from the supermarket, appeasing his conscience for yesterday no doubt, she has pulled on her shell, is ready for battle and has emptied all their joint bank accounts into her own. After all, when it comes down to it, it's all about the money.

*The bigger the lie...the more punishment you'll get.*


### Lottie 1980

We'd had a great day in the Shambles. All the stall holders agreed and that night I had over two hundred pounds to take to Cal on Tuesday. I was so proud I thought I would burst, so I told my Mum.

The minute the boast left my mouth I knew I'd made a mistake. I thought that Cal's money would be safe, that Mum would be proud of me, that for a brief moment, we lived a normal life and she was a normal mother. I was wrong.

I saw it in her eyes. A light, a flick of greed, it was the same look when she was going to do anything reckless, something she would later regret: excess with drink, sex with a stranger she'd brought home, shoot her mouth off...steal Johnny Caldwick's money?

But still, as I climbed into bed that night, a part of me didn't believe she'd actually go through with it. When I woke the next morning I checked the money and it was still under my pillow where I'd fitfully slept on it. I let out a sigh of relief.

Sunday passed uneventfully and I checked the money again when I woke on Monday morning. It was still there. I toyed with the idea of staying off school to guard it, but if I managed just one more week of full attendance I'd get my prefect badge and I was so close, *so* close.

I was fairly confident she wouldn't take it. It *was* Cal's money after all, and nobody messed with Cal. Not even her. Still, to be on the safe side I hid it in one of my wellies in the bottom of the wardrobe. It was hardly a locked safe, but at least it was out of sight. Even I knew under my pillow was too much a temptation for Mum, regardless of whose money it was.

That night the house was empty when I got home. I rushed up to my bedroom, tore open the wardrobe door and plunged a hand into the wellie. It was still there and my heart skipped a beat for joy. I could barely believe Mum had left it alone. Had she looked and been unable to find it, or was she just too afraid of Cal to take it? I didn't care, it was still there and I was seeing Cal the following night so I could hand it over and tell him that I couldn't keep this sort of money at home in future. It was too dangerous, too tempting for her.

When I got home the following night the house was empty again. It was odd for Mum to be missing two nights in a row but I was in a rush and gave it no more thought. I ran upstairs and changed out of my school inform. Cal's taxi would be here in less than an hour and I had an essay on Othello and Iago's relationship for English that I wanted to make a start on.

I was enjoying Othello. It was full of twists and turns, deceit and manipulation. I found it amazing how easily Iago could manipulate Othello, simply because he lacked experience in love or was it his self confidence, or his ego? I decided that was precisely why Mr Selleck had set the essay, to explore that very question and find out for ourselves.

Before I got my books out I went to the wardrobe door and pushed my hand into the welly. It was empty. I checked the other one. Nothing. I pulled them out of the wardrobe, turned them upside down and shook them hard. It definitely wasn't there, but I checked it again, just to be sure. My stomach set hard as concrete.

Then I thought that perhaps I had dreamt I'd put it there and it was still under the pillow. I ran to the bed and whipped off the pillow. Nothing. Had I put it somewhere else last night just to be on the safe side and forgotten?

I felt sick. I fell on my hands and knees and, head spinning, scanned under the bed. I was so frantic I was unlikely to see the money even if it was right there in front of me, so I took a deep breath and went back to the beginning of the search, starting with my wellies. I checked the back of the wardrobe...just in case. Under the pillow, the bed, the wardrobe. I looked under the clothes and debris strewn about my floor. Nothing.

I looked everywhere I had already looked and then I looked again. And then again. Nothing. It was gone. The bag of takings had been taken.

I sat back on my heels, in the middle of the chaos and wept out my frustration, and when I heard the honk of the taxi I filled with fear for what this meant for me.

When I arrived at Cal's I was physically shaking. He knew something was wrong as soon as he saw me. I hated my mother more in that moment than I had ever hated her before, to steal from Cal was bad enough, but to leave me to face him. I couldn't believe how low she had stooped this time.

'What?' he said.

'The takings.' It was all I could manage.

'How much?'

'About two hundred.'

I thought I saw a smile flick across his face but it was gone in an instant so I must have been mistaken. This was no laughing matter so why would he smile?

'Who?'

'I...I don't know,' I lied. God, when did I start lying so much!

'Your mother?'

I shrugged but felt relieved he didn't take me for the thief, then I realised what a Judas I'd be if I ratted her out. I felt torn. Angry at her leaving me in this position, but fearful for her safety. Cal wasn't someone you messed with, what was she thinking?

'I don't know for sure,' I said quickly. 'I haven't seen her to ask her. She was out when I got back from school.'

'We both know your mother.'

I didn't say anything to that, and for a brief moment I wondered if he'd planned it. Anyone who knew my mother, knew what she was like, could guess what was likely to happen, but I dismissed the idea. It didn't make sense, why would he?

'Where did you stash it?'

'In my welly in my wardrobe.'

To my surprise he started to laugh. It unnerved me. 'What?' I asked, wanting him to stop.

He turned and looked at me. 'Don't worry lass, I'll sort this out with your mam.'

'It might not be her,' I said, quickly.

'Well, it was someone and I'm gonna start with her.'

'You...you won't hurt her will you?' Despite all her faults, she was all I had.

'Nah we'll come to some...' he paused and licked his lips before continuing. 'Arrangement.'

His reassurance didn't reassure. I wanted to ask what he meant, but I was too scared to question him further, and relieved that Mum would have to sort it out. After all, it *was* her doing.

The rest of the evening went much the same as Thursday. I spent the hour or so naked, and as he moved me into different poses, he touched me more intimately and frequently than before. He didn't take any photos this time, said I was too uptight. I didn't feel as shocked as the previous week, but he was probably right, I wasn't relaxed either. It was getting easier, but I knew he wouldn't be able to put me in a proper studio yet.

When I got home the house was in darkness. With two hundred pounds in her pocket, Mum was unlikely to return for several days.

I wondered again what Cal had meant when he said he'd come to some arrangement. Maybe he'd get Mum to work it off for him in one of his businesses, though she wasn't very good at holding a regular job down.

As I entered the cold dark house the memory of his face made me shiver. What did Johnny Caldwick have in store for her?

Mum still hadn't returned by Thursday morning. Fortunately I had half a loaf of bread leftover from the weekend to see me through, and there was my school dinners. So whilst I was hungry, I didn't starve.

The loaf was less appetising by Thursday evening, but I cut the green bits off the final two slices and toasted them. I had just forced the last mouthful down when I heard the toot of the cab to take me to Cal's.

When I had children they'd always have enough to eat I thought, as the cab made its familiar way across town. Even if I had to do without. Isn't that what parents were supposed to do?

The cab didn't pull away as usual when I got out and I walked up the dark path to the front door with my stomach clenched.

As I arrived the door opened abruptly making me cry out. Cal's huge frame filled the doorway. I couldn't see his expression because the light was behind him, but his body language told me he was in no mood for jokes.

'Come on,' he barked. He closed the door and strode down the path. 'We'll be late.'

I followed him back to the taxi, not daring to ask him what we'd be late for. He'd tell me eventually, or I'd find out when we got there. At least I wouldn't have to pose around his living room freezing my arse off for an hour while he gawped and pawed at me.

After a silent fifteen minute taxi ride we pulled up outside a large semi-detached house. It was on the new estate and I knew some of the posher kids at my school lived round here.

'Come on,' Cal growled, as he hoisted himself out of the car. I never saw him pay for these taxis we took I realised, as I climbed out after him.

The taxi pulled away, so I knew we were staying, at least for a while.

I took a deep breath and found the courage to speak. 'What are we doing here?' I asked, as we waited for the door to be answered.

'We're visiting a pal of mine,' he said.

'Who?'

'Chap called Paul. Nice fella. Loaded. Someone worth knowing.'

Just then the door was opened by a thin balding man. He had a weasel face and long deep lines down either side of his mouth. He looked over our shoulders and down the street, his neck giraffe like long.

'It's fine, Paul,' Cal said, irritation peppering his words.

Paul opened the door wide to allow us in.

'This her?' he said, looking me up and down in the hall.

'Paul meet Lottie, Lottie, Paul,' Cal said, over his shoulder as he headed down the hall. 'You got anything to drink?'

Paul didn't take his eyes off me as he spoke. 'Kitchen cupboard. Right hand side. Whiskey. Do you want a drink, darling?' he asked me.

'I don't like whiskey.'

'I've got Pernod. You like Pernod?'

'I don't know. I've never had it.'

'Come on, come and have a glass. See what you think.' He put his hand in the small of my back and gently guided me down the hall to the kitchen at the end of the corridor.

It was breathtakingly beautiful. Fitted cupboards, chrome kitchen appliances. I was dazzled and breathless for a moment. How the other half live, I thought.

Cal was sat at the table with a bottle of whiskey and three glasses.

'Lottie doesn't like whiskey Cal, so I'm going to give her a drop of Pernod and lemon instead.'

Cal nodded and drained his glass.

In any other circumstances I would have thought the two men looked amusing. Cal was the size of a small shed, whilst Paul was small, weaselly and insipid. They were chalk and cheese, like a comedy duo. Only, I wasn't finding any of this funny. I was confused as to why we were here, and worried about what might be expected of me.


**Andrea 1980**

With my purse stuffed to the gills with more money than I had ever dreamed of, I hooked up with a bloke in a pub off my usual circuit, Jack was his name, or was it James, possibly John. Anyway, we'd had a blast and I lost track of time, but within two days the money had run out and I had sobered up enough to realise what I'd done

I don't know why I did it. Maybe it was the realisation of what we'd got ourselves into and I just wanted to get hammered.

The point was, I'd stolen money from Johnny Caldwick. No one did that and survived, not unless they had the ability to pay him back with interest, I didn't. When would I ever learn? In life I seemed to lurch from one disaster to another.

I spent all of Thursday evening nursing a port and lemon, trying to get my alcohol fuddled brain to function sufficiently to get me out of another mess. At kick out time I still had enough alcohol in my body to give me the courage I needed to do, what I decided I needed to do.

I stepped into the cold air and walked to the taxi rank, I was heading to Cal's house. I was going to put this right, for once in my life I was going to do the right thing.



When the taxi pulled up at the house it was dark apart from a light on in the kitchen. I asked the taxi driver to wait for me and tiptoed up the path. I later found out it was the same night Lot was introduced to Pernod Paul, so I was already too late to change anything. Would I have done anything differently? Who knows.

I tapped on the kitchen window, praying it was Cal who was still up and not Rosie. That would just top off everything, having *her* answer the door.

The door opened and I was relieved to see Cal's bulk.

'What the fuck are you doing here?' he hissed.

Not the start I was hoping for and relief turned to fear. I wasn't sure I could I do this but I had to. Had to, I reminded myself.

'Can I come in?'

He paused, then opened the door and nodded towards the kitchen. I stepped in, enjoying the warmth of the house round my bare legs. I had tights on when I left the house two days ago but I wasn't sure where they were now.

'I needed to explain about the money,' I said, as soon as we got into the kitchen.

'There's nothing to explain.'

I paused, and I meant to confess. I did, but when I opened my mouth something entirely different came out.

'But there is, you think it was me but it wasn't.'

'Oh right, so who took it then, Rumpel-fucking-stiltskin?'

I took a deep breath, I didn't want to let my fear get the better of me. I had another chance here. Another chance to make this right.

'Baz,' I said.

'Baz? Who the fuck is Baz?'

'A boy Lottie's been seeing, it's nothing serious,' I added quickly, when I saw his face turn purple.

'So how long's she been seeing him?'

I shrugged. 'A few weeks, I'm not entirely sure, but that's not the point. I need you to know he's the one.'

He didn't say anything for a while.

'Everyone knows he took it,' I said.

Cal nodded. 'And you just happen to go on a two day long bender at the same time did you?'

'My cousin won on the bingo, we've been celebrating.'

'I didn't just come up on the fucking banana boat, Andrea. I know for a fact you fucking took it and you're going to fucking pay me back.'

A voice called down the stairs. 'Cal?'

He glared at me then walked over to the kitchen door and opened it. 'It's alright love, go back to bed.'

'Who is it?' I recognised Rosie's voice and suddenly everything looked hopeless. My brilliant plan was in ashes. Not, I realised, that it had been that brilliant, or difficult, all I had to do was tell the truth. What was the matter with me? Why wouldn't the words come out. It wasn't as if I was fooling him anyway.

'Go back to bed.' It was a command rather than a request, and I caught a brief look into Rosie's life. I was glad.

Cal closed the kitchen door and returned to stand in front of me, arms folded, looking impenetrable, and it occurred to me that he could finish me here and now and no one would know.

I swallowed. 'But you know we have nothing.' My voice was smaller than I would have liked.

'Oh, I wouldn't say that.'

Silence hung. We both waited. Finally I capitulated.

'What do you want?'

'Leave it with me, I'll talk to Lottie.'

'Leave her out of this, Cal, please?'

'I didn't bring her into this in the first place Andrea, you did.'

'Well, then…' I opened my arms and adopted a pose. 'I'll pay it off.'

He looked me up and down. 'No offence pet, but you couldn't.'

I felt my insides shrivel in shame. I was beautiful, desirable, I always had been. Men loved me, he was mad, clearly didn't know what a man wanted. A man wanted a woman, not a child.

155

I dropped my arms. 'It's only two hundred fucking quid for fuck's sake.'

Cal laughed, it was a mean, nasty nasal laugh, produced to scorn and scorch. 'Like I said, you couldn't.'

'It was the boy,' I insisted. 'Everyone knows it.'

'So how did he get at it? How did he know it was there?'

I cursed myself for drinking so much, sure that if I hadn't I could have handled this whole thing much better, could have thought on my feet.

'Well...I guess Lottie must have told him.'

He reached out and I flinched. He put his hand around my shoulder and pulled me into his side gently, fondling one of my breasts. 'In that case, you and Lottie have nothing to worry about. I'll sort it out with him,' he said, quietly.

I still felt uneasy. 'He must have made Lottie give it to him, forced her. She wouldn't steal from you.'

'I know.'

'Neither would I,' I added.

He released me. 'Go home. We'll sort something out.'

'Sure?' I wanted to ask if he would leave Lottie out of it, but I couldn't find the courage, probably because I knew he wouldn't. Regardless of anything I said.

'I'm sure.'

As the cab was pulling away I looked up to see a small white face at an upstairs window with a raised hand. Bloody Rosie. It was all *her* fault.


### Lottie 1980

When I woke up, I thought I could smell bacon and for a brief moment I forgot about Cal and Paul and Mum and the money and everything except my maths homework. But I had woken so many times with the apparition, especially when I was this hungry, that I dismissed it. Then it all came tumbling in on me and I thought I would drown in the horror of it all. What had Mum done this time?

The previous night hadn't been too bad, I reasoned, and there was no reason to think it would get any worse than that. I bit of looking and touching I could cope with. It wasn't much more than Cal had done. I could cope, if I really tried. Anyway, the truth was, I didn't really have a choice. Mum had got us into this mess and I had to get us out.

A noise from the kitchen interrupted my thoughts. Mum was back, sooner than I thought. I wasn't sure if that was good or bad news. Had she spent all the money already or had she run into Cal?

I pulled on my jeans, they were cold against my skin but they'd soon warm up. I could put the oven on in the kitchen to get warmed through while I made breakfast. Then I remembered I'd eaten the last of the bread the night before.

I ran through my school schedule as I finished dressing, it was Friday, double maths and my homework wasn't done. I had tried when I got back the night before, but the Pernod had made my head fuzzy and I couldn't concentrate. Great, another tongue lashing off Mr Wright, I thought as I braced myself at the kitchen door. I hoped Mum was in a good mood but I was prepared for the worst.

As I opened the door the smell of toast and bacon was overpowering, I could hear sizzling in the pan and Mum was standing at the cooker, oven door open to warm the room, spatula in hand. She turned her head as I entered and smiled at me. Smiled at me, cooking bacon, in the morning...my heart soared with joy.

'The kettle's just boiled. Make yourself a coffee,' she said.

'You want some tea?'

'I've got one. Breakfast will be ready soon. Toasted bacon butties,' she announced.

I was in such shock I couldn't speak. I must be dreaming, that's what this was, a dream. I made my coffee then hung around not sure what to do next. I wasn't used to Mum being busy and me being idle. It felt...wrong.

'Sit down Lot,' she said.

I took my coffee over to the table and sat down. Shortly after she joined me with the bacon butties.

'Brown sauce?' she said, holding up the bottle as if I might not understand. I almost didn't.

I nodded and took the bottle off her. She only ever behaved this way after she'd beaten me, and she hadn't so...what was this all about?

'I wanted to apologise,' she said, out of the blue, as if she had read my thoughts.

'What for?' I said, my mouth full of the salty bacon, sweet margarine and tangy sauce.

'What happened.'

I thought she meant last night. I was about to tell that it wasn't too bad, all part of the training really. That's how Cal explained it on the way back. I had to get used to being naked in front of people other than just him. The touching...well, that was part of it too.

Cal had been kind really, letting me do that with his friend. I'd frozen up at first. Imagine if I'd done that on set? I'd have been mortified, and my career would have ended before it began.

No, Cal knew what he was doing. Paul was a bit rougher, a bit more...grabby than Cal. I heard Cal say 'Steady on mate,' a couple of times. That's when I knew I could relax. This was training and Cal had my back.

I felt ashamed now of what I thought Cal was doing. He was a decent bloke. The money was between him and Mum. He knew I wouldn't steal from him. I felt a twinge of fear for her. Yes, he was a decent bloke, but you didn't cross him. I wondered what he would do.

'I mean, it wasn't really my fault.'

'It's okay, Mum.'

'No, I guess there are worse things a person can do but still, I've cleared it with Cal, and I'm sorry for what I said.'

'Cleared what with Cal? What did you say?'

'About the money numbskull,' she laughed, it tinkled round the room. She had a beautiful laugh, it wrapped round you like a feather boa. 'I went to see him last night.'

'When?'

'Late.'

'Were you drunk?'

'A little.'

'What happened?'

'I just explained the mistake.'

'What mistake?'

'That you thought I'd took it but I didn't.'

'But you did.'

'*I* know that, and *you* know that, but Cal doesn't have to.'

Fear clutched my stomach and the butty set like concrete in my mouth. 'So what did you tell him?' I swallowed the hard lump. It took two goes.

'Don't look so worried, it's all sorted out.'

Fear foamed in my mouth, making it difficult to form the words. 'What did you tell him?' I asked again, my voice a whisper as I forced them out. She had told him I'd taken it. I just knew it.

Mum looked at me directly. She had that warning look on her face, the one that said I'd be sorry if I continued.

'Don't make a scene Lot,' she said, her tone weighted with the the same warning.

I looked down at my half eaten butty. 'I'm not, I just wondered,' I mumbled.

'I told him you'd taken it. Sort of.'

My eyes flew up to her. 'You what?' I had hoped I was wrong, that she hadn't done it.

'Oh calm down. He's much more likely to forgive you than me so where's the harm?'

'He has a gun,' I said.

Mum laughed. 'He's not going to shoot you for two hundred pounds. Besides I told him you'd stolen it for someone else, that someone else *made* you do it.'

'Who?'

'Baz.'

'Baz! You brought Baz into this? Why?'

She shrugged. 'He looks like he can handle himself.'

'Oh, Mum.' My eyes prickled and I blinked hard. This was not a time for tears.

'Calm down, it'll be fine.' There was that tone of displeasure in her voice again, but I foolishly ignored it.

'What exactly did you say to him?'

'I told him Baz took it and he made you tell him where it was. I'm not sure Cal believed me but that's the story and we're sticking to it. Your back's covered so don't start getting all hysterical on me. Just leave it the fuck alone now.'

I knew I shouldn't, the warning signs were there, as soon as she swears I know I should back off, especially when she's been on a bender, but I couldn't help it. Baz. Why Baz? It was bad enough to blame me, but to implicate Baz.

'What the hell were you thinking?' I said, before I could stop myself.

I didn't see her move, but felt the blinding flash of pain across the left side of my face. The blow so hard it lifted me off the chair and I fell to the floor. She stood over me.

'Don't you ever speak to me like that again you little bitch, you hear me?' Her words were distorted by her anger. A globule of salvia fell from her mouth onto the floor. It glistened beside me. 'Do you hear me?'

I couldn't speak. I tried, but nothing came out. She kicked me hard in the side. All the air left my body and it assumed the foetal position of its own accord. Natural instincts taking over.

'Do you hear me?' she screamed over me, circling my curled up figure.

I knew I looked pathetic and I knew that made her worse, but there was nothing I could do. My body was balled up and would not do anything I told it to. A foot connected with my kidneys and I knew that would hurt for days. Kidneys always did. Again I tried to speak, but only a snivelling wail escaped. I was ashamed of my weakness, of my cowardice.

'Look at you, you're pathetic! I do my best, make you a wonderful breakfast and you go an spoil it all, all I get is lip.'

Another kick, this time in the back of my head. I moved out of my physical body, so her blows would stop hurting, and observed from a safe distance in the corner of the kitchen. I judged that a couple more minutes, three maybe four more kicks, possibly a couple of punches, and her anger would be spent. She'd leave me alone then.

'You're a cheap slut. Don't think I don't know what you and Baz get up to. This is for your own good, d'you want to end up like me?' A kick to the coccyx. Now *that* would smart in the morning.

'You little fucking whore,' one punch and another kick.

There was at least another kick and punch to go before she'd finish and I was bound to be late for school, not ideal with double maths and unfinished homework. Still, what could Mr Wright do...shout at me? Give me a detention? I decided to concentrate on one problem at a time and closed my eyes, tightened into a ball, and waited for the storm to pass.

It took longer than I thought.


I didn't make it to school that day, or for sometime after, which would wreck my chances of a prefect badge. I must have passed out because when I woke up Mum wasn't there. I sat up and immediately threw up on myself. I felt dizzy and knew enough to know that I probably needed to see a doctor.

I moved slowly. First I cleaned myself up as best I could in the kitchen, then I crawled upstairs to finish off, washing in icy water in the bathroom. I undressed and put on clean clothes, leaving the soiled ones in the corner of my bedroom. I'd deal with them later.

Any sudden movement made me feel sick and I didn't want to vomit over myself again. Once I was dressed I gingerly made my way round to the GP surgery on the estate. After a thirty minute wait I was beginning to think I might be okay, that perhaps I was being the drama queen my mother thought me, but when they called my name and I stood up I realised that no, something *was* wrong.

'I got jumped on my way to school,' I explained, to the greasy haired doctor with dandruff when I finally managed to find my way to his office. 'I went home, but I've been sick and I feel a bit dizzy. I hope I'm not wasting your time, but I thought I should get it checked out.'

He asked me where my parents were and I explained that it was only me and my mother and she was already at work when I got back home. I liked the normal way it sounded.

He looked cross and my stomach clenched. I *was* wasting his time, the waiting room was chocker with people who were proper ill. Still, despite his anger, he examined me. When he finished he rang the reception desk and asked them to call an ambulance.

I was beginning to zone out by this time so I can't remember much after that. There was a ride in an ambulance and there were police at one point, but I didn't remember anything much until I woke, tucked up tightly into fresh hospital linen, with a mattress that crinkled when I moved and the smell of antiseptic in my nostrils.

The police returned to take a statement, their big blue uniforms taking up the space, demanding attention. I was suitably vague. I'd been attacked by a group of young people on my way to school. No I didn't know them, no I wouldn't be able to recognise them again, it had all happened so fast, I didn't have time.

He didn't believe me, and I could hear how lame it sounded, but there wasn't anything they could do. I know they only wanted to help but they didn't get it, none of them did. This morning's beating was bad enough, but if I told them the truth I might not survive the next.

Besides, this time it was my fault. I knew better. I could have avoided it.

Finally they left and I lay back my head, glad to finally get some peace. Then I remembered Baz. I had to warn Baz.

## Andrea

She doesn't come.  Andrea waits and she doesn't come.  She can't say she blames her, but still, she thought she would.  She hoped she would.

The regrets are piling at her door.  There are so many things she wishes she'd done differently now.  *'If wishes were horses…'*  Mark had said.

If they were, Andrea would be one of the most successful horse traders in history.

## Andrea 1980

I wasn't happy about beating her.  I never am.  But she goads me, she knows not to give me lip and she still does it.  She *knows* the consequences.  I just see red, especially when I'm coming down from a session.  It's not as if I can help it, or that she doesn't know that.

Still, later that day when I'd calmed down I did regret laying into her as much as I did.  I'm not sure why I couldn't stop, and it frightened me when I thought back on it.  Though not as much as when the police arrived on the doorstep.  I thought she'd finally told them what I'd done.  It was a relief when they told me she'd been attacked on the way to school.  *Good girl.*  I softened and felt bad again for what I'd done.

'Can you give me a lift to the hospital?' I asked.

'Sorry love, we've got another call to make on the other side of town.'

It took me two buses and ninety minutes to get there and then I had to wait another thirty minutes in the waiting room with a broken coffee machine and a wailing kid.  There was nothing wrong with him that was a good clip round the ear wouldn't fettle, and I was on the verge of smacking him myself when they called me in.

By this time I was nearly as mad as I'd been that morning, but I took a deep breath to calm myself.  I couldn't afford to lose my temper again.

When I entered the room Lot was tucked into a trolley bed, her arms neatly laid on the blanket.  She moved her head to me as I opened the door and the sorry in her eyes was haunting.

'Hello darling,' I said, fleeing to her bedside, feigning concern.  I did it so well that I fooled myself and found tears coming into my eyes and a clog of hard emotion in my chest.  I fought it back until I realised it was okay.  In fact, it would be useful, so I relaxed, sat by her bedside and let the tears flow.

In moments I found myself engulfed, sobbing, great wracks that pulled so hard on my insides I thought I might be sick with it. I felt a hand on my shoulder and realised a nurse was crouched beside me.

'Fancy a cuppa?'

I nodded, unable to speak and I begun to pull myself together. 'Sorry,' I managed moments later. My voice was hoarse and broken.

She patted my shoulder and left us alone.

I looked at Lot. 'I'm sorry, Lot,' I started, but the emotion rose up again and took over.

As I bent my head and cried I heard Lottie say, 'It's okay.'

Why couldn't she be angry at me? Why didn't she rail at me like I had against my mother? Her softness made me want to hurt her again and that made me cry harder and, as always, I vowed I wouldn't do this again. I'd do better in future, I'd be a better person, a better mum, this time would be different. This time I *meant* it.

Was my mother was watching me? Could Andrew see me? What did they think of me, of the way I'd turned out and of the life I was living? As if the thoughts were too heavy for my head I laid it on the bed and let some more of the pain out.

## Lottie 1980

Two days later Mum came to collect me in a taxi. As the car rode us gently through town Mum prattled on. She didn't need conversation, she needed to forget what she had done, being overly friendly was her way of saying she was still sorry. Personally, I wished she'd just come out and say it, but I knew she couldn't. That scene in the hospital was either a momentary lapse or a scene for the nurses, either way, she was back to being herself. So I sat back and bathed in the glow of her infrequent attention.

As Mum's words washed over me, my mind began to wander. I had never got so many taxis in my life, it felt like I was never out of them these days! The gas and electric were reconnected, we had a colour television, and there was coffee at home whenever I wanted it. I used to dream of this kind of luxury, yet I couldn't remember being so miserable, so confused.

My whole body hurt from the beating, and life seemed strange and out of control. It reminded me of the feeling I sometimes got when I was watching a film with Mum and she laughed and I did too, but I didn't know what I was laughing at.

As the taxi rocked me, with the smell of leather and car freshener tickling my nostrils and my mother's constant verbiage washing over me, I thought of Baz. I had to warn him of what had happened, but how could I do that without telling him what had *been* happening. I thought he'd like having a model for a girlfriend but now, when it came down to it, I didn't want him to know what I was doing. It was as if some part of me was being tainted by it all. I was selling my soul for a few pieces of silver. Like...like one of Shakespeare's characters, though I couldn't remember which one now. Shylock...was it Shylock?

As much as I reasoned it out with myself, something felt wrong about all this. At first I thought it was my discomfort in getting naked, but that was getting easier. The real problem was that the more involved I got with Cal, the more uncomfortable I felt. My insides seemed to be in a constant twist these days. Something didn't add up.

Whenever I questioned it Cal's logic won out. He was helping me, I was much more relaxed than a few weeks ago, but I still felt as if there was something fundamentally wrong with it all. Was I a prude? Was that it? Did I have to face the fact that, fundamentally I wasn't cut out to take my clothes off in front of people?

Mum's voice twittered on, melodically up and down as she relayed an incident in the pub the previous night. I tuned in to make sure nothing was expected of me. She was the heroine of course, funny and bright and beautiful. I returned to my own thoughts.

Did she know what Cal was up to? She had to, he'd said as much. So if she was happy for this to go ahead surely Cal was legitimate? Then there was the money. And Baz. How could she point the finger at him? If she could do that...could she be trusted to take care of me? Of course she could. She would see Baz as dispensable, and she was using him to deflect Cal from her, I knew Mum was afraid of him. Baz was a solution, I was her daughter, and despite all the beatings she gave me, I knew she wouldn't let anyone else hurt me. And yet, thinking back to the Pernod Paul situation, the only person who had ever really protected me was Cal. He had my back, my mother...not so much.

The taxi pulled up outside the house and as Mum leant forward to pay I knew I didn't want to do this stripping, naked modelling thing anymore, I wasn't cut out for it. It was wrong, for me.

The problem was, I thought as I tentatively climbed out of the car, wincing as I stood upright, I wasn't sure what I could do to unpick this mess.

I watched Mum, wrapped up in her own little world strolling up the garden path to the front door, and limped after her.

If I wanted to get out of this, clearly I was on my own.

## Lottie

It's ten and Dan has gone to bed. Lottie is not ready to sleep, things are churning too much inside.

Things are polite between them, Dan watches her, he knows something is wrong but he doesn't know what. He keeps asking and she just smiles and says, 'nothing', but she can see he's not convinced.

He doesn't know about the money yet, and she wonders how he'll react when he finds out. It makes her insides tighten so she refocuses on the television. It's another reality TV programme and she would be barely interested at the best of times.

She stands and walks the floor three times and then flops back into the sofa. The past has made her restless, the present isn't much better. Her thoughts turn to Jenny. Thoughts that are as uncomfortable as the ones about Dan.

What is happening to her? What is that junkie bitch thinking, letting her stay with her paedophile of an uncle? The answer sets her on her feet, striding across the carpet again.

*Using her, like my mother used me.*

Before she has thought through what she is doing Lottie tears out into the hall, grabs her coat, handbag and the car keys and leaves.

It's a few minutes before she realises where she's heading, and when she does she knows she has no choice, it is simply something she *has* to do. The visit to the Craigs' on Wednesday has played on her mind, and she has to make sure she's done everything she can for the girl. Including this.

Jenny isn't Tracey, she still deserves a chance. Maybe there's something redeemable in the girl if she could get away from her abusive family. She could wash her hair, lose weight, get an education, make something of herself.

If people had taken a closer look at Lottie when she was Jenny's age, they'd have seen the signs, found the evidence, been able to put a stop to it all before it was too late. Miriam has criticised her in the past for being too removed from their recipients, for not caring. It is the only criticism that sticks to Lottie. Well, *this* is caring. This is *doing* something. This isn't sitting in some meeting or swanning about at a conference. She has to do this. She has to *do* something.

Twenty minutes later she pulls up on the opposite side of the road to the house, pulls on the handbrake and switches off the engine. Lottie sits back in the car , the silence disturbed only by the clicks of the engine as it cools down, and takes a few deep breaths.

As she starts to calm down, she wonders if this is such a good idea. Wasn't she simply playing into Miriam's hands by being here? Breaking protocol in this way? It was gross misconduct and if anyone should find out... Besides, what does she expect to gain from this? Shouldn't she be leaving this sort of thing in the hands of the police? The professionals.

She thinks back to the children trust board meeting and the policeman there, whose name has escaped her again, making quips with his slicked back hair and bright buttoned uniform. He didn't care about people on this estate. It reminds her of how disposable she felt as a child. How the authorities made her feel as if all she was just another problem to deal with, something to sort out. They never had all the facts anyway, didn't understand the repercussions of their 'help'.

Still, she reminds herself, that's why she went into the work she does, to help change things from the inside. But there's process and protocol, does she really think staking out the Craigs' house is a sensible idea?

Just as she decides it would be best for her to leave, a taxi rounds the corner and pulls up outside the house. It hoots its horn then sits, chugging and waiting. It causes a shudder in Lottie as she remembers.

Moments later the door opens and Lottie's heart jumps as she sees Jenny emerge with a dark haired older man. The way they interact leads Lottie to believe that it is Uncle Bob. They both get into the taxi and it pulls away.

Lottie switches on her ignition, swings the car round and presses her foot on the accelerator to follow the taxi.

They leave the estate and Lottie follows as the car makes its way through the middle of the town, the traffic is light, making it easy for her to follow them at a distance. All her questions, concerns and self flagellation about her decision is forgotten, as she focuses on keeping the taxi in sight.

After twenty minutes the cab pulls into a new estate, full of small mock tudor houses. Lottie slows her car to a stop at the side of the road far enough away not to be noticed, but close enough to see what's happening, and switches off her lights.

Jenny emerges from the taxi, Bob and the driver exchange banter that Lottie can't hear, and then the taxi pulls away, leaving Jenny and Bob to walk up the path to the front door. Bob knocks.

There's a dim outside light that makes Jenny look drawn and pale, but she smiles at Bob as the front door opens and she steps into the house. Lottie is sat at the wrong angle to see the person who opens the door.

After a few minutes Lottie switches off her engine and settles down to wait in the dark car. Time passes, the cold settles around her and rain starts to patter gently on the roof of the car.

*If you want a job doing right...*

### Lottie 1980

I didn't have to go to see Cal that week, everything has a silver lining, even a beating. He visited us on the evening I came out of hospital, walking into our house with a proprietary air and my mother seemed to shrink down in his presence. It was both satisfying and irritating.

He pointed at me. 'Go to your room,' he said.

I looked at Mum and she nodded so I went, with some relief if I'm honest. I didn't like either of those two people very much at the moment. I lay on my bed with the latest Jane Austen book, Northanger Abbey, I wasn't enjoying it as much as Pride and Prejudice. I hadn't read more than a couple of pages when I heard Cal shouting.

I put it face down on the bed, careful not to lose my place, and crept out onto the landing to listen. My blood was pumping through my body, perhaps they were arguing about me and this meant it was all over. I would be sorry to lose my job at the book stall, but it was a small price to pay to get out of this mess. I crouched at the top of the stairs.

'...damaged goods Andrea!'

My Mum said something, but it was too quiet for me to make out. That made me nervous, Mum wasn't one for keeping her voice down.

'There's a debt to pay. You, her or this Baz lad.'

When I heard Baz's name on Cal's lips it sent an electric current through me, and everything inside reared up to protect him. He had nothing to do with this and I hadn't been able to see him to warn him yet.

I crept down a few stairs to see if I could hear what my mother was saying. I thought I heard my name, but I couldn't be sure.

Then the door handle rattled and I rushed as fast and as quietly as I could back up the stairs, wincing as I went. I hid on the landing, holding my breath, listening, my heart beating hard.

'So, it's settled,' Cal said, as he came into the hall.

'Yes,' my mum's voices sounded small.

'And will you tell her or shall I?'

'Let me ask her.'

'Ask? Ask? Did you hear me? I said, shall I *tell* her or will you?'

'Okay, I heard you, leave it with me.' She was being placatory, not her usual angry lilt when she was being pushed.

'And no more beatings,' he warned.

'Understood.'

Cal left and I slipped into back into my bedroom, discomfort eating at my stomach.

The following week Baz and I were walking back from the park. I knew Mum was going to get home early tonight and I wanted to be home and in bed before she got back. Baz had stopped asking me about my aunt and I was pleased. I didn't like to keep lying to him.

I didn't know how to broach the issue of Cal to warn him. I'd rehearsed numerous ideas in my mind but nothing sounded likely. Once again I cursed my mother for making my already complicated life even more so. She was a greedy cow and I vowed I would do everything I could not to be like her when I grew up.

'Baz?' I said, as we walked along the river, unsure what I was actually going to say.

'Yeah,' he said, he was kicking a coke can he'd found outside the park gates that had accompanied us on the journey home since. Sometimes he kicked it ahead and we walked up to it, at other times he dribbled it along as I walked beside him. The rattling was beginning to grate.

'You know Cal?'

'Yeah.' He continued to dribble.

'Well, he lost some takings recently.'

Baz said nothing, just focused on his can. I wondered if he was listening but pushed on.

'Well, when I say lost, I mean someone took it. And he's looking for the guy who nicked it.'

Still he didn't respond. I continued.

'Anyways, someone told him it was you.'

He didn't say anything and I was convinced then that he hadn't been listening when he stopped and shouted, 'What?'

'I know. I thought I should tell you.'

'Who fingered me then?'

'I don't know,' I lied. 'But he's a bit...scary, so you might want to just be on the look out.'

We walked together in silence for a while. The can left behind and forgotten.

'It'll be alright,' he said. 'Nothing to do with me.'

But I could see he was worried.

He reached over and took my hand. 'You worry too much,' he said, giving it a squeeze.

There was nothing more I could do, at least, not right now. Next week I'd talk to Cal again, straighten things out once and for all.


### Lottie

Lottie's mobile rings. It shatters the silence and makes her jump, bringing her back from the past. Her heart racing, she scrambles in her handbag to find it's Dan and she switches it off. She doesn't want to speak to him. He would ask where she was and what could she say?

When she switches off her phone she glances at her watch. They've been in there for over an hour and she leans her head back against the seat, feeling tired and cold, questioning again the purpose or even the use, of what she is doing.

Without hearing the conversation or seeing something, isn't it pointless? Shouldn't she at least get out of the car and check the house? Her mind reels back to another young girl, a taxi and a living room. Was the same happening in there, right now? Or worse? She can't think about that time. She never thinks about it. But something bad could be happening that she could prevent and instead she is just sitting here.

In frustration she slams the heel of her hand into the steering wheel and the force causes a shooting pain to arc up into her arm.

'Oh, that's great,' she whispers, but it calms her down.

As her anger subsides, the cold settles deeply into her bones and the tiredness reasserts itself. Just as she admits she is on a pointless mission the door to the house opens. Lottie sits upright and peers through the rain splattered windscreen.

A taxi chugs passed her car and three figures emerge. Lottie leans across the steering wheel, trying to see the third figure, but it's dark and the windscreen is steaming up and speckled with raindrops. She switches on the electrics and sweeps the wipers across the windscreen whilst she leans forward to wipe the inside.

As Jenny and Bob trot to the taxi, the third figure steps out onto the doorstep to watch them leave. He looks familiar but she can't quite make him out, can only see his profile against the light of the open doorway.

She leans over further to get a better look of the third figure and catches the horn. The loud blast makes her jump back and the heads of all three figures turn towards the car. *Fuck! Shit! Piss!*

169

Frantic, her heart pounding she grabs her bag from the passenger seat and pretends to rummage in it, keeping her head down, her face hidden, desperate to climb in it if she could. After a few moments she glances up to see the taxi pulling away, and the third figure retreating into the house. *Shit! Missed it all.*

Lottie throws her bag onto the seat, starts the car and once again follows the taxi. After another twenty minutes through town she is disappointed to find herself pulling back into the Craigs' street. She stops a little way down the street and switches off the engine. The rain has stopped and she sees Jenny and Bob getting out of the taxi.

Bob leans in to say something to Jenny and she laughs. Then she looks directly at Lottie and it makes her heart stall. Did they recognise the car? Her? No, it was impossible, not in the dark and the rain, but Bob is now making his way down the street towards her.

Lottie's eyes widen and for a moment, she is unsure of what to do. Then, wits gathered, she starts the car, puts it into gear and speeds off. Bob shouts something at her but Lottie can't make it out.

As she drives away, her heart thrumming in her ears, the vision of Jenny laughing burns into her retina and she has an epiphany.

*Jenny and I are not the same, and no one needs saving here. No one, except perhaps me.*

# Sunday

### Andrea

She still doesn't visit, and Andrea waits. She's not sure how long has passed, these damn drugs confuse her. Why doesn't the stupid girl just come back? If she did Andrea could explain, or at least try to. So much to say, so much to mend, so many misunderstandings, and so much confusion. Anger rises. It wasn't *all* her fault. She did try to stop it. She wants Lottie to know that, and she wants her to know that, what Andrea did in the end, was to save Lottie as much as herself.

### Andrea 1980

Beating Lot was a vent for my frustration but clearly wasn't a solution to our situation. I needed help and there was only one person I trusted enough to call.

We'd agreed to meet in Durham. I didn't want to meet in Darlington, someone was bound to see me and I couldn't afford for Cal to hear I'd been seen talking to the police.

As I stepped off the train and pulled my gloves on to protect against the nip in the December air, I was nervous. Mark had risen in the ranks, he was an inspector now. I didn't really know what that meant, but it sounded impressive, it sounded intimidating. He'd done well for himself but then, I always knew he would.

I'd heard he was married, probably to the woman I'd seen him with in the pub that day, but I didn't know if he had kids. It made me wonder again about the past and chances and decisions. Those forks in the road of life where you can go one way or another, small decisions that you think aren't important but lead to a series of consequences that change your life completely.

As I walked from the station down the steep bank towards the hotel where we'd agreed to meet for coffee, the Christmas decorations only made me feel more shit about what lay ahead.

I had never been in a hotel and I was sure it would be obvious to everyone the moment I stepped inside the door. How would I know where to find him? Was there a special meeting room or place? I desperately hoped I wouldn't stand out. Maybe it would be like the Ritz, only northern style, with the crusts left on the bread and meat paste instead of ham. I chuckled to myself as I came to the bottom of the hill and spotted the hotel across the road. *Easy to find at least,* I thought. One less thing to worry about.

Moments later I was approaching the doors, and when I saw Mark standing outside my stomach did sixes and eights. He spotted me and waved. I waved back. I wondered if we looked like two lovers meeting, then pushed the idea from my mind.

I smoothed out my coat as I hurried up to him and arrived breathless and hot and unsure. I wasn't used to feeling unsure, although recently with Cal on the scene it had become something I was getting more familiar with.

'Hi,' I said.

He smiled. 'Hi.'

He looked just the same. I took a breath, looked out across the road then back again.

'This is a bit...posh,' I said, wrinkling my nose.

'Don't worry, there's a pub round the corner. I just thought this would be easy to find.'

Relief flooded through me, along with a bit of disappointment. Did he think I couldn't handle myself in a posh place? I bet he and his wife went to hotels all the time.

We turned and walked along the street in the direction Mark had indicated.

'So, how are you? You look tired,' he said.

'Do I?' I felt affronted. In the past he'd always told me how good I looked. I smoothed out my hair. 'I'm fine, you?'

'Good.'

'It's been what...four, five years? What's new?' I asked, in an attempt to keep the conversation up.

'Got promoted, got married.' Even though I knew it still pulled at my insides when he said it. 'And you?'

'Same old same old,' I said in a sing song voice. *What is wrong with me?*

Mark stopped. 'Here we are, the pub,' he said.

It was an old pub, the kind we used to frequent when we were kids and I smiled.

'Would you have found it?' he asked.

'Me, find a pub? You joking?'

We laughed. His trailed off, I laughed too long and too hard I realised.

I coughed. 'Looks like the Red Lion. Only smaller.'

'It does, doesn't it?' He pulled the door open for me. 'Shall we?'

It *was* small. The bar would only seat five stools maximum. A bench ran along one wall opposite the bar with two rectangular tables in front of it. No more furniture would fit into the room. It was early in the afternoon and empty apart from the proverbial old man propped up at the corner of the bar reading a newspaper.

As a token nod to the looming celebrations, tired paper decorations hung limp from the ceiling and a white plastic tree stood at the end of the bar, a handful of chocolate Santas for decoration.

'Okay?' Mark asked.

I nodded, pleased that he cared what I thought.

'What'll you have to drink? I can run to a port and lemon these days.'

The memory came flooding back and I had to catch my breath, stop myself from falling into nonsense.

'Half a lager and lime will do fine.'

'Sure?'

'Yes, thanks.'

'Grab a table I'll bring them over.'

I took a seat on the bench. It was covered in black leather that had seen better days. I watched Mark get served by a man whose stomach was a walking warning against overindulgence, and noticed another snug through the hatch behind the bar.

Mark returned, placed the glasses on the table and sat down opposite me.

'Cheers,' he said, lifting up his pint. 'Merry Christmas!'

I mirrored his image then drank, wishing I had said yes to a port.

'I see Rosie from time to time.'

'Oh,' was all I could think to say, and I remembered her face at the window.

'I don't think I've ever seen such unhappy eyes.'

I shrugged. 'You make your bed...'

Mark put his glass down and looked at me. 'So, I'm guessing this isn't an old times reunion.'

'No.'

I shifted through my head trying to find the right words to begin. Mark sat watching, and I found myself wondering if his wife knew we were here. What had he told her? Where was she? Did they have children? He hadn't mentioned any so maybe not. I was pleased about that. Mark broke into my thoughts.

'Andi?'

'Sorry, I was just thinking how to begin this...where to begin.'

'You know what they say, start at the beginning.'

The beginning. Did this all really start back that night he and I went out with Andrew and Rosie, or was it earlier?

'It's Cal,' I said eventually.

173

Something crossed Mark's face but I couldn't make it out, it looked like irritation.

'What about him?'

'Are you any closer to...nailing him?'

'Andi, is this about Andrew?'

'No. Yes. Sort of, but no, not really.'

'Care to elaborate?'

'You know those rumours about Cal, about the sort of things he's involved in, you know...'

Mark leaned forward. 'Andi, listen to me. Stay away from him. Leave his sort to us. He's dangerous.'

'You think I don't know that?'

We sat in silence. A radio was on low somewhere in another room. The old man's paper rustled as he turned the page. A chair scraped in the room through the hatch.

'I don't want you doing anything to jeopardise your safety and getting involved with Cal will do that. No one comes away unscathed.'

'It's too late.'

'What?'

'I'm already involved.'

'You're what?'

'You heard.'

'How? What possessed you to even go near him?'

He looked at me for a long time, the silence stretching between us, then put his head back and he closed his eyes. 'What have you done now?' he whispered. He wasn't really asking a question.

I looked at his exposed throat, the contours of his face. Noticed he needed a shave, there was a darkness under his eyes and the hairs in his nose needed a trim. All signs he had been working to hard, when we were young Mark had always taken pride in his appearance. I wondered if his wife took care of him. Did she bring him tea in bed? Did they make love on Sunday mornings? Did she watch him shave?

He brought his head down and looked at me.

'Mark...I, I thought I could catch him.'

'But?'

'But now we're in a bit of a pickle.'

'We?'

'Me and my daughter.'

'Your daughter?'

I nodded and realised that I was more upset and afraid than I had dared to admit.

'Jees, Andi. What on earth possessed you? Do you think this is a *game*?'

'I had this idea of getting something on him and bringing it to you.'

'This something, is it to do with your daughter?'

I nodded, not trusting myself to speak. For the first time I realised just how despicable it sounded. How despicable it *was*.

'Does your daughter know?'

I swallowed then spoke. 'No, I just got her a job on Cal's book stall.'

Mark didn't say anything and we drank our lager in the quiet for a few minutes. I noticed mine was nearly finished.

'What was the plan, exactly?' he asked eventually, when he'd calmed down.

'I didn't intend to involve her. I was trying to get inside his business, get close, see if the rumours were true and if I could find anything out. But,' I paused. I really didn't want to say what I was about to say, to anyone, let alone Mark. 'But he wasn't interested in me.'

'Let me guess, too old?'

I nodded and he sighed.

'It didn't take long. He's now 'training' her to be a model.'

'Model?'

I repeated the words using my fingers as speech marks. He nodded to show he understood.

'Anyways, she goes to his house every Tuesday and Thursday for photo shoots.'

'Does he take pictures?'

'I think so, yes but I've never seen them. I did ask him about it once.'

'What did he say.'

I shrugged, trying to look casual but it didn't work. Inside I was horrified. 'All I know is they're not appropriate.'

'What's that mean.'

I glared at him. 'Really, Mark?'

He lifted his hands as if to ward off my look. 'Okay, okay.' He sighed heavily and thought. 'Have you asked your daughter?'

'No, I haven't said anything. I don't know what to say.'

'Well, that's something at least.'

'What's that supposed to mean?'

'What do you *think* it means, Andi? I mean seriously?'

I felt my cheeks flush. I couldn't remember the last time I blushed. I looked down at my empty glass waiting for the feeling to subside.

'I'm sorry,' he said.

'No, you're right. I've messed up. Story of my life,' I laughed.

'Carry on. Tell me the rest.'

'So now he's talking about Lottie's boyfriend-'

'Who's Lottie?'

'My daughter. Cal's telling me she can't have this boyfriend, that they're getting too close. Anyway, that's when I realised I'm in out of my head and thought of you.'

'It's in "over" your head.'

'What?'

'You said, "out of my head"? The term is in "over" my head.'

I looked at him for a moment. 'Are you seriously giving me a grammar lesson?'

'No, I'm just saying-'

'Well don't, I don't give a fuck what the saying is, I need help.'

'Okay, okay, keep your voice down, we don't want to attract attention to ourselves.'

I wasn't sure if his warning was because of his wife or Cal.

'Okay, so Lottie works on his stall on Saturdays and she goes to his house on Tuesdays and Thursdays, and we know he hasn't had sex with her because he wants the boyfriend kept away, to keep her a virgin presumably. Have I got it so far?'

'Yes.'

'How old is she?'

I faltered. If I told him the truth would he guess? Of course he would, he was a copper, it was his job to work things out. So I lied.

'Fourteen.'

'What the hell has the bastard got planned?' I could tell by the way he said it that he wasn't expecting me to reply. 'Have you told me everything?'

There was one other thing I thought, the money, but I couldn't bring myself to tell him about that. How could I? Besides, what did it matter?

'No, that's everything.'

'Oh, Andi,' he whispered.

'I know, I know, stupid huh?'

'What am I going to do with you?'

I just smiled at him and he smiled back. We looked at each for too long and then he broke the connection. I was sad he'd broken away, though I knew I had no right to be. He was married, we had our chance, I blew it. Besides, he looked at me differently now. I wasn't sure if it was because he was married, or because he didn't like what he saw anymore. I immediately dismissed the last idea, that couldn't be true. I still had it. I was like a fine wine.

'Do you know anything else?' he asked, leaning back on his stool.

'He has a gun and he goes down to London.'

'Whereabouts in London?'

'I don't know, I'm not his fucking travel agent.'

'Andi, I'm trying to help.' He sounded tired.

Finally he finished off his drink.

'Another?' he said.

'It's my turn,' I said, reaching for my bag.

'Let me,' he said, and went to the bar before I had a chance to respond.

'Get me a whiskey chaser will you?' I called over to him.

He nodded without turning round.

'Do you think you can help us?' I asked, when he returned with the drinks.

'We'll work something out, don't know what yet but don't worry, we will.' He put the glasses on the table and sat down. 'But I'm glad Lottie isn't my daughter.'

When I stood up to leave four drinks and thirty minutes later, my heart froze and I turned my back to the hatch.

'Mark,' I hissed.

'What?' he said, pulling on his coat.

I used my eyes to indicate the hatch. He glanced through and nodded at me. We left quickly. Outside the cold air hit me and I wobbled.

'I'll get you a cab,' Mark said, holding onto my arm.

'Do you think he saw us?' I asked.

'I hope not,' he said, waving down a cab.

'I've got a return ticket I don't ha-'

'It's on me,' he said, understanding my reluctance. 'You can't get the train in this state.'

'What state? I'm not in a state, I only had a few drinks.'

'Yeah, well, Andrew would never forgive me if I left you here like this.'

He opened the car door and as I climbed in I tripped and ended face down on the back seat. I was so mortified I wanted to cry, instead I laughed as I righted myself. 'My foot,' I said, giggling.

Mark handed the driver some money and then bent down and gave me a tight smile. 'You okay?' he asked.

'Of course,' I leaned over to say something to him, became aware of how close our faces were and I forgot it.

'It'll be fine,' he said. 'I'm sure he didn't see us.' He stood up, took his closeness away and I sat back in the seat as he closed the door. I watched him walk away. He didn't turn round, he didn't wave, he hadn't said goodbye.

'Where to, pet?'

I gave the driver my address and laid my head back. What were the chances? All I could hope was that Mark was right, and Pernod Paul hadn't seen us.


## Lottie

Lottie sits opposite Dan at the breakfast table and realises it's the first breakfast they've had since the day they were told she couldn't have children. She blamed his distance then on anxiousness: about the process and the impending news. Now she knows the truth she's not sure it helps. She wonders how long he can keep up the pretence, she wonders how long she can. *How does this end?*

She stands up. 'I'm going for a shower,' she says. 'I'll be back before you go.'

'Okay,' he says, without looking up from the paper. 'We've got dinner at my parents tonight,' he calls after her. 'Wear that purple dress. It looks good on you'

Dan bought it for her birthday two years ago as a surprise. A Karen Millen in deep purple that drew from her body an hour glass figure she didn't even know she possessed. He chose well and she would have lived in it, if it weren't for one thing.

She hates purple.


## Lottie 1980

'Here,' Mum said, shoving a bag in my hand.

'What's that?'

'It's what you're supposed to wear. Tonight.' She didn't look at me.

I peered into the bag and pulled out silky purple fabric that morphed into a dress as I unfolded it against me. It was long, slim fitting, with a draped kick out below the knee. Long wizard sleeves added to the dramatic effect. It was the most beautiful piece of clothing I had ever seen, let alone touched, worn or owned.

'God, it's beautiful, Mum,' I said, breathless with excitement.

'Yeah, okay, well...go and put it on then.' Still she didn't look at me.

'You okay?' She looked defeated and small.

Finally she glanced at me. 'Sure, why?'

I shrugged, not wanting to provoke her, aware I needed to tread carefully. 'No reason, just checking.'

She gave me a little shove, 'Go on then or you'll be late.'

I skipped upstairs, so excited to see it on. I placed it carefully onto the bed, then with speed removed my clothes. As I pulled it over my head the cool silk gave me goose bumps. It slipped easily over my body and I smoothed it over my hips. I went to the mirror and the overall effect was every bit as wonderful as I had imagined downstairs. It clung in all the right places, skimming my hips and breasts, making me look and feel considerably older than my fifteen years. I hugged myself with pleasure, all Cal's failings forgiven.

### Andrea 1980

As soon as I saw her in that dress I knew I had to find out, one way or another, what the hell was going on. I couldn't speak to her, I'd tried and I just couldn't find the words. It all came out wrong. So when they left I went to the phone box.

### Lottie 1980

Cal picked me up at seven on the dot. I quivered inside my brand new dress. I knew I looked better than I ever had and just wished Baz could see me. But then, what would be the point? I had a suspicion that Baz and I would not make it through this ordeal together, and the thought created a hungry ache in the pit of my stomach as I walked down the path to Cal in the waiting taxi.

I didn't understand anything anymore. I had grown to hate and fear Cal, even though he was taking care of me. I'd looked up the word hate in the thesaurus: loathe, detest, abhor, abominate, despise. Abhor was my favourite.

'We're going to The Red Lion,' he said, when I was seated in the cab.

'In town?'

He nodded. 'Pal of mine owns the place.'

I was surprised Mum hadn't tagged along, which added to my nervousness. Nothing was right about this, I could feel it.

'Why are we going there?' I asked, I tried to be relaxed but my voice came out funny sounding.

'You'll see.'

We rode the rest of the journey in silence.

### Andrea 1980

I dialled the taxi company that Cal used.

'Hi, Johnny Caldwick has just left my house in one of your taxis and he's left his wallet behind. Can you tell me where the taxi was taking him?'

'Hang on, love and I'll check.'

The line went quiet for a few moments.

'Hello?'

'Yes, I'm still here.'

'Red Lion. Want a taxi love?'

'No, thanks, I'll get a friend to drop it off.'

I hung up and dialled the only other taxi firm in town.

### Lottie 1980

The dress was beautiful but wholly inappropriate for the winter weather and, not wanting to crease it, I hadn't put a coat on, so I was frozen by the time we got into the pub. The warm beery smell wrapped itself around me, and I was glad to get inside.

Cal shook the hand of a man with a mop of back hair behind the bar.

'John, good to see you, how's it hanging?'

John had a pudgy face, not quite fat, but it was going in that direction, probably as a result of all the alcohol he consumed. Cal didn't introduce us, but I saw the man glance in my direction several times as they chatted. He smiled at me one time, and I thought he had a nice face, kind eyes, so I smiled back.

'Can we go up then?' Cal asked.

John nodded, and as Cal led me to a door at the back of the pub I could feel John watching us go. My nerves returned, and as I followed Cal up the stairs that lay behind the door, my legs shook and I bit my lip so hard I drew blood. The sharp pain and the subsequent warm iron liquid that filled my mouth soothed me, released some of the tension, and I let out the breath I didn't know I was holding.

We entered a spacious room that smelt damp. The black leather sofa in the centre looked lost in such a big space. The only other furniture was a dark wood dining table pushed to the wall between two large bay windows. Thin greying curtains hung limp, barely disguising the view of the decorated town square beyond and I could just make out the Christmas lights.

A large television covered in dust stood in the corner by an wide open fireplace. The grate had not been cleaned out for some time, heaps of grey ash spilled onto the fireplace and the brown rug that lay in front of it.

There was a chill to the room and I wished again I had worn a coat.

'Right then,' said Cal, rubbing his hands together as he entered the room. 'I've got you a little test, right?'

I nodded, not knowing what to say. I had so many questions they crowded against each other, banging together like thunder clouds giving me no space to think.

'I want you to sit on the sofa and just slip the top part of your dress off.'

'I'm not wearing a bra!' I told him. The moment I said it I knew that was the point. It was why he'd given me the dress in the first place, and I wanted to weep with disappointment. Couldn't I have one beautiful thing in my life, I thought, just one thing?

Cal just gave me that look, and so with reluctance I went over to the sofa and did as he said.

Cal went to the door and turned to look at me. 'That's right, back straight love,' he told me then, nodding with satisfaction he called down the stairs for John.

Oh god, no. John, really? That nice man behind the bar? Were there no nice men in the world anymore? Perhaps there never had been. Then I remembered Baz.

Cal sat down next to me. 'Now, when John comes in that door you smile, you hear me, regardless of what happens you just sit there and smile. Understand?'

'Yes,' I said. It came out as a whisper, full of grief. When I heard my own voice I thought any person with any conscience would let me go, but not Cal. I was beginning to think he didn't have a soul, or if he did, a black one, and I realised he wasn't looking out for me. Not anymore. If he ever had.

I heard a creak on the stairs and put a smile on my face, my heart hammering, my face bright red. I was sat bolt upright, beasts bared, my hands resting gently in my lap.

As John rounded the corner Cal caught hold of one of my hands and I felt something soft in my palm. Instantly I realised I was holding Cal's flaccid cock in my hand. It was warm and silky, curled up like a pet in his lap. I sat rigid, smile fixed, breasts bared, holding onto this old man's cock as John turned the corner.

I'm not sure why I didn't pull away. Was it shock? Was it a desire to please? Was it a need to appear more grown up than I actually felt? Perhaps it was all three. All I do know is that my body froze, and my smile cemented to my face as John came into the room.

He was smiling and I didn't know if this was a good or bad thing, until I noticed a brief twist to his face. A fleeting moment of something, I wasn't sure what, but spending a lifetime of dodging my mother's blows had taught me to know when someone wasn't happy, and John wasn't happy.

'Alright pal?' Cal asked, lifting his pelvis so his penis rubbed against my hand.

Smile still fixed, I glanced at Cal. The delight on his face was evident. I looked back to John to see his features rearranged to hide whatever it was...a fleeting glimpse of disgust perhaps?

'Choice, nice one Cal,' he said, and stuck his thumbs in the air.

'Corker, what?'

John nodded, his eyes darting between us.

'Told you, didn't I, son?'

John nodded, looking down at the floor, then back at us, I noticed his eyes careful to stay on our faces. Even I, with my inexperience, could tell he was as uncomfortable as I was, that despite outward appearances, we were both in the same position.

He indicated behind him with one of his thumbs. 'Better get back to the bar,' he said. He waited, and I realised he was waiting for permission from Cal to leave.

That's when I realised *just* how powerful Johnny Caldwick was.


### Andrea 1980

I was stood directly opposite the entrance of the Red Lion, hidden behind one of the pillars that held up the indoor market. I stamped my feet to stave off the cold and wished the cafe was open so I could get a cup of tea.

Thirty minutes later I was wondering if I was in the wrong place and considered leaving when Cal and Lot appeared in the door of the pub. Lot

182

looked desperately young tottering across the market square in high heels and that shiny dress. A vision of her at four, dressed in my shoes in the bedroom came to me, and I wondered how I could have ever thought I didn't love her.

I waited until they rounded the corner then crossed the road and entered the pub. John acknowledged me with a nod and a wink and, feeling shaky I made my way over the quiet pub to the bar.

'What brings you in here alone, Andrea?'

'I'm meeting a friend,' I said.

'What'll it be?' he asked.

'Half lager and lime,' I said.

'You just missed Cal,' he said, as he put a glass under the tap and clicked the switch.

'Shame. Was he on his own?'

John flicked a look at me. 'No, had a young lass in tow.'

'Oh?'

He placed the glass on the bar, turned to get the bottle of lime cordial from behind him and poured a shot into the lager. I was itching to ask him for more details but held my tongue, knowing John preferred to offer information.

I handed John a pound note and watched him ring up the sale.

'I'd heard he was seeing someone new,' I said, and took a sip of my drink, watching John over the edge of my glass.

He screwed up his face. 'Yeah, sweet little thing.'

'Young?'

He scoffed. 'Very.'

I leaned forward and gave him one of my best smiles. 'Really?'

John came and stood opposite me, and I could tell from his body language that he was settling down for a chat, the bar being so quiet.

He shook his head. 'Outrageously so.'

I raised my eye brows and licked my lips. 'Tell me more,' I said.

'I'd doubt she's even sixteen.' His voice was filled with disgust and I wondered what had happened for him to feel that affronted. After all, older men and younger women were hardly a revelation.

I decided to make a joke to keep the conversation light. 'You didn't serve her did you, John?'

'Andrea, she was with Cal. Of course I bloody served her!'

I laughed my sweetest laugh and leaned over further. 'Oh John, you'll have it wrong. What would a man like Cal be doing with a girl, man like that needs a woman. She's probably one of the family.'

John leaned closer and lowered his voice. 'She's not a rellie, I can tell you that for nothing, but I couldn't begin to tell you the rest,' he said. 'In fact, I'm still in shock.'

He looked a little shaken now he'd said it, and I thought if I was going to get anything out of him now was the time. 'Really? That sounds interesting.'

He pulled a face and shook his head. 'Not interesting, Andrea. Sick's what I'd call it.'

'I'm sure it's all above board.'

'It's disgusting is what it is. I fear for the kid, I really do.'

The last came out as a whisper and my heart skipped.

'What d'you mean?'

He stood up straight. 'Nothing, forget I said anything.' He picked up a cloth and wiped down an already clean bar.

It was clear the subject was closed. For a change I didn't want my drink, there was a sour taste in my mouth, but I forced it down, leaving it would have looked suspicious. Everyone knew my reputation and now was not the time to be drawing attention to myself.

'Well, looks like I've been stood up,' I said, as I put my empty glass on the bar.

'Beautiful woman like you? Doubt it.' He smiled.

He was a nice man, I decided, too nice for me. Whatever he had witnessed had made him uncomfortable but it was clear I wasn't going to get anything out of him unless...I'd slept with worse for less good reasons.

I leaned forward and smiled my best smile. 'Aw thanks John, and you're probably right. Think I might have got my facts mixed up.'

He smiled back. 'Another drink? On me?'

The implication was obvious and I paused. Was this the right thing to do?

'That would be lovely,' I said, and John beamed at me.

I left the pub well after closing time, pissed, with damp knickers but no more information. John knew more than he was letting on, and maybe, just maybe, enough to get Cal, but I hadn't been able to get anything out of him but his spunk.

Perhaps it was time to call Mark again.

**Lottie**

'See you about three,' Dan says, standing by his golf clubs in the hall. Golf is today's excuse.

'See you later.'

He doesn't even pause, he doesn't even look back or raise a hand goodbye as he drives away. They say it doesn't take much to tip you over the edge. It's the small things apparently.

Lottie picks up her mobile and dials. 'Emergency locksmith in the Darlington area please,' She says

She waits.

'Put me straight through.'

Two hours later the locks are changed, Dan's clothes are packed in suitcases on the door step and she is sorting through her wardrobe. The purple dress is the first thing to go. *Bastard!*

**Andrea**

Andrea knows that she can't stand another day without the morphine, the pain is too bad. She also knows that once she starts taking it, Lottie and she are doomed. She laughs, just a spurt, like a car engine that can't quite get going. They're already doomed There's no fixing of them.

Lottie is so...so...rigid. Always was. Even as a child Andrea would have to force her to go out and play. Left to her own devices she would sit and read all day, that's no good for a child, it's not healthy, it's not...normal.

She never came home dirty and covered in mud like the other kids. She came out of the womb middle aged. Still, Andrea supposes it had its uses, one of them had to be the grown up.

She chuckles when she thinks back to her earnest face cleaning the house. She was so small. Seven or eight. Always independent, always self sufficient. She had Andrea to thank for that. She was much more competent than any of the other kids in the street. Their neighbours would often comment on it to her in the the club.

In those moments she was proud of her, but to be truthful, most of the time, Lottie just got on her nerves. It was like living with Mother fucking Teresa, she was so pious and...good. It leaked from her. It wouldn't have surprised Andrea if her daughter had become a nun.

That was what was so surprising about all that Cal business. Andrea *never* thought Lottie would go through with it and couldn't imagine what made her agree.   Still, Cal had said to leave it to him, he'd find a way. Clever bugger, that Cal.  Manipulative fat bastard that he was.

She wants to explain, she never meant for it to go that far, never meant for it to turn out the way it did.  She knows Lottie blames her, but Lottie was the one who agreed to it all.  She was the one who said yes.  If she'd said no, like Andrea had expected…

The bastard really did them over, and how does she explain it to Lot? How does she do that?  How can she make her daughter understand that it was *she* who lost everything and everyone?  Not Lottie.


## Andrea  1980

When Cal left with Lottie that Saturday morning for the stall, I was already awake, though I stayed in bed, waiting for them to leave.  It didn't take me long to dress.

I stopped at the corner shop to buy fags and get some change and then made my way up to the telephone box outside the post office, lighting a fag to steady my nerves.

When I opened the door the smell of stale piss hit my nostrils and my stomach lurched.   I held my breath to stop myself from gagging, then started to take small breath until I got used to it.  If I threw up I wouldn't be able to make the call, and I couldn't afford to let anymore time pass.

My hand shook as I set the pile of two pence pieces on the shelf next to me and my heart beat so hard I could hear it on my ear drums.  I lifted the receiver and breathed a sigh of relief when I heard the dialling tone.

I had memorised the number on the scrap of paper in my pocket and I put my finger into the hole over number six and pushed the dial round, listening to it buzz back round to the beginning, then I dialled the next number, and the next.  It took forever, and as it whirled round for the third time, I looked out across the forecourt outside the shops to check no one was about.  Judy Ward was coming out of the shop and had stopped outside the post office to talk to old Mrs Wright from number 53.  Nothing to worry about there.

I dialled the last number and waited for it to connect and ring.   I wasn't sure he would be there but he'd said to leave a message if he wasn't. My anxiety built again, I'd practised what I would say if I needed to leave a message, but I held the phone tight to my ear, praying he would be there, praying it would be him that answered.

It stopped ringing and I heard his voice.

'Mark? It's Andi. There's been...developments,' I wasn't sure how else to put it.

'What?'

'I can't explain it really, it sounds like nothing.' I felt silly suddenly, a new dress didn't mean anything, but the conversation with John, what could be something, couldn't it?

'Try.'

I paused for a long time.

'Andi?'

The pips in my ear alerted me to the fact that I was running out of time and I shoved another two pence piece in the slot, then another one just to be on the safe side. I didn't want to lose him now.

'You still there?' I asked.

'Yeah. What is it?'

'It sounds silly now, but...he bought her a dress.'

'A dress?'

'An expensive one. And there's something else, I followed them.'

'You did what? Andi, for christ sake, just do as I said.'

'It was fine. I had,' she paused, before continuing, 'an interesting conversation with John, the landlord of the Red Lion?'

'Go on.'

'He didn't say much but I'm sure he knows something. He seemed...shaken by something. He said it was sick, then he clammed up. No matter how I tried I couldn't get anything more from him, but I think he knows something.'

'Okay, I'll go and have a word with him, see what I can find out.'

'Be careful,' I said.

'No more following anyone, you hear me?'

'Yes,' I whispered. 'Mark, I'm scared.'

'I know, me too.'

It was hardly the reassurance I was expecting from a police officer.

'What if it all goes wrong?' I asked, trying to get the reassurance I needed.

'It won't, we'll figure it out, I promise. Okay?'

'Okay.'

Silence hung on the line between us and I wanted to fill it by telling him how I felt about him, how I had always felt, how I would always feel. The words started to form but as I opened my mouth Mark spoke.

'I've got to go now, but you'll be fine,' he said. 'And be careful.'

'Mark? Thanks again.'

'It's my job.' I heard the implied message and it wormed down under my armour and struck deep.

'Yes,' more words were there, hanging on my lips waiting for me to drop them into his ear so I hung up before I could make a fool of myself. If I'd known it was the last time I would get the chance I might have told him. *If wishes…*

By the time I reached home I was back in the present, and ready, well as ready as I would ever be, to do battle with the man who had ruined my life.

Later that day, weeks after I'd seen her face at the window, *she* turned up on my doorstep. To see her standing there, wrapped in an elegant red coat, with an air of expectation, made my blood boil, but I let her in anyway.

As she passed by me I caught a whiff of expensive perfume. I signalled the door to the living room and followed her in, wondering what had brought her here after all these years. I watched her take in her surroundings, remembering the last time she had spoke to me, whispering in my ear.

'I know what's going on and I want it to stop,' Rosie said, turning to face me, her hands plunged deep in her coat pockets.

I was too angry to respond directly. 'Tea? I'd offer you a sherry. But we haven't got any.'

'What are you playing at?'

I cringed at this question, it's one I have asked myself a thousand times. As usual I just went crashing in with some half baked idea, but I couldn't admit this to *her*.

I sighed. 'What do you want, Rosie?'

'I want it to stop.'

'Oh yeah, you said.' I retrieved my fags from the mantelpiece and lit one, staying on the other side of the room in case I could no longer control the urge to smack her face. She had no idea how kind I was being, stuck up bitch!

'I want it to stop because she's the one who'll get hurt. Nobody else.'

I knew it was true and I wasn't sure I was doing enough to stop it. So I didn't respond, I drew on my fag instead.

'Is she Mark's?'

I wasn't sure if I was more surprised by the sudden change of subject or that she'd guessed.

'Your daughter?' she clarified for me.

I nodded to indicate that I knew what she's referring to. I wasn't stupid. Well, not all the time 'What makes you say that?' I asked, eventually.

'I'm good at maths.'

I took a long drag then released the smoke slowly, watching it rise to the ceiling.

'Why didn't you tell him?' she asked.

'None of your business.'

She didn't say anything to that and I glanced at her. She was looking down at her feet but then looked up and caught my eye.

'I loved him, you know?' she said.

'So did I.'

'It wasn't my fault. It wasn't anyone's fault.'

'Not even Cal's?

'I meant us,' she added quickly. 'You, me and Mark.'

'There was no *us.*'

'Andrew and I thought so.'

I leaned forward. 'You thought wrong,' I spat.

'Well,' she paused. 'I should be going, don't want Cal asking awkward questions.'

'Keeps you on a tight leash then?'

'Yes, as a matter of fact he does.'

I already knew the answer from my visit that night, but her candour surprised me.

'But I keep my eye on him too.'

'You should never have gone out with Andrew,' I said. 'If you really loved him you wouldn't have.'

Rosie raised her face towards the ceiling momentarily, took a breath and then looked directly at me again. 'Is that why you didn't tell Mark?'

'I told you, mind your own business.'

'You can't control people, you know, Andrea? '

'So, Cal know you're here then?'

She looked back at her feet and shook her head in exasperation.

'Why do you stay with him?'

She looked at me. 'You know why.'

I laughed, nervously.

'I'm waiting, and I'm a patient woman,' she said. 'Like I said, I keep my eye on him.'

I didn't know what she was talking about but suddenly felt tired of it all. Rosie looked hard, I knew I looked the same. The years had not been kind to either of us I realised then.

'Well, thanks for dropping by, let's make it another couple of decades before we do this again, eh? ' I returned to focusing on my fag.

'Look, Andrea, I know you've never liked me and I understand why, but if there's anything I can do…' she drew one hand from her pocket and held out a piece of paper. 'Here's my number. Don't call after five, he's almost always home by then.'

I didn't take it. Just left her standing there, holding it out towards me.

'I'll leave it here.' She placed it on the coffee table. 'If there's anything… I haven't forgotten,' she turned and left.

I heard the front door click shut and stared at the paper, wondering what she knew that I didn't.

## Lottie

Bang. Bang. Bang. 'Lottie, open up!'

Lottie sips her coffee and flicks over a page of OK magazine, looking at the pictures of another Z listed celebrity wedding. *She needs to eat more pies,* she thinks, taking in the sharp collar bones sticking up from beneath the lace dress.

'Lottie!'

She turns the page and pain stabs at her as she takes in the child bridesmaids. She gleams from the caption that they are five and three. She looks at them again, cherub ringlets under a ring of small pink roses. *Sweet.*

'You can't do this, be reasonable!'

Moments later her mobile buzzes against the kitchen cabinet but she doesn't get up to answer it, she knows it is Dan. She did warn him, sent him a text telling him not to come home.

'Lottie! Let me in, let's talk about this. Please.'

She turns another page. Takes in the massive cake. The pearl encrusted wedding dress. Remembers her own.

He bangs on the door one last time before it falls silent.

Lottie holds her breath and waits. Nothing. Is he sitting outside in the car catching his breath, or has he gone to his parents? She wonders what he will say to them. She wonders if he knows about the bank account yet.

She feels a twinge then reminds herself that he has a credit card. Besides, he shouldn't have been dicking around

For the first time in weeks she feels as if she finally has some control over her life, then wonders how long it will last before some bastard comes and pisses on it.


## Lottie 1980

Unusually Cal's in the cab that picks me up for our session and he tells me I'm auditioning tonight. If they like me, I might get some work.

Just when I think I'm going to quit something happens. 'So, you think I'm ready then?'

He shrugged. 'Dunno, we'll see won't we?'

It didn't exactly inspire confidence, but I was used to people having low expectations of me, and I was used to surprising them, I thought cockily.

191

I had tenacity, it was my new word, it meant 'grim determination'. I had tenacity to keep on going, and I was beginning to think that with a little tenacity, I could do anything I set my mind to. Tony on the stall was right. He'd said if I could succeed at school, what couldn't I do?

I sat back and relaxed, warming to the challenge as the taxi moved through the dark wet streets towards our destination.

The house we arrived at was posh! It was so big I held my breath as the taxi pulled through the wrought iron gates into the drive.

'Here?' I gasped

Cal laughed. 'Here,' he said.

The tyres made a crunching noise on the stones as we drove up. It was only a short drive, not the golden gates and sweeping lawns of my imaginary father, but it would do, and a shock of excitement ran through my body.

I wished Baz could see it. To keep him at arms length I had seen less of him recently, it was the only thing I could think to do to keep him safe. Once this was all over I promised myself I'd see him *every* night. Although I still hadn't figured out how I could get out of what ever 'this' was.

We got out and stood on the doorstep and Cal pressed the bell. I wondered if a butler would open the door but I was disappointed when it was opened by a balding man wearing glasses and a green 'v' necked pullover.

'Gerald!' Cal boomed, as if the man were on the other side of a crowded pub rather than standing right there in front of us.

Gerald beamed. 'Cal my man, please *do* come in.' He was as posh as the house.

We stepped into a disappointing hallway, I had expected a sweeping staircase and a chandelier, still it was big. The hall was long and wide with at least four doors leading from it and a large stair case wound up from the back wall. A door underneath the staircase straight ahead of us was open, and I caught a glimpse of a huge flagstoned kitchen and a conservatory beyond that.

'The other gentlemen have already arrived and the room is prepared. I've had Mrs Fenick put some refreshments in there, tea, coffee, wine, beer, as well as a few plates of food in case we get...peckish' he said, as he led us down the hall to the door on the right.

'She gone now?' Cal asked.

'Oh yes, as requested all staff have left the premises.'

Staff! So he might not have a butler, but he had 'staff'. *Dead* posh.

When we reached one of the dark wood panelled doors Gerald opened it and stood back.

'Please,' he said, gesturing for us to enter.

Cal went first and I followed. I didn't see anything at first because of his bulk but as he stepped into the room I gasped as my feet sank into the sumptuous burgundy carpet.

Leaded windows ran the length of the far wall draped top to toe in gold brocade. Below the window stood a long dark cabinet with a range of plated food. The light from two heavy chandeliers glinted off a set of silver pots which I assumed must be the tea and coffee Gerald had referred to.

But the piece that dominated the room was the dinning table in the centre, it must have been big enough to sit twenty people and when I quickly counted up the chairs I discovered to my satisfaction I was right. Twenty.

My attention turned to the two men sitting at the far end of the table drinking red wine. Pernod Paul I knew, but the other man was a stranger to me. I was taken with his dark wavy hair, olive skin and big brown eyes. He reminded me a little of David Essex, which was nice. I assumed he was the one I was auditioning for, him and perhaps Gerald.

'Allow me to introduce you,' said Gerald, stepping forward. 'Johnny Caldwick, Rupert Wainwright. Rupert is *very* interested in your offer, as am I of course.'

The two men nodded at each other from different ends of the room.

'Would you like something to drink?' Gerald asked. 'Perhaps a little wine for the lady?' he turned to me, it was the first words he had addressed to me and I found I couldn't speak.

Cal glared at me and I swallowed. I couldn't let him down now, a lot was riding on this. I coughed to clear my throat.

'I'm fine, thank you,' I said, hearing the feigned posh clip to my voice. Cal smirked at me.

Rupert stood up. He was taller than Cal, though much leaner. He walked along the length of the table towards us without taking his eyes off me. It made me feel twitchy and my throat went dry. I prayed he wasn't going to ask me any questions.

He stopped in front of me and looked me up and down. 'Shall we begin?' he asked me.

I looked at Cal and he nodded so I started. I knew what was expected of me, I'd rehearsed it a thousand times now and I'd been naked in front of John at the pub and Pernod Paul now. Still I faltered as I undid my blouse.

'She's nervous,' said Rupert. 'How charming.'

'She's new to it,' Cal explained.

'I like it,' said Rupert and licked his lips. I looked down at the burgundy carpet to avoid looking at any of them and continued to unbutton my blouse.

193

The room was warm so when I removed it and stood in my bra I didn't feel the loss quite so much as I did at Cal's.

'Is that it?' Rupert said, his voice soft.

'Skirt too, love,' said Cal.

I put my hands behind me to undo the clip. It was then that Rupert reached out and cupped my left breast. I took a sharp breath in and caught Cal scowling from the corner of my eye.

'We need to check the goods,' Rupert told me. 'See what we're getting for our money.'

I nodded mutely and waited. He squeezed and rubbed my breast for a few moments and then dropped his hand. He turned, 'Gerald,' he called. 'What do you think?'

Gerald was now seated at the large table watching, his eyes squinting through his glasses. 'Very nice,' was all he said.

Rupert turned back to me. 'Continue, please,' he said.

I unfastened my skirt and let it drop, then stepped out of it, the way Cal had told me to.

Rupert smiled. 'Neat,' he said.

Cal had warned me many times that my face needed work so I forced a smile. Rupert laughed and I suddenly felt foolish. My mind went blank and I didn't know what to do next. I glanced over to Cal and he nodded encouragement, but I didn't understand what he was encouraging me to do.

'And the rest, lass,' he said, impatiently.

I put my hands behind my back to unhook my bra then Rupert held up his hand.

'Wait! I'm not sure we want to see it all today,' he turned to Gerald. 'Or do we?'

'No, no, no Rupert, you're absolutely right. Don't want to rush these things, spoils it you know? This is something to be...savoured.'

'Quite.'

Rupert turned and stepped forward, he was so close I could feel the heat off his body. I found it disturbing. It was one thing to practice with Cal and a few of his mates, but this seemed a whole different thing. More serious somehow. Then I reminded myself that it would be, it was an audition. They were like an interview, they were meant to be serious.

'Will she take it?' he asked.

'Steady,' said Cal.

'Just the mouth,' Rupert said, brushing my lips with his thumb then slipping it into my mouth.

It tasted of soap, which was a relief, but I still didn't like it. It was rude.

'I said steady, Mr Wainwright.'

He pulled away, laughing. 'I'm just kidding.'

194

'Still, it's a shame,' said Gerald. 'I'd pay good money to see that.'

'Consenting?' Cal asked, he seemed suddenly interested.

I had no idea what they were talking about.

'Of course! Good god man, what do you take me for?'

'I wouldn't be bothered either way,' said Rupert, and he looked at me in a way that made me feel as if he would devour me right there and then. My insides quailed.

'I take it the meat is...unseasoned?' he said.

'Of course,' said Cal. 'It's sweeter that way.'

'Quite,' said Rupert.

I was standing in my bra and pants and these guys were talking about meat!

'More wine anyone?' asked Gerald, and Rupert returned to the table.

'You can get dressed now,' Cal told me, and joined the men at the table. 'You got any beer Gerald old man?'

As I pulled my skirt on I was full of questions, but I knew better than to ask anything in front of the others, I'd talk to Cal in the car on the way home.

When I was dressed Pernod Paul put me in the car and told me to wait. I sat and watched him disappear into the house wondering how long they would be.

During the wait I decided it was time for a frank conversation with Cal. I was confused about what I was getting myself into. It seemed a long way from the modelling we discussed on the market stall that day. Something felt wrong, and I was determined to get to the bottom of it.

'Do you think I got the job?' I asked him as an opener, testing the waters on the way back.

'You did alright.'

'But do you think they'll hire me?'

'Dunno. They've got others to see.'

'When will I hear?'

'A week or so. I don't know.'

That seemed a long time, but I wasn't sure how these things worked.

'What did he want me to take?'

He didn't say anything so I watched the houses pass, counting the door numbers in twos: 244, 246, 248, 250 and I started to relax. There was a break in the road and I wasn't sure if the next house was 252 or a new road name which would start the numbers again. I searched the houses as they passed, trying to find the number, anxiety building in my chest until I saw it, 258 and relaxed.

'Drugs,' he said, breaking into my reverie. The word was quiet, almost a whisper, I guessed so Mickey didn't hear. Cal trusted no one.

'Drugs?' I looked at him, but could only see his profile in the dark of the car. I saw him nod.

I leaned into him and whispered, 'Why'd they want me to take drugs?'

Again there was a long pause and I was about to go back to counting when he spoke.

'They deal, they see you as a potential customer. Don't worry about it,' he put his hand on my knee and squeezed it softly, then left his hand there.

I thought for a moment and then whispered back, 'So why did they ask about consent?'

'Just checking.'

'Checking what?'

His voice rose above a whisper. 'Jesus, what is this, twenty questions? You could give the coppers a run for their money.'

'I wouldn't want to be in the police,' I informed him, speaking normally now.

He just nodded, rubbing my leg up and down with his hand.

'I want to own a book shop,' I told him. I wasn't sure why I said it, it just popped out.

'What, like my stall?'

'Yeah, sort of, only, I want a shop rather than a stall.'

'Nothing wrong with a stall,' he told me. 'Here that Mickey?' he called out to the driver. 'My stalls not good enough for her now.'

Mickey looked in the mirror, caught my eye, laughed then turned his attention back to the road. It wasn't real laughter.

'No, no it's great,' I added hastily, realising my mistake, thinking frantically. I didn't want to get on the wrong side of Cal. 'I just want a shop so...so...so I can live above it.'

'Right,' he said. 'You'll need some money for that.'

'But I'll have it, won't I? From the modelling?'

'Oh, yeah,' he said.

My stomach did that knotty thing again. 'You said,' I reminded him.

He nodded in the dark, it was frustrating not being able to see his face, his eyes. They gave away a lot, the eyes.

'So do you think I got the job?' I asked again.

'Probably.'

Whilst I wasn't keen on the whole modelling thing and had decided to quit, I didn't know how. Cal scared me and I wasn't sure how he would react. If I was stuck in it I wanted it to be a success, to get me away from here, give me choices in life. I could quit after, when I had some money, when I had my book shop. It would all be worth it in the end I told myself.

'Course, if you really want to make money, and fast, you'd be better off doing movies.'

'Movies?' He'd said some models became actresses. 'Do you think I could?' I wondered if they had book shops in Hollywood then gave myself a shake. Of course they did!

'Sure you could. Are you interested?'

'Absolutely!' I said.

It wasn't until later that evening, when I was lying in bed alone with my thoughts that realisations began popping in my mind.

He wasn't a legitimate business man, and nothing he did suggested it. I had been a fool to have ever believed him.

If he was a legitimate agent surely he'd have an office, a secretary? He most definitely wouldn't have a gun. As for movies, how had I been so gullible? How had I even *thought* that it was mainstream stuff? God, it was so obviously now that he'd meant porn.

My mind reeled back over the last few months as it reorganised events in light of this new information and realisations dropped in one by one, building on each other.

I had spent months taking off my clothes in various places, for various men, being touched up, gawped at, pawed, groped, humiliated, all for the promise of a modelling contract that was never going to materialise!

I had been tarted out! The dirty fat old bastard, and his scummy mates, had been getting cheap thrills off a young gullible fool. Me!

And did my mother know about it? Of course she fucking did! That's how we got the electric back on, the new television, her extra booze money...oh god.

It was too awful to even think about. Tears formed, and I pushed my face into the pillow, unable to believe she could do this.

I had thought Cal had my back. I thought my mother would use Baz but not me...how could I have been so stupid? I wept my humiliation out quietly into my pillow and when that was done I braced myself for what was to come.

I might be young and alone, but I was no longer gullible, and this was going to stop. All I had to do now, was come up with a plan.

# Monday

### Lottie

'I hate this,' Poppy declares, throwing down her pen.

They are discussing how they can make the most of the likely opportunities that will arise in the next twelve months as a result of political policy changes.

'It's always the same. The North East gets shafted by the Tories.'

Lottie sips her coffee and waits for Poppy's storm to pass. She's vehement but it rarely lasts. It can be quite intimidating at first, all that passion and anger wrapped up in a red crew cut and doc marten boots, but Lottie is used to it now.

She has heard it said that their sector, the charitable sector, is made up of, and led by, damaged people, and taking a step back and looking at the pair of them, she thinks there might be more than a grain of truth in it.

Poppy's tirade is interrupted by a knock on the office door and moments later Sandra puts her head round, clearly anxious.

'Everything okay?' It isn't, Lottie can tell just by looking at her, and Sandra isn't easily phased.

'Lottie, sorry to bother you but the police are here and they want to talk to you. They say it's urgent.'

'The police?'

She nods.

'Okay, put them in the meeting room and I'll be there in a minute.'

She turns to Poppy. 'Sorry about this.'

'No worries. I'm taking it she's not referring to the reformed 80's band?'

Lottie smiles. 'I doubt it.'

'So what you been up to now?'

'Nothing, that I'm aware of.'

'They probably heard the news that we're planning another night out.'

'Are we?'

'No, but I think we should.'

'D'you want to wait while I sort this out or shall we reschedule?'

'Laters. I've got paperwork up to here,' she indicates just below her nose. 'I'll have a chat with Sandra on the way out and fix up a date.'

'Thanks,' Lottie says, and leaves Poppy to pack up and find her own way out.

As she makes her way to the meeting room her stomach starts to churn. What could this be about?

She hopes, when she reaches the door, that Dave Saunders from the the partnership meetings isn't there. He's a bit of a prick and she doesn't want to see his smug face, but as she enters the room she's disappointed.

She nods. 'Dave,' then turns to the policeman she doesn't know, extending her hand. 'Hi, I'm Charlotte Logan, the Manager. I believe you wished to see me?'

'PC Jeff Walker,' he says, taking her hand.

'Shall we sit down?' Lottie suggests, and they gather round one end of the long table.

'So, what's this about?' Lottie asks. She suddenly thinks she knows, but hopes she's wrong.

'We've had a complaint, Lottie.' It's Dave.

'About?'

'That you've been harassing a family.'

'What? That's impossible. We have the strictest procedures in place to protect both our staff and our clients. We also have a very robust complaints procedure should any client feel that are not being properly supported.' Lottie realises she sounds a little pompous, a little like Miriam in fact, and the thought makes her smile genuinely for the first time in a long time. The next comment removes it.

'The complaint is about you.'

'Me?'

'Apparently you sat outside the Craig family's house and then followed two members of the family to another address where you sat outside until they left, and then you followed them back home again.'

'Well, I...how do they know it was me?'

'They didn't. They reported the car. The description and number plate are registered to you.'

'I don't know what to say,' Lottie sat in silence, her mind whirring.

She sits, feeling like her fourteen year old self in front of the truancy board. Only this time she can't blame her mother.

'Were you in the vicinity of the Craigs' house on Saturday evening?'

She frantically tries to think of a lie. What can she make up? Car stolen? Lent it to someone? Complete denial? What proof do they have, it's her word, a professional, against them - addicts and thieves. My god! When did she start thinking of them like this? Maybe always, deep down... So what is she doing here, in this job. She's one great big lie, she's one great big hypocrite.

'Mrs Parker?'

Lottie takes a breath. 'I wasn't there.'

'Can you tell us where you were?' asks Dave.

'At home, I think...I guess.'

'But you're not sure?'

'Can you remember where you were every minute of the day?' She hears the sharp tone her voice has acquired. The two policemen exchange a glance.

'Do you have any idea why they think it was your car?'

There's something about the way he asks, the look in his eye.

'I have no explanation for that,' she says, slowly, carefully.

The two policemen stand. 'We have further investigations to make and may need to come and back to talk to you,' says Dave Saunders.

'Of course,' she says, her heart thumping. Surely it was just a matter of time before they found out, then she'll lose her job, her reputation, everything.

Dave Saunders turns to exchange another glance with his colleague, and his profile against the sun coming through the window causes a jolt of recognition in Lottie.

She nods. 'Ironic, isn't it?' she says, assimilating this new piece of information, as she shows them to the reception.

'What's that?' Dave asks, at the front door.

'The fact that they have so little to do with police on the estate, and yet...they know *exactly* how to work the law. You'd think they were getting some...inside advice, wouldn't you?' She looks at him pointedly.

Dave blanches. 'They know their rights alright,' he says, but she's made herself understood.

As she returns to her office she passes Miriam and wonders how long it will be before she knocks on the door.

Lottie isn't sure, as she packs up an hour later, if the lack of the knock is more ominous. Still, she has more pressing questions now. Like: why were Bob and Jenny visiting Dave Saunders, and what, if anything, is she going to do about it?

On the way home Lottie takes an unplanned detour and finds her car back in the hospice car park. She gets buzzed in, signs the register of visitors and finds her way easily to the small ward her mother is on. It's only her third visit but, as Jenny the volunteer said on her first visit, you soon find your way about.

She enters the ward and walks to the end of the bed, watching her mother. She is sitting up, has the magazine Lottie brought last time open on a trolley table in front of her, and looks stronger than she did last time, but then she was asleep and looked close to death, so it wouldn't be hard.

Lottie just stands there, she doesn't have anything to say, no words. She wasn't expecting to be here. She hasn't even brought grapes this time.


**Andrea**

200

Andrea isn't sure how long Lottie has been standing there, but when she looks up from her magazine she's confronted with a face like a slapped arse.

'Hello Lot.'

'Mum.'

'So you came back then. Grab a pew if you're staying,' Andrea tells her.

Lottie sits on the edge of the chair as if she doesn't want to commit to anything.

'You okay?' Andrea asks. It's what you say to make conversation, break the ice, and there's a lot of ice to break.

'I'm fine. Tough day at work that's all. You? How are you?'

'Dying,' she says, then laughs at her own joke. Not too hard, she doesn't want to start coughing and scare her away again. 'What do you do?'

'I run a children's charity.'

Andrea doesn't really know what this means. Her only experience of charities are shops and the christian aid envelope that came through her door once a year, collected a week later by women poorly dressed and past their best.

'What's the weather like?' Andrea asks. She's not interested in the weather, but it's another source of conversation.

'Not bad, considering the time of the year.'

Andrea looks at her closely. Is she really her daughter? Where's the resemblance. Who is this dowdy looking woman who would fit right in with those woman who collected those envelopes? Why doesn't she say something, make some bleeding effort? Make it easier on a dying woman.

'You look like me,' Andrea tries.

'Oh please, spare me.'

'You do!.'

'We both know that's not true.'

Andrea falls silent, realising there is no way in. Charlotte sits there upright, intractable, solid, everything in fact, that Andrea despises.

'You put me through hell,' Lottie says out of the blue. *Such a drama queen.*

'Oh you do exaggerate, Lot.'

'Really? Then what about the time you stole from Cal and left me to face him?'

'I don't remember.' Andrea says, but Lottie insists on reminding her. She wonders if Lottie is going to lay all her sins before her feet. If she is, this is going to be a very tiresome visit. Tiresome and long. *Be careful what you ask for.*

Still, dying or not, it's time for the truth.

'Why did you want to see me?' Lottie asks, breaking into her thoughts.

'Eh?'

'Why did you phone me, why did you ask me to come here?'

Andrea shrugs lightly. 'It's what you do isn't it? When you're dying. You make up with the living.'

Lottie turns and looks her squarely in the eye and says, 'Have we got that much time?'

Acid drops drip from her tongue and burn Andrea.

'You tell me,' Andrea says, right back at her, like a shot. *She never was as quick as me.*

'God, where do we start?' she asks, and Andrea's heart plummets. She hasn't got any fight left in her. Not that she ever was that brave. But she did do one brave thing in her life, and she wants Lottie to know about it and the need makes her go soft.

They have changed places, Lot has gone hard, whilst Andrea has softened. Andrea was soft once, a long time ago, before life toughened her up. Funny, how life cycles like that. Soft and young, hard and middle aged, soft and old...Life toughens you up and then, as you realise how little time you have, and you start to understand what really matters, it tenderises you again. How can she explain it?

One thing's for sure, this isn't going to be as easy as she thought.


## Lottie

'So, you came back then,' is her mother's greeting.

She really is the most despicable woman. Why did she call? What possible good could come out of it? Unless, like every other time in her life, she just wants to break down everything Lottie has struggled to build. One last kicking before she goes.

'God where do we start?' Lottie says, when her mother tells her she wants to make up.

Her mother doesn't say anything to that, she could never deal with anything remotely like emotional intelligence, waved it off, dismissed it as navel gazing or drama. Drama! The words; kettle, pot and black, come to mind.

'Where do we go from here?' her mother says, eventually.

'I don't know.'

*Is this another of her games?*

The air boils between them, the hatred putrefying the atmosphere. Or is that just her? She glances at the nurse checking something on the side, or perhaps pretending to be busy in an effort to be inconspicuous.

She has the same feeling creeping up on her every time she comes. Utter despair. The utter pointlessness of it all. *Why I am here, what is the point?*

Andrea lies rotting, waiting. Lottie sits watching, waiting.

'Why did you call?' she says again, exasperated. It's the only thing left to say.

Her mother's words both surprise and chill her.

'To tell you the truth,'


### Andrea

'To tell you the truth,' Andrea says, knowing it's rather dramatic but what the hell, it's allowed, she's dying. 'It's not all been about money you know, not *all* of it, and I want to tell you about your father.'

Lottie turns ghostly pale at the answer. Well, she did ask. Typical of Lot. Always the same, wanting to know what's going on and then when you tell her she freaks out.

Andrea tries to soften it. 'There's things I thought you should know.'

Lottie nods. 'My father?' she says.

Andrea should have expected it she supposes. She wanted her to see the bigger picture, but she always did hone in on the detail.

'You know who he is? All those years...you told me you didn't...' her voice comes out in a whisper, Andrea can barely hear her, you'd think it was *she* who was dying, the weakness of her.

'Yes, well, I had my reasons.' Andrea tells her, hoping to cut through her mood.

'Who is he?'

This was the question Andrea has avoided all her life, so naturally she stalls.

'Was,' she says.

Andrea wishes she hadn't done what she did, but she did, and at the time she thought she had good reason. She knows now that she has never had a good reason for any of the decisions she's made and it's time to face the truth of it.

The realisation hurts.

### Lottie

The pain of her loss over the past eleven days floods her. Was it only eleven days ago when she got the call from her mother, when she still had hopes of a family, the belief in a faithful husband, a spotless career?

She stands and glowers at the woman. Lottie read somewhere that hate is just the flip side of love, heads and tails, love and hate. She doesn't know if it's true, but her mother evokes strong emotions and she's afraid of what she is capable of doing to her if she stays.

So she turns and leaves. It's all she can do right now. Her mother will have to die alone. It's what she deserves, because those small losses when she was young, hurt just as much as the rest.

### Lottie 1980

My heart sank when I looked at my January timetable and saw double religious studies with Rowell. I wondered what the delightful Rowell had in store for me today. Although I was doing better at school, I still struggled with some subjects, *and* some teachers. Mr. Rowell in religious studies was one of those. He was always looking for something to pick on, it went beyond the usual stuff, my poor grades and attendance, besides, all that was improving. I was now convinced it was personal, he had labelled me a write off like so many others in authority, and now he had it in for me, and he took every opportunity to embarrass me in front of the class.

I had taken to sitting at the back, quietly keeping my head down. I didn't want to answer questions because he ridiculed me, even when I was correct he managed to twist it round so I looked like an idiot. I had decided that he was a bastard. End of. And I wasn't playing anymore.

I shuffled in and took my seat at the back. His class was one of the more well behaved, probably because he was such a bastard, and when he began talking the class hushed into silence. After a few minutes I began to relax, my eyes wandered to the window and across the green fields as I wondered again what I would say to Baz this evening. It was not a conversation I was looking forward to.

Two days previously Mum had demanded I finish it with Baz.

'He'll get hurt again, Lottie,' she said, referring to the recent beating he had taken, and I knew this was no manipulation, it was the truth. She seemed to have conveniently forgotten that she was the reason he was in the picture in the first place, but arguing with her was not going to change anything.

Baz didn't know who had jumped him and he didn't suspect I had anything to do with it, but I knew. And I knew, from what my mother had said, that he had got off lightly. Keeping him at arms length hadn't worked so I could see no choice, but my stomach clenched when I thought about packing him in.

He made my world a better place and a blanket of sadness sat heavily on my shoulders when I thought about him not being there anymore.

'Charlotte? Charlotte?'

It was Rowell and I sat up straight. 'Sir?'

'Glad you could join us Miss Parker,' a couple of people sniggered.

He walked back and forth in front of the class before stopping by his desk and turning to me.

'What does the Bible say about Christians?'

'Can you be more...specific, sir?' It was my new word.

'More specific?'

'Yes, sir. It's a big book, it says a lot about a lot of things.' It was a serious question but now I was the one who got the laugh.

'Are you trying to be funny, Parker?'

'No, sir. Just trying to answer the question.'

'If you'd been listening you'd have the context.'

'Sorry sir, clearly I wasn't and you've made your point. If you could repeat the context I'd be happy to answer your question,' more laughter from the class.

'Don't get smart with me, Parker'

The class now looked at me to respond. I'm not sure why I did what I did next. Perhaps it was because it was a stupid thing for a teacher to say, perhaps it was because I was fed up of being pushed around, perhaps it was because of Baz, probably because I was showing off and it was an easy goal.

'Sir, make your mind up. I'm either funny or smart, or perhaps I'm both? Anyways, aren't we here to get smart? Isn't that your job?' I saw his face change colour. I felt powerful and, knowing what was coming next, I saw another opportunity for a score. 'Let me guess, go to the headmaster? Did I get the context right, *sir*?'

'Get out, Charlotte Parker! Go directly to the headmaster's office. I'll deal with you later.'

I stood and packed my bag as slowly as possible to cause the most amount of irritation, smirking to heighten his irritation.

'Hurry up, girl!' Rowell said, rewarding me for my efforts.

205

Finally packed up, I stomped out of the class heading straight for the main doors. I'd have to face the wrath of Rowell sometime, but with only one more lesson left for the day there was no way I was going to spend time standing outside the headmaster's office waiting for it. I was smart, Rowell had just told me so. My joke brought a small smile of satisfaction to my face but it didn't last long.

I might as well see Baz sooner rather than later I reasoned, get it over with. As I started the long walk home the blanket of misery wrapped itself around me again, and an hour later I was standing on his doorstep.

When he opened the door his face filled with delight. Seeing his broken eye made me wince. The left eyeball was red instead of white and it made me cringe to look at it. At least the swelling along his top lip had gone down.

'Hi! Hang on I'll get my coat,' and he was gone.

Moments later he was back and we were heading down the road.

'Reccie or park?' he asked.

'Park,' I said. It was closer and there were benches. I thought this was something best done sitting down.

As we made our way to the swings I rehearsed again what I was going to say. I had decided to tell him the truth, explain the situation and why we had to finish. Truth was always best. Course, he might be appalled at my taking off my clothes, he might hate me forever and walk away and not want anything to do with me, but it was a chance I had to take.

We sat on the swings, side by side in silence. He must have known something was up but he didn't ask. I glanced at him, sitting nonchalantly on the swing, rocking back and forth ever so slightly, and I knew I couldn't. He would argue. He wouldn't hate me and walk away. He had too much damned stupid pride for that. He would try to fight my battle for me, and inevitably suffer the consequences. I couldn't let him do that.

With a sinking heart I knew I was going to have to be savage with him, make him think I didn't like him, even though it would splinter me inside.

Decision made I steadied myself on the swing, looked at the ground in front of me and blurted it out. 'Baz, I'm packing you in.'

The swing stopped and he looked at me. 'You're what?'

'You heard.'

'You can't.' He laughed, nervous.

I glanced at him. 'I just did.'

'But...why?' I saw the pain and confusion on his face and looked away.

I shrugged. 'I'm...' I didn't want to finish the sentence, I didn't want to strike the final blow.

'You're what?' he prompted.

I took a deep breath and looked at him, keeping all expression from my face. 'I'm bored with you.'

He flung himself of the swing his beaten face twisted in anger.

'Bitch!' A drop of saliva flew from his mouth.

He walked back and forth for a few moments and then turned to me. I remained expressionless, immobile, moving slightly outside my body in order to keep my equilibrium. My new word.

'You're a fucking slapper,' he said, then strode off, his hands plunged deep in his pockets, head down. At the end of the path he turned back and shouted. 'And I only went out with you because of Johnny Caldwick. You ugly fucking bitch.'

I watched him walk away and returned to my body. The pain in my chest I could accept, that was where your heart was so I was expecting that. What I wasn't expecting was the ache in the pit of my stomach, like I hadn't eaten for a week. A gnawing ache of hunger that I knew, no matter how much I ate, would never go away.

I watched him disappear into the dark and let fat tears fall, remembering his words and wondering if any of it had been real.

# Tuesday

### Andrea

Andrea barely feels the edges of her body anymore. She is slowly being effaced. The pain, once you get used to it, isn't so blinding. She was never good with pain, but now she has to be there's something quite pure in it.

She's frightened. Not of death. She came to terms with that weeks ago. No, She's afraid of going before she's settled everything. But what if the stupid cow doesn't come back? There's no guarantee that she'll return. She always was a law unto herself. Not rebellious, but she had her own ideas of right and wrong, fairness and justice, and she was never afraid to follow her own path.

She might just stay away to stop Andrea finding peace, and quite frankly, she wouldn't blame the spiteful little cow. Still, she hopes Lot comes back, before it's too late.

She hears them, the staff. They think she doesn't but she does. Whispering in the corridor. She knows she hasn't got long. They hover, like white death angels, waiting. They don't know how stubborn she is. She has to hold on. She has to wait for her Lottie. She has to come back. She has to.

### Andrea 1981

'I don't have sufficient evidence to bring in the police in an official capacity. We need some sort of physical evidence.'

Mark and I were back in the Durham pub. The faded decorations were gone and it looked the better for it.

'So you didn't come up with anything with John at the pub?'

'Nothing.'

'What about an anonymous tip off?' I said.

Mark shook his head. 'Too dangerous. We already know how slippy Cal is. They'll investigate and find nothing, then he'll start asking questions about who tipped them off.'

Mark was right and my heart sank.

'So what do we do?'

He shook his head. 'I'm not sure yet, but you need to get her away from him.'

'How do I do that?'

'Send her to a relative or something, anything. And we need some evidence.'

'What kind of evidence?'

'Some of the photos would do it, although it still might be difficult to pin it on him.'

'Not with my statement surely.'

He shrugged. 'Possibly, and Lottie's.'

'No, not Lottie's'

'Andi-'

'Not Lottie's.' I was clear about that. I'd done enough.

Mark sighed and rubbed his face. 'Okay, fine.' It didn't sound fine but I didn't care. 'Perhaps we can talk to someone else who's been involved in this?'

'I don't know who else is involved. It was luck I stumbled on John.'

'Then you're going to need to start talking to her about what's going on.'

'I don't know what to say to her.' To my horror I felt tears prick my eyes.

'Andi,' it was soft and he reached out to place a hand on my arm.

I pulled away.

'Sorry,' he said. He took a breath and then carried on. 'You need to keep a close eye on things. If anything else changes, call me.'

'What sort of things?' I asked, taking his lead and returning to the task in hand.

'*Anything.*'

'Like?'

He shrugged. 'A change in routine, she goes to a different place, something new is discussed, anything at all. *Anything* that makes you feel...wrong.'

'The whole thing feels wrong.'

He nodded and we both knew he was biting his tongue. It didn't need to be said.

'Okay?'

'Okay.'

'And if you can get any physical evidence at all, or get someone to agree to talk, let me know immediately. But be careful. Don't go following him around again. You were lucky, but next time...'

I nodded. He didn't need to finish that sentence either.

He stood up. 'I have to go, you want a lift to the station?'

'No thanks, I could use a walk.' Truth was, I didn't trust myself in a car with him alone and I had done enough damage for now. I couldn't risk losing Mark's help. Maybe after this was all over...I turned the idea over in my mind slowly until Mark interrupted me.

'We'll talk soon,' he said. 'And Andi, talk to her.'

I watched him leave, then returned to my drink and my thoughts.

So we had a plan, of sorts. All I had to do was keep Lottie safe until he could figure something out. Maybe I'd send her to Babs'. She would be safe there.

The second part was harder. I didn't know who else was involved and I didn't know how I could get the photos from Cal. Besides, as Mark had said, them alone wouldn't be much help in nailing him. Anyone could have taken them.

So, we had the beginnings of a plan, a poor one. I should have sent her to Babs' the minute I got home.


### Lottie

Lottie's chair, Chris Wallis, sits in the seat opposite her. He's a man unafraid to take up the space he occupies, which is just as well as he is a man of some girth, made of a 'significant number of dinners, pies and beers', as he is frequently fond of saying. He has an unapologetic habit of slapping his belly, as if he is showing off some accomplishment. Intelligent eyes sit beneath a balding head, shaven and equally unapologetic.

Lottie liked the man the instant she met him at her interview. His air of self confidence gives him a measured, composed air, that she likes. More importantly, it is reassuring to her, and she needs that right now.

'It's a lot of nonsense,' says Chris. 'But we have to follow protocol.'

'I understand, Chris. You obviously know the circumstances?'

He shrugs. 'Of course.'

There is a moment's silence and she can't help feeling that Chris is holding something back. She says nothing, waiting, knowing it will come out eventually if she remains calm. For all his good points Chris does have one small flaw, if it could be considered a flaw. He feels he has to protect women, that they have to be handled gently. It is frustrating to her sometimes, but she decided some time ago that there were worse traits he could have.

Lottie sips her coffee, her calm exterior belying the tumult of emotions that lay beneath the surface. She replaces the cup in its saucer, enjoys the bitter deep taste of the coffee, rearranges her fringe, and waits.

'There is something else,' Chris says eventually, as she knew he would.

'Oh?' she says, and smiles encouragement.

210

He seems to take heart from this and launches into what has been on his mind.

'Miriam didn't just complain about you not following protocol and, truth is, from what you've said, I'm not concerned about it.'

'But there *is* something you're concerned about?'

Lottie's heart beats faster and she blames the strength of the coffee, even though it hasn't had time to take effect. Does he know about the police visit yesterday? Already?

'She, well, I don't want to worry you too much about this, Lottie, but...'

'Go on,' she says, holding her breath, waiting.

'She's made an official complaint against you personally.'

'About?'

'She claims you've been bullying her.'

As if that isn't bad enough, his next words feel like a punch in the stomach.

'And she's not the only one.'

Her brain scrambles through her staff, unable to conceive of any of them accusing her of bullying. She is a good manager. She cares. She spends time with her staff. Miriam she can understand, there is no love lost between them, but who else would claim she was a bully? Who would even have grounds to?

When the answer comes it hits hard.

'Hilary Collins,' says Chris.

She nods, and despite her best efforts the room blurs a little.

'I'm sorry, Lottie.'


An hour later, Chris's reassurances still ringing in her ears, she packs up her desk. It's barely eleven in the morning.

They agree that whilst the investigation of the grievances are underway she'll take a few days off work.

'You've earned it,' Chris booms.

He isn't wrong, so why does she feel so rejected?

The official line, once she has succinctly and professionally confided in her chair, is that she has been given compassionate leave to attend to her dying mother. It seems, to her surprise, that her mother has finally helped. It will hold the gossipers in the sector at bay when the investigator arrives to question the staff.

She doesn't tell him about the police visit. She had every intention of doing so when he arrived, but with his revelation she suddenly feels on shaky ground, as if Chris might remove his support, as if the police visit might add credence to the complaints. Was it lying? Probably, lying by omission, withholding evidence. It *felt* dishonest. *The bigger the lie, the more punishment you'll get.*

The complaints have sealed her fate. She knows the police won't be back. Dave will make sure of it. They have an understanding. Lottie knows why Jenny was there, and he knows she saw it. *We are uncomfortable bed fellows.* Gross misconduct for both, the end of careers and reputations.

As she loads her bag she shudders at the decision she has just made and her mind scrambles to make sense of it all. The complaints have forced her hand, she reasons, that's what has pushed her to do the unthinkable. Lie.

No, she realises, it's worse. By turning a blind eye to what's going on she is, in effect, selling out Jenny.

She feels the mercury in her blood rise. It is so unfair, so unjust, so...unnecessary. Hilary has no idea what she's done, what she's forcing Lottie to do.

Unable to contain herself any further, she leaves her half packed bag on her desk, and makes her way down the corridor to the other side of the building to the open plan office Hilary shares with the three other family workers.

She stops at the door way, taking in the piles of paperwork on the desks, the posters, pot plants and family photos that adorn each desk, personalising the area for each worker.

Hilary's desk sits in the far corner, a poster of Daniel Craig is pinned to the wall by her chair, a dancing purple flower sits on her desk. She remembers Hilary bringing it in to her office, showing her how it danced when you clapped your hands. The memory squeezes her heart. We do have a good relationship, or at least, we used to.

Ben and Stu look up from their desks at her standing in the door way. Ben is on the phone and smiles, raises a hand in welcome. Stu smiles too, raising his eyebrows in enquiry.

'No, Hilary?' she asks.

'Day off,' Stu tells her.

*Clever.*

'Gone shopping for a dress for the wedding.'

'Wedding?'

He looks surprised. 'Hers,' he says. 'It's only six months away.'

Lottie blanches at her mistake, but covers it quickly by laughing. 'Of course,' she shakes her head and rolls her eyes, then stops. *Don't over do it.*

'Want me to give her a message?'

She shakes my head, 'No, it'll keep, it's fine, thanks.'

She retraces her steps slowly back to the office. How did she forget about Hilary's wedding? Had she mentioned it recently? She rattles through her memory but can't recall anything.

Perhaps she's not connecting to the staff the way she thinks. Is she so wrapped up in her past that she has failed to read the signs here, in the present? Has she really been too forceful about Jenny? Has she underestimated Miriam?

Inside her office her hands tremble as she finishes packing up. Sandra appears in the doorway and Lottie looks up, forces a smile.

'Hi,' she says.

'Chris just told me,' Sandra says. 'I'm sorry.'

'Thanks,' she's not sure if she's talking about the official line of her compassionate leave, or the complaints. Then she realises it doesn't matter, both will be known to the staff soon enough.

'I'll just be on the end of a telephone if you need me,' Lottie tells her.

'I've cancelled all your appointments.'

'Thanks,' she says, as she picks up her bag.

She moves through the offices like a woman condemned, but when she gets into the car she is surprised to feel relief. She is not expected to return here anytime soon, and no one expects anything from her. She thinks about Dan, then her mother springs to mind. Well, not from here anyway.

She lays her head on the back rest of the car and closes her eyes. Dan, what is she going to do about Dan?

With steely determination she opens her eyes, plucks her phone from her handbag and dials Dan's number.

'Hi,' she says, when he answers. 'We need to talk.'

They avoid their usual cafe in Norton and Dan suggests they meet instead in a pub in Yarm. It's a much longer drive for both of them but Lottie forgives him the moment she climbs out of her car.

She had forgotten how quaint the market town is, and as she steps over the cobbles and passes the elegant buildings that host an array of boutiques and funky shops, she makes a mental note to see if Poppy fancies a shopping trip sometime soon. *Very* soon.

As Lottie enters the pub she sees Dan sitting at a table in the corner and her resolve not to drink disappears when she sees two glasses of red wine in front of him. She was going to pass. She has a ton of work to do, then she stops short, remembers she doesn't and the thought is both uplifting and terrifying. *What am I going to do with myself?*

Dan stands to greet her, smiling, nervous.  He leans forward and kisses both cheeks.  It feels as alien and formal as if he'd shaken her hand. She catches the scent of his aftershave, CK One, she remembers buying it for him for Christmas and the memory barbs.

Lottie settles in the chair and studies the menu, even though they both know what she'll order.  She tries to convince herself that she fancies a salad.

'Fish and chips?' Dan asks.

'No,' she says, to spite him.  Then after a brief reconsideration she capitulates, feeling her skirt dig into her flesh in protest.  The wine, the fish and chips, he always did tempt her.  Still, she could say no.  She *is* a grown up.

While Dan nips to the bar to order she reaches into her bag for her work phone to clear a few emails, then she remembers she left it behind, along with all the paperwork, files, and other paraphernalia she usually carries around with her.

When he returns she is sitting back in her chair, taking in her surroundings, trying to look relaxed.

'So, this is a far cry from Stockton High Street,' she says.  She has rehearsed what she was going to say while he was at the bar.  'People wouldn't believe you if you told them.'

'It's like every borough though, isn't it?  Everywhere has its pluses and minuses.'

There's a hiatus in the conversation and it makes Lottie nervous. Ordering food was a mistake.  The wine was a mistake.  This whole thing was a mistake.  She should have just sent him a solicitor's letter.  After all, that's what she wants...isn't it?

'The charity shops in Stockton High Street seem to be the only thing thriving at the moment,' he says.  'But we've got a major restoration plan in store for the High Street,' he adds.

Lottie nods and the conversation dies again.  She sips her wine.

'You're like salmon swimming against the tide,' she says, finally. 'You know, cut after cut from central government.'  Sip, sip, sip, snip, snip, snip.  It's the longest conversation they've had in months.

He nods.  'Did you know the biggest employers of public service workers are in the North East?  The last time the Tories were in power...'

Lottie stops listening.  She's heard his political rant before.  It's never changed in all the time they've been together.

Dan stops and the conversation grinds to a halt again, until she can't stand it anymore.

'We need to-' but Dan interrupts her before she can finish.

'Thanks for seeing me, Lot,' he says.

'Don't call me that.'

214

'Sorry,' he pauses. 'I'm glad you called. I missed you.'

It brings back a lifetime of them, and it cuts her, slices like a blunt knife.

'I was...' he looks round and Lottie waits, wondering what he's about to say. 'Worried about you.'

'I'm fine,' she snaps, pushing distance between them.

She's alone, he isn't, she reminds herself, and grief bubbles deep inside, banging like overheated water in a copper tank.

'I wanted to tell you how sorry I am...for...everything.'

She takes a swig of the wine to swallow what she's afraid might come up. The tannins shrink her tongue. She is too raw for this, too much has happened, she has lost too much and she fears it will undo her.

His physical presence is too much of a reminder. The warmth of his body, the smell of his aftershave, the taste of his tongue, all come flooding back till she thinks she might drown in the memories, and the pain of betrayal reasserts itself. She wonders if it will ever stop.

'You and me, well...' he doesn't finish his sentence. Is he leaving a gap for her to fill?

She refuses. Let him sit there with his words and his excuses and his pathetic attempts at an apology. Sorry isn't enough. You can't just do stuff and say sorry and get away with it. It isn't fair. There has to be some...retribution, some punishment, something to balance it all out. You can't just say *sorry*.

Lottie looks at his contrite face, his sheepish eyes and realises he's never been particularly nice to her. Not in the way other husbands are. He doesn't bring her flowers, he doesn't leave her notes or take her places or unexpectedly smile at her or cuddle her or do much for her at all in fact. Not for a long time. Not since the early days. She thought it was the fertility thing, but really he's never been there for her. Not really.

She has forgotten why they got together in the first place. Lottie thinks of Murtaugh and the rush of blood that coursed through her body on meeting him. How the words stopped in her mouth when he walked into the conference room, how her heart pounded in her chest when he approached her. Nothing like that had ever happened with Dan.

'Lottie?' he says, and she realises that he's been talking all this time and she hasn't heard a word. She hung on every one of Murtaugh's words, could repeat them verbatim now if anyone asked.

It is both of them, she realises, and now it has to stop.

'What do you think?' he smiles.

'I want a divorce,' she says, and as soon as she says it she knows it's true.

Dan's face registers shock and without another word she stands up and strides out.

Thirty minutes later she is sitting on her sofa. The heating isn't on at this time of day and she can't motivate herself to get up, besides, the cold squeezes into her and she enjoys the numbness it brings.

She feels too old to live anymore, life is too heavy. Is this what her mother feels like?

Why did she have to die in this slow and painful way? Bringing up the past to haunt them. Couldn't she just have gone off and died somewhere, got run over by a bus, fallen over a cliff, drowned in a lake, died peacefully in her sleep even?

But no, not her. How could Lottie expect anything else? Her mother would die as she had lived, with the maximum amount of drama, and causing the most inconvenience and pain as possible.

Lottie breathes deeply, the cold air burning the edge of her nostrils as it enters. She breathes again, it isn't helping anymore. She tries to recall those therapist's eyes, anchoring her, keeping her safe, but she fails, they're not really here. No one is here anymore. She is alone. Her career and marriage are in tatters. Any hope for the future lost.

As if on cue Emily, the neighbour's child, wails through the wall and it occurs to her that her death, like her mother's, would not have much of an impact. Oh, they'd be shocked for a while, a day, maybe two, some people even a week, Poppy and Dan for example. But then life's events would take over and they'd forget. Today it's tempting. Then nothing would matter. The black rises, clouds her head, threatens to drag her deeper into the abyss.

She stands up, she must do something otherwise…she picks up the phone and dials the only person left in her life she can trust, remembering she has survived bad days before.

### Lottie 1981

There was never any love lost between Tracey Craig and myself so I should have expected the ramp up on the assaults as soon as I packed Baz in. Still, for some reason there was a tiny part of me that hoped she wouldn't start up on me again. Maybe I hoped she'd got out of the habit, found some other poor soul to inflict her fat stupid bitch ways on. I was wrong. Everywhere I turned she was there, making up for all the lost grief she could have inflicted on me during the truce called when I was Baz's girl. All the lost opportunities were not lost at all, simply stored for future use.

I hadn't had the best day. I'd had the usual run in with Rowell, still unable to understand why the miserable bastard hated me so much, but that was par for the course. What upset me was my run in with Mr Wright.

I liked him. I could have a laugh with him usually but today...

It had started innocently enough. He had called me to stay on after the class had finished and asked me *again* if I'd given anymore thought to taking the exam. I had been my usual 'truculent' self. That's my new word it means 'eager or quick to argue'. I was never 'truculent' with my mother of course, only my teachers, and only when I thought they were wrong.

'Charlotte, it's not funny you know?' There was a bite to his words that I didn't like.

'Didn't see anyone making a joke, sir.'

'I see, it's going to be like that is it?'

'Like what?'

He sighed and his forehead creased. 'I have better things to do, you know,' he snapped, 'than hound your sorry little hind?'

'Then stop,' I said simply. It wasn't as if I was asking him to bang on about exams.

He shook his head, his face growing redder. 'You are a silly little girl at times,' he said. 'Go on, sod off.'

With that he dropped into his chair, slapped a student's exercise book down in front of him and began marking it.

I hesitated, unsure what to do, he'd never talked to me like that and it didn't feel good, but I wasn't sure how to smooth it over. I watched his red pen scour a tick deep into the page.

'Charlotte?' he said, without looking at me.

'Yes, sir?'

'Go away please, I have nothing further to say to you.'

I left with my heart in my stomach. It was one thing to have a run in with Rowell, but to upset Mr Wright. It made me wonder if it there was something wrong with me.

Maths had been the last lesson of the day and I trudged down the long corridor, jostled by the crowds. It would be just my luck to have missed the bus home too, that would just put the cherry on top of the shit cake of a day I'd had.

I didn't miss the bus, but I ended up wishing I had.

My bus was just signalling to pull out as I rounded out of the school gates. I began to run and raised my hand, waving frantically at the driver, there was no way he couldn't see me. This one wasn't a bastard and stopped for me, the doors hissed open and clanked hard against the sides as I jumped on.

'Cheers,' I said as I showed him my bus pass.

The doors closed behind me and the bus lurched forward, causing me to grab onto the poles to stop me from toppling onto someone.

'The bitch's as pissed as her mother,' a voice called across the seats.

I didn't need to look to know who it was and my stomach clenched. Really? I asked whoever was up there in the sky, could you not give me a fucking break for once in my life. I really wasn't in the mood for a confrontation, not tonight. My patience was pulled painfully thin and I thought that today of all days, it might just snap.

I ignored the catcall and looked quickly along the seats, praying for that break, but there were no seats at the front. I made my way slowly down the aisle, holding tight to the metal bars on the back of each pair of chairs, to the last remaining seat, two rows from the back and right in front of Tracey Fucking Craig.

I dropped into the seat, pulled my heavy bag onto my lap and waited for the inevitable, wondering what form it would take this time. The material prickled the backs on my knees where my skirt ended.

I waited so long I forgot what I was waiting for and my mind wandered to Mr Wright and how I could make it better with him. The answer was obvious, take the bleeding maths exam of course. I thought about Baz and wondered where he was and how he was, safe I hoped, at least something good had come out of finishing him. I missed him, no it was worse than that, I had this hollow feeling inside as if someone had removed an organ or something, but it was for the best. My mind turned to the situation developing with Cal and the future. I had to get away from him and I needed a plan.

I was dragged from my thoughts when my head was wrenched backwards and hit the metal grab rail at the back of the seat. Instead of it righting again it stayed there, was held there I realised, by Tracey's vice like grip, her fist wrapped into my hair.

I opened my eyes to see her looming over me, forming a spit ball. She slowly dropped it onto my cheek, my stomach lurched. I was powerless to do anything.

'Hello, bitch.' she said. 'I hear you've been fucking with a mutual friend of ours?'

She meant Baz.

'I have a message for you,' she said, rolling another glob of spit together and letting it drop onto my face. It fell onto my forehead and slid

218

towards my left eye. I closed my eyes which only heightened the feeling of the warm spit on my face, sliding into my eye socket.

'Yes, you bitch, close your eyes and pray.'

She savagely let go of my hair forcing my head forward violently so I hit my head off the bar on the seat in front of me. Except for the rumble of the engine the bus was silent, everyone holding their breath, glad it wasn't them.

Mercifully we had reached her stop and I watched her make her way down the aisle to the middle of the bus and the exit. I used the sleeve of my blazer to wipe the spit off my face.

The doors slammed open and a group of kids got off, laughing, Tracey among them. I looked out of the window as the bus pulled away just in time to see Tracey turn and draw her finger across her throat.

Great, I thought, that's all I fucking need. If I was going to survive the next few weeks it looked as if I was going to have to fight back, regardless of the promise I had made myself.

Could my life get any shitter, and was 'shitter' even a word? If not it should be. Still, at least it was Friday.


### Lottie

'Thanks for coming over,' says Lottie.

'Not a problem. I was thrilled to have a reason to cancel my three o'clock.'

Lottie smiles and they fall into silence.

'I need to go back and see my mother.'

Poppy stirs her coffee over and over in silence, waiting.

'We have some...unresolved stuff.'

Poppy nods and places the spoon by the side of the cup.

'I can't keep...hiding or...running away.'

'Oh I wouldn't be too quick to dismiss them as management techniques. They've worked for me,' say Poppy, as she picks up her coffee

Lottie smiles. 'I think I'm going to leave work too.'

'What?' Poppy drops her cup into the saucer. 'You can't let a couple of complaints ruin your career, Lot.'

'I'm not. I need a change of direction. The complaints have just...focused me, that's all.'

'What will you do?'

Lot shrugs. 'No idea, but I do know I want to be out of the line of work I'm in.'

'Maybe you can foster kids?'

'Hardly.'

'Why not? You've always wanted them. We both know there's a massive demand for foster homes.'

'More kids than homes at the moment.'

'So...?'

'I think I need to get my head sorted before I try to help anyone else. There's Dan for a start. That hasn't been resolved.'

'You took all the money, kicked him out and told him you want a divorce. Apart from the paperwork, job done I'd say.'

Lottie laughs. 'What would I do without you?' she asks.

'Oh I don't know. Get drunk less? Eat the right foods? Not know the recipe for fuck off pie?'

'Exactly.'

It feels as if the cloud has lifted, that she won't drown after all. She glances at her watch.

'There's still time,' Poppy says.

Lottie nods.

'Want me to come with you?'

Lottie shakes her head. 'I need to do this on my own,' she says.

Lottie sits in the car outside. She knows she has to go in, knows that if she doesn't there will be no peace for her in this lifetime. Knows in fact, that whether she goes or not, she will lose herself in that dark place again, so she might as well go into it with some of the answers.

Andrea must be still alive, she reasons, otherwise she would have been notified, wouldn't she? It was only yesterday that she walked out, yet it seems like much longer. Time can play tricks like that.

She takes the key from the ignition, pulls her bag onto her shoulder and opens the car door. It feels like she is moving through cotton wool, that everything is in slow motion, as if she is only half in her body. She is holding on tightly, like a helium balloon that needs a tight grip. She doesn't want to slip outside as an observer. She needs to be present for this.

She locks the car and feels her feet eating up the distance to the entrance, one step at a time. She rings the bell, sees the receptionist on the other side of the door peer at her, checking before she releases the doors. They open with a swoosh and the distinct smell of hospital assaults her nostrils, disinfectant and the underlying faint stench of death and misery.

She signs in against an innocuous welcome from the receptionist.

'Do you know where you're going?' she asks.

Lottie nods and turns away.

She listens to her heels clacking off the linoleum as she makes her way down the long corridor, passes a volunteer pushing a squeaking book trolley, a nurse and doctor heads together talking as they walk, an old couple holding hands. Reaches the silver door of the lifts and watches her finger press the large button that lights up red. Waits. Hears the clanking as the lift responds. Waits some more as it gets closer. The doors open and she steps in, turns, presses the button for the next floor. Waits as it makes the slow journey heavenwards. It would be quicker to take the stairs, if she knew where they were. The lift stops with a jolt, the doors struggle open and she steps out onto the area furnished with armchairs, two seater sofas and a coffee machine.

She turns right and makes her way to the ward. Through the double doors, along the corridor passed the private rooms, into the four bed ward and then she stops dead. The bed is empty. *Her* bed is empty. Lottie is too late. Her mother has gone.

*Revenge had never worked, and the best laid plans...*

## Lottie 1981

Over the weekend I had made the decision. I *would* fight back, I'd had enough, and the old Lottie was back. She was only coming for a brief visit I decided, once I'd beaten Tracey to a pulp everyone else would leave me alone.

In Monday's registration Tracey loomed over my desk.

'Morning, bitch,' was her greeting.

I continued to sit, waiting for the right moment. I was going to enjoy this I thought, and I didn't want to rush it.

'What's the matter...cat got yer tongue?'

Her two lackeys laughed. I eyed them and decided they were no threat. If they decided to step into help I could handle them. It was Tracey I needed to take down, and quickly.

'I said-'

'And I heard you,' I growled.

'Ohhh, get you. What happened, grow a pair over the weekend?'

I stayed silent, letting the rage build, letting the red slowly seep over me.

'I'm fucking talking to you,' she said, leaning right over me, her soft bulge pressing into me, her cheap perfume adding fuel to the mist inside me.

221

As soon as her head was lent right over me I lowered mine and then jerked it back hard as I stood up, making contact with her face as I knew I would.

Tracey stumbled back from the force.

'Fight! Fight! Fight!' chorused from the class.

I spun round to face her, bringing my fist round and hitting her straight into her nose with all the force I could muster.

I knew I'd made contact and done some damage by the shock of pain that ran up my arm from the contact. She staggered back again and I noticed from the corner of my eye that Susan and Jane took several steps back. I didn't need to worry about them.

My blood was up now and I stepped forward and hit Tracey again in the face with my other hand, she took another step back and fell into the desk and slid to the floor. I should have stopped there, but I had four years of anger lashed down that had been released and I couldn't have stopped even if I wanted to. And I didn't.

I punched and kicked her again as she lay writhing on the floor. The chorus started to fade, this wasn't so much fun for them to watch. I meant business. One kick landed in her kidneys, and I knew how much that would hurt, not only now, but later too, my mother's beatings had taught me well.

I leant over, picked her head up by her hair and pulled my fist back to punch her in the face when rough hands began pulling me off her and back into the room.

I stood, my arms held on either side by teachers, my breath ragged and surveyed the damage. I looked round the class at the shocked and horrified faces of my classmates that encircled me, and I knew I was in trouble.

The teachers escorted me and Tracey to the headmaster's room and after Tracey was cleaned up and we answered a few dull questions Tracey was sent home to recover and I was given six lashes of the cane.

It was worth it. No one would ever try anything with me again, though I suspected I'd never make a friend for the remainder of my schooling either. Fuck 'em. Fuck them all.

The next day I arrived at Cal's with swollen knuckles. It was our first session since the 'audition'. He didn't comment when I told him what happened.

This was my other plan and I hoped it would go marginally better than the one I had implemented the previous day.

I had decided to 'vacate' my body. It was a trick I had learnt to do when Mum was dishing out one of her more severe beatings. I left my body and stood to one side, literally watching. It never bothered Mum, she's just enjoyed the release of beating me, didn't mind if I was present or not, which

I now understood a whole lot better, so I wasn't sure it would work with Cal, but it was worth a try.

'Come on, lass, you look half dead,' he said, after about thirty minutes. 'Smile for fucks sake, the punters don't want a photo of a corpse.'

He was still pretending he was teaching me. He wasn't to know that I had figured out his game. My body smiled. It was a fiendish grin. I could see his point, no one would want that, surely? Which was precisely my point.

Cal dropped his hands and gave my naked body a shove. It fell onto the sofa. I could see, now that Cal had shown me pictures of naked women, that the breasts were still buds, they hadn't matured, I would probably have a decent pair of breasts when they finished growing and the thought pleased me.

'Put your clothes on,' Cal said.

I watched myself dress, not yet ready to return, it was not pleasant to be in there. Out here, nothing could hurt me. Cal sat on the sofa and beckoned my body. I watched with interest, wondering at this new turn of events.

'What's up?' he asked. 'It's bad for business this...this..attitude.'

Though I didn't want to, I could see it was time for me to return. My body could move, but not hold a conversation properly, besides, this was part of the plan. I could see I had an opportunity to get myself out of this. I slipped back in and took a breath, righted myself before we continued.

'I'm...I'm..I'm not sure I'm cut out for this Cal,' I whispered. I had to be careful, deliver my lines in the right way.

'Not cut out for what, lass?'

His tone was gentle, kind even, but I knew, I had seen that dark underbelly of him, and I was careful where I tread, mindful that one wrong step could wake it up. I couldn't afford to make a mistake.

'I think I might be wasting your time,' I ventured.

He laughed and laid a hand on my leg. I held my body rigid so as not to flinch at his touch.

He patted my knee. 'You'll be fine, now off home.'

I was not disappointed. A few more vacant sessions and he'd let me go, he'd get bored and move on. He didn't have any alternative.

I smiled as I sat back in the taxi. It was all going to work out.


Cal had more patience than I gave him credit for, but by the end of our third session he was beginning to lose it.

'Seriously Lot, this isn't any good love.'

'I know,' I said, pulling on my clothes. I kept my face suitably contrite, but my insides were dancing to Singing in the Rain. I'd seen the film on telly the previous night and it had sang through my head all day. It was my talisman, I decided. This was how I was going to approach life in future, no matter how difficult things might get, I was going to dance in the rain.

'That's what I was saying Cal, I just don't think I'm getting it.'

'Do you want it, love?'

This was the question I'd been waiting for, the one I'd held my anger in check for, the reason I'd continued with more nude session with Cal, and I had to handle it carefully if I was going to escape. I was so close now.

I slumped onto the sofa as I pulled my sock on. 'Honestly Cal?' I maintained a long pause. 'Yes, I do. It's just, I don't seem to be able to do it. I'm no good at it. The book stall? Yes. This?' I shook my head, then reached for my trainer.

Cal didn't respond. I tied my lace, my head down, hiding behind my hair in case I smiled, my heart hammered. Finally, when I was suitably composed I sat up and faced him.

'What are we going to do?' I asked.

He smiled and his response froze the blood in my veins.

'I've got one last idea love, don't you worry. After all, we don't want your little friend Baz to get hurt, do we?'

I shook my head. So he wasn't safe then, I had finished it for nothing.

'Good. Wear that dress I bought you next time.'

I nodded. He smiled.


## Lottie

Lottie stands, unsure of what to do next. It is done, all over, and she is left with a sea of emotions she cannot even begin to name. Left with the desire to curl up and weep, a desire to lash out and maim, a desire to be left alone and to be held at the same time.

She doesn't know how long she stands there before a voice says, 'Can I help?'

Lottie turns and recognises the volunteer Jenny.

'I...I don't think so,' she tells her.

'You after your Mam?' Jenny asks.

'Yes,' it comes out as a whisper, as if she can no longer speak her name now she has gone.

Jenny's reply brings Lottie back from a far away place.

'She's been moved to a private room,' she says. 'Follow me. I'll show you'

Lottie follows as if she is in a dream, sleep walking down the corridor and into a room where her mother lies in the bed, still alive, but she sees at a single glance, barely.

She looks up at Lotte. Her eyes widen and Lottie thinks her mother might start to cry, and she is so relieved to see her mother she thinks she might too.

For a long time they just drink each other in.

'Mum.'

'Lot.'

She moves closer to her bed, taking her in, seeing her properly for the first time. Lottie knows her mother is doing the same thing. It's as if they've known each other for ever yet have just been introduced. She hates to say it, but it's like seeing a long lost love. You know they're not the same person you once loved, that they are different, a stranger, but there's a bond of shared memories that keeps you connected. It's twisted, she abhors it, but it's true.

Lottie walks in and sits in the chair beside the bed, not taking her eyes from her mother. Eyes locked in astonishment they drink in each other. She can't believe her mother's still here, her mother can't believe she's here. It must be the first time in her life where they have shared the same emotion. No, not the first time, perhaps the second.

As they sit in the silence, the past comes roaring back between them, no longer something they can move around, no longer something to negotiate, no longer something they can ignore.

'Tell me,' her mother says.

So she does.

## Lottie 1981

When the cab arrived that Thursday I was wearing *the* dress and I shivered as I stepped out into the cold, snow was forecast and you could feel the tightness in the air. I wobbled down the path in my new high heels, my clutch bag clamped under my arm.

'Alright Cal?' I asked, his face was set in stone and tension oozed from him, setting my teeth on edge.

He nodded, but said nothing more. We drove in silence, until I couldn't stand it anymore.

'Where are we going?' I asked, trying to keep my voice light.

'Photo shoot,' he said.

My stomach somersaulted. 'Really?'

He nodded.

'For who?'

'It's a try out,' he said.

'For who?' I asked again.

He looked at me for a long time, and for a moment I thought he could read my mind, see into my soul. I shuffled, glanced out the window, looked back at him.

I forced a smile. 'Well?' I said.

He glanced at the taxi driver and then gestured to keep quiet. It wasn't Mickey so I nodded and sat back, looked out of the window, trying not to let my imagination run away with me. He was bound to try something new, I thought. He'd said as much when we last met. I just had to keep doing what I'd been doing, and soon he'd see it was a waste of his time. And if this really was a photo shoot, well, it was bound to the be the end of it all.

The taxi took us out of town. I'd assumed we were going to do a photo shoot in a friend's studio, so when we turned into a trading estate about fifteen minutes later, I was reassured. Perhaps this was legit, I thought. Well, as legit as Cal got anyway.

'Just drop us here mate,' Cal said, after a few minutes. We got out beside the road and started to walk.

'Where are we heading?' I asked. I stumbled a little, unused to the balancing act that was required to wear heels. *I must look drunk.*

'Not far,' he said, his face still stone.

I felt the same foreboding I did when my mother wasn't pleased with me, but reassured myself it was just my programming. What more could Cal do to me?

We walked along the deserted road of the trading estate and passed a couple of turns. My feet began to hurt, I didn't understand why Cal had made the taxi drop us off so far from our destination, and when I asked him he just said, 'Not sure where it is.'

The units were becoming less and less attractive. We had passed the prefabricated ones built recently, and were now moving into the estate where the old broken and derelict brick ones stood, waiting to be replaced.

Eventually Cal took a turn to the left towards a disused unit with broken windows and weeds growing out of the wall. He wrenched the peeling door open and stepped to one side letting me enter first.

It had a dank musty smell and I could hear water dripping in the distance. It was cold and dim inside, and looked nothing like the setting of a photo shoot to me.

I remembered seeing a few urban shoots in Jackie magazine recently, perhaps that was what this was about, the thought that I might be on those pages, instead of one of the thousands of girls reading them, sent a frisson of excitement through me despite my resolve that it ended tonight. Then I remembered that the girls in the magazine wore clothes and it fizzled out.

I looked at Cal quizzically.

He smiled. 'We're meeting Mickey,' he finally explained.

I followed him down the corridor until we reached a large disused room. There were no cameras, no lights, no props, just two men standing together. They turned to us as we entered.

One whistled and I recognised Pernod Paul straight away. 'Nice dress,' he said.

The other one was a dark man with a receding hair line and crooked teeth, he had a lopsided leer on his face. It took me a few moments to realise it was Mickey, I had only seen the back of his head before.

'Yeah, nice,' he said. It was one of the few times I had heard him speak.

'Alright lads, that's enough.'

My blood started to pump in my ears and I stopped. Where were the cameras? The lights? The make up artist and photographer? This wasn't a photo shoot, this wasn't anything, except an abandoned old trading unit. But before the thoughts could register with my limbs, before I could act, Cal grabbed my arm, his fingers digging viciously into my flesh, and pulled me across the room towards the men.

'Micky, take her will you?' he said as shoved me into the man's arms.

'No problem,' he said, his hot breath on the back of my neck.

'Have you got the money from them?' Cal said, to Pernod Paul.

'Yeah.'

'Right, where's the car?' this was directed at Mickey.

'Round the back, as instructed.'

'Good. Let's go, I don't want to be late.'

Mickey and Paul walked either side of me, holding tight to my arms as Cal led the way back out of the unit and round to the side of the building. Their fingers dug deep as we picked our way through the debris of pipes, bricks and piles of rubble, and my feet started to hurt.

At the back among the trees sat a gold car like the one on The Sweeny. Mickey pushed me into the back seat and Paul sat next to me. Cal got into the passenger seat and as usual, Mickey drove.

'Cal?' I said, my voice shaky.

'What?'

'Where are we going?'

'I told you, a photo shoot.'

He'd said that before, he'd said that when we arrived at the unit, 'but you said-'

'Shut the fuck up and do what you're told.'

My heart beat fast and my mouth dried up. This didn't feel right, but more questions would only exacerbate Cal's already dark mood, so I sat back and watched the scenery pass by. Pernod Paul twitched next to me and I wondered whether he had some affliction, or if it was because he was as nervous as me.

After about twenty minutes I started to recognise the area and realised we were returning to the Posh House. My heart began to really pound now and my palms were sweating. I tried to reason my fear away, this was where I came for the audition, obviously they were happy with me and now wanted to do a photo shoot. I recalled some of the photos Cal had shown me, one in particular with the woman reclined on a four poster bed across silk sheets. Perhaps that's what they had in mind.

But I could not stop thinking about Rupert and the way he had looked at me, as if he were ravenous and I was a tasty snack. Mickey pulled into the drive and my body started to shake.

'Cal...I...' but I couldn't get any words out.

Pernod Paul pulled me out of the back of the car. It was harder to walk on the gravel drive in my heels so I held onto him.

'That's better, eh?' he said, patting my bottom. Mickey arrived at my other side and we three stood behind Cal at the front door.

The door opened and Gerald went through his reassuring spiel again about his staff as he led us to the same room as we had been in before.

Pernod Paul and Mickey guarded me on both sides as Cal shook hands with Rupert and turned to face another man.

'Johnny,' said Gerald. 'Let me introduce you to Nathan Hamilton. Our newest...investor.'

'Good to meet ya,' Cal said, taking the man's hand.

He was the oldest in the group, with silver grey hair and deep wrinkles round his blue eyes. He was also the shortest man I had ever seen. Not quite a dwarf, but he wasn't far off. He must have been about an inch shorter than me.

'Beer?' Gerald asked.

Cal laughed. 'You learn fast, Gerald,' he said.

'I try,' Gerald said, smiling as he poured a bottle of lager and passed it to Cal. 'And how about our lovely Lottie?' he asked.

All eyes turned to me and the heat I felt from all the attention must have been how Icarus felt when he flew too close to the sun.

'I'm...I'm fine, thank you.'

'Well, at least sit down little lady,' said Nathan, pulling a chair out. 'It's nice to finally meet you.'

I looked at Cal and he nodded. I went and sat down, Nathan stood behind the chair and placed his hands on my shoulders. 'I've been hearing great things about you,' he said.

I didn't like his compliments, I liked him touching me even less, but I couldn't afford to get too involved in what was going on. If I cared, if I got emotionally involved, I'd find it difficult to vacate my body, and that would ruin everything.

Today, this ended, this whole sorry mess I'd got myself into.

'Does she meet expectations?' Rupert asked Nathan.

'Oh yes,' he removed his hands and came to stand in front of my chair. 'Exceeds I would suggest.'

Rupert turned to Cal. 'Gerald tells me you've been successfully supplying him for some years now.'

'We aim to please the punter,' Cal said.

'He certainly does that,' said Gerald, grinning.

It all became clear and I finally understood what they were talking about. I couldn't believe I had been so naive, and my mouth ran dry with the realisation, this was not simply taking my clothes off and being touched up, this was going to be much more.

I stood and started to cross the room towards the door. I don't know what I was thinking, they were hardly likely to just let me walk out.

Mickey caught up with me and grabbed my arm.

'No you don't little lady,' he said, his fingers pressing spitefully deep when I tried to wriggle free.

I opened my mouth to protest but found I couldn't. I had lost my voice, crippled by the rush of realisations hitting one after the other.

'So, Gerald, as you've been the man who made it all happen, might I suggest that you go first? Show us how it's done,' Rupert said.

'I'll pass on this one. This sort of thing is a bit...rich for my blood,' Gerald said, to my relief. 'I'm more of a...spectator when force comes into play.'

Micky wrestled me back into the chair, though there wasn't much of a struggle. I was too stunned, my brain still processing all the information.

Cal turned slowly, facing the men. 'So who *will* be first then? You've paid good money for this gentlemen, silly to be shy now.'

'I want to see what we're buying?' Nathan asked.

'Of course. Cal, Nathan wasn't present at our last meeting. He's only our word for the quality of the goods.'

'No problem,' said Cal.

I watched him walk across the room towards me and he winked when he reached me, as if we were in some kind of ruse together. I wondered if we were, if this was some almighty hoax on these posh men.

'Come on, Princess,' Cal said, as he reached out and pulled me into a standing position. 'Let's get your dress off.'

When I didn't move Cal growled out my name. When I still didn't move he reached out and pulled off my dress over my head.

I clung onto some faint hope that this was a genuine audition, or perhaps a joke, or something other than what I knew it was. I just couldn't believe Cal would do this, that my mother would allow it. This sort of thing didn't really happen.

I stood in my knickers, my breasts bare, and Cal circled his finger as a request for me to spin round, so I did, taking in the room and the escape points. There were the windows hidden behind the curtains, and the door we'd come in. There were no other doors or exits that I could see. Cal stood directly in front of me, and Mickey and Pernod Paul were either side of the door, so I ruled that out, which left the windows. On the plus side we were on the ground floor, on the negative the curtains were drawn so I couldn't see how they were latched or even the size of them. I tried to remember what they had looked like from outside but nothing came to mind.

*Think, Lottie, think!*

Rupert, Nathan and Gerald moved closer to get a better look and a wave of fear and hopelessness loosened my insides, despite my plotting there was no escape, unless I intended fighting through Cal, Mickey and Pernod Paul.

'Very nice,' said Nathan. 'Very nice indeed.'

'More where that's come from,' Cal said, and for a moment I forgot he was talking about me.

Nathan came and stood beside me, with my heels on he only came to my shoulder. He reached out and brushed a finger across my nipple and I lashed out, swiping his hand away. I held my breath, wondering what he was going to do next.

He looked at me, raised an eyebrow and laughed. That made me mad and I took two steps backwards towards the door.

'Going somewhere?' asked Rupert. He stood behind Nathan, smiling.

Cal came up behind me and put his hands on my shoulders, pushing me forward gently. It reminded me of the first time I met him, when my mother's hands had pushed me forward to greet him. Had she known? Did she know what she was offering me for? I pushed the thought from my mind, she couldn't, she wouldn't.

230

Nathan moved forward again and this time took my full breast in his hand. Involuntarily I stepped back into the wall that was Cal. That's when I knew for sure that there was no escape, that whatever these men had planned for me was going to happen, and I swallowed hard as it occurred to me that I may not escape alive.

When I found my voice and screamed. One of the hands left my shoulder and clamped tight across my mouth wrenching my head back into Cal's chest. I could smell his sweat through the small breaths I took through my nose. He lowered his face and whispered into my ear.

'Make a scene and you'll only make it worse for yourself. Relax, it won't hurt as much that way.'

The room blurred as tears formed.

'Now, I'm going to remove my hand and you're not going to scream anymore, are you?'

I nodded agreement, he removed his hand and I gasped a deep breath though my mouth.

'Tears, Cal?' asked Rupert.

'Novice,' he said. 'Comes with the territory.'

'I suppose,' he answered, sounding bored.

'Please, don't,' I begged, pleading to their better nature. 'Please?'

Nathan laughed. 'How quaint,' he said.

'Mickey,' Cal said, letting go of me.

Mickey grabbed me and I pulled away from him, trying to get my arms free, until he took my feet from under me and slam dunked me onto the floor. One of my shoes flew off. All the breath left my body and I lay on my back, helpless.

'Careful Mickey, for fuck's sake!'

'Sorry Cal, she's a handful.'

Cal leaned over me and pulled my other shoe off. I was still catching my breath and there was nothing I could do at first, but moments later as my breath returned I found enough strength to kick out. I didn't make contact, and my leg flayed around in the air.

'Mickey, hold her,' Cal ordered.

Mickey dropped down and pinned my arms back. I bucked my body, then kicked out again, desperately trying to release his hold on me.

'Christ! Paul, give us hand here,' Mickey said.

Another pair of hands got hold of my legs and held me down. I threw my body from side to side, heaving it up and twisting.

'I'll get one side, you the other,' Mickey said.

Paul grunted, and as they moved into different positions to hold me down more effectively I knew I couldn't stop what was about to happen. I held back my tears, they wouldn't do me any good. Instead I looked up to catch Paul's eye, I thought there was a flicker, a moment of softening, but then he looked away and I knew he would't help me.

I was now prostrate, naked apart from my knickers, legs apart. The carpet scratched my skin and I noticed the chandelier over head, thought how pretty it was, decided I would never buy one.

'Gentlemen,' Cal said. 'Dinner is served.'

Rupert and Nathan came and stood on either side of me. I noticed Gerald stayed in the background and thought perhaps he wasn't as keen as the others, maybe he would intervene? My hope faded with his next words

'Although I'm not a joiner, Mr Caldwick, I do enjoy a good show. I wouldn't mind a film of this lady in action...when she's had a little more...experience of course. I'm not so keen when they're in that no man's land.'

'No man's land?' asked Pernod Paul.

'The bit after they've been broken in, but before they've learnt to ride properly,' said Cal.

Gerald laughed. 'Precisely.'

Cal addressed the room. 'Who's first?'

The words ripped through my body and I thrashed beneath the men's grasp, desperate to be free.

'Now, now, this isn't how I envisaged it, as exciting as it is,' it was Rupert's silky voice and I hated him.

'I aim to please,' said Cal. 'Just tell the boys how and where you want her.'

'I'm not one to be picky, but partially clothed was *not* what I paid for,' this was the dwarf and I hated him more.

Cal nodded to Paul and Mickey and they released me. I had a moment of relief before I realised why. They began to pull at my knickers and I lashed out with my clenched fists, catching Paul on the chin and knocking him backwards.

'You daft bastards! Why didn't one of you hold onto her?' shouted Cal.

'Ha ha! She *is* a feisty one,' said Gerald.

Mickey slapped my face and the sting rang round my head, disorientating me for a moment.

'Steady Mickey, just go steady.'

'Sorry Cal,' Mickey said, as he fought to hold me down. 'She's just a bit ouff-'

I cut his words short with a smack under the chin with my knee, but before I could scrabble away Paul was up and on my shoulders, pinning me down.

'Come on, Mickey, move yerself,' he shouted.

Mickey righted himself as I writhed beneath Paul and flailed out with my feet, unable to connect to anything.

I heard chuckling from the watching men which only seemed to incense me further. How dare they! How dare they! I lashed out again, hard this time and this time my foot hit something hard. Pain shot through my big toe turning my insides to vomit and I realised we'd scuttled across the floor and my foot had hit one of the legs of the heavy dining chairs. I held my breath, waiting for the intensity of the pain to ease, and the two men took advantage of this pause and ripped off my underwear then dragged me back to the centre of the room. I felt tears forming in frustration as my tired limbs flopped.

Rupert came and stood over me, one hand in his pocket, the other holding a glass of red wine. 'That was a lot of unnecessary fuss young lady. Relax, you might even find you enjoy it.' He smiled and took a sip of his wine before turning and handing the glass to Cal.

He bent down beside me, sliding a hand down my body and pushing a finger into me, making me wince. He removed his finger, winked at me and then stood up, retrieving his glass from Cal.

'She's dry as a bone,' he said.

'Tight though,' Cal said.

'More than likely,' Rupert sipped from his glass as he looked down on me.

'So how d'you want to do this?' Cal asked.

'Well,' Rupert said slowly. 'I did have other plans but given her...energy I think we'll need to revise them.' He turned to dwarf 'Heads or tails?'

I couldn't see the dwarf properly and I heard him say something, but it wasn't clear.

'Well, it seems her little display has put them off their game,' he leaned down to me. 'Good show little one.' He turned to Cal. 'Just me. I'll break the little filly in.' He laughed, 'you should be paying me.'

I heard the tinkle of a belt buckle and his zip. 'Hold her still,' he said, and before I knew what was happening his weight was on me.

I could feel the roughness of his clothes between my legs, the smell of red wine on his breath and my body froze. There was nothing I could do. So I waited for the inevitable, and as I had no experience of what was about to happen, I braced myself for I knew not what, wishing I hadn't said no to Baz..

He pushed against me, once, twice, grunting and jerking on top of me, stabbing me with something unyielding. When it came it slit into me causing a sensation that ripped into my stomach, and tore up through my body. The movement of his thrusts caused the tears I had held back to spill down the side of my head and fill my ears.

My body went limp and my mind misted over at the second full thrust. I remembered a rag doll I had years ago, Flossy. Another thrust brought me back. The pain heightened and my mind groped for a foot hold to keep my sanity. I tried to remember the words of singing in the rain, but another thrust dragged me back.

Another thrust, and I found myself standing beside a man thrashing himself into a young girl, another holding her left side, a third sitting to her right, Cal standing watching, with two others beside him. It took me a moment before I realised I had moved out of my body.

Two more plunges brought Rupert to a shuddering stop, panting he collapsed on top of the girl.

'Steady,' Cal said. 'I don't want her suffocated.'

Rupert pulled himself up. 'Christ!'

'What?'

'She really *is* a fucking virgin!' I wasn't sure if it was delight or horror that caused the rise in his voice.

'That's what you paid for.'

Rupert pulled up his zip, shaking his head. 'I thought she was just...young...inexperienced.'

I looked down at the girl. She *was* young. I took in the exposed breasts, the small hairy mound between her spread legs and the blood coating the inside of her thighs.

'Didn't Gerald tell you? I don't disappoint.' It was Cal. 'Nathan?'

'Actually, the bloods up now, so don't mind if I do.'

I watched as the little man undid his trousers and mounted the young girl lying prostrate on the floor. The two men who had held her down sat back, there was no need to restrain her anymore. Nathan didn't last very long.

'My god,' he said, as he stood up, blowing out a deep breath as he zipped up his trousers. 'That *was* tight!'

Rupert laughed. 'We noticed.'

'Well, you hardly lasted much longer,' Nathan said, he sounded angry.

'Gerald? You sure?'

'No, Thank you. It's not my thing.'

Cal came forward, pulling on his belt. 'Well gentlemen, if you've finished and you don't object? I'll have a go. Clear the pipes before we talk further,' he said, with a wink.

'Go right ahead, we're finished with her,' said Rupert.

'Paul, grab hold of her will you?'

'I don't think there's any need, Cal,' Paul said.

Cal looked down at the girl, she wasn't moving, there was no struggle left.

Cal shrugged. 'Fair enough,' he said, as he knelt down to get ready. 'But stay close, just in case.'

And with that he took out his hard cock and thrust it deep into the body, jamming it in over and over again as he grunted with pleasure. It took a while and the men stood around in awkward silence, sipping their drinks, until he gasped his final thrust.

As he tided himself up he said, 'Mickey, put her in your car will you? I've got some business to sort.'

'I think, based on today's quality, we can come to some arrangement,' said Rupert.

'That's what I like to hear. You got another beer, Gerald?'

As Mickey scooped up the girl's body I found myself slamming back into it. It was broken, the pain filled my head with red, and I wondered if I could ever feel normal again.


## Lottie

Neither of them speak. They are back there, reliving those awful few days, when they were both incapable of doing anything.

Cal was a dark cloud that hung over them, and they were each waiting for the inevitable storm to break, unsure of the depth of damage it would wreck when it did. Neither of them talked about what had happened in that house, but it was in their eyes when they looked at each other, so they stopped looking.

Lottie watches her now, and can see the pain of those days etched in her eyes. She is glad, she is glad to finally see some remorse in the bitch. She hasn't had to live with it like Lottie has. Every day. Every day it lurked in the back. A shadow cast across her life that finally robbed her of her future. And her mother's selfish phone call, the one saying she was dying and would Lottie please come, has only served to bring it all back.

She lies there, dying, wanting once again something from her. Has she ever, ever in her life thought about what her demands do to those around her? To Lottie?

Right now, as she looks into the dying face of her mother, she hopes she burns in hell. She can't imagine what the bitch has to say that will make any difference.

'Now,' she says, anyway. 'You tell me.'

### Andrea

There's pure hatred on the face looking at her. She's had people dislike her in the past, and it hasn't bothered her much, a bit if she's honest, but not much. Still, she doesn't think she's ever seen anyone look at her like that. A look like that chills the blood. She can already feel the maggots feeding off her body.

It stops her. Lot won't forgive her, no matter what Andrea says, and now she knows it all, she can't blame her. She should have died quietly and just let them inform Lot after the event. Then she realises that for once this isn't about her, and from somewhere, Andrea has to find the courage to tell Lottie what she needs to know.

She opens her mouth and in a voice barely above a whisper, she starts to tell her the truth, or at least, her version of it. She starts at the beginning when Andrew met Rosie, before Lottie was even conceived...

'It was a Saturday night in the Red Lion,' she begins.

### Lottie

'When Cal brought you back, all battered and broken like that, I didn't think I could bear it. It was one thing to give you a smack when you were getting on my nerves, but to see you broken like that, half dead.' Andrea stops and points to the water on her bedside.

Lottie automatically steps forward to assist, cradles her mother's head in one hand, holds the glass in the other, watches the cracked lips sip. Her mother nods she has finished and Lottie returns the glass back to the cabinet.

Her mother lays her head back and closes her eyes. She is quiet for so long Lottie starts to wonder if she's finally slipped away, then she opens her eyes and starts to speak again.

'I realised then, it's your own flesh and blood, and I know it sounds awful now, but I realised that regardless of how many times I had wished you had never been born, suddenly I was glad you were. Really glad you were. Except...except for the mess you were in. I'd have spared you that, had I known.'

Lottie stops herself from pointing out that she *had* known. She had known what that man was capable of, she had invited him into their lives, she had put Lottie within reach of him, and she had failed to protect her.

So far, Lottie didn't see the miraculous redemption she had expected. Perhaps there was no such thing, except in soppy films and novels, perhaps in real life there was no redemption.

'I was angry with myself,' her mother continued, breaking into her bitter thoughts. 'You were due to go to Babs' the next day. If *only* I had acted more quickly. Arranged it a day earlier. *If horses were wishes...*' she looked at Lottie and smiled. Lottie didn't return the smile and Andrea turned back to looking at the ceiling.

'I didn't need to ask what had happened. I could guess the worst and didn't want to know the rest, not until today anyways. I was never very good at just...facing it, you know?'

She paused to catch her breath, gain some strength. She didn't expect an answer.

'Even Cal looked as if he knew he had gone too far this time. I just hoped that now it was the end of it. That now he would leave us alone and we could just get on with our lives.'

Anger bubbled in Lottie. How could her mother expect her to 'just get on with her life'?

'I undressed you. Do you remember?'

Lottie nodded, not trusting any words.

'I cleaned you. Cosseted you like a baby. And you were so broken and bruised you let me. It was as if you had just been born and finally, finally I had found the mothering instincts I had always lacked.'

They heard voices coming down the corridor and then fade away again as they passed through a door.

'I could blame my mother for interfering and not letting me near you when you were a baby, she constantly made me feel inferior, made me feel that, even when I did so something I was doing it all wrong. But the truth was, it suited me to let my mother get on with it. I was young, grieving and angry. I hated the baby, but I didn't hate her anymore. Do I sound heartless?'

Lottie stayed silent.

'I know I do. You don't need to say anything. After I had cleaned you up and put you to bed I went downstairs and wept until I was empty, then I drank. It was a long night, I think I even prayed a little. Prayed that if there was a god, and I'd seen precious little evidence of him, that my baby would wake the next morning. It was a long night. But the next day when I went in you were awake! You looked so...so well. I could hardly believe it. I thought it was all going to be okay. I think I might have even said that.'

'Yes, you did,' says Lottie. 'I remember.'

## Lottie 1981

I woke the next day feeling sore and swollen and exhausted, even though I had slept all night.  I had expected nightmares, but it was as if my mind had shut down.  It could barely remember anything and the little I did remember seemed dreamlike and unreal, cut images and muted noises.

I was laid in bed staring at the ceiling when mum appeared with a cup of something.

'Oh good, you're awake.  Alright love?' she asked, she was bent in supplication and I knew then that she knew what had happened.  Not necessarily the details, but she knew.

I pushed myself into a sitting position to take the mug from here, wincing as I did so, hoping it was coffee.  It was tea.  I sipped at it anyway, and found that, for once, I didn't mind, then realised I hadn't eaten or drank anything for over twenty-four hours.

Mum sat on the bed, her voice quiet.  'I've made some arrangements for you to go and stay with Barbara for a few days.'  Barbara was my cool tomboy of a cousin.  I was a bridesmaid for her and I thought she rocked, it was the last place I wanted to go.

'I'm fine,' I told her.  'I'll be okay.'  I corrected, when I realised I was lying.  I wasn't fine.

'Lot, it's for the best,' my mum said, her voice still soft.

I looked at her and for the first time in my life she looked genuinely sorry, lost even.

I practiced a smile,  'I'm okay mum,' I told her.

For one horrible moment I thought she was going to cry and the air hung tight around us, as if the earth was holding its breath.  Then she shook her head and said, 'You're going to Barbara's,' in that way that said it was not a discussion item.

I nodded and sipped my tea in resignation.

'It's going to be okay now,' she said, patting my knee.  The touch was like an electric shock and I jumped, spilling the hot tea on the bed clothes and my legs.

She jumped up and fussed around me, whipping the tea out of my hands and flapping the blankets until they cooled.

'I haven't got anything clean,' she said.

What she meant was we didn't have any spare sheets.  She brought a towel from the bathroom and tried to dry it.

''S okay,' I muttered, wanting to be left alone.

'You sure?'

I nodded.

'If you need anything just give me a shout. You best stay in bed today, get some rest,' she hovered in the doorway for a few moments. 'It *will* be okay now,' she said, and finally left.

Her words battered down on me. How could it be okay? How? The question brought images that made me shrivel. Images that my mind had not allowed me to remember until now. Images of the men who had circled me, stood over me, been inside and outside of me. Distorted images flashed. Hands, flesh, sounds, smells, words, grunts.

Anger, humiliation and shame pushed and raged inside me as I sat in bed, holding my tea. I couldn't cry. I couldn't move. I was raw and exposed and terrified, and I knew I had to do something to let it out, otherwise my skin would stretch until it burst.

The heat from the mug was building in my hand, pulling me from inside, pulling me from the rage and the darkness. I wrapped my hands round it further, enjoying the burn, the release, but it didn't last, it wasn't enough. I put the mug down, climbed out of bed, and looked underneath.

As I suspected a plate from my tea a few days ago was still there. I picked up the knife and climbed back onto the bed. Holding it in my hand, I gritted my teeth and made a tentative cut into the skin on the top of my foot. It wasn't a deep incision, but it was enough for a drop of ox red blood to emerge. I gasped. The release was instant, and as I breathed out, fat tears began to run down my face at last.

### Andrea 1981

'It's over Cal,' I told him, two days after he brought Lottie back.

When he had turned up on the doorstep my insides had shrivelled at the sight of him.

'You knew what you were getting the pair of you into,' his previous sheepishness replaced by his usual belligerence.

'Not that. *Photos*, you said. *Photos!*'

'Aw, come on, Andrea. You're not that naive.'

I shook my head. This wasn't what I believed we were doing. It wasn't. Photos, maybe movies, but not this. And we still had nothing on him, nothing.

'But she's just a bairn,' I whispered. It came out as a plea.

His reply made me shrivel even further.

'She was all woman from where I was standing,' he sniffed and hitched his trousers over his bulk of a belly. 'Besides, I've invested.'

'Oh what have you invested?' I snapped.   I knew I shouldn't, it wasn't going to help.

Cal's face went red with anger and my heart beat speeded.

'Look, Cal,' I said, softening my voice.   'Regardless of what you think, she *is* just a bairn.  I mean, have you seen her?  She's a mess.  What use is she to you now?'

'She'll pull round, given time.'

'Cal, you'll destroy her.'

'Like you care.'

'She's the only family I've got left now, Cal.'   We both chose to ignore the underlying message.

He pushed his face into mine.  'You forget love, I've seen the results of your good hidings.'

I waved the comment away.   That didn't matter in my book, nor Cal's.  We both knew that.  'Shit happens, doesn't mean I don't care about her.'

He looked thoughtful for a moment and I began to hope.

'You owe me, Cal,' I reminded him.

He shook his head.  'You owe *me*.  You came to me asking for a job and I gave you one, and extra money and you robbed from me, remember? That's how you repaid me.  Well, you started this, and you can't pretend you didn't know what you were getting her into.   This was your decision Andrea, yours,' he walked into the hallway and paused.  'I've invested, and I don't make bad investments, you understand me?'

I nodded and he left.

I stood in my hall, my broken daughter lying in her bed upstairs, no longer wondering *how* I was going to fix this, but if I could.




Later, after I'd taken some chicken soup up to Lottie, I sat on the back step for some fresh air and lit another fag, listening to Jean and Pat next door going at it hammer and tong.  I wondered if Pat would smack her, she was a pain in the arse so I could hardly blame him.  Still, it wasn't right and I didn't like hearing that crack of skin again skin.

Had they heard me going at Lot?  Probably, I decided.  But they knew better than to poke their noses in, same as me with them.

I sat on the back step in the last of the day's bleak January sun, racking my brains trying to think of something, some way out of this mess, but each time I drew a blank.  We had no evidence for the police, not enough to guarantee a conviction according to Mark.  Not that I'd told him about the recent events. I couldn't bring myself to. I'd ring him tomorrow, once Lot was at Babs'.

We couldn't take off, we didn't have any money, and where would we go anyway? There was Babs' place, but it would only be a matter of time before he found us. Cal had invested time and money, he'd 'shown her around', he had a market for Lottie now. He couldn't be seen to lose her, his reputation wouldn't stand for it, his pride wouldn't stand for it. Lottie was his now, and if we did a runner, we'd be easy to find and he *would* find us.

I'd known Cal most of my life, and I knew that he never let something go if he didn't want to. It was how he'd got Rosie, it was the reason my brother was dead, and if we weren't careful...I couldn't bring myself to finish the thought.

As the shouting next door reached a crescendo and I heard the sharp crack of skin against skin, I turned my attention to what I was going to tell Babs.

### Lottie 1981

Barbara and her husband Dave welcomed me into their home. A semi-detached on the other side of town. A nice part of town. Babs made me a coffee and we sat on the leather sofa in the front room. It had a massive bay window that beckoned the light in. Everything was right about this house and I envied my cousin and her life.

No one would marry me now. Why would they? No matter how often I washed, and it was often, I couldn't wash the filth away. The feeling of being used. I carried it now in my DNA. Filth was a part of me and I was convinced that anyone who got close would see it, smell it. Besides, I wasn't sure I ever wanted to get married. The little I knew about men didn't inspire me to want to shack up with any of them. Except perhaps Baz and that wasn't bloody likely.

I was still bleeding heavily and I had fainted occasionally. I wondered what Mum had told Babs, but as we sipped our drinks it wasn't long before I found out.

'So, I thought we'd have a chat,' Babs said.

'Oh?'

'Yeah,' she looked a little uncomfortable, then launched into it.

'You're young, perhaps too young, but still, you're young and bound to want to experiment.'

I said nothing. I couldn't, I had no idea what she was talking about.

241

'It would be better if you waited but, as you're not, you need...protection.'

I did, she was right, but I couldn't help feeling that perhaps we had different ideas about the kind of protection I needed.

'What kind?' I ventured, It was a safe question.

'Well,' she shuffled in her seat, adjusted her jumper needlessly. 'Condoms,' she said, and then proceeded to discuss the various merits or otherwise of contraception. It was a long and brave speech, and I was touched that she cared enough for me to do it, it was clearly uncomfortable for her.

'Right,' I said.

'That way you can stop this happening again.'

'Stop what?'

'It's okay,' she leaned forward, put her hand on my arm and I flinched. She sat back. 'You're Mum told me,'

'Told you what?'

'About the baby.'

'What baby?'

'Lot, you don't have to pretend to me, your Mum told me everything. I realise it must be upsetting, losing a baby isn't a nice thing to experience at any age, and it must be especially difficult at your age. But there's plenty of time for all that in the future, when you're older, married and in a stable relationship.'

I nodded. Appalled. So that was the story. More lies. Was this a story she was telling everyone, whether they needed to know or not? Was she spreading it round the estate now in my absence? Covering for Cal and his cronies? Is this what Baz had heard? We had never had sex, and I hated that he would believe I had with someone else. But then I realised I had, and the thought made my heart ache.

More shame heaped up. Layer upon layer until I thought I would stop breathing. Would my mother never be satisfied? Would she destroy every part of me until I was a husk? Was I to lose everything that was even the tiniest bit good in my life? Would she take away everything? Would I ever be free of her?

The ache inside deepened and I missed Baz's arms round me more than ever. Would I ever find my way back from this place, into that place of safe arms again.

But then, would I even want to?

**Andrea 1981**

It was clear Cal wasn't going to let Lottie go and, by implication, me. The money I'd taken had sealed our fate after all. I had broken our deal and that had given Cal permission to do the same. I was stupid to ever have taken it but then, I never did think through the consequences of my actions.

It was the following week when an idea came to me. I had plucked up the courage to ring Mark the previous week to tell him what had happened. I didn't see I had a choice.

'Oh god, Andi. I'm sorry.'

'It's my fault,. You told me to send her away. I was going to...' to my horror bubbles of grief filled the back of my throat and I hung up.

Today this call would be better I thought, as I lined up my two pence pieces and dialled. I'd made the story up for Babs, it could work for Cal. I explained my idea, talking quickly so I didn't run out of money.

'So, you think it'll work?' I said, when I'd finished.

'It might....it'll certainly spook him. I'll follow him, see where he goes, who he speaks to. He's bound to want to cover his tracks.'

'That sounds good.'

'He'll show his hand, Andi. He's bound to.'

'So you think it'll work?' I asked again.

'I think it's genius!'

I returned the receiver, buoyed by the call. Cal had destroyed one member of my family, I couldn't stand by and let him it it to another and now I had a plan it no longer looked hopeless for Lottie and me. Finally, I was going to nail that bastard.

Everything was in place. Lottie was with Babs and I'd started spreading the rumours. It wasn't difficult, all I had to do was tell Pat from next door and Sheila from Wordsworth Avenue. I knew it would just take off after that. It was an awful thing to do to Lot, but what else could I do?

The timing was tight, the 'incident' had happened only a few weeks ago, but I was counting on Cal not doing the maths.

Within two days, as I thought, it was estate gossip, and that's when the looks started, but it wasn't until Friday night at the club that anyone tackled me straight on, cowardly bastards..

It was Brenda. Didn't like the woman myself, always wore cheap polyester, nasty stuff, Didn't dare touch the women for fear of an electric shock. Anyways, she came up to me bold as brass on the Friday night just

243

after the bingo, before the turn, so I knew she'd had a drink but not so much as she didn't know what she was doing.

'Here, Andrea, I hear your Lot's up the duff.'

'Don't know where you heard that.'

'There's word going round.'

'Don't know what you're talking about. Our Lot's gone for a holiday at her cousin's.'

Everyone would see through the lie. Few went to stay with the rellies, and never during school time. Don't get me wrong, none of us were adverse to keeping the kids off school, it just never occurred to anyone to send them away.

'So, she's gone on a little holiday has she?'

'That's right,' I said, brazing it out. I needed people to believe Lottie was pregnant. I had made a lot of mistakes with Cal, but I couldn't afford to mess this up.

Brenda took a swig of her cider and black. 'Well, I just thought you should know what people were saying love.'

'Appreciate it, Brenda.'

Now it was done I just wanted to get away from the woman before she electrocuted me with one of her touches.

The following day I was up and dressed, ready for when the cab came for Lottie, as I knew it would.

It was four weeks since he had brought my daughter home battered and bruised. She was still at Babs' but she would need to come back soon.

Cal was in the cab and I went out to see him, knowing he wouldn't move, knowing he would expect Lottie to trot out and jump in like she did every week, that he believed the world tipped along on his axis. Still, it always had so I couldn't blame him for it, and I recognised that I too, desired the same. I just didn't get it. Well, things were about to change for Johnny Caldwick, finally.

When he saw me he hoisted his bulk out of the cab and walked up the path to meet me. This wasn't a conversation that either of us wanted to have within earshot of the taxi driver.

'Where is she?' he demanded.

'I've sent her to rellies,' I told him.

'Is she alright?'

'Of course she's not fucking alright.'

A look of anger flicked across his face. 'You know what I mean.'

'Cal, you have no idea of how *not* alright she is.'

'She'll be fine,' he said, regaining his composure.

'No, she won't.'

We stood on the path, the taxi chugging in the background.

'I can't do this now, taxi's waiting. Get her back here. I'll come round in the morning, when Rosie's gone to church.' He turned and walked back to the taxi. In his mind it was settled, no further discussion was needed.

'She's pregnant, Cal,' I said, to his retreating back.

He turned. 'She's what?' he hissed.

'You heard me.'

'Since when?'

'Do I need to spell it out for you?'

He didn't say anything and that's when I knew for sure. Whilst she hadn't said anything explicitly, I had hoped, despite the obvious signs, that Lottie was just being an hysterical teenager, over dramatising the situation. But Cal's lack of response confirmed everything.

It all came rushing back to me and I wondered how I could ever have denied knowing what was going to happen. 'That was the point, wasn't it?' I said, the words twisting out of my mouth. 'Unbroken, in-tact! Remember?'

'Didn't you have her on the pill?'

'Why would I? You didn't give me the whole story, did you?' I leaned forward. 'And it *wasn't* ever part of the deal,' I hissed.

'You stupid fucking bitch,' he said, and a sudden pain struck my cheek. I found myself face down on the lawn and it took me a moment to realise he'd smacked me across the face.

'I told you, you steal you pay. Get her here tomorrow,' he said and strode off. As I lay in the grass, the damp seeping into my clothes, I heard the door of the taxi open and close and then it pulled away.

He was taking a chance, smacking me like that in front of the taxi driver, until I remembered that Cal never left witnesses behind. He always dealt with them, one way or another. That was why he was still walking around. Free. Damaging people. No doubt the driver was being paid for his cooperation, and if he didn't Cal would have plans for him. He would have plans for me to.

I stood up, my face screaming. It had been a long time since someone had hit me and I'd forgotten what it felt like. Not just the pain, though that was bad enough, but the humiliation, the feeling small, the helplessness of it all. I remembered with shame the beatings I had given Lottie over the years.

I returned to the house, shaking as I closed the front door. Was my plan good enough? Could I really do this? I needed to make sure it was

245

flawless because if not, if there was even a chink of weakness, Cal would tear us apart.

I lit a fag with shaking hands, Cal always took care of witnesses, one way or another.


The following morning dragged. I'd slept badly, woke up early and felt dreadful. As much as a told myself everything was set, as much as I convinced myself that Cal was as good as gone from our lives, and much as Mark has reassured me yesterday on the phone, there was still a part of me that wouldn't believe it until it was over.

He'd slipped through so many people's plans for his downfall, including mine, could we really do it? After all, what had changed really? Then I reminded myself that this time it was different. It had to work, Mark was a professional policeman, he knew what he was doing and he was risking a lot to help me.

I lit a fag and drew the smoke in deep, hoping it would calm my jangled nerves. Did our response to the shit that happens in our lives define who we are at the core, our true natures, or could that be changed?

Both Mark and I suffered loss at the death of Andrew, but whereas I had gone on to lurch from one disaster to another, never daring, I realised now, to get truly close to someone again, Mark had gone on to use that same incident as a springboard to a new and better life.

Lemons and lemonade.

I'd made a mistake there, perhaps if I'd chosen differently, told him…I stopped. I couldn't afford to go meandering into what if's. I couldn't afford to be anything but strong. It had never counted more than now.

I took another deep drag and after I released it, a swig of cold tea. What would Lot make of her life after this? Would she do as I did, or take after her father and strike out, be more, not because of it, but in spite of it? Lot was good at her core, like her father. She would be alright, if I could just free us from Cal.

The idea of facing him made my stomach knot and when the knock came at the door, I'm ashamed to say I almost soiled myself.


When I opened the door Cal filled the space, bigger than I'd ever seen.

'Cal,' I said, as I opened the door and stood to one side to let him in.

He passed me and went into the living room.

'She here?' he asked, taking all the oxygen with his question.

I shook my head mutely.

'I'm not pissing about,' he warned.

I swallowed and found words from somewhere.

'I know, Cal, she's still not well.'

'Still?  It's been weeks.  What's the matter with her?' his eyes flickered for a moment so I knew somewhere her health bothered him.

'You mean apart form being pregnant?'

He just glared at me.

'She's running a temperature.'

'Is it serious?'

'I don't know, but I'm told it's high.'

'You mean you haven't been to see her?'

I shrugged and he shook his head.

'I can't take her to the doctors can I?  Anyways,' I took a breath. 'The police have been, yesterday.' I saw with satisfaction the surprise in his face.

'The police?  Why?'

'There's been a report, a complaint,' I licked my lips involuntarily, quick, like a lizard.  I mustn't do it again, I mustn't look too nervous.  He'd pick up on that, mustn't look too relaxed either, that would make him suspicious too.

'What sort of complaint?'

'Mark Harvey's involved in the investigation,' I said, ignoring his question.

'That bastard.'

I didn't say anything.  If I agreed Cal would know I was lying.  If I disagreed I risked him loosing his temper.

'He's been fucking hounding me for years.'

'Since Andrew,' I told him needlessly.

He turned and put his face into mine.  'You put him up to this, you bitch.'

I stepped back, needing some room to find the courage to speak.

'No, I'm not daft.  I'm as guilty as you are.'

'Yes love, and don't you forget it,' he said, stabbing with his blunt sausage fingers.

He stepped back, blew out a breath and whipped his greasy hair over his bald patch.

'So, now what?' I asked.

'Well, what's the complaint?' he asked.

'God, you want a list?'

'Not what they could *do* us for you daft cow, what was the *complaint*?'

'Something about reports of child abuse.'

247

'Child abuse!'

'Well, she is a *child*, Cal.'

He waved me aside, ignoring my comment and started pacing, his agitation growing, spewing out into the room.

'What do we do now?' I asked, I needed him to feel we were both in this.

'Harvey won't be after you,' he said.

'He's known as a copper that does it by the book. You know that. If I'm implicated, which I am, he'll be after me just as much as you, and your...friends.'

'Fucking hell!' he said, as the wider implications rippled out and hit him. 'This is a right fucking mess. Where did this complaint come from?'

I shrugged. 'No idea. There was a spot of trouble at school, maybe that was it.'

He stopped pacing in front of me. 'I told you to make sure she went to school precisely for this reason.'

'I did! And I told you we shouldn't change anything. That's probably why there was some trouble.'

'What sort of trouble?'

'Kids stuff, some name calling, a fight, rumours starting. She was suspended for awhile. Might have been that, might not. Let's face it Cal, it could have come from any number of people. My neighbours, your neighbours, stall holders who were watching, even one of your punters. You were hardly discreet were you? They could have let their mouths run, done some bragging, Who knows, problem isn't *where* it came from, it's what we do about it now.'

Cal had resumed his pacing, his great hulk storming back and forth, wearing out my carpet and my nerves. So far it was going alright, but I wasn't going to relax, not yet.

I waited, this couldn't be rushed, Cal had to think that I was in as deep as him, if truth be told I was. More importantly, he had to believe that there was a legitimate serious report that was being investigated.

'Wouldn't this be dealt with by social services?' he asked, out of the blue.

I hesitated. He was right of course, but I hadn't expected him to know that.

'I dunno,' I said, thinking quickly. 'Wouldn't it depend on the source...or...or...or where the complaint had been filed?'

He paced again while I held my breath.

'You've got a social worker haven't you?'

I nodded.

'How come they weren't sent out to talk to you?'

My voice rose. I was frightened now. 'I don't know Cal, I'm not in charge of the investigation.'

Did he hear the bite in my voice? If he did, he chose to ignore it.

'Fuck, fuck, fuck, fuck, fuck.' He turned to me. 'What are we going to do?' he asked.

'I don't know. Lot's pregnant but I can do something about that, on the QT so to speak, but the rumours, the investigation, they're out of my hands, and you know Mark?'

He grabbed my arms. 'Fuck Andrea, you've got to help me.'

I had never seen Cal like this and a feeling of triumph went off like a rocket inside me. The great Johnny Caldwick, look at him now. Of course, it wasn't enough for me, I wanted him on his knees, snivelling like the worm he was, but this was a close second.

'I'm doing all I can, I'm keeping Lottie out of the way for a start. That's why she's still with Babs.'

He let go of me. 'That's good,' he brought a sausage finger up to his chin in a parody of someone thinking, but I could see nothing was going on. There was blind panic in his eyes. Then something changed, a dawning occurred on his face and my previous feeling of triumph was quickly replaced by a dreadful drawing down of my stomach.

'What do you mean...that's why she's still with Babs?'

Something in his manner wrong footed me, made my heart quicken. 'I told you, the police came.'

'But she's been there for a while now...two, maybe three weeks?'

'About that,' I said. It was nearly four now.

'So if the police didn't come round till yesterday, why did you send her away weeks ago?'

'I dunno, she just needed a rest. She was in a bad way, Cal,' I said, my insides twisting in fear.

'Unless you've known all along...' he turned slowly to face me square on.

I felt the blood drain from my face. 'I don't know what you mean,' I said. My fists clenched and my shoulders started to hunch.

'You're trying to set me up,' he said quietly.

'No!' I said quickly, recognising the danger.

'You and fucking Mark Harvey, you're trying to set me up.' He stood up straight, his fists clenched, if he hit me now I was sure I'd never get up. 'You bastards.' he whispered, taking a step towards me.

I swallowed hard and put my hands out, in what I hoped was a placatory manner.

'How Cal? Why?'

'For Andrew.'

'What, my daughter for Andrew?'

'You're a witch Andrea Parker, everyone knows that. A spoilt little witch, if you couldn't have it, no one could. You'd split your own mother in two for a fiver.'

Then he lashed out and I felt the heel of his hand crack across my cheek sending me reeling to the floor. The pain took my breath away for a moment and as he loomed over me, a great mountain of a man, I knew I had to act quickly.

'Cal stop!' I could only manage a whisper, so I held out my palm towards him. 'Please, that's not it. I could go down too, think about it.'

He stopped. His breathing was heavy and I knew I only had moments to stop this.

'I sent Lot away as soon as I heard the rumours, before the police or anyone could speak to her. I *lied* for you. If you don't lose your head you're in the clear.'

'What rumours?' he asked.

'I don't know,' I said and I didn't. I couldn't think straight. I was saying anything that came into my head.

He leaned over, poised to punch me, his face in mine, so close I could smell his dog breath and whispered. 'If you don't tell me everything now, I'm going to beat you to a pulp. I'm going to mash your fucking face so hard your own mother wouldn't recognise you.'

Small hairs rose all over my body, my mouth went dry and I wet myself.

'I don't-'

He punched me hard in the face and pain exploded across my cheekbones.

'Everything,' he growled.

I swallowed hard to find my voice, determined to tell him nothing, and then, before I knew what I was doing, I told him everything. About the plan, the phone calls, the conversation with John the landlord at the Red Lion, that Mark was operating on his own, that the pregnancy was a lie. I lay cowering beneath his raised fist and told him everything. Every. Last. Thing.

He took a step back, I considered staying on the floor but decided that if he was going to give out any further punishment, I'd rather have another slap than a boot in the ribs and scrambled to my feet.

'Anything else I should know?'

I stood in clothes soaked in my piss, my face throbbing, with one eye starting to close and I shook my head, not trusting myself to speak in case I burst into tears.

'If I hear anything, *anything*, about you shooting your mouth off you'll die...slowly,' he said, as he made to leave. 'Especially if you talk to Harvey. And don't think I won't find out, bitch!'

I raised my head to look at him and, as I did so he slapped me again. I fell and hit my head on the mantlepiece as I went down. Small sparkles appeared in front of my eyes.

'That's just a little reminder of what I'm capable of,' he said. 'Just in case you'd forgotten. Remember, one word to Harvey, just one.'

As I lay there, in my own piss, humiliated, in pain and quaking with fear, I listened to him leave and I didn't doubt any of it.

A few minutes later there was a knock on the door. I pulled myself up and, knew who it was. Not wanting him to see me like this, I called through the door to hang on a minute and dashed upstairs to get washed and changed.

When Mark saw me five minutes later I knew I still looked a mess, despite my best efforts.

'What the hell happened?' he asked, his mouth open.

'I got into a fight, you should see the other guy,' I tried to laugh, but my head hurt too much and I winced.

'Did Cal do this to you?' he asked, as he took my arm and led me into the living room.

'Yes, just a friendly warning.' I could feel my bottom lip starting to swell and realised I must have caught it with my teeth. It would balance out my eye, I thought.

'So what now?' he asked.

I sat down, realising how exhausted I was. 'I can't go through with it.'

'What?'

'I can't. I'm too scared, it won't work. He's gone, it's enough.'

'But what about everything you said, what about Andrew, what about Lottie?'

I sighed. I knew Mark wouldn't want to leave this. but I needed to get him to agree, for his own sake.

'Andrew's dead, it's over. You were right, I should never have started this thing with Cal in the first place. It's got way out of hand and I need to protect Lottie.'

Mark sat down on the sofa and looked at me. 'It's a bit late for that don't you think? You're going to let him walk away, again? After everything he's done? Look Andi, I never liked this whole situation you'd got yourself into, you know that, but you've put your daughter through hell, and now you tell me you want to pull out, just at the last minute? It doesn't make sense.'

I nodded. 'I know, but that's what I want.'

I watched the blood drain out of his face.

'Really?'

In that moment I wanted to explain, I wanted him to understand, didn't want him to think badly of me, wanted to tell him who Lottie was, then I remembered what Cal had said. Those hurtful words from a man I detested were hurtful because they were true. I was spiteful, I always wanted things my way and I had done untold damage to all sorts of people to get it.

If I told Mark the truth now, he wouldn't leave us alone. God knows, what he would do, or what would happen to him in the process of him doing it. Telling him wouldn't give Lottie a father, or Mark the daughter he didn't know he had. If he knew the truth about Lot he would hunt Cal down, regardless of the consequences. If I was ever to tell him about Lottie, it had to be for the right reason, and the time for that had passed. So I held my tongue.

'I just can't do it,' I said, instead.

He shook his head. 'I always thought you were better than you let people believe, I guess I was wrong.' He stood up, 'You are so impossibly selfish,' he said. 'And I'm sorry I ever met you.'

They were the last words he would ever say to me.


### Lottie 1981

After several weeks at aBbs' I finally returned home a few days before Valentine's day. I couldn't help but think of Baz as the taxi passed the end of his road, and a short stabbing pain hit me in my solar plexus.

'Your face!' I said, when she opened the door. Her eye was puffy and her cheek bruised.

'It's nothing,' she said, and refused to discuss it further, but I knew who was responsible and I shuddered.

She gave me an enormous hug when I came through the door, then held me at arms length as if I'd been away on some epic journey.

'Has the bleeding stopped?' she asked. Her bluntness never failed to stop me in my tracks.

'Murm.'

'Lot, it's important. Answer me.'

'Mostly, yeah.'

'Good. That's good.' She let go of me and ran her hand over her forehead, She looked genuinely distressed, not the feign drama and concern she usually displayed, not the syrup sugared saccharine voice that I thought I might drown in, this was different. It was...I thought for a moment, it was real. The realisation frightened me.

I considered tackling her about the story she had told Babs then decided against it. What was the point? It was done now and I wasn't convinced that any amount of reasoning or protesting would make any difference. What was done was done. As always, I simply had to find a way of dealing with the aftermath of my mother's actions.

'Cuppa?' she asked.

I nodded and smiled.

'Coffee?' she said.

A small spurt of joy went off inside me and I nodded again, perhaps things would be different this time.

Later that day I went to the shop for some ciggies. It was good to be out in the fresh air, walking around as if nothing had happened. Good, but strange, as if I were walking in a dream. I wasn't sure if *this* was the dream, or the horrifying events of a few weeks ago.

The window of the shop was decorated with large red hearts and the familiar dull throb of my heart started again. I half hoped and half dreaded bumping into Baz, and practised scenarios and conversations as I joined the queue in the shop.

I was so engrossed in my fantasies that I wasn't immediately aware of the sly looks and whispered comments from those ahead and behind me. I was next in the queue and shuffled forward and swallowed hard before I spoke.

'Ten regal blue,' I said.

'You back then, Lottie?' Sheila asked.

'Looks like it.'

She placed the cigarettes on the counter and I handed her a pound note as I slipped the packet into my pocket.

'Heard you were at your cousin's?' she said, ringing up the sale.

'That's right.'

She counted out the change into my hand.

'Heard other stuff too,' she smiled.

'Is that right? Thanks,' I said and left quickly.

As I walked home, cigarettes in my pocket, I held my head up, if they sniffed any weakness in me, life on the estate would be intolerable. I couldn't afford for that to happen, not now I had no escape. This was my life and I had to accept it.

My mother's story about me was obviously being passed round, exchanged like contraband. I had been pregnant, I had lost the baby, or worse, I had had an abortion. People would think it was Barry Johnson's and only he and I knew we had never had sex. *I wish we had.* I wished with every fibre of my being that he was the one who had taken my virginity.

253

As I put the key into the front door there was one thought that shook my insides every time I thought it. *He would think I had sex with someone else, he would think I never cared for him.* And even though I didn't think I had anything left inside to break, I did.


## Andrea 1981

A week after Lottie returned Mark Harvey was found face down in the river Skerne. Beneath the grief of losing him was a layer of sheer terror. No one had seen anything, no one knew anything.

But I knew, and I knew he'd be back.


I jumped at every knock at the door, every taxi that pulled up in the street and my nerves were shoot after two months, but still he waited.

You notice I don't say he didn't come, because that was never an option. Jonny Caldwick never forgot, never forgave, debts had to be balanced, scores settled.

And here we sat, Lot and I, still owing. Waiting for the bill.


Cal left it long enough for things to die down, Lot's pregnancy to fade into the background and my blood pressure to reach an all time high.

Then, one sunny Sunday afternoon in April I heard a taxi chug in the street. I jumped like one of Pavlov's dogs to a ringing bell, then my mind kicked in to remind me it was fine.

Lot and I were in the living room, watching Seven Brides for Seven Brothers. Even though it was April and the sun shone, it was unusually cold and I'd lit the fire in the living room. It was cosy, the rest of the house was freezing.

The recognisable knock on the door saw Lot and I stare at each other in shock. It could only be one person.

'Upstairs,' I hissed, 'And don't make a sound.'

She was so quick and light I almost didn't see her leave. I licked my lips, but my mouth was so dry they stayed cracked. My breathing became shallow and I couldn't get enough oxygen, making my head feel light as I made my way to the door.

I let him in, I had no choice, but I hadn't been idle while waiting for him. I had a plan, and this time it *would* work.

'Andrea,' he said, nodding as he pushed passed me and went into the living room.

I followed him in. 'It isn't safe, Cal,' I told him.

'It is. Mark and his family are taken care of.'

I didn't know anything about Mark's family, but Cal seemed to think I did, and it was safer not to contradict him.

'Still, I don't think it's safe for you to be here.'

'You know why I'm here,' he said.

I nodded. 'Meet me Wednesday about seven at the bridge, it's out of the way of prying eyes and it will be starting to get dark,' I suggested. 'Just in case. We can talk better there. Come to some...arrangement.'

I held my breath while he considered it. He had to say yes for my plan to work, if he declined I was buggered. Finally he nodded in agreement and left. I called up to Lottie that it was safe for her to come down and let the air leave my body in relief.


## Lottie 1981

When I heard him leave, I went to the bathroom, washed my face and took a long hard look in the mirror.

My eyes were wide giving me the look of Mrs. Rochester in the attic. My face was puffy and I had black bags under my eyes because I still had nightmares. Hearing his voice brought it all back again, making my heart beat so hard it hurt. I could barely breath. I would never be safe again.

I turned away from the mirror, I was a mess, I was broken, I was disgusting, I was used and no one would ever want me. Ever.

I went into my mother's bedroom but the pills had gone from her bedside. I checked the drawers and the cupboards, then I went back into the bathroom to check the cabinet, Nothing, not even paracetamol. She was one step ahead of me and for a moment, just one moment, I thought she might care after all.

But I did find scissors and her razor.


255

## Andrea 1981

When I saw her it shocked me.

'Lot!' I whispered.

Her beautiful long hair was all gone, her shaved head covered in nicks and cuts, her scalp vulnerable and raw. She looked like something from Belsen with her haunted black eyes and drawn face.

'I'm sorry,' she whispered, her eyes filling with tears.

I opened my arms and for the first time in our lives, we took comfort from one another, and it steeled me for what I had to do.

There was only one way to get rid of Johnny Candlewick, and all I had to do was find the courage to go through with it...

Cobba on the estate went rabbiting with his greyhounds. A few years back they tore my cat to pieces in the front garden. The cat was old and he did me a favour, I'd have only had to take the old moggy to the vet, but I didn't let on. That way he owed me. I didn't know what use he would be at the time, but it never hurt to have a few favours in your pocket. Now I was calling in the debt. I knew he'd be discreet. That was the way of our estate. Gossip was rife, but nothing left the estate. The authorities were authority, and not to be trusted.

So I made my way to his house late that night and told him what I needed. He didn't ask any questions.

Thirty minutes later I left with a 410 shot gun, ammunition and a basic understanding of how to fire and reload it. I also made him a promise to take it out into the fields beyond the estate at least once to practice before I pointed it at anything.

'Or anyone,' he said.

The bridge where Cal and I had arranged to meet sat in a bowl of fields with the estate sitting above it on the left and the road that ran around the estate running along the length of the ridge. I had everything set up. I'd hidden the gun in a bush along the lane running from the bridge, just round the first bend, so it wasn't visible from either the bridge or the road that ran along the top of the fields.

All I had to do now was wait. My palms were wet, my heart thundered and I wondered, not for the first time, if I could go through with it, until I remembered I had no choice.

The light started to fade and a chill had fallen. I pulled my coat tight round my body, for comfort as well as to keep out the cold. I hadn't told

Lot where I was going and she knew better than to ask. I would tell her to piss off out later, I wasn't sure what state I would be in and the less she knew the better. It wasn't to protect her, it was to protect me. Lot didn't have the stomach for lies and I knew if she found out what I'd done, assuming I was successful, she'd blab.

I took a breath and the cold air burnt my nostrils on the way in. My lungs didn't seem to be functioning properly, only partially inflating, not taking in all the oxygen I needed. I regretted now not having a drink to steady my nerves. I thought I needed a clear head but now realised that it was the last thing I needed. I was going to kill a man, or try to, a man who was bigger, meaner and stronger than me. A drink was exactly what I needed.

My insides tightened and I swallowed hard when I saw a familiar silhouette across the evening sky. Cal appeared over the brow of the bowl, walking from the estate and the road that encased it, like a giant and I let out a whimper. 'Get a grip, Andrea' I whispered.

I needed to stay calm, keep my nerve, otherwise I wouldn't be able to do this. I cursed myself. *Pathetic bitch!*

Cal trudged across the field, moving closer to me and I took another breath, swallowed again, stomped my feet, moving to stave off the impinging cold and fear. It was taking him ages to get to me and I wasn't sure if that gave me the time to get my shit together, or lose it completely. I decided that I would just have to wait and see. I'd know soon enough.

I thought about the consequences of this going wrong, what he'd do to me, and my insides went watery. Then all to soon he was stood in front of me, on the bridge with the rising black river swirling beneath us, in the rapidly fading light. I was almost tempted to jump in.

'Andrea,' he nodded.

'Cal,' I said. It was all I could say. It came out clear enough, I thought. I sounded nervous but he'd expect that. Probably better that way than sounding overly confident. All in all, not a bad start, although it had hardly started.

'Shall we walk?' I said, nodding in the direction behind me. The lane, towards the bush round the corner. I had to get him to the bush otherwise all was lost.

'Here's fine,' he said.

'Fair enough,' I looked up at the road. 'Just thinking we can still be seen, but it's up to you.'

He looked back in the direction I was looking and I knew he'd be able to see how obvious we were, even in the dim dusk light.

'So?' I started, wanting him to suggest we move from here. 'You sure you want to do this here?'

He looked back at me and nodded. 'I'm assuming this is about Lottie?'

'You *are* aware that she's fifteen, a minor?'

His eyes tightened at that and he nodded his head, he looked back over his shoulder. 'Let's walk,' he said, and my heart leapt.

Pleased, I turned to walk beside him, then I remembered that getting him to walk down the lane was barely half of my plan.

'You nearly killed her, you know?'

I didn't know the details but seeing the state of her, I didn't need to. Had Cal…? I didn't finish the thought, instead I concentrated on listening to our footsteps on the broken shale that had been spread to create the footpath.

'It got out of hand,' he said.

I looked ahead. We were walking slowly, Cal's bulk ambling along beside me. I had never been more aware of how big he was. I bit my lip, trying to gain some control over my jelly legs. The bend in the lane seemed miles away.

'What do you want with Lot?'

He stopped walking and turned to face me. My heart sank, I needed him to keep walking.

'What do you care?' he asked.

I shook my head, pretended I was angry and started to walk, not too fast, hoping he'd follow.

'Hang on, Andrea,' he called after me. I stopped but didn't turn round, to my relief I heard his footsteps. When he reached me I resumed the walk, but slowly. I didn't want to lose him, I needed to lure him round the corner. I *had* to.

'Look, I think Lot's a pretty lass. She could have a future.'

'What makes you think she doesn't have one now? She's bright, not doing too bad at school by all accounts.' I had to keep him talking, had to keep him walking.

'Come on Andrea, we both know that kids off the estate stay on the estate, and if they get off it's not through the education system.' He laughed at his own joke and I forced myself to laugh too, not sure what the joke was, he was right.

'So, what *are* you proposing?' I asked, feigning interest.

'The original idea, with a few extras.'

'Modelling with a few extras. What does that mean?'

'Oh, come on Andrea, you've been around.'

The bend was getting closer, we were nearly there. I needed to get him round the corner and a few steps further, but it was getting dark and I was concerned that at any moment he might suggest we turn back. I picked up the pace a little, just a little, hoping he wouldn't notice. He didn't.

'Look,' he said, he had a reasoning tone to his voice. He'd taken my silence as disagreement and was trying to cajole me, but I wasn't fooled by this friendly approach. If he couldn't cajole he'd threaten. I knew, I did the same.

'Lottie has a great future, she could earn a lot of money, get off the estate, see the world, meet some *very* interesting people. All she would need to do is model during the day, and be a little...friendly at night.'

We had turned the corner and Cal was engrossed in his vision for my daughter. I was focused on the bush ahead, I could just make it out in the dim light.

'What do you say?' he asked.

'What kind of money?' I asked, knowing this would keep him talking for the few steps I needed to get him a bit past the bush. Then I could run back and get the gun, that way, if he ran towards the bridge I'd be able to get him. My heart speeded up for a moment and my throat tightened at the thought of what I was about to do.

'Well, it would depend on what we decided to use her for,' he said, as if we were talking about a working dog or livestock.

'Oh?' I said, inviting him to continue as we passed the bush. My heart hammered so hard I could barely hear his reply. I would have to make my move now, but suddenly my arms and legs were like lead.

The more I thought about it, the heavier my limbs became and the harder my heart beat. There wasn't a moment to lose, if I waited for much longer I would be crippled by my fear. I'd never get another opportunity like this, so before I lost my bottle, I took a deep breath and turned.

I ran back and charged into the bush. I heard a sound of surprise from Cal but refused to think anymore. I grabbed the shot gun and plunged back out of the bush into the lane, standing between Cal and the direction we had just come from.

It felt heavier than it had when I'd practised with it. I only had one shot. I'd have to spend time reloading it to take another one, and if I missed...I tried not to think what Cal would do to me if I missed.

Cal started to laugh. 'What is this?' he said, with a smile.

I tried to speak but nothing came out. Instead I raised the gun and aimed, my hands shaking. I took a breath to calm myself. Reminded myself that I hated this man, hated him with every fibre of my being, so why couldn't I just shoot him?

Cal's arms went up, 'Hey!' he said.

His movement panicked me and the gun went off. The noise was deafening, echoing across the fields into the dusk and the smell of burnt oil, like acrid fireworks, filled my nostrils. I froze, waiting.

Cal took a step or two back but I didn't know if I'd hit him. Then he straightened up and I realised I'd missed.

'What the fuck-' he gasped.

My ears were still ringing as I reached into my pocket for another cartridge. I wasn't concerned about the noise, I knew it would be ignored, people who lived on the edge of the estate were used to the sound of rabbiting. But I was concerned that Cal had started moving towards me.

I cracked the gun the way Cobba had showed me and I'd practised, but my hands were trembling as I took a cartridge from my pocket and I dropped it.

'Fuck, fuck, fuck,' I said, plunging my hand into my pocket to pull out a second cartridge. I had little time left and couldn't afford to drop this one.

I glanced up and Cal was about half a dozen steps away from me. His face twisted with loathing. I took a few steps back. Stopped. Bent over the cracked open gun and focused. Cal's heavy breath got closer. He could only be a foot away. With shaking hands the cartridge finally slid in and I shut the gun with a snap.

I looked up to feel Cal's left hand coming down on my shoulder. The shock of him being so near made me jump. The gun jerked and fired, and I pissed myself in fright.

I dropped the gun and made whimpering noises as I braced myself for the inevitable pain that would hammer down on me, wondering what Lot would do when I was dead. It had been a stupid plan, I realised now.

Then to my amazement, I heard another shot and Cal crumbled to his knees, clasping his stomach.

'Oh fuck,' he said. 'Fuck. Fuck. You bitch.'

Relief flooded my body. I had shot him! But how? I didn't have the gun. Had it gone off when I dropped it? It didn't matter. He was wounded.

His breath was raspy and I knew he was hurt bad, but was it enough to finish him off? Stomach wounds could kill, but they took time, and I didn't want him found.

He shook his head, straightened up and roared in pain, a huge bull of a bellow. I jumped back, convinced he was going to come for me. The movement made the blood ooze between his fingers. In the dusk it looked black, appropriate I thought, for a bastard like him.

How long would it take for him to die, assuming he was going to? Could I leave him? The trouble was, I didn't trust him to die. If I left him I wouldn't know for sure, I would never know, and I had to.

He curled up on the floor, 'Andrea, please,' he said, quietly into the growing dark.

I thought about Andrew, lying in the gutter, bleeding, in much the same way as Cal was now, and I was pleased. Finally. Finally.

'Rose,' it came out as a whisper.

I thought these were the words of a dying man, until Rosie stepped out of the shadows, she was holding Cal's gun in her hand, the one he had brought to my house.

'Rosie!'

I could smell iron on the breeze and realised with a jolt that I was smelling Cal's blood, his life force spilling out of his guts. Black and iron. My stomach turned over and I gipped.

'Come on, we've to get out of here,' Rosie said, pulling at my arm. She had picked up my gun and was holding it in her other hand. 'And don't be sick, don't you *dare* be sick.'

I started to cry as Rosie dragged me back towards the bridge.

'You...you...' I tried, through the sobs.

'Yes, I finished the job. I told you years ago we'd do it. Now come on, my car's not far away. If we're quick we can be away before anyone sees us. But you've *got* to hurry.'

'Rosie, I can't, my legs...they won't...'

She stopped, dropped the shotgun and grabbed me with both her hands, squeezing my arms till it hurt. 'You *have* to. You have to get home and take care of Lottie. For Mark, for Andrew, for once in your life you have to think of someone else! Now come on!' She picked up the gun and ran off ahead. I followed her on shaky legs, I had to do something right.

We got to the bridge and Rosie wiped down the shotgun and threw it into the river. I heard the splash as she retrieved the other gun from her bag, wiped it and threw that one away too.

We ran across the bridge, across the field and up to the road where Rosie's car sat. She had parked on the side of the road that opened out onto the field with no street lights. It was dark now and it was safe to assume we had managed to get across the bridge and field without being seen. The car was another matter but it was a chance we would have to take.

Moments later we were driving away. Rosie put the heater on and I was glad to feel the warmth against my feet

'Why are you helping me?' I asked, eventually.

There was a long pause before she responded. 'Not everything's about you,' she said, her eyes glued to the road ahead.

I wondered if that was what she meant when she'd said she was waiting, that she hadn't forgotten. The day she visited me and said she was keeping an eye on him. Had she followed him here? Is that how she knew what was going on? But I was too exhausted to ask, and I wasn't even sure I cared. It was over. It was done.

We rode the rest of the journey in silence. Rosie dropped me a few streets away from home and I walked the rest, going straight upstairs and locking myself in the bathroom. As I ran the bath, Lottie knocked on the door.

'You okay?'

'Fine. Having a bath.'

'Want a cuppa?'

'No, thanks.'

I knew she was lurking outside the door. 'Fuck off, Lot,' I said, over the thundering water, and heard her footsteps retreat down the hall.

I peeled off my clothes, bundled them into a tight ball and climbed into the bath to wash away the sweat and blood.

Later that night, after Lottie had gone to bed, I collected the bundle hidden under my bed and burned my clothes piece by piece.

Rosie and I never spoke again.


## Lottie 1981

The Saturday after Cal had visited I got up, got dressed and was ready at eight as usual, waiting for the taxi to take me to the stall. Things would go back to how they had before, now Cal had returned. That's the kind of man he was. You just got on with it, did what he wanted.

It didn't stop my body feeling heavy with dread. I just hoped Cal wouldn't be at the stall, I didn't want to see him. Wasn't sure what looking at his face would do to me. Wasn't sure I would be able to hold myself together. I rubbed my scalp and the scratchy feeling of the hair growing back soothed me. When I turned my head I was still surprised at how light it felt, I had dreams of long hair and woke up the next morning feeling grief.

By eight thirty I started to think it might not arrive. My heart leapt at the thought but I tried to keep it in check, knowing that just as I relaxed the cab would come round the corner. I wondered if Cal has said anything to mum, but she was asleep and I knew better than to disturb her.

I curled up in the living room with A Tale of Two Cities and tried to concentrate on reading while I waited.

I wasn't sure what I was waiting for: the cab, an explanation, Mum waking. I just sat, tried to read and hoped the taxi wouldn't come for me. It wasn't much of a book, too much description for me, but by ten o'clock I started to relax into it.

Just before twelve I heard Mum moving around upstairs and slipped a piece of paper between the pages so I didn't lose my place. Things were better between us, but I knew she didn't like to see me reading, and I didn't want to push it, especially as I had no idea what the future held in terms of Cal.

262

She came into the living room, sat in her chair, lit a ciggie and threw one at me.

'The taxi didn't come,' I said, as I caught it.

'What?'

'The taxi? For the stall? It didn't come.' I smiled.

She took a couple of drags before she spoke. 'Oh yeah, you don't have that job anymore.'

I felt a flood of relief.

'And Cal?'

'Buggered off.'

I didn't ask anymore.

'You want some beans?' I asked, standing up and realising I hadn't eaten anything.

'Nah, just a cuppa,' she said, and I made my way into the kitchen.

As I fought with the tin opener I felt the relief wash over me again. Cal was gone.

Mum left later that day. She didn't come back. Ever. A week later our social worker came to collect me. They'd had an anonymous call that I had been abandoned. I was put into care.

The ghosts continued to haunt me in my dreams for a long time. And nineteen years later I would discover that one of them had left a legacy inside me...one that would rob me of children. My marriage. My future. The same day she called me to tell me she was dying...

## Lottie and Andrea

'I don't believe it,' Lottie says.

Andrea smiles as she lays there. 'It's the truth.' she says, in her fading voice.

'You *killed* him?'

'No, not exactly, but I started it.' There's a hint of pride in her voice. She is proud, of that at least.

'And then you left...'

'I had to.'

'You could have come and found me later...after…'

'Would you have wanted that?'

'Yes.'

Neither of them say anything. Andrea closes her eyes. She feels so tired now.

'I'm sorry,' she says, without opening her eyes.

'I was *fifteen*!'

'I know.'

'I thought I knew what I was doing. I thought it was my choice but you only *think* you know what you're doing at that age.'

'I know.'

'That's why it's illegal,' Lottie adds.

Andrea opens her eyes. 'Why what's illegal?'

'Everything.' Lot catches a sob in her throat and takes a breath before speaking again. 'It ruined me. It's ruined my *life*.'

'Not yet, your life isn't over yet, you can stop it, trust me.'

Silence hums between them and Lottie feels her body go tight as she holds herself in, afraid of what she might do to the woman if she lets herself go. *Trust her? Did she really just say 'trust me'?*

Andrea tries to sit up and despite herself, Lottie goes to her side and helps her, rearranges the pillows, lays her back against them. Before she can step back out of reach Andrea clasps her hand. 'What do you want me to do?' she asks her daughter quietly. Desperate that something good comes out of making the telephone call, of calling Lottie here, to this place and their past.

'Nothing.'

'I want to make it right!'

'You can't, nothing you can do will do that.'

Lottie pulls her hand away and returns to the chair. They sit in desperate silence until Andrea finally breaks it.

'So what do we do?'

'There's nothing *to* do. It's done.'

The tears spill as Lottie stands. She can't bear sitting anymore. Hot anger courses through her, causing her head to hurt. She needs to release the pressure or her eyeballs will explode. She wipes the tears from her face with the back of her hand and reaches for the pillow at the bottom of the bed, clasps it tight against her. Venomous hatred surges as she steps towards the bed. She would dearly love to hold the pillow over the woman's face, except what would be the point? She's almost dead anyway.

'You're a hypocrite,' she says instead. 'You say one thing and do another.'

'It's called being human,' Andrea says, in a tired voice as she leans back and closes her eyes. 'It's what we all do when we're trying to be better than who we really are.'

Lottie doesn't respond. Her mouth is twisted as she takes another step. *This will never end,* she thinks.

Andrea looks up and sighs. 'Look, I don't want you to waste the rest of your life hating me.'

'This is just another of your shitty games. You never could face up to what you did. What YOU did!'

'Maybe. I don't think it matters anymore,' she pauses, so very tired. 'We're not so different, you know?'

The thought fills Lottie with horror and she clasps the ends of the pillow tighter. Her teeth fuse. 'We're *nothing* like each other,' a piece of spit lands on her chin.

'I wanted to come back, but I was too...I don't know,' she shakes her head. 'Have you any idea how painful it was to look in your eyes, know what they had done?' Andrea sighs, looking at the angry face staring back at her. Her intractable daughter. 'And I had lost Mark, worse, I was responsible for his death. That was tough. I nearly ended it all. Trust me, I had some lonely years.'

'You want me to feel sorry for you now?'

'No, I'm just trying to explain. It was...hard for me.'

'It was nothing more than you deserved. Do you know what I was going through? The years of therapy, the inability to get close to anyone, to trust anyone again. That hug we had, after I shaved my head? That was the last time anyone touched me for three years. Three years!'

The words hang between them like ghastly halloween decorations.

'I didn't think I would ever have a relationship with a man, then I met Dan. He was sweet and patient and kind, at least in the beginning. And now our marriage is over because one the those bastards gave me a disease,' she pauses, catches her breath, forces herself to say it. 'I can't have kids. You have taken everything from me, but then, you always did.'

Andrea closes her eyes, tries to catch her breath, this isn't how she pictured her final days. This isn't what she wanted and she is running out of time to make it right. She opens her eyes to see Lottie glaring at her. She said she wanted the truth, she just didn't expect it to be going both ways.

'I'm sorry,' she says. It is so lame in the face of such tragedy, but it makes her message all the more important so she forces herself to press on. 'All I'm trying to do is stop you from making the same mistake I made. I don't want to die with you hating me, for you as much as me.'

'Right,' Lottie spits.

'Whether you believe me or not is up to you, but I spent my life hating someone, someone I thought had ruined my life, and I ended up doing it all by myself because of it. The hate I mean,' she pauses, catches her breath, wonders if she has the strength, the courage to continue, then forces herself. *This isn't about me anymore.*

'I got my revenge in the end, but there was a price to pay. There always is. I didn't pull the trigger, but it was no less satisfying to watch the bastard die,' Andrea stops for a moment, returns to another place, catches her breath. 'Anyway, that actually isn't the point. The point is, carrying that hatred, getting that revenge, it cost me everything. It cost you too and I'm sorry for that, more than you'll ever know. I deserve to be hated, I'm not disputing that, but I know what it will do to you.'

'It's the clinic...the news.' Lottie's eyes shine with unshed tears.

Andrea nods.

'It's the last straw. I just can't forgive you that.'

'I understand, I'm not saying it's fair. It's not about fairness.'

They fall into silence against the background hum of the oxygen. The sounds of the hospital shuffle around them.

Lottie releases her grip on the pillow as her anger ebbs and puts it back at the bottom of the bed. Each end is creased, a spiral of lines where she clasped it.

'Were you going to suffocate me with that?' her mother asks, she smiles to show she is joking.

'I was thinking about it,' Lottie says, as she sits down, her body heavy.

'What stopped you?'

'Didn't want to put you out of your misery,' she tries not to smile but fails.

Time moves forward. 'I've decided to leave work. They'll probably fire me anyway.' She's not sure why she says it.

'Why?'

'I did something stupid.'

Andrea laughs. 'If I had a penny for every stupid thing I'd done...' her voice peters out before she can finish what she is saying.

'You're tired.'

Andrea nods.

Lottie sits, trying to assimilate the new knowledge. Her mother has done things for her, from guilt, from love, who knows? It is a warped love, if love is what it is, it is probably even too little too late. But Andrea has tried, in her clunky, selfish manner, she has tried to put right what she has made wrong, even if she failed. Lottie thinks about her actions recently with Jenny. Perhaps her mother is right, perhaps they aren't that different.

Finally she looks at her mother. 'So, what do we do now?'

'I'm not sure I've got that many options,' says Andrea, and this time Lottie smiles too.

Each woman grapples through strong emotion towards the other. Lottie not knowing if it's what she wants, Andrea unsure if she's capable of giving it to her anyway.

'But there was that time,' Andrea says, thinking about the hug Lottie mentioned previously. Lottie nods. It was only a moment, but bigger things have been built on less.

*It wasn't all bad*, thinks Lottie. When she was eleven she had mumps and her Mum stayed up all night laying cold flannels across her burning forehead. Her mother taught her that when sewing, the thread should measure no longer than to her elbow or it would knot up. She still measured it the same way. Was there more...surely there was more...

'I fancy a cuppa,' Andrea says.

She doesn't look like she could drink anything, but Lottie stands. 'I'll go and see what I can find,' she says and leaves to fetch coffee for them both, for what else can she do?

When she finds the kitchen and begins to prepare the drinks it seems childish to take her mother coffee when she knows she prefers tea. She doesn't want to be childish. She wants to look mature and grown up, she wants her mother to be proud. For some inexplicable reason, she wants to do something nice for her. So she decides to take extra care when making her tea, the way she did that day on her fifteenth birthday. The day she got the job on the book stall.

As she waits for the kettle she wonders if she could get a job in a book shop? It was something she had a real passion for when she was a child, and she loves books, loves reading. She could do anything now. The kettle comes to a boil and Lottie finishes the drinks.

When she returns ten minutes later her mother lies with her eyes closed. She has that same skull like appearance she had when Lottie first saw her. Was that really less than two weeks ago?

Lottie places the mug on the beside table and sits, her hands clasping her own mug, sipping her coffee and allowing her mother to sleep. Mulling over what her mother has told her. Wondering how long they have together before she leaves.

The warm room suddenly chills, and an ice blanket wraps itself around her. She feels a light breeze on her face, her cheek. No, not a breeze, more like someone's breath. That's when she knows. She touches her fingers to her face, and the breath passes, filling Lottie with a deep sadness, and an even deeper gratitude.

For all her mother's faults and cowardice, when it really mattered, Andrea was brave enough to come back for her.